"You're a minor using an untested device that isn't even supposed to exist. This is tricky."

"But it's stuck on me, so what else am I supposed to do? Besides, I'm actually getting better at using it, so there's no reason to worry. I'm stronger, faster, and probably better at fighting and defending myself and my friends than any of you. And you're going to need me to rescue my dad. Unless you have a better idea."

"I know you're faster, for sure," Dr. Sharma said carefully, moving through traffic, "and I don't have a problem with you defending yourself or others. But I am not your mother, and I'm not so sure she's keen on the idea of putting you in danger." She hesitated, then said, "We don't even know if we'll need to do any fighting. Maybe we'll be able to go in and get your dad without any altercations."

Charlie raised an eyebrow. "You don't watch many superhero movies, do you?"

Also by Lisa McMann

Going Wild

LISA McMANN

PREDATOR VS. PREY

A GOING WILD NOVEL

HARPER

An Imprint of HarperCollins*Publishers*

Library of Congress Control Number: 2017949434

ISBN 978-0-06-233718-4

Typography by Sarah Creech

18 19 20 21 22 CG/BRR 10 9 8 7 6 5 4 3 2 1

First paperback edition, 2018

To Brandi and Faith,

and superhero booksellers everywhere

PREDATOR vs PREY

A **GOING WILD** NOVEL

CHAPTER 1

The Ultimate Threat

Dr. Victor Gray held out the photo of young Charlie Wilde. In it she was scaling the side of a burning house like a lizard. She wore a silver bracelet on her arm. Victor tilted his head at the girl's father, who was tied to a chair. "No sense playing innocent, Charles. I suspect you know full well that your daughter has been using your Mark Five. I'm not an idiot."

"Where did you get that photo?" With a surge of fury Dr. Charles Wilde lunged at his former friend, nearly knocking into the unconscious biologist, Dr. Jack Goldstein, who was tied up in a chair next to him. He lost his balance and tipped over, landing hard on his side on the floor. "What have you done with her?" He struggled, completely unable to do anything but wriggle helplessly. Pain seared through his shoulder, which had taken the brunt of the fall. "Give me that! This is blackmail!"

Dr. Gray watched him curiously with a bit of sympathy. A strange look crossed his face. "You're starting to convince me, actually," he mused. "Either you've been taking acting lessons or you really didn't know. Hmm." He tapped his lips with the corner of the photo. "I'm surprised you'd be that careless with such a powerful device."

"I told you I don't know what you're talking about," sputtered Charles. His face burned. Years had gone by since he'd spared a thought about Victor Gray, and he could hardly believe he was sitting here, tied up, like this. Decade-old memories of his job at Talos Global, working on Project Chimera, had come screeching to the forefront of his mind ever since the soldiers had abducted him earlier that day. Reminders of Victor returned, too—how his personality had seemed to change as their work had progressed. It had been hard to pinpoint exactly what it was about Victor that had become troublesome. Perhaps it had been his growing obsession with the project or his irrational overreaction when the government shut it down.

Charles hadn't been alone in his concerns. Two of the other scientists had noticed that Gray was coming unglued, too. They'd considered reporting him, but Gray hadn't actually done anything wrong. Instead, the scientists had decided to stay in touch. They'd put together an emergency contact plan, just in case they learned of any strange behavior from Dr. Gray—or in case anything more serious ever happened. But nothing had, and the three scientists eventually got busy with their lives, lost touch, and forgot about Victor.

Now Dr. Gray seemed truly unhinged. He called to a couple of his soldiers, and they came quickly. "Pick him up, will you?"

While the soldiers acted on his order and righted the chair with Charles in it, another one approached. "The other two teams have arrived," he said. Dr. Gray beckoned him closer, and the soldier whispered something in Gray's ear.

Gray reared back. "They failed? Both of them? Against *children*? I'm . . . shocked."

"And . . . it seems the kids may have taken the three devices we had retained."

Charles watched them, confused. *Children? Three devices?* Was he talking about Charlie again? What was going on?

Dr. Gray stood rigid, angry, staring at the soldier, who shrank back as if he hoped the doctor wouldn't strike out. *Had Victor become violent, too?* But after a moment he turned sharply and paced to the other side of the desk. He pinched the bridge of his nose thoughtfully. "I don't need *any* of the bracelets," he muttered. "I have something even better now." Then he shrugged and said icily to Charles, "It appears your daughter got away from my soldiers. I imagine your wife knows by now that you've disappeared."

Charles, bewildered and red-faced, looked like all the veins in his neck were about to explode. "Leave my family alone," he warned through gritted teeth.

Dr. Gray turned his head slowly to look at Charles and Dr. Goldstein next to him. "If you agree to help me, I will," he said patronizingly. "It's very simple, Doctor."

"Help you with *what*?" Charles hated asking it. It made him feel weak. But he wouldn't sacrifice his family for anything. "What on earth are you trying to do?"

"I need you to build a new device," he said. "If you can convince Jack to help, all the better. Maybe he'll feel sorry for you—if he ever wakes up, that is."

Charles let out a frustrated sigh. "Why are you doing this? The government shut down this project for a reason, Victor. It was too risky. And now you've ruined these people. For God's sake, look at them! When the government discovers this, how are you going to explain that you've continued Project Chimera on your own? Have you lost your mind?"

"I won't be discovered until it's too late for anyone to stop me," said Dr. Gray coolly. "Besides, I think it's the perfect solution."

"Solution to what?" asked Charles.

Dr. Gray blinked at him, as if he thought the answer was obvious. "Solution to the threat of human extinction."

Charles's eyes widened. "What on earth are you talking about?"

"The idea behind Project Chimera was a good one—I believed in it wholeheartedly. And now that I've been successful making these hybrids, I want to pursue the direction you were headed in with your device by giving my soldiers powers from multiple animals."

Charles was completely bewildered. "B-b-but the project was shut down—it's too dangerous! Why are you doing this?"

Dr. Gray continued, growing impassioned while explaining his plan. "We need a stronger hybrid race to jump-start evolution. That's what we're setting out to do here. That's why I need you." He gazed at the largest soldier in the room, then turned sharply toward Charles. "So. Will you work with me to create a new device? Or do I send my soldiers after the bracelet on your daughter's arm again and do this myself while you sit here with Jack? The lab is just down the hall, and the choice is yours."

Dr. Wilde clenched his jaw and tried to breathe. Gray sounded like a psychopath—he had grown so much worse. The options he had given . . . obviously neither was acceptable. Charles glanced at Jack, ragged and half-starved for refusing to help. He'd do the same if he didn't have his family to worry about. The soldiers had already messed with Charlie. Was she panicking? Would Diana remember what he'd told her all those years ago? Would she know what to do? He held out little hope. It had been too long.

He closed his eyes in defeat. There was no way in the world he could let those thugs go after Charlie again if he could do anything within his power to stop them. There wasn't a choice to make—it was already made. Now all he could do was stall for time.

"Charles?" Victor prompted, interrupting his thoughts. "What is your decision?"

Dr. Wilde could see no way to get out of this—not at the moment, anyway. "If I say yes, you need to take care of Jack *immediately*. He's no use to us in that condition. And . . . the job will go

5

faster with two of us." He stared grimly at the floor.

"Cyke will make that happen," said Dr. Gray. He nodded slightly to the large soldier. "Take care of Goldstein."

"Of course," said Cyke.

"And keep your soldiers away from my family," warned Charles.

"I told you I will." He narrowed his eyes. "But if they cause trouble, all bets are off. Do we have a deal or not?"

Charles blew out a resigned breath. There was no other way. "All right," he said. "Take me to the lab."

Dr. Gray seemed pleased. "I will," he said, pulling a cell phone from his pocket. "But first, let's make a little call to ensure everything will go as planned."

CHAPTER 2

The Scene of the Crime

Charlie Wilde expelled a breath of relief when her mother pulled up to the curb at Andy's school. "There's Mom! Come on." She and her brother sprinted to the car and got in. Charlie flung her arms around her mother's neck. Andy leaned in from the backseat and hugged them both.

Mrs. Wilde held her children tightly. "Are you all right?" she asked. She drew back a little so she could see their faces. Andy was crying.

Charlie's lashes were wet. Her stomach was in knots. "We're okay, Mom," she said. "I'm so glad you're here."

"So am I," Mrs. Wilde said, her face filled with emotion.

"I'm scared," said Andy in a small voice. "What are we going to do about Dad?" Andy's earlier annoyance with his father for not picking him up on time had quickly turned to fear when Charlie revealed that someone had broken into their house and abducted him.

"We're going to figure this out," their mom said, "and everything's going to be okay." Diana Wilde's voice was firm and reassuring—the kids could always count on their emergency room doctor mom for that in stressful times. "So let's not panic quite yet." But she couldn't hide the worry in her eyes.

Charlie nodded and let out a held breath. "Okay. No panicking." She released her grip. Her mother's presence provided some relief—at least three out of the four of them were together and safe. But she didn't feel any better about her father's situation. She'd seen how bad the house had looked, especially his office. They had to find him.

Charlie settled into her seat and closed the car door so they could get moving. Andy sat down too and put his seat belt on. He wiped his eyes on his shirtsleeve and sniffed.

"This could all be a big misunderstanding," Mrs. Wilde said as she put the car in gear and pulled away from the curb. She started driving quickly toward home. "Charlie, are you positive Dad didn't just walk to the Summit soccer field for your game? Maybe he didn't get your text message about it being canceled. Or maybe he took the bus to do some errands, and he just left the house a mess and accidentally forgot his phone at home?" Her phone rested in the console cup holder—no doubt she'd tried calling him too.

"I'm sure. Dad's phone was smashed to pieces." Tears sprang to Charlie's eyes again, and she choked up. Hadn't her mom been listening? "Don't you believe me? I'm not exaggerating. His office was totally trashed."

"Oh, Charlie—of course I believe you. I'm just trying to . . .

I don't know . . . process all of this. And I'm so sorry you had to face that alone. That must've been very frightening." She punched the gas pedal and the car roared through a yellow light. "Tell me everything from the beginning."

The question made Charlie hesitate, feeling a little guilty. *The beginning? Which beginning?* There had been a lot of shocking and unusual events recently that she had been keeping secret from her family, and she didn't know how to start explaining them all. Besides that, she didn't understand half of what was going on. Charlie knew that strange soldiers in black bodysuits were after her . . . and her bracelet. They'd broken into Maria's house and kidnapped Mac—though luckily Charlie and Maria and Kelly had found him in the soldiers' warehouse and rescued him. But the soldiers were after Dad, too. And that's the part she didn't quite understand. What exactly was his connection to them and the bracelet? There were several pieces to the puzzle floating around in her brain, but she hadn't yet had the time to put them together.

Charlie pushed up her sweatshirt sleeve and peeked at the silver device, which she'd found in a mysterious package with her name on it. The sleek Chimera Mark Five gave her five different animal powers and basically turned her into a superhero when necessary. Unfortunately it was also stuck on her wrist, and she couldn't remove it no matter how hard she'd tried. And it was somehow at the root of all the horrible things that had happened in the past twenty-four hours. But suddenly trying to explain to her pragmatic, no-nonsense mother the powers it gave her—the speed of a cheetah, the strength of an elephant, the healing ability of a starfish, the climbing skills of a gecko, and the night vision of a bat—seemed completely overwhelming, not to mention how ridiculous it would sound to anyone who hadn't experienced them. The thought of explaining the soldiers, like the leopard man with fur growing on his face . . . And the Project Chimera folder . . . And the envelope with the Talos Global logo on it, which was the company her father used to work for, and the top secret papers inside, at least one of which had her father's name on it. . . . Where exactly was the beginning of a tale like that? Charlie's throat felt tight and numb, and she could hardly concentrate on any of it with her father missing. *Abducted*. The soldiers had gotten to him.

But she had to say something. Charlie collected her thoughts and decided to start with the most recent events, from the time she'd headed home after rescuing Mac and fighting the soldiers in the warehouse. "Well," she began, "I came up the street and saw Jessie running around the yard, barking her head off. Big Kitty was crouching under the bushes near the front door, which was open. So I ran inside—"

Andy interrupted, sounding anxious. "You probably should've gone to a neighbor." Both children had been taught plenty of rules about what to do in an emergency, not only from their parents but also from classes at the local Y in Chicago, where they'd lived before their recent move to Arizona.

"Yeah, I know, but I wasn't exactly thinking straight," explained Charlie. "I'd been trying to call Dad for a while, so I was already worried."

"Me too," said Andy. His voice hitched. "Is he going to be okay?"

"We're trying to figure that out right now, sweetie," their mom said. "Keep going, Charlie."

"I went inside," Charlie repeated. "Stuff was knocked over and thrown everywhere. I called for Dad and rushed to his office. It was totally ransacked. His cell phone was on the floor in pieces, and he was gone. So I ran straight to Andy's school and called you. Did you talk to the police?"

"Not yet." Mrs. Wilde put her hand on her phone, then frowned and pulled away. She glanced at Charlie. "What do you mean, you *ran* to Andy's school? From home?"

Charlie froze. Her cheetah ability on her bracelet had activated, allowing her to run at a speed of seventy miles per hour. She'd gotten there quickly, but a normal kid might take forty-five minutes to go that far on foot. Her mom didn't know Charlie was abnormal as long as this bracelet was stuck on her. "Um, yeah. I mean, I was scared. I guess my adrenaline really kicked in."

From the backseat Andy was straining forward against his seat belt so he could hear everything. "Did you put the pets back in the house?"

"Yeah, buddy. Of course I did," said Charlie over her shoulder.

She turned back to her mother. "Why haven't you called the police?"

Mrs. Wilde turned down their street and gunned toward their driveway. "I just . . . I wanted to see what we're dealing with first."

Charlie stared at her. "So you actually don't believe me. And now we're wasting time that we could use to find Dad!" It wasn't as though Charlie *wanted* the police to come, because she'd probably have to tell them about the bracelet. But that didn't matter now. This was serious. It was life or death! Why would her mother wait to call them?

"Charlie, trust me. I know you wouldn't lie about something like this," Mrs. Wilde said firmly. "It's just . . . there's something . . . strange. . . ." She shook her head slightly and parked the car in the driveway. As she turned the engine off, her cell phone buzzed. All three of them stared at it in the cup holder, as if expecting to see Charles's name appear as the caller, even though they knew his phone was smashed. But instead of a name or number, the screen read "Private."

It buzzed a second time, and Charlie and her mother looked at each other, alarmed. Then Mrs. Wilde picked up the phone. "Hello?"

A man's voice came through, loud enough for Charlie and Andy to hear in the silent car. "Diana, this is a friend of your husband's. He has something he'd like to tell you."

Andy clapped his hands over his mouth. Charlie gasped and

leaned closer to her mother, eyes wide.

"Diana," said Charlie's father. His voice sounded shaky.

"Charles!" cried Mrs. Wilde. "What's happening? Where are you?"

"Listen to me, Diana. Have you called the police?"

"No, not yet—I just—"

"Good. Don't call them. Okay? If you don't call them, I'll be okay. I'll be safe."

Diana frowned. "But—who? Where?"

"I'll be *safe*," Mr. Wilde repeated. "And they'll leave you alone. Okay? Don't call the police."

"But Dad!" Charlie cried, unable to stop herself. "Where are you? When are you coming home?"

"Charlie," Mr. Wilde said, and she could hear the relief in his voice. "Thank God." But he didn't answer any of their questions. Instead he grunted like somebody was hurting him and said again, more urgently, "Diana, do you understand?"

Mrs. Wilde held her hand up to keep Charlie from saying anything more. "Okay," she said, frustration apparent in her voice. The expression on her face was full of anguish. "Where are you?" she repeated. "Hello?" But then she lowered the phone and looked at the kids. "They hung up."

"Call him back!" said Andy.

"She can't," said Charlie. "It was private. They blocked the number."

Charlie's mom sat in stunned silence for a second, then shook her head, as if trying to comprehend what was happening. "Come on, kids." She got out and strode quickly to the door with Andy and Charlie right behind.

The three weaved through the house, gasping and exclaiming as they looked at the destruction. Some of the furniture was over-turned, stuff had been flung out of cupboards and drawers, even the TV in the living room was smashed. "I told you," said Char-lie, slipping in front of her mother and grabbing her hand. "Come with me. You've got to see this." She headed to her father's office.

"Whoa," said Andy, taking it in. He looked like he might start crying again.

Mrs. Wilde stared at the disaster in the office. Her hand flut-tered to her throat. "Oh my word," she murmured. She took a few cautious steps toward the stacks of Talos Global boxes that had been torn apart, contents stolen. A few loose wires and cords lay across the desk and on the floor—the computer they'd been attached to was gone, too. She let a fearful breath escape. "Oh, Charles. Who did this?" She pushed her hair back, looking dazed, and puzzled over the mostly empty Talos Global boxes. "Who on earth would want . . . ?" she murmured, and then her eyes wid-ened. "No. Could it be? After all these years?"

"What are you talking about?" asked Charlie.

Mrs. Wilde slid one of the empty boxes aside. She didn't seem to hear Charlie. Then she quickly moved the others, finding only a few remaining files of the dozens that had once been contained inside.

Charlie looked at a sheet of paper that had slipped out of one of the folders and lay on the floor. It had her dad's old company logo on it, like the paper she'd seen in the envelope she'd grabbed from the warehouse. Suddenly Charlie felt sick. She broke out in a cold sweat as she thought about the phone call. The soldiers. And the connection to Talos Global. What did her father have to do with those thugs? Where were they? And what were they doing to him now?

Mrs. Wilde knelt and continued riffling through the remaining items. Then she stopped and stood up straight, turning to look wildly around the room. "Where . . . ?" she murmured, her face more frantic than Charlie had ever seen it before. Then Mrs. Wilde's eyes alighted on the broken cell phone. She reached for it. It fell apart in her hand.

"Mom!" said Andy, his anxiety level clear on his face. "What are you doing?"

Instead of answering him Mrs. Wilde looked up. "*Safe*," she murmured. "Yes. He said it right to me." Her gaze landed on the closet, and she dashed over to it.

"Mom," Charlie said urgently. "What's going on?"

"Kids, please," Mrs. Wilde replied, distracted. "Just give me a minute. I need to think this through." She flung open the closet door and stepped inside, then dropped to the floor, where a safe was bolted down. It appeared untouched by the intruders.

Mrs. Wilde muttered under her breath, focusing on the dial lock. "What's the combination?"

Charlie and Andy exchanged a confused glance, and Andy sidled over to his sister. She put her hand on his shoulder to offer some reassurance. It was all she could think to do.

Momentarily halted, Mrs. Wilde turned and saw her children standing together, staring at her. She opened her mouth, then closed it. Then she said, "I can't explain now. You have to trust me."

"What are you looking for?" said Charlie.

Mom looked from one child to the other and pushed back a lock of hair that had fallen onto her face. "I . . . You have to understand there's something more going on here. It's . . . This might be something your father warned me a long time ago could happen. And it never did, and thank goodness for that, but we sort of stopped expecting it."

Charlie and Andy grew even more confused. "What?" asked Andy, eyes widening. "Mom, you're scaring me."

Mrs. Wilde's expression was a mix of fear and concern. She got up and went to the children, gathering them around her to comfort them. And then she blew out a measured breath. "Look," she said softly. "This is going to be difficult to understand. You heard your father—we can't call the police. But he . . . he said . . . he said the word 'safe' in a weird way. And repeated it. And I remember that's where he left . . . something. Back then. All right? Just sit here quietly with me while I figure this out, and don't say a word about this to anyone—don't text your friends or post anything online. Understand? And we stick together—we do *everything* together—until further notice."

The children stared at her, frightened by her mysterious manner.

"Okay?" Mrs. Wilde prompted.

"Okay," said Charlie, and Andy echoed, "Okay." Charlie put her phone away.

Mrs. Wilde went back to the safe and began turning the dial to the left, then right, then left again. She tugged at the handle. It didn't open. Undeterred, she spun the dial several times around, then tried another combination.

Charlie pulled up her sweatshirt sleeve and glanced at the bracelet on her wrist. She clicked through a couple of screens. Of the five colorful animals represented, only the starfish was animated at the moment. The bracelet's healing power was working fast after all the fighting Charlie had done just a short time earlier. Thanks to that ability, she hardly felt any pain anymore from the leopard man's long sharp claws. As she watched her mother wrestle with the safe, trying more combinations, Charlie was reminded of how she'd yanked the door off the safe in the warehouse using the elephant-strength power of the device. But that animal wasn't animated now.

Mrs. Wilde sat back against the closet doorjamb and closed her eyes, rubbing her fingers on her temples, thinking deeply. She got up and looked at the underside of Charles's desk, then searched through all of its drawers, one of which was overturned on the floor.

"Now what are you doing?" asked Andy.

"I'm looking for the combination for the safe. I really need to get in there."

Charlie swallowed hard. Should she tell her mother about the bracelet? About how she could open the safe if her strength ability kicked in? But her mom had told them to stay quiet, and she was intensely searching the room, and Charlie's strength ability wasn't activated, so it was useless to try to explain—at least right now when her mother seemed to be so focused on her task.

"Why don't you know the combination?" Andy asked his mother after a while.

"Well, I *should* know it," said their mother, sweat beading on her forehead now, "but your father resets it periodically. When we moved to this house, he told me where I could find it, but I'm afraid I was a little distracted with my new job at the time. And . . . I can't remember."

"Oh." Andy looked troubled but kept quiet as Mrs. Wilde continued her search.

"Do you want us to help you?" ventured Charlie.

"I want you to keep quiet and not touch anything until I figure this out." She gave an exasperated sigh, then looked at Charlie apologetically. "I'm sorry. Maybe you and Andy could look around the room for a spot that might be a good hiding place for a safe combination. Can you do that?"

Andy nodded and obeyed, his eyes darting around the room, but the task seemed useless to Charlie. Instead, she tried to activate the bracelet again by thinking about her father and the break-in and all the events at the warehouse. But since she was relatively safe at the moment, the device didn't detect a need for anything other than healing Charlie's bruises and wounds. After a while she gave up on the bracelet and gazed once more at the Talos Global paper on the floor, thinking things through.

Charlie's mom's weird searching and vague statements were startling, but in a strange way, something about her behavior also made sense after everything Charlie had just gone through. After all the crazy things she'd learned earlier. Her dad, who always called himself a lowly biologist, had been part of something far beyond anything the children had ever known or could have guessed until now. Did her mom have any clue who the "friend" was that called? Did she know that Mr. Wilde was somehow connected to soldiers who abducted him and were capable of attacking Charlie and Maria and kidnapping Mac?

Charlie reached out her foot, grabbed the paper with the sole of her shoe, and pulled it along the floor toward her so she could read it. Her eyes went to a phrase she'd seen before. "'Project Chimera,'" she whispered. The same words had been written on the outside of the warehouse envelope. Her bracelet was called the

Chimera Mark Five. Did her father's company make the devices? She broke out in a cold sweat. Did her *father* make them?

Charlie's mom looked sharply at her. "What did you say?" she demanded.

Charlie gave her mom a fearful glance. Her heart rate began to speed up uncontrollably, though she hardly knew why—there was something in her mom's voice that frightened her. She felt her fingers tingling, the device growing warmer on her arm. Her breath hitched. "I said, 'Project Chimera.'" Her eyes widened. "Why? Do you know what that means?" She picked up the paper and handed it to her mother.

Mrs. Wilde took it and studied it. She wiped her forehead on her sleeve and didn't answer.

Charlie quickly peeked at the bracelet and clicked through to the screen that would tell her which of her abilities had activated. The lizard and the elephant had pulsed to life alongside the starfish. A surge of hope mixed with her fear. Her strength had turned back on. But did she dare use it? How could she not, when her father's safety was at stake?

"Mom," Charlie said slowly, looking up, "I know you're trying to concentrate, but there's something I really need to tell you—a lot of things, actually. But first . . ." She cringed, hardly daring to suggest what she was about to suggest, but knowing she couldn't wait another second. "I can probably open that safe for you if you want me to."

CHAPTER 3

Coming Clean

"You . . . what?" asked Charlie's mom, seeming to forget about Project Chimera for the moment. "Did you find out the combination?"

"Not exactly," Charlie hedged.

"Well, I need it opened. If you think you can do it, be my guest."

Charlie decided not to mention that she would also be destroying the safe by opening it. She figured seeing her in action was probably the best way to start explaining the device to her mom. Mrs. Wilde moved out of the way, and Charlie sat down and grabbed on to the safe handle. Her sticky gecko fingertips ensured a tight grip. "Stand back," she said. She put her feet against the edges of the box.

Mrs. Wilde looked dubious. "I'm not so sure that's the best way to go about it," she said. "Don't hurt yourself."

Charlie didn't reply. Feeling the warmth from the bracelet, she took a deep breath, concentrated, and pulled until her knuckles turned white. At the same time she pushed her feet hard against the frame. The door to the safe groaned and shivered. It bent at the corners. Then, with a loud *THUNK*, Charlie flew backward. She hit the closet wall hard, safe door in hand, and felt the drywall collapse against her back. "Oof," she said as all the breath was forced out of her. Pulling off safe doors was one of her least favorite things to do, she decided. She sat up carefully, little bits of drywall dust slipping down the back of her sweatshirt, and peered out of the closet.

"Charlie!" Mrs. Wilde cried.

Andy stared at his sister, incredulous. "What the—?" said Andy. "How—?"

Mom hurried to Charlie's side. "Are you okay? How in the world did you do that?"

Charlie set down the door and peered inside the safe. It was half full of papers, envelopes, and some important-looking documents. "Welp," she said, easing gingerly out of the way so her mother could look for whatever she needed, "it's kind of a long story."

Mrs. Wilde recovered her wits and checked Charlie over. Then she sat down in front of the open safe while Charlie told her and Andy about the bracelet. She explained how she'd found a package among their moving boxes with her name on it. How the bracelet had gotten stuck on her arm and wouldn't come off after the school bathroom incident, where she'd torn the sink right out of the wall. How she'd even saved a mother and child from a house fire using a variety of the five distinct animalistic powers the device had given her. "Sometimes the bracelet powers turn on when I don't need

them," she explained, "but that can actually come in handy some-times."

"Wait," Charlie's mom said. "Go back. You're saying *you* are the one who saved that woman and her baby from the fire? I worked on them in the ER." She shook her head in disbelief. "I can hardly . . . What on earth possessed you to go inside a burning house? Didn't you see how dangerous it was? Charlie! I—I don't even know what to say." She looked around the torn-apart office, utterly perplexed and bewildered by the developments.

"But I'm fine because of the healing powers," Charlie argued. "Remember my leg after I got hurt in soccer tryouts? It healed completely—by *morning*. Plus, I have an *obligation* to help people. . . ." She trailed off, remembering her talk with Maria about that.

"You're a maniac," said Andy, his voice filled with awe.

Mrs. Wilde stared at Charlie for a long moment, like she still couldn't believe what she was hearing and wasn't sure how to respond. "This is so . . . shocking," she murmured. "I don't—I almost can't fathom what you're saying. But your leg and that fire rescue? And now the safe . . . ?" She shook her head, almost dazed, then turned to look at Charlie. "I can't deny that those abilities seem beyond normal. I'm almost afraid to ask, but what else has happened?"

"Yeah," said Andy, like he couldn't believe there might be more. "What else?"

"Well," said Charlie, "people are after the bracelet . . . and they might be the same people who kidnapped Dad." Hesitantly Charlie trudged onward with the story, telling her mother and Andy about the three strange soldiers in full bodysuits who'd attacked her and Maria on their way home from school earlier that day. "And three different ones kidnapped Mac and brought him to an old abandoned warehouse. But he's okay. We rescued him."

"You did *WHAT*?" cried Mrs. Wilde. "By *yourselves*?" All semblance of the steady, even-keeled doctor had flown out the window—their mom had uncorked.

Charlie cringed but plowed forward because she knew she had to get to the most important part. "After we fought off the soldiers, we found some papers in the warehouse. They had Dad's old work logo on them, like these." She pointed to the paper she'd been looking at earlier. "And Dad's name was on at least one of the papers, too." Charlie ducked her head in preparation for her mother to explode again, but that didn't happen.

Diana Wilde stared long and hard at her daughter. Everything was so farfetched, so inconceivable. Charlie held her breath and waited for her mother to deny that any of this was possible. The last thing she expected was for her mother to actually believe it.

"Project Chimera," Mrs. Wilde murmured.

Charlie looked up, searching her mother's face. "That's what was written on the folder we found. And this bracelet is called

Chimera Mark Five—it says it on one of the screens."

Charlie's mom put her hands up to her face, as if she were trying to pull her thoughts together. Then she expelled a deep breath, dropped her hands in her lap, and opened her eyes. She wore a new expression of resolve. "I really can't believe this is happening," she said.

"Do you think she's making it up?" Andy asked. He sounded like he wanted to believe Charlie but wasn't sure that a grown-up might.

"I'm not lying," Charlie implored. "I promise. Look." She held out her arm and shoved her sleeve up high, then clicked the bracelet and showed her mother the message scrolling in red letters, CHIMERA MARK FIVE . . . DEFENSE MODE INITIATED . . . KEY IN ACCESS CODE TO DEACTIVATE.

Then she showed her the screen where the animated silver elephant, green lizard, and pink starfish pulsed.

After a long moment Charlie's mother placed a comforting hand on the girl's wrist. "I believe you," she said quietly. "It's seems impossible, but because of the little bit I know about your father's old job, I do. And since I believe you, I need to find what I was looking for now more than ever." Quickly she began to flip through the items in the safe, shoving things aside that she didn't need. Finally she discovered a small white envelope at the back. Charlie's mom snatched it up and held it. Her first name was on it, written in Mr. Wilde's familiar scrawl. "This is it," she said. Her fingers shook as she ripped open the seal and pulled out a piece of paper.

She unfolded it, and the kids moved to look over their mother's shoulder so they could read it too. It was a printout, dated ten years ago.

> *My love,*
>
> *If you're reading this, the worst has happened. I had hoped you'd never need this—hoped that my colleagues and I were being ridiculously cautious. Unfortunately our instincts must have been right.*
>
> *I'm sorry I've had to be so secretive all these years, and that this letter is cryptic—it was necessary in case it fell into the wrong hands. In the event that something tragic has befallen me, this should help.*

Andy and Charlie looked sidelong at each other with troubled expressions. What was their father talking about? It had to be about his top secret work at Talos Global—that was the only thing that made sense. But what had he been so worried about back then to make him write such a letter and have some sort of conversation with their mom about it?

Charlie pressed her lips together, wanting desperately to ask questions but knowing now wasn't the right time. She continued reading.

> *Instead, I need you to contact someone who will help you—someone you can trust completely. You have the information at your fingertips. I know you can find it. And . . . apologies for the extra precautions.*

"What does he mean?" asked Andy. "This letter makes no sense."

"Shh," said Charlie.

> *I love you and Charlotte and the baby with all my heart. You're the strongest, smartest person I know, and you will get through this.*
>
> *Yours qlways,*
>
> *Charles*

"I'm the baby, right?" whispered Andy.

"Shh," said Charlie again, poking her brother with her elbow and nodding once sharply in their mother's direction.

Charlie's mom was studying the letter. "I have the information?" she muttered. She dropped her hand with the note and closed her eyes in despair. "An entire decade has passed since then, Charles. I barely remember the conversation. If something was

28

going to happen, we expected it to be years ago."

"You were right about the 'safe' clue," said Charlie, trying to be encouraging.

"Yes. I just had the most unusual feeling when he said it like that, which is why . . ." She got to her feet and began looking around the room. "This clue is so random. I have the information? Where?"

"Didn't he say it was at your fingertips?" asked Charlie. "Maybe that's the clue."

"Yeah," said Andy. "Maybe he means it's on your computer. Because, you know. Typing. Fingertips. Get it?"

Mrs. Wilde nodded thoughtfully, then her eyes widened. "I hope that didn't get stolen too." She darted out of the office and went to the living room, where she kept her laptop. The kids followed.

The laptop was gone.

"Oh no!" cried Mrs. Wilde. "All my stuff!" She looked around the living room in case she'd only misplaced it, but it wasn't anywhere. "Now what?"

They thought for a moment, trying not to despair, but Andy struggled to hold back his tears. Charlie wondered if her brother fully understood what was happening. She doubted it. He could see how upset their mom was, and he was probably taking his cues from her.

Charlie went over all the information again in her head. "It's weird that Dad would put a clue on your laptop when he knows you don't carry it with you to work and stuff. But you also use your fingertips for your phone, and you never go anywhere without that."

Mom studied Charlie thoughtfully. "Good point. You might be onto something, Charlie." She pulled her phone from her pocket and placed the letter from Charles on the coffee table, then sat down on the couch and began looking through her apps. Andy's tears dried up, and he and Charlie sat around her, watching and offering suggestions on which apps could hold a clue.

"Wait a minute," said Charlie, her heart sinking. "You didn't have this phone ten years ago when Dad wrote the note. Maybe he put a clue in the phone you had back then, and it's gone for good."

Mrs. Wilde's shoulders sagged, and she closed her eyes momentarily, then opened them again. "Okay, you're right in that I've upgraded phones several times since then. But I think they've all been smartphones for at least that long. The information transfers—contacts do, anyway. And he's smart enough to put it somewhere that would back up to my computer, too." She abruptly went to her contacts list and checked her husband's information, but there was nothing unusual about the entry.

After several minutes of fruitless scrolling Mrs. Wilde set the phone in her lap and returned to the letter, muttering as she reread the key phrases.

Charlie and Andy read it over again, too. *At your fingertips.* *Smartest person.* Were any of these words supposed to be a code for something else?

"He spelled 'always' wrong," Andy pointed out.

Charlie rolled her eyes. Now was not the time to criticize their father's typing abilities. "It's just a typo," Charlie said. "The 'q' is right above the 'a' on the keyboard. Simple mistake."

Mrs. Wilde paused in her search. "That's odd, though, isn't it? Spell-check would have picked that up."

"Did you even have spell-check back in the old days?" asked Andy.

Mrs. Wilde almost smiled. "Yes, son. Amazingly we did, even way back then." She studied the typo and mused, "Your father hates typos. He would never print such an important letter with a mistake like that in it."

"Do you think he spelled it 'qlways' on purpose?" asked Charlie.

"Maybe." Mom scratched her head. "But what's the significance? Is the absence of the 'a' or the presence of the 'q' the important part?"

"I think the 'q' is the clue," said Charlie. "He could have just left the 'a' off if he didn't want it there."

"You're right," said Mrs. Wilde. "So what does it mean?"

Andy inched closer. "Search your contacts under the letter Q!"

Mrs. Wilde was already going back to her list of contacts. "I've had a lot of friends and colleagues over the years, but I don't think I know anybody whose name starts with Q," she said. She entered the letter and hit the search button.

There was one entry—a very mysterious one, at that. First name Q, last name S. And in place of a phone number, there was a jumbled mess of numbers and letters.

"What's that supposed to mean?" asked Charlie, staring at the string of letters and numbers. "That's not a phone number. Who is QS?"

Charlie's mother examined the contact entry. "I don't know. I certainly didn't add this."

"So you think we found the clue?" asked Andy.

"I really hope so," Mrs. Wilde said. She studied the strange code as a feeling of hopelessness settled over them. What were they supposed to do with this nonsensical clue? She swallowed hard and her eyes pooled.

Charlie watched her. "Are you okay?" she asked.

"Just . . . worried." She sniffed and took a deep breath, then let it out slowly. "All right, kids," she said, shaking off the tears. "We have to be brave. Let's figure out this clue so we can find your father. Andy, can you get me a notepad and pencil?"

Andy hopped off the couch and made his way around the mess to the kitchen near the landline phone, where they kept such things. He brought the items back to his mother.

"There are ten characters," said Mrs. Wilde, "which is good. It means this is probably a coded phone number. I'm trying to figure out how to decipher it."

"I've worked with ciphers in school," said Charlie, eager to do something to help.

"Me too," said Andy. "First you write the alphabet in a line."

Their mother was already scribbling the entire alphabet on the paper in a long row. Below that she wrote a row of numbers, one through twenty-six, a number under each letter.

Then the three of them looked back at the contact information and studied the strange phone number for QS. There were five letters alternating with five numbers. The first character in the string was a letter.

"He gave you five of the numbers," Andy pointed out.

"I don't think those are the right ones, though," murmured Mrs. Wilde. "That would be too easy. But we'll get to that. Let's start with the letters." She matched all five letters from the code on her phone screen to the numbers they corresponded with on the paper in front of her. She wrote those numbers down, keeping them in the same order as in the code. "How am I doing so far?"

"Looks good to me," said Charlie, and Andy nodded.

"Here's the tricky part." Mrs. Wilde thought for a moment, then looked at her phone again to check the code. She took all the numbers Mr. Wilde had given her and matched them up with their corresponding letters in the alphabet cipher. She wrote those letters down too and plugged them into the empty spaces. Now all the letters in the original code were numbers, and the numbers were letters.

"I don't see how that gives you a phone number," said Charlie, who was watching intently. "You just have the opposite of the jumbled mess you had before."

"Just hang on," said her mother. She hesitated, thinking hard. "Your father always knew how much I despised his little coded puzzles," she said with a sardonic laugh. "But he adores them. What do I do now?"

The three of them stared at the code. It didn't offer anything to let them know they were on the right track. Andy started searching common ciphers on his phone, while Charlie wondered aloud if the letters were supposed to spell something. But if they did, then what? They needed numbers. After a while she gave up and looked over Andy's shoulder as he continued to search different options. They tried a few, but none of them seemed to be right.

"Sometimes people use numbers to mean letters," Charlie said. "Like three for E, or one for I."

"Yeah," said Andy, looking hopeful.

"Wait," said Mrs. Wilde, suddenly inspired. She opened the keypad on her phone and pointed to the numbers. "That reminds me of a code Charles used before, when he made me figure out a clue in order to open a present he'd bought me. See how each number on the keypad has three letters that go with it?"

The kids nodded.

"I'll bet that's our secret. For each of the letters we have here, we match them up to the number they correspond with on the keypad." Mrs. Wilde took each letter, found the number it went with on the phone, and wrote those numbers in place of the letters in her new code.

"That's so cool," said Andy. "I always wondered what those letters were good for."

"Tricky," said Charlie. She nibbled on her thumbnail anxiously, thinking of her father. "I hope it's right."

By the time Mrs. Wilde was done, she had a ten-digit phone number scrawled on the paper. "Okay," she said, cautious confidence growing in her voice. "It's a Chicago area code, which makes me think we did something right. Here goes. Cross your fingers that we've got this." Her hand shook as she dialed. After she finished entering the numbers, she pressed the speaker button.

The phone rang. Four times. Five. Six. It didn't go to voice mail. Charlie and Andy exchanged a glance. Finally, on the seventh ring, someone picked up but didn't say anything for several seconds. Then a woman asked guardedly, "Who are you trying to reach?"

Mrs. Wilde swallowed hard, her eyes darting to her children.

"Say something," Charlie whispered.

Their mom leaned over the phone and spoke clearly and distinctly, "Q. S." She paused, then added, "Please."

"Who's calling?"

"It's . . . I'm Diana. Diana Wilde."

There was silence on the other end. For a moment the three Wildes thought the person had hung up. Mrs. Wilde put a finger to her lips to ensure her children wouldn't say anything. They remained quiet. Charlie thought she could hear a faint sound of clicking on the other end, like someone was typing.

The three looked at one another, confused. And then the woman spoke again. "Hello, Diana," she said. "I'm very sorry to hear from you. This is Dr. Quinn Sharma. Is anyone forcing you to make this call?"

CHAPTER 4
Top Secret Stuff

Dr. Quinn Sharma? The name sounded vaguely familiar to Charlie, but she couldn't quite place it.

Charlie's mother hesitated. "No. I'm here with my children. You're on speakerphone."

"How can I help you?" Dr. Sharma asked guardedly.

"I—we found a note that led us to . . . you."

"Has . . . has something happened to Dr. Wilde?"

"He's been abducted."

Charlie could hear a small intake of breath on the other end and a momentary silence.

Mrs. Wilde continued. "How do you know him?"

"I worked with him at . . . in the past."

Charlie sat up, her eyes widening as she realized why Dr. Sharma's name sounded familiar. It was one of the names listed on a cover sheet inside the envelope she'd taken from the warehouse. But did that mean she was on their side? Or on the side of the soldiers?

Mrs. Wilde paused and narrowed her eyes. "How do I know I can trust you?"

"You don't." The words landed hard. "But your husband left you my number, so it seems he trusts me."

"That was ten years ago."

"True. And I understand your hesitation. Maybe I can tell you a few things that might help."

"Okay," said Mrs. Wilde, her voice guarded.

The woman continued. "I'm a genetic biologist. I worked with Charlie at Talos Global ten years ago."

Charlie could hear more typing, and then Dr. Sharma said, "You have two children, Charlotte Paige and Andrew Finn, ages twelve and ten. Your husband's middle name is Alexander, and yours, Diana, is Rae. You lived at 15538 Balder Street in Chicago until recently."

"Whoa," whispered Andy and Charlie together.

Mrs. Wilde blinked, her face still betraying a hint of uncertainty. The woman seemed trustworthy enough to Charlie—after all, her dad had said this person could help them. Still, it felt a little weird talking to a complete stranger.

It appeared that Mrs. Wilde had similar doubts. She proceeded cautiously. "Do you know anything about a . . . a package?"

"Ah," said Dr. Sharma. "Yes. I had a package delivered to Charlie. And a note. Right before you moved."

"But *I'm* Charlie now," Charlie blurted out before she could stop herself. "He's *Charles*."

Mrs. Wilde silenced Charlie with a look. "And the package

contained . . . ?" she prompted.

Dr. Sharma hesitated. "A wrist device that he created. One that alters . . . things. Wait. Charlie, did *you* open it?"

"I thought it was for me!" she cried.

Mrs. Wilde placed a comforting hand on Charlie's. Charlie swallowed hard and fought the urge to say anything more. She knew her mother had to handle things right now, but she had a lot of questions for Dr. Sharma.

"I'm sorry—I never thought—" Dr. Sharma's distress was evident in her voice. She stopped abruptly and then whispered, "Oh dear," like she was imagining all the things that could have happened with the bracelet finding its way into a twelve-year-old's hands. "Okay," she said after a moment. "Let's figure our way through this mess."

Mrs. Wilde closed her eyes and sighed. "Thanks, Doctor."

"Please—you can call me Quinn. I'm just a lowly biologist."

Charlie almost smiled despite the dire circumstances. Dr. Sharma talked like her father. That "lowly biologist" line—it was something her father had said frequently about himself in the same manner. Somehow it made her trust the woman completely. She caught her mother's eye and nodded. This person was safe. It was such a relief to find someone who could help them fill in the blanks. Mrs. Wilde squeezed Charlie's hand and gave Andy a reassuring smile. They were getting closer.

* * *

Charlie's mom finished telling Dr. Sharma everything she knew. Charlie chimed in to answer some of the more specific questions about the soldiers and the bracelet. They could hear the biologist typing occasionally on the other end of the phone. "You did the right thing in calling me," she told them. "The project was a top secret government contract. When it was shuttered, Victor Gray was acting suspicious, so we set up this emergency system. I'm glad we did, because Victor's obviously up to something. I suspect he's the one who called you."

Charlie, Andy, and their mother looked at one another, confused. "Who is Victor Gray?" asked Charlie.

Dr. Sharma paused. "Our fellow scientist on the project. Dr. Victor Gray—wasn't he there with the soldiers you fought?"

"I don't think so," said Charlie, "but nobody exactly took the time to introduce themselves before attacking me."

"Of course not," the woman murmured thoughtfully. She hesitated, as if weighing her options. "I feel like I need to let you in on some of this intel now that you three and Charles are facing danger. But I'm not comfortable doing this on the phone after what happened to your house."

"Can you at least tell us why you think Dr. Gray would do this to Charles?"

Dr. Sharma was silent for a moment. "If he abducted your husband, it's because he needs him to help further whatever his cause is."

"So you don't think he's going to hurt my dad?" asked Andy.

"I don't think so. As long as you keep the police out of it like he said, he should be fine. But," Dr. Sharma went on, her voice worried, "if Gray has moved his lab and all his soldiers across the country in pursuit of your device or someone who can re-create it, I worry he's doing something . . . big."

Charlie, Andy, and their mom waited, expecting Dr. Sharma to explain. But the woman was quiet for a long moment as she typed something. After a while she spoke decisively. "I'm looking at flights for first thing tomorrow. I'll text you my details once I have them. I think it would be better to discuss all of this in person."

While Mrs. Wilde and Dr. Sharma firmed up details, Charlie snuck a peek at her phone screen for the first time since her mother had told her and Andy not to text their friends or go online. There was a text message from Maria.

"Mayday! Mayday!" it read. "I've got a little problem over here. HELP."

CHAPTER 5

Pulling It Together

Charlie's mind started spinning again after seeing Maria's text message asking for help. Was Maria just being dramatic or was something really wrong? Had the soldiers gone back to her house? The thought was enough to make her bracelet activate. Quickly she unlocked her phone to reply. But as she began typing, the cracked corner of her screen split straight across the bottom of the phone's face. The lower one-third of the screen no longer responded to Charlie's fingertips.

"Crap," she muttered. Her strength ability was completely destroying the thing. Why did it have to happen now? Andy looked over and his eyes widened at the sight of her Frankenphone, but for once he wisely stayed quiet.

Charlie tapped the delicate screen lightly, wondering if maybe the cursor had just frozen momentarily, but soon confirmed that she couldn't type another letter. The message box was right in the middle of the damage. A second later the screen faded and went black. Now what was she supposed to do?

A flood of anxiety, anger, and frustration washed over her. This whole situation was hard enough without her phone giving her problems. She glanced at her mother, who was still talking to Dr. Sharma. Andy had curled up in the chair with their dog, Jessie, and was talking to her quietly as he petted her.

"Hey," Charlie said to Andy, going over to him. "Can I borrow your phone? I need to text Maria back and mine's dead."

"Mom said not to text our friends."

"Yeah, but this is an emergency."

"No," he said. "Go plug yours in if you need to do it so badly."

Charlie grimaced. "Come on, please?"

"No. Do you want me to tell Mom on you?"

Charlie sighed and gave up. She went back to the kitchen, spying the landline. Her mom was standing right next to it. She went after it, but when she reached for it, her mother automatically pulled it out of her hands and put it back in the holder, shaking her head and frowning.

Charlie tried to explain that she wasn't about to tell anyone what was going on—she just needed to check in with Maria. But Mrs. Wilde turned away and plugged her free ear so she could hear what Dr. Sharma was saying.

Out of options, Charlie dropped into a chair and hoped Maria's "little problem" was just that—little. Her mind turned back to the other urgent situation of the day, which was playing out like a horror movie. She was hardly able to comprehend that her father had been abducted, probably by the same strange, animal-like soldiers she'd fought off hours before. And it was because *he* had created the bracelet that was stuck on her wrist right now. Her *dad*. Had made *this* insanely powerful bracelet. No wonder he'd been abducted! Mr. Dr. Wilde, as her friends called him, was no lowly biologist. He was amazing. And Charlie couldn't tell anyone. Not even him.

Not that it mattered. She closed her eyes, overwhelmed and exhausted by the bombardment of otherworldly events. School that morning seemed like it had been a week ago. Like Andy, she needed to curl up and process what had just happened.

She hoped the soldiers hadn't been rough with her dad like they'd been to her. It was a relief to know that Dr. Sharma believed Dr. Gray needed Charles, so he wouldn't hurt him. But Charlie's imagination was going crazy after everything she'd experienced, and she couldn't shake the thought of more terrible things happening to him. What if her father wouldn't help Dr. Gray? Or worse . . . what if he would? It was a terrible situation no matter what.

Charlie's mom hung up and came back to the living room. "Quinn assured me that now that Dr. Gray has your father, he won't need you or your bracelet, Charlie. So you don't have to worry about them coming after you anymore." She let out a sigh of relief. "We're all going to be okay. And we're going to find him." She searched Charlie's face, then checked Andy's response too, making sure they were both handling the news all right.

Charlie frowned. "Are you sure they won't come after me? Why would they suddenly not want the bracelet when that was all they wanted earlier today?" She wondered if that meant her friends would be safe too. That would be a big relief.

"Well," said Mrs. Wilde, a bit of worry creeping back into her voice despite her intentions, "I guess nothing is sure anymore. But they probably found your father sometime after they attacked you. And I guess it makes sense that they'd want him more than the bracelet—your father made that device over ten years ago. With today's technology, he could make something more advanced now."

"Maybe one without any glitches," said Charlie, thinking of how the wrong powers sometimes activated.

Andy sat up. "But I still don't understand *why* that Dr. Gray dude kidnapped Dad. Why doesn't he just make a new device himself? Isn't he a biologist too?"

"Quinn said that Dad and the other scientists were all creating different types of devices. I imagine Dr. Gray wants to skip all the work that Dad already put into the Mark Five and have him improve on what he's already done."

While Charlie absorbed this new information, Andy just shook his head. "I can't believe our dad can do crazy junk like that. Who knew? And you too, Charlie," he said, their previous disagreement over the phone apparently forgotten. "You're pretty cool."

Charlie shrugged. Seeing Andy able to let some of this intense stuff fly right over his head was a relief—she didn't want him freaking out inside like she had been. But hearing her mom explain things made her feel a lot better. Maybe that had helped Andy, too.

"So . . . what do we do now?" Charlie asked her mother. She inched toward the landline phone again, growing more and more anxious to reach Maria and find out what was going on with her.

"We sit tight and wait for Quinn to arrive. She's going to give us further instructions once she reaches her government contact."

"Do we get to stay home from school?" asked Andy.

"I think that would be best, at least for tomorrow. Even if Quinn is right about her theory, I'm not confident enough to let you two out of my sight quite yet."

"I have tests coming up," Charlie murmured automatically, knowing at least two of her teachers were planning them at the end of this week before spring break began. She hadn't had much time to prepare with everything that had happened. But tests seemed so much less important now.

"Well, I guess that's pretty cool," said Andy. "A day off tomorrow, then only two more days of school." He looked up with a consternated expression. "Oh, Mom, I forgot. Juan asked me at school today if I could go camping with his family on break. But . . . I guess I should say no."

Charlie's mother blinked. "What? Who?"

"Juan is one of Andy's new school friends," Charlie reminded her. "He's been over a few times but maybe not when you've been here." Diana Wilde had been working extreme hours since the move to Arizona a month ago, and Charlie was getting used to having to fill her mother in on everything.

"Oh, of course I remember him," said Mrs. Wilde, distracted. "I drove him home once and met his mom. Nice family. Maybe that's not such a bad idea." She looked at Andy and trailed off, lost in thought. "Do you want to go?"

"Well, I mean I *did*. But with Dad missing, I don't know." His face screwed up and he buried it in Jessie's fur.

"Actually . . . ," Mrs. Wilde began, then shook her head, looking overwhelmed. "I can't handle one more thing to think about right now. I'm sorry, buddy. Let's figure this out later."

Andy lifted his head and nodded solemnly. Everything was up in the air, their mom was trying to deal, and Charlie knew Andy didn't handle this kind of stress very well. She thought distraction might be good for him. "Hey. I have the second *Ms. Marvel* for you," she said quietly. "You want it?"

Andy breathed a sigh of relief. "Yeah, sure."

When Charlie returned with the comic, she caught her mother's grateful gaze and returned it with a solemn, brave one of her own. A certain, unusual kind of energy passed between them. A bond of trust, perhaps, or a deep sense of understanding. It felt like one of those looks between two adults when there were children in the room—and this time Charlie wasn't the child. She'd seen it dozens of times between teachers at school. Between her parents across the dinner table. All sorts of unsaid things passing through the air. It was Charlie's first experience being on the receiving end of it, and it made her feel like she was in on a special secret. Like her mom was silently asking Charlie if she wanted to be a member of the secret looks club. And if she was ready for the responsibility that went along with that.

Charlie was. She thought so, anyway. She swallowed hard and nodded slightly.

Her mom's eyes grew shiny. She leaned in and embraced Charlie in a long, tight hug, and stroked her hair. "Let's try to keep things light for Andy's sake, okay?" she whispered.

"Okay."

"Atta girl." Mrs. Wilde released Charlie and gave her a half-smile, and then reached for Andy to hug him too.

Charlie's phone vibrated again, jolting her back to Maria's problem. She looked at the screen to find another text message. "Seriously, Chuck," it read. "Help needed pronto. I think you're the only one who can help me at this point."

"Maria!" Charlie murmured, tapping and swiping desperately on the alert to try and open the message, but it soon faded. She had to find out what was going on. She stood up quickly and excused herself to the bathroom, grabbing the landline phone on her way. But once in the bathroom she realized she had no idea what Maria's phone number was and she couldn't look it up. This was so frustrating. She had to do something about her phone— what if her father tried to call and she couldn't answer him? What if Maria was really in danger? What if the soldiers came back and she couldn't let her mom know?

This was a terrible time to throw one more problem on the pile, right when her mother had so much else on her mind. But Charlie knew it was the right thing to do. As she went back to the living room to confess about her broken cell phone, she wondered if she could recall Maria's number from memory. But she'd barely looked at it—she'd just added Maria as a contact. She hadn't written it down anywhere else. Just then she remembered she'd seen it one other place. It was on the soccer team roster on Charlie's bulletin board in her room. Maria Torres's name and contact information were at the top of it. She made a detour to her bedroom.

But when Charlie tried calling Maria from the landline, the phone rang five times and went to voice mail. *Why didn't she answer?*

CHAPTER 6

Maria's Big Problem

Charlie left a message. Why hadn't Maria answered? Maybe she didn't answer unknown numbers, and there was no reason for Charlie to think Maria would have her home number plugged into her phone. That had to be it. Hopefully she'd check her voice mail soon. Charlie tried calling again. And again, no answer. Had something bad happened to her?

It was no use looking for Mac's number—his phone and iPad had been stolen by the thugs who attacked them. Charlie flopped down on the bed and put her head in her hands. She had to help Maria. But there was no way her mom would let her go over there—not tonight. She'd have to sneak out.

Just then Charlie heard a voice outside, followed by the sound of pebbles bouncing off her bedroom window. Her lungs froze in fear. Were the soldiers after her? But that was silly—they wouldn't waste time throwing pebbles to get to her. They had already broken into the house once. Nevertheless, she felt her bracelet heat up.

"Hey, Chuck! Are you in there?"

Charlie's eyes widened, then her breathing resumed and she ran to the window. She peered out into the darkness, shading her eyes from the light behind her, but couldn't see anything. "Maria?"

"Charlie! Are you all right?"

"Are *you*?" Charlie replied. "My phone broke! I tried to call you from the landline but you didn't answer. Things are a little crazy here right now. My dad . . ." She felt her throat constrict and she blinked hard. She couldn't get herself to continue.

"Not *your* phone too!" exclaimed Maria, sounding more devastated than Charlie would have expected. "It's bad enough not being able to text Mac."

"Hey, I didn't break mine," said another voice. "It was stolen."

"Mac, you're out there too?" Charlie asked.

"Yep."

Charlie moved over and turned off her bedroom light, then returned and looked out the window again. Now she could see the silhouettes of her friends below, and beyond them the line of trees and the walls that enclosed the backyard.

"Can you come down?" asked Mac. "You need to see this. We have a huge problem."

"Yeah," said Maria miserably. "Huge."

"Why didn't you just come to the door? It's not too late. You can come inside."

"Um . . . well, no," said Maria, her voice taking on the tiniest quiver. "I can't. I don't want your mom to see me."

Charlie looked over her shoulder. The hallway was deserted. Mom and Andy were still downstairs. "Hold on a sec." She ran out of her room to the top of the steps and listened, trying to figure out if she could get around them without her mom seeing her. She could hear Andy sniffling and her mother talking to him in low, reassuring tones. "Nope," Charlie muttered. She'd have to find a different way.

She went back into her room and closed the door softly, leaving her in total darkness. Immediately she began to chirp uncontrollably—her echolocation power had kicked in. She hoped it wasn't loud enough to summon Andy or her mother upstairs wondering what sort of bird was on the loose. She flipped on the light switch and the chirping ceased.

Leaving her shoes off, Charlie went back to the window. She carefully removed the screen and pulled it inside the room, then climbed out backward and hung there, her stomach flipping as she hoped that would be enough to activate her climbing ability. An instant later she could feel her fingers and toes tingling. "Okay, cool," she muttered. She gripped the window ledge and her toes latched on to the rough stucco siding, the stickiness feeling a little like Velcro. Awkwardly at first, then more smoothly as she became reacquainted with the sensation, she made her way down the side of the house.

"So, my dad was abducted," Charlie blurted out as she neared the ground. It felt weird and horrible to say it out loud. It made it feel real. "The soldiers got him."

"Oh no!" said Maria. "That's horrible!"

"Are you serious?" asked Mac.

"Totally serious. But you can't tell anybody. Promise? I'll explain later."

"Okay," said Maria and Mac together, both sounding uncertain. Then Mac said, "What can we do to help?"

"My mom got in touch with someone who's going to help us, so it's under control at the moment." Charlie landed on the ground and turned around, searching for her friends in the shadows. Suddenly she began chirping again. "Ugh," she said. "Can you hear that?"

Mac started laughing. "Is that your echolocation? You sound like a bird with hiccups."

"Yeah. You both look like silvery shimmers to me. Let's step over here." Charlie guided them to the swath of light that came from her bedroom window. The chirping stopped, and Charlie got a good look at Maria. Her eyes widened, and she took a step backward. "Whoa. What the—?"

Maria's cheeks were tearstained, but those weren't what surprised Charlie. It was her hair. Or whatever it was on top of Maria's head. And . . . on her chin.

Charlie sucked in a breath and peered closer. Maria had a furry beard. "What happened to you?" she asked as gently as she could.

Maria started crying, and she held out her wrist. "This bracelet," she said. "It turned me into a monkey." There was fur on Maria's arms, too.

"Oh no," Charlie breathed. She glanced at Mac, who looked

solemn, and then at Maria. "Can't you turn back?"

"We tried all the buttons," said Maria. "And the bracelet's stuck on me, like yours is."

A horrible feeling began to grow inside of Charlie, on top of the already horrible feeling that wouldn't go away because of her dad. This was beyond awful. Charlie could hardly imagine how Maria must feel. "There has to be some way for you to change back," she said, trying to be logical. "There just has to be."

"Do you really think so?" asked Maria, her voice practically begging Charlie to confirm it.

"Of course I do," said Charlie, but she didn't feel very confident. "Maybe Dr. Sharma will be able to fix you—she's the person who's coming to help us rescue my dad." Charlie quickly filled them in on Dr. Sharma's and her dad's roles in creating the devices and what they'd suspected about Dr. Gray.

"That's incredible," marveled Mac. "Your dad worked on these? Is that why Dr. Gray had the soldiers abduct him when they couldn't get the bracelet from us?"

Charlie nodded and looked solemnly at Maria. "I know you must hate what your bracelet has done to you, but we might need to use these things if we're going to save my dad."

Maria looked doubtful but then said, "Well, of course I would want to help with that. But right now I just wish I hadn't ever put this thing on." She looked down. "Or at least picked a different one."

Charlie thought she understood. "What about checking the Project Chimera folder and the envelope? Maybe we can find some answers there so at least we can get you turned back to normal now."

Mac held up the large manila Talos Global envelope with the folder stuck inside. "I brought them from Maria's house."

Charlie sighed in relief. "Smart thinking. So your parents haven't seen you like this?"

Maria shook her head. "Not yet."

"Good," said Charlie. "Even if we can't figure out how to fix this right away, you could wear a scarf or something, right? And long sleeves?" She tried to sound hopeful.

Maria's lip quivered. She tried to speak but could only look miserably at Mac.

Charlie was confused. Was there something else going on?

Mac pressed his lips together. "It's not just the fur," he told Charlie. "Show her, Maria."

Maria began to cry. Slowly she turned around and pulled a ropelike coil of something out of the back of her jeans.

It was a tail.

CHAPTER 7

Skills and Complications

"Oh my," said Charlie, staring at Maria's tail.

"Right?" said Mac.

Maria turned to face them, leaving the tail swishing in the air behind her. "This is a nightmare!" she howled. The sound pierced the air louder than any of them expected.

Mac patted her shoulder sympathetically but warned her to keep her voice down. He pointed to Charlie's open window. "We don't want anyone to hear," he said.

"I know," sobbed Maria, softer now. She stepped out of the light to be safe.

Charlie reached out and hugged her, trying not to recoil when she felt the scratchy fur against her neck. Hastily she pulled away and looked at Maria's tail. "I'm so sorry," she said.

Maria sniffed and wiped her eyes. "I look hideous."

"No you don't!" said Charlie. "Don't say that." She looked at Maria all over. "So, you've got some fur and a tail. Is there anything . . . else?"

"That's all I know so far."

"She doesn't feel like testing out her monkey abilities quite yet," Mac warned Charlie, as if he'd had the conversation with Maria earlier. "We started looking through these papers in Maria's bedroom, but she got nervous that her mom would come in and see her like this, so we came here." He opened the Talos Global envelope and pulled out a large stack of loose pages along with the Project Chimera folder. He showed the top document to Charlie. "We found this page, but we didn't get very far with it—you'll see why."

Charlie squinted at the top paper in the light streaming from her bedroom window. The heading said, "Proposal: Mark Two." Charlie scanned the page and saw a lot of big scientific words she didn't recognize. "Is Maria's the Mark Two?"

"We think so," said Mac. "Her device has two lines around the TG logo. Yours has a pentagon and it's the Mark Five, so it makes sense. Which means mine's the Three and Kelly has the Four."

"What does this say about Maria's bracelet?"

"We didn't get that far," said Mac. "Basically all we know is that Maria is part monkey, so we figure she can do what they can do. Jump, swing from trees, parkour type moves."

"We need to find the section about how to change back," Maria pointed out.

"I know. We have a lot to read here." Mac sat down on the patio in the lighted spot and spread out the Project Chimera papers in front of him. He squinted and held one up to read. Maria sat next to him in the shadows, glancing furtively up at Charlie's window.

Charlie noticed and realized Maria didn't want to sit in the light. "I'll get a flashlight for you," she said. She climbed back up the wall to her bedroom window, went inside, and grabbed the emergency one from the upstairs hallway. She could hear the soft drone of her mom's voice downstairs, so she knew the coast was still clear. She ran back to her room, closed the door, and went out the window and down the stucco siding again.

"Check this out," said Mac when Charlie sat down. "There's your dad's name." He handed her a paper.

Charlie looked at it. It was the one she'd seen in the warehouse. She glanced over the other names, spotting Dr. Quinn Sharma's, then read the page, which was like an introduction letter to the project. "Basically there were five biologists from Talos Global assigned to Project Chimera, including my father. This is talking about how each of them would experiment with a 'device of their own making.' So they each got to choose the animal powers."

"Cool," said Mac. "I wonder what mine is." He glanced at Maria, then added, "But figuring out Maria's is more important." He turned back to his papers.

Maria flashed him a weak smile. "Thanks." She looked at Charlie. "Did Dr. Sharma say why she sent the Mark Five to you?"

Charlie explained how the device had come to be in her garage and the confusion with the names.

"That is so *weird*," Maria said, sounding a bit brighter now.

"Mr. Dr. Wilde doing crazy inventions like this—did you freak when you found out?"

"Totally." Charlie looked at the letter again. "It also says here that the government wanted my dad and these other scientists to make devices that would enhance the United States military. To make our soldiers unbeatable."

"Wow," said Maria. "So, are the soldiers who fought us part of the military? That doesn't seem right."

"No, they're not, since Dr. Sharma said the government shut down the project before they had a chance to experiment on humans. So they must be something that this Dr. Gray guy created."

"Who are the other scientists?" asked Mac. "Do you know them, too?"

"Nope. Besides my dad, we just know Dr. Sharma so far. And she told us about Dr. Gray and Dr. Goldstein. The fifth one's name is . . ." She hesitated, then found it on the paper. "Dr. Nubia Jakande."

"Hmm." Maria turned back to her research. She set a page down and picked up another one, then set that one down too.

Mac studied the one in his hand. "Here's some more about what Talos Global does. Biogenetics." He skimmed the page, then frowned. "It's all just superscientific terms that I don't understand, about DNA and junk like that."

"There's got to be something more about my device," said Maria, growing anxious again. "Isn't there an instruction manual? Or anything written about the Mark Two after it was already made?"

"I haven't found anything like that yet," said Mac. "Maybe since they shut down the project before the devices were finished, they never got around to writing manuals. That seems like something you'd do after you have the device just the way you want it, right?"

Charlie's heart sank. She'd been hoping for an instruction manual for her device, too. "Yeah, that makes the most sense. But maybe at least we can find out what kind of monkey DNA they used in Maria's. And also figure out what animal they used for yours, Mac." She scoured the pages.

After a while Maria set down the flashlight. "None of this is helpful. I'm stressed out." She looked frustrated and tired of trying to read through the scientific gobbledygook. They were getting nowhere. She stood up and hugged herself in the chilly night air, then bounced up and down a little. A few minutes later she began testing out her jumping in the shadows.

Charlie and Mac saw her and exchanged a look. "See if you can get her to try out her ability," Mac whispered. "At least that'll give us some information. We're not finding anything good in here to help us."

Charlie turned to Maria. "You look pretty light on your feet," she said, trying to be casual. "How does it feel? Any different?"

"A little. I feel springier, I guess." Maria stopped jumping and looked self-conscious.

"I'll bet you can do stuff like that soldier named Miko. Remember her? She's the one who swung around the street sign."

"Yeah," said Maria. She crossed her arms over her chest and stopped jumping.

"Why not give it a try?" suggested Charlie. "Nobody can see us back here. Maybe if we can watch you in action, we'll be able to figure out more about your device."

Maria shrugged and looked doubtful. "I don't know. It feels . . . embarrassing."

"Come on, Maria," Mac said, standing up. "I'll put my armor on too. And Charlie can stand in the dark and chirp like a weirdo. We'll all look ridiculous together."

"Yeah," said Charlie. "Please?"

Maria sighed. "Fine. I may as well."

Mac grabbed the papers and Charlie picked up the flashlight, and they followed Maria over to one of several large Ficus trees that lined the cinder-block wall around Charlie's backyard. Charlie automatically started chirping in the darkness, and the trees shimmered and turned into silvery shadows. After a moment she grew annoyed by the sound. She lifted her sweatshirt up over her mouth and the noise stopped. Things went dark again.

"Well?" Maria said to Mac. "Aren't you going to put your armor on?"

"If you insist," said Mac with a grin, like he'd been dying to mess around with his device again but was valiantly putting Maria's problem first. He clicked the buttons like he'd done in the warehouse.

Maria smiled. "It doesn't feel so bad when you two are doing weird things too."

While Mac's silvery suit flowed out of his device like mercury and encased him, Maria reached up for the lowest branch. It was just a little too high. She jumped halfheartedly, which sent her springing nimbly into the air. She grabbed on to the branch and swung on it, hanging above the ground and moving slowly back and forth like a gymnast preparing to start a routine.

"This feels weird," Maria said.

"Try something else," encouraged Charlie through her sweat-shirt. "Pull yourself up, maybe."

Maria frowned, then went along with what Charlie suggested. She did a pull-up, then swung her foot around, hooking the back of her knee over the branch. She made it look effortless.

"Wow, that's great!" said Charlie. "Keep climbing!"

Maria continued cautiously, reaching for the next branch. "There're a lot of leaves here," she muttered. "A whole lotta leaves."

Charlie turned toward Mac, who had set the envelope on the

ground and was punching buttons on his device. A second later, a laser light zipped around his neck so quickly Charlie almost thought she'd imagined it.

"Hey!" said Mac. He brought his hands up to the helmet and lifted it off. "It's removable. How about that!"

"Cool!" said Charlie. She glanced at Maria, feeling sorry for her friend, then bent and picked up the envelope to try to decipher the papers again. She trained the flashlight on the Proposal page they'd looked at before. "Hey, Mac, do you see any familiar words at all on this page that might give us a clue to what kind of monkey she is?"

"I noticed some Latin. I was planning to look up the words at home." He put his helmet back on and peered over Charlie's shoulder, then pointed to the terms and sounded them out the best that he could. "Genus *Alouatta* monotypic. Subfamily Alouattinae. Those words sound like they might be animal details."

"Hmm. Well, you of all people would know." Mac was a pretty big animal fan and knew all sorts of random facts about them. Charlie took the sheet from him and scanned it. "What's this?" She pointed to a line at the bottom of the page and read it aloud. "I predict any enhancements will subside naturally once subject's chemical levels return to normal."

"So Maria's fur will go away on its own?" asked Mac. "But when?"

"When whatever with her chemical levels," muttered Charlie.

It wasn't terribly helpful, since they had no idea how to know what Maria's chemical levels were or what normal was. Charlie handed the paper to Mac, who studied it, then shoved it back into the envelope and started messing around with his device buttons again.

Charlie turned to watch Maria, who was still swinging gingerly by one hand, then the other, reaching out to get an idea of how far it was to a branch in the next tree. She pumped her legs to gain momentum, then squealed in fright and let go, flying through the air in order to reach the next branch. For a second Charlie thought Maria would come crashing to the ground. But she caught the branch and hung on.

"That was great!" said Mac, forgetting his device for the moment. "Can you try to use your tail for something?"

"I'm not sure how to control it," Maria began. And then, "Whoops! There we go." Her tail began batting from side to side. Maria's face wore a look of sheer concentration as she tried to direct the tail to move the way she wanted it to. Eventually she flipped it up into the air and its tip wound around a higher branch. Immediately the tail released and flopped down. Maria's face fell. She concentrated and flung it up again, and it wound around the branch. This time it stayed put. Maria let go of one hand, hung on with the other, and tugged on her tail to see if it would stay stuck. It did.

"Prehensile tail!" said Mac, as if that were a good thing.

"What does that mean?" Charlie asked.

"It means she can use her tail like an extra hand," Mac said, growing more excited and impressed as Maria cautiously let go of her other hand and hung from the branch by her tail. "She should be able to grab on to things with it and use it to swing and make her stride longer." He clunked over to her. "You're doing great, Maria. That's so awesome."

"This is sort of fun," Maria admitted, growing bolder. She began swinging back and forth from her tail, holding her arms out at her sides. "Look, I'm flying."

Suddenly her tail grip slipped and she began to fall. As Charlie automatically sprang forward to catch her, Maria reached out a hand instinctively and grabbed a branch, catching herself and swinging around it. Then, with a look of terror on her face, she let go, flew through the air, and reached for another branch. After a few more moves like that, her look of terror turned to determination. She swung around each limb, found her rhythm, and soon she was moving from tree to tree around Charlie's backyard. After a moment she came back around to where Mac and Charlie were standing and landed only a little shakily on her feet in front of them, out of breath but grinning.

"That was seriously cool," Charlie said.

"Yeah?" asked Maria.

Charlie nodded.

"Can you scale the wall?" asked Mac.

Maria looked at the wall, which was about eight feet tall. "I think so," she said. She ran and jumped and caught the top of it with one hand, then pulled herself up. "Easy," she said. "Give me something harder."

"Hmm. Okay. Come back down and try a horizontal wall run," suggested Charlie. "Run along the ground, then keep running sideways up the wall. Then see if you can push off and leap for a tree limb."

Maria raised an eyebrow and tugged at her beard. "All right," she said.

While Maria made a few unsuccessful attempts, Mac muttered something excitedly under his breath. Charlie turned. "Hey," she said, looking more closely at him. The moon glinted on his armor, but instead of it being completely smooth like it had been earlier at the warehouse, she could now make out thin lines in a large leaf-like pattern covering the suit. "How did you do that?"

"I'm not sure," he said excitedly. "It looks like I have some sort of scales. But they're stuck flat and they don't do anything cool as far as I can tell." He clicked his device and Charlie watched. The images on the screens on Mac's bracelet were in black and white, not color like on Charlie's, and it looked like they were missing some words of explanation.

"What's that supposed to be?" Charlie asked, pointing to the screen, where a dotted outline of an animal was the only thing represented.

"I think the media part of my device wasn't quite finished when the government shut down the project," said Mac. "It's all pretty low tech compared to yours. This drawing looks like an anteater."

"Is that your device's animal?" Charlie wrinkled her nose. "An anteater?"

"I hope not," muttered Mac, but he sounded worried that it might be. "I don't think eating ants is an especially useful ability. Besides, anteaters don't have shells. Maybe it's an armadillo."

"Whatever it is, at least you have protection." She pounded on his shoulder. "Can you feel this?"

"I can feel the pressure, but it doesn't hurt at all." Mac continued clicking through the screens. There didn't seem to be very many options for Mac's suit. When he found himself coming across the same tabs again, his shoulders slumped. "That's it?"

"Do you think you just overdid it with clicking the buttons and you're stuck in some weird part of it?"

"Maybe." Mac looked up. "Especially if the media part wasn't finished—could be like a website glitch, where they forgot to put in the code for a home button on one of the pages. Know what I mean?"

Charlie nodded.

"I should probably shut it down and see if it will reset." Mac clicked a couple more times and suddenly the suit liquefied and started swiftly pouring back into his device.

"I'll bet there are more cool things you can do," said Charlie. "Whoever made this one wouldn't have put all the fun in just turning the thing on and off. It's got to have more features, like the helmet thing, that you just haven't found yet."

"You're probably right," said Mac, somewhat cheered by the prospect. Soon he looked completely normal again.

Maria came jogging back to her friends, sweating and breathing hard. "I saw you looking through the papers again. Did you find anything else about my device?"

"Only that the 'enhancements' will 'subside naturally.'" said Charlie. "That's good news but not very specific."

"So there's no button to turn it off?"

"It doesn't look like it," said Charlie. "But there are a lot of papers that we haven't read yet—we'll keep searching."

"Maybe now that you've actually used the abilities, your chemical levels will change," suggested Mac, though the look on his face made it obvious that he was just grasping at straws to make Maria feel better. "The device could have some sort of sensor that can detect when you're done needing it."

Maria remained dubious. "I hope so," she said. "This fur has got to go away soon or I'm in big trouble."

Charlie handed the envelope to Mac and glanced at the house. "Maybe you two can keep searching for more information tonight. I . . . I've got to go inside soon. My mom will freak out if she can't find me after everything that happened today."

Their energy deflated. "I'm really sorry about your dad," Maria said. "I hope we didn't take you away from important stuff.

I really appreciate you coming outside. I feel a little better."

"Yeah, I'm sorry too," said Mac. "Are you . . . okay?" His eyes shone with concern.

"I think so," said Charlie. "It's not like I can do anything to find him at the moment." She took in a deep breath and blew it out. "Besides, I care about what happens to you, too. You're my best friends." She looked at Maria, trying to ignore the beard. "What are you going to do now?"

"Go home and hope my stepbrothers are keeping my mom and Ken so busy that they don't notice me. And pray that I turn back to normal by morning."

"I'll help by distracting them," said Mac.

Charlie thought for a moment. "I have a scarf you can borrow. Maybe you can cover up most of it."

"That would be great, thanks."

The three walked back to the house. Charlie climbed up the side and disappeared into her bedroom. A moment later she returned to the window and tossed a scarf down to Maria. "My mom's keeping me home from school tomorrow. If you need me, call my house. You've got the number now."

"Thanks, Charlie. If this doesn't go away, I might be staying home too. I hope you find your dad soon."

"Me too. Good luck," said Charlie, feeling helpless.

Maria and Mac waved halfheartedly. Charlie watched them head out through the gate into the darkness.

"Charlie, where are you?" called Mrs. Wilde, her voice faint through the closed door. "I could use some help down here."

"Coming!" Charlie quickly replaced the screen and closed her window. She grabbed the house phone and ran downstairs with it, returning it to its charger in the kitchen.

Her mom was there, cleaning up. "Quinn said it's pointless to leave the house a mess. It's not like there'll be any fingerprints because the soldiers wore those bodysuits."

"I'll bet their fingerprints would look really different, anyway," said Charlie, remembering Prowl's claws. She started resetting the dining room chairs. "This feels weird."

"Very," said her mother. Almost in a daze, she and Charlie finished straightening up the kitchen and moved on to the dining room. Andy, back in the chair with Jessie, stayed focused on his comic book while the dog occasionally licked his face.

"Hey, Andy," said Charlie. "Wanna come help us clean?"

Andy didn't move.

"Leave him alone for now," Charlie's mom said quietly. "I had a good talk with him while you were upstairs. This is a lot for a ten-year-old to handle. He's trying to cope the best way he knows how."

Charlie watched her brother thoughtfully. There was a big part of her that wanted to crawl into bed with a book and hide inside it forever. She didn't blame Andy for wanting to escape with a comic.

They continued cleaning. When Charlie grew warm from

all the work, she took off her sweatshirt and was reminded of the warehouse all over again—she still wore the T-shirt that was covered in blood and full of rips from her fight with Prowl.

"Charlie!" said Mrs. Wilde. "What in the world? Are you okay? When did this happen?" She rushed over to examine her daughter while Andy looked up from his chair. His face turned pale.

"It's okay," Charlie assured them. "I'm fine. The healing power is working fast. It doesn't even hurt anymore." She glanced at Andy and gave him a reassuring smile. "I'm okay, really. See?" She pulled down on her sleeve, revealing her shoulder through the neck hole. The cuts had all closed and were scabbed over, well on their way to healing.

"Well, that's a relief," said Mrs. Wilde.

Charlie went over to Andy so he could see up close. Then she knelt and showed him the starfish pulsing on the device screen. "That means it's healing me."

"That's pretty cool," said Andy. "I want one."

"Your bracelet really is incredible," Mrs. Wilde said. "It would be amazing to have something like that in the ER, you know? To slap it on a trauma patient for a bit and watch him heal right up . . ." She paused, lost in thought, then murmured, "It would change the world."

"Maybe then you wouldn't have to work so much," said Charlie wistfully.

Mom looked at Charlie. "Maybe," she said. "But for now I'm going to take a leave of absence from my job until this nightmare is over." She looked at Charlie's shirt again. "Let's throw this thing away, okay?"

It didn't take as long as Charlie expected to get the house looking back to normal, though reminders of the break-in remained. One of the six dining chairs was broken beyond repair and two of the family pictures that had been on the walls were smashed, the photographs scratched. While Mrs. Wilde went for the vacuum cleaner, Charlie picked up the loose photos and focused on her dad's smiling face. Carefully she wiped the shards of glass away, then brought one of the photos to the refrigerator and secured it there with magnets so they'd be able to look at the family every time they walked by.

Once their nerves had settled enough to allow them to grow hungry, it was already way past their bedtimes. They rummaged through the kitchen looking for food.

"Do you think we could all camp out in your room tonight, Mom?" asked Andy as he fixed a peanut butter and jelly sandwich. "I don't want to sleep in my room alone."

Under normal circumstances Charlie wouldn't want to do something like that. But tonight wasn't normal. "Yeah. Can we, Mom?"

"I'd love that," she said. "I get the bed." Her smile was strained.

"I guess that means we get the floor, kid," Charlie said to Andy.

"Rats," said Andy.

After they finished their late-night snacks, the kids pulled sleeping bags out of storage and set up their area together. Charlie was worried she wouldn't be able to sleep because of all the crazy things that rushed through her head. Had Maria made it inside without anyone noticing her monkey-fur head and beard? Was Dad okay? Was he thinking of them, too? Charlie hoped he wasn't worrying about them like she was worrying about him. But after all the physical and emotional exertion she'd been through that day, it didn't take long before she drifted off into a dreamless sleep.

When she woke, the sun was streaming into the bedroom. Her mom's blankets were tousled, but she wasn't in bed, and for a moment Charlie panicked. But then she smelled breakfast cooking. Andy was still passed out on the floor beside her, with Fat Princess curled up next to his face and Big Kitty on top of the sleeping bag near his feet, keeping watch through slit eyes. Charlie could hear Jessie's dog collar tags jangling in the kitchen. She stared at the ceiling. Her stomach churned and her heart sank as she was jolted into remembering everything that had happened the previous day. How had her father slept? Was he all right? And Maria—had she changed back into her normal self?

She sat up and searched the area for her phone and found it on the dresser, attached by the charging cord to an outlet nearby. Her mom must have plugged it in for her. Charlie grimaced—no doubt her mom had also noticed the rough shape it was in. She crawled over to it and checked the time. Nearly ten o'clock. Maria and Mac would be in school. Or at least Mac would be.

She unplugged it, got up, and went into the kitchen in search of her mother, who was cracking eggs into a bowl.

"Hi, Mom."

"Good morning. Hungry?"

"Sure." Charlie decided not to mention that this was the most cooking she'd seen her mother do since they'd moved here.

"Mac stopped by. Nice kid. He was just making sure you were okay."

"Was Maria here too?"

"No, just him."

"Why didn't you wake me up?"

"We had such a late night last night—I wanted you to sleep. Besides, he couldn't stay. He was on his way to school and he looked kind of anxious, like he was worried about being late or something."

"Did he say anything about Maria?"

"He said she was staying home from school today. Sounds like she's not feeling well."

"Dang," Charlie muttered. That meant she hadn't changed back.

Mom looked sidelong at Charlie. "I don't suppose you know if your friends have told anybody about what happened to you all yesterday."

"Mac and Maria wouldn't." Charlie looked guilty and confessed, "They've known about my bracelet for a while. It's top secret. Mac's been trying to deactivate it so I can take it off, but we haven't had any luck so far finding the access code." She frowned, thinking she needed more time with those Project Chimera files. "I'm not sure about Kelly, though. She promised not to say anything, but I don't really trust her all that much."

Charlie's mom poured the egg mixture into a skillet. "I'm really not sure what to do," she began. "I don't want more people to know about this because that would put Dad at risk, but what about their parents? I feel responsible for telling them what happened." She sighed. "This is complicated."

"Maybe we can ask Dr. Sharma what we should do. I don't want my friends to get in any trouble or anything. When will she be here?"

"In about an hour. She called a few minutes ago and said she just landed at the airport. She's bringing someone else to help us—I'm not clear on exactly who."

"That's a relief. Then we can try to find Dad?"

"I hope so. I'm glad she's not wasting any time. I can't stand not knowing what's going on."

"Yeah, me too." With her father, for sure, but also with Maria.

Charlie was quiet for a moment. Then she dug her toe into the rug and twisted it around. "So-o-o . . . you saw my phone."

"Yes. We'll get you a replacement today. I don't ever want you to be without a phone. Not anymore."

Charlie nodded. "Thanks, Mom."

"Just stay out of situations that would do *that* to your phone again, okay? They're expensive."

Charlie couldn't promise that. What if someone needed her? "Sure," she said uneasily. But she knew that if those soldiers came back, or if they got between her and her father or anyone else she loved, she wasn't going to worry about keeping her phone in pristine condition. She was going to fight with everything she had.

CHAPTER 8

Getting Some Answers

By the time Dr. Quinn Sharma's rental car pulled into the driveway, Charlie, Andy, and their mother were anxious to get moving on a rescue plan. Every minute that passed with Mr. Wilde's whereabouts unknown made them feel more and more helpless.

Two women got out of the car. The driver started toward the house while the other woman went to the backseat to get a duffel bag. Andy held Jessie back so she wouldn't run outside or jump on the visitors, and Mrs. Wilde opened the door, not even waiting for the woman to knock. "Hi, I'm Diana."

"Quinn Sharma," said the driver. Dr. Sharma was a medium-sized woman with dark golden skin, glasses, and thick brown hair pulled back into a low ponytail. A few loose wisps framed her face. She wore a navy-blue business suit with a slightly rumpled white blouse, and she looked tired but alert. She held out her hand in greeting.

Mrs. Wilde shook it warmly as the other woman closed the back door of the rental car and walked briskly toward them.

"This is my former colleague and friend, Erica Sabbith," Dr. Sharma said. "She's an engineer at Talos Global—she's been there since Charles and I and the others were working on Project Chimera."

Erica was tall, broad-shouldered, and had the athletic build of an *American Ninja Warrior* contestant, Charlie thought. She had short, spiky, jet-black hair and didn't smile. Tattoos started near each of her wrists and ran up and out of sight under her sleeves. "Nice to meet you."

"Did you work on Project Chimera too?" Mrs. Wilde asked her.

"I was in a different department, but I knew about it," said Ms. Sabbith.

"We've been friends for a long time," said Dr. Sharma. "When I reached a dead end trying to contact our old government liaison, I turned to her. She was able to get away to help us—she has access to equipment we'll need. Shall we go inside and talk?"

Charlie's and Andy's eyes widened and they stepped aside.

"Of course," Mrs. Wilde said. If she was intimidated, she was hiding it well. She shooed the cats out of the way and ushered the women inside. Immediately Ms. Sabbith pulled a black wandlike device out of her bag and began to wave it around the furniture, walls, and air vents. "Excuse me, what are you doing?" asked Mrs. Wilde.

"Looking for bugs," Ms. Sabbith said softly.

Andy looked confused until Charlie whispered in his ear, "Recording devices, not insects."

"Oh," said Andy.

Soon Ms. Sabbith finished her search. "All clear," she said, and sat down with Dr. Sharma and the three Wildes around the dining table. Quinn opened her briefcase and took out a folder. "Here are some photos of Dr. Gray," she said, sliding them to Mrs. Wilde. "I thought they might be useful so you know who we're dealing with."

"Thanks." Mrs. Wilde glanced at the photos and showed them to the kids.

Charlie studied the photos of a gangly man in his midfifties with salt-and-pepper hair. He wore a white lab coat in one of the photos.

Ms. Sabbith turned to Charlie. "I understand from Quinn that you can't get the Mark Five off your wrist. Would you mind if I have a look?"

"Sure," said Charlie. She hesitated, then got up and went over to the woman and held out her wrist.

Dr. Sharma leaned closer so she could see too. Erica gently turned Charlie's wrist so they could get a view of all sides.

"Quinn, is this metal titanium?" Ms. Sabbith asked.

"Yes. All of the bracelets were made with it."

Ms. Sabbith nodded. "And what would happen if we lasered this off her? Would it still work?"

"You might be able to cut cleanly through the clasp without destroying it, but I can't guarantee that."

Charlie cringed. Now that they had the files, she was hoping to find a clue that would tell her how to unlock the device. But if she did, would she have to give them the bracelet? She wasn't sure she wanted to be without it now.

"We don't want to risk that." Ms. Sabbith turned thoughtfully back to Charlie, who sighed with relief and showed her how to get to the other screens on the device. She talked through what each one was for.

"Charlie," said Dr. Sharma, "I'm curious about a few things. Can you describe the attackers? And why do you think they're soldiers?"

"We call them soldiers because Mac heard them talking, and they said soldier kinds of words, like 'ten-four' and junk like that. And one of them called the other 'soldier' once too. All of them wore similar full bodysuits. All black. They had goggles covering their eyes so you couldn't really tell where they were looking. And they all had different abilities. Like Cyke," she said, growing a bit more comfortable the more she talked. "He was just huge and strong and could run really fast, but he couldn't climb a tree—not even a little bit without falling. But then Miko was small and super agile, swinging around a street sign and leaping off." She thought of Maria's tail and realized Miko hadn't seemed to have one. "She might be a chimpanzee."

"So you know their names?" asked Dr. Sharma.

"Not all of them."

"How many soldiers are there all together, would you say?"

"Three from the first attack on Maria and me. They were Cyke, Miko, and one with really sharp claws—I call her the Claw Woman. And three different ones kidnapped Mac, but Maria and I met them in the warehouse. It's not always easy to tell them apart—until you fight them. Then you get a better sense of who they are."

Dr. Sharma almost smiled. "I can imagine. Sounds like you're pretty tough."

"I have to be now," said Charlie solemnly. "I have a responsibility."

"Well, you're like me, then," said Ms. Sabbith. "My responsibility is to set you all up so you can find your dad and get him home."

"That's good," said Charlie.

Andy broke in. "Ms. Sabbith, did you know my dad when he worked at Talos Global?"

"Yes," said Ms. Sabbith, "I knew all the biologists."

"So you would recognize him if you saw him?"

"Yes, definitely."

"Oh," said Andy. He seemed pleased with the answer.

Dr. Sharma leaned in. "Next question," she said. "Where is this warehouse?"

Charlie described how to get there, then found it on a map on her mom's phone, since hers was broken.

And then Dr. Sharma asked the question Charlie was dreading. "Did you happen to see any other devices in the warehouse when you were looking around?"

The words hung in the air. Charlie didn't want to get her friends in trouble. But she couldn't lie to this woman. Not with her father's life in danger.

"Well," Charlie began, "yeah, we did." She looked at the floor, feeling very guilty. "My friends Mac, Maria, and Kelly each have one of them."

Mrs. Wilde, Dr. Sharma, and Ms. Sabbith all looked surprised. Mrs. Wilde gave Charlie a sharp look. "Charlie!"

"You didn't mention that," said Dr. Sharma, alarmed. "This could be a serious problem—none of the devices were finished or tested on humans." Then she narrowed her eyes, confused. "Wait. All three of them, you said? Do they have Victor's prototype too? Because Jack has the one he made. Or . . . at least he did." Her confused look turned to concern. "I wonder if he's . . . ," she began, then she paused and sighed, closing her eyes.

Charlie wondered what was going on. But then Dr. Sharma opened her eyes again and looked sternly at Charlie. "We need those bracelets back."

CHAPTER 9

More Trouble

"Are my friends going to be in trouble?" asked Charlie. "I mean, I don't want them to be. They helped me and it isn't even their dad who's missing and—"

"They're not in trouble," interrupted Dr. Sharma. "But those devices are very powerful, as you've already figured out. And they're also supposed to be top secret, so I'd feel a lot more comfortable if they are back in our hands."

Charlie gave her a fearful look. "But the soldiers know who they are now, so they need the bracelets to protect themselves and their families! That's why we took them in the first place!"

Dr. Sharma paused and was quiet for a moment, thinking it through. "But if they're seen with or using them, that could cause Gray to be suspicious or think we're up to something. Have any of them activated the devices?"

Charlie pressed her lips together. "Yeah, Mac used his," she said in a small voice. Yesterday she'd conveniently left out the part where Mac had fought alongside her, but she didn't see any way to protect him now. "Maria did, too—she turned into some sort of monkey. Kelly put one on her wrist, but I don't know if it activated or not. Nothing happened when she did it."

Dr. Sharma stared at Charlie. "A monkey? With monkey features?"

"Y-yes. She stayed home from school."

"What?" cried Mrs. Wilde.

The biologist frowned. "I don't like how this is going. Have Maria's parents found out?"

"I don't know," said Charlie miserably.

But Dr. Sharma had made up her mind. "We can't afford to let word get out about what these devices do. If Maria's parents learn that Maria's DNA has been altered and they go after anybody, we won't be able to stop the information from traveling. And if Dr. Gray finds out and feels threatened, it'll put Charles in danger. Erica, let's bring the three kids and their parents here now. We'll come up with a plan in the car. Meanwhile, Diana, if you could get Charlie a working phone, that would be great."

"You're going to tell their parents?" asked Mrs. Wilde. "I think that's best—they need to know what's been happening."

"We'll tell them something, Diana," promised Dr. Sharma. "I'm just not sure what yet. But this is our responsibility now—I need you to follow my lead and let me handle things. Okay?"

Mrs. Wilde looked relieved. "Okay."

"We'll meet you back here." Dr. Sharma looked to the Wildes for confirmation that they understood. They nodded solemnly.

"Good. Once we have your friends here and the equipment

accounted for, Erica and I will set up reconnaissance at the warehouse to see if the soldiers are still there, or if they've left any clues about Charles. Okay?"

"Sounds good," said Mrs. Wilde.

Charlie quickly called Maria before they left. When she didn't answer, Charlie started worrying about her again. She left a voice mail letting her know Dr. Sharma was coming. Then Charlie and her brother and mom went to get a new phone.

A couple of hours later, Dr. Sharma called Diana to say they were heading back to the Wildes' house with all the parents agreeing to meet them there. Shortly after, Charlie had a brand-new phone with all of her contacts transferred.

As soon as Charlie got back to the car, she texted Maria. "Got a new phone. Is everything okay? Why didn't you answer when I called?"

A moment later the reply came. "Long story. We're in your family room, and boy, is my mom mad." After that she put a string of sad-face emojis.

"What do you mean?" Charlie texted.

There was no reply for a long moment, and then Maria texted, "You'll see when you get here."

A few minutes later, Charlie and her family arrived home. Mrs. Wilde guided Andy toward the stairs and sent him up to his room to give the older kids some semi-privacy to talk. Charlie flew into the family room. Ms. Sabbith sat in a side chair with a wireless device in her ear, watching something intently on her phone. Kelly looked sullen in another. Maria and Mac were on the couch. Maria wore a baseball cap on her head and Charlie's scarf around her neck, and she sat . . . lopsided. The device was still on her wrist, and her face wore an expression of misery.

"What's going on?" said Charlie. "Is everybody okay?"

Maria looked up at her friend, and Charlie could see her eyes were red from crying. "Maria," Charlie said, going over to her. "It's going to be okay. These people are on our side. I promise."

"It's not that," Maria said quietly. "It's . . . I couldn't answer my phone earlier because my mom *saw* me. With the scarf off."

CHAPTER 10

Scrambling for a Story

Charlie paled, trying to imagine what Maria's mother must be thinking after seeing her daughter with monkey fur. "Oh no," she whispered. "What happened? What did you tell her?"

Maria started crying. "When I told my mom I was sick and had to stay home from school, she was busy helping get the boys ready, so she didn't check on me right away. I thought I was in the clear. But later she came into my room and made me take the scarf off. Obviously she freaked—thank goodness she didn't see the tail. I panicked and came up with a story about it being a science experiment—I'm sorry, I didn't know what else to say! I didn't tell her anything important. She was about to take me to the hospital when Dr. Sharma and Ms. Sabbith came to the door. So I babbled to them what I'd told her. Dr. Sharma is in your den with the parents now, fixing things."

"That was a really smart thing to say, actually, Maria," said Ms. Sabbith, looking up from her phone. "If there's something we know about, it's science. And you clued us in right away so we could run with it. Don't worry. Sharma and I are working on it as we speak." She flipped apps and typed something.

"See?" said Mac to Maria. "I told you. You did good."

"Did you try taking the bracelet off again?" asked Charlie.

Maria nodded and Mac spoke up. "I read some more of the Project Chimera papers this morning and found out her device won't come off when it's in Active mode. Her screen says it's locked for safety measures. I guess that's so no enemies can take it off during fights."

Charlie went over to Maria and attempted a gentle hug. Maria stiffened, and Charlie quickly let go and tried not to stare at the wisps of fur that poked out from under the scarf. "I'm so sorry," she said softly. She turned to Mac. "Did you figure anything else out?"

"She's a howler monkey," said Mac. "I looked up the Latin name. She resembles pictures I found of the monkeys at the Phoenix Zoo."

Maria's face screwed up and more tears came. "Worst monkey ever."

"Well," said Charlie gently, trying to be positive, "there are a lot of really great things you can do now."

Mac began nodding. "Yeah. The way you were running up walls and leaping all over the place—you're destined to be a parkour professional," he said. "Maybe you could show Kelly some of your tricks."

Kelly raised an eyebrow.

Maria gave Mac a look of death. "Not right now. I'm sort of

freaking out here about my mother, in case you can't tell."

"Sorry," said Mac.

After everything that Maria had done the previous night, Charlie was dying to see what else she could do. If she could use her feet like weapons the way Miko had done, Maria could be really helpful in a fight. And with the prehensile tail, even better! But Charlie knew better than to say anything right now when her friend was feeling so bad. It must've been a huge shock to her mother. How was Dr. Sharma going to explain this? And even more stressing was wondering if the changes were permanent, like the soldiers' features seemed to be. "Maybe we can make you a bodysuit like the soldiers have," she said weakly.

That made Maria cry even harder. She bent forward and put her hands over her eyes. "I don't want that. Charlie, you've got to help me. I need to change back. Like, now. Or my mother will never believe them."

"I'll help you, I promise!" said Charlie, though she had no idea how. She whirled around to Ms. Sabbith, who was typing furiously. Charlie waited until she looked up, then asked, "What can we do about Maria?"

"Do you have the envelope Mac mentioned a few minutes ago?" Ms. Sabbith asked.

"No," said Mac. "I left it hidden under my bed."

"Hmm," said Ms. Sharma, distracted by what she was listening to. "Sorry, I'm an engineer, not a biologist. Hopefully Dr. Sharma will be able to help you soon."

Maria cried harder and began to howl. She clamped her hands over her mouth.

Charlie glanced helplessly at Kelly, unsure what to do.

Kelly shrugged. "It's probably better just to not talk about it right now," she said quietly. "Everything anybody says just makes her more upset."

Charlie nodded. "Yeah, good point. I'm sorry, Maria." She glanced at Kelly's wrist. She wasn't wearing her bracelet, which was a good sign. "You haven't tried out your bracelet yet, have you, Kelly?"

Kelly's eyes flitted to the side, then she returned her gaze to Charlie. "Uh, no."

"Where is it?"

"It's a dud, actually. Doesn't work."

"So you tried to activate it?"

"I don't know. Yeah. I pushed the buttons, okay?" She glanced uneasily at Ms. Sabbith, who had looked up from her phone again.

"Didn't you bring it with you?" asked Charlie. "Dr. Sharma needs it."

"No. Like I said, it doesn't work, anyway. I threw it in the trash. Don't worry about it."

Charlie gave an impatient sigh. But then she realized that she was no longer in charge. Kelly was Dr. Sharma's problem now. A flood of relief washed through Charlie—it was awesome not having to wrangle Kelly. "Okay, fine, whatever," she mumbled. She looked at Mac, who was awkwardly trying to console Maria, and gave him a small smile. His bracelet was on his wrist, and Charlie knew for a fact his worked. "Did you have a chance to search for information for your device, Mac?"

"No. I was focused on Maria," he said. "But like we were guessing last night when we saw that screen, the suit is probably some kind of an exoskeleton, like an armadillo."

"Or one of those roly-poly bugs?" asked Kelly.

Mac smirked. "Sure. Just like that."

"I mean it. Your device makes a silver suit of armor for you, after all. Silver is close to gray, like those icky bugs."

"Yeah, well, I won't be just rolling up and hiding when I'm faced with danger, you know. I did pretty good fighting yesterday."

"True." Kelly shrugged and looked out the window.

"So, what about you two?" Charlie asked Kelly and Mac. "What do your parents know?"

Mac's face turned glum. "My mom and Kelly's dad were with Dr. Sharma when they came to pull us out of school. I don't know what she said to them, but somehow they agreed to come here to talk things through."

Ms. Sabbith looked up suddenly. "Okay, kids," she said. "I've been secretly on FaceTime with Dr. Sharma all this time, so that I'd know what she's been saying and could tell you. She told your parents that what happened to Maria is a harmless science experiment gone wrong. She's saying the bracelets are simulators, and Maria's created the illusion of a monkey's beard."

"Whoa," said Maria. "Not sure Maytée's gonna buy that."

"Now she's telling them that Diana just got home, and she's asking the three parents to sit tight in the den for a few minutes while she gets her."

Charlie heard the sound of the den door. A moment later Dr. Sharma came into the dining room. Spying Mrs. Wilde in the kitchen, she went quickly to her and spoke quietly for a long moment.

Mrs. Wilde frowned, then nodded and went to the den. Dr. Sharma stopped in the living room. "Everybody keeping up with the story?"

Ms. Sabbith nodded. "Smart idea to FaceTime."

"I just sent Diana in there to tell the other parents that the devices were Charles's for his college class and that you kids got into them unknowingly—you thought they were cool-looking and tried them on."

"My mom's not going to believe this," Maria said, still crying.

Dr. Sharma walked toward the girl and softly laid a hand on her shoulder. "I know this is hard. Just trust me. I think I can get her to believe me. Though it would help if you could change back before I get done with them."

Charlie sat up. "We read something last night from a Project

Chimera file. It said that Maria would change back naturally when her chemical balance returned to normal. Or something like that."

"Hmm," said Dr. Sharma. "I'd like to see those files."

Charlie explained why they didn't have them at the moment.

Dr. Sharma looked at Maria's wrist. "What device do you have?"

"We think it's the Mark Two," she said.

Dr. Sharma tapped her lips thoughtfully. "Dr. Jakande created that one." She paused for a long moment, then looked at Ms. Sabbith in the chair. "Any luck finding her?"

"Not yet."

"What's happening in the den?" Dr. Sharma asked.

"They're asking questions, saying it was careless to leave the bracelets lying around where kids could get them. Diana is agreeing and being regretful."

"She's great." Dr. Sharma looked back at Maria. "So, how long have you been like this?"

"Since I activated the bracelet yesterday."

"You haven't changed back at all?"

"No," said Maria.

"From what Charlie said, it sounds like the Mark Two is designed to affect the wearer only when he or she is under duress. And then you should change back to normal once your body calms down. Sort of like . . ."

"Like you're a werewolf?" asked Mac.

"A werewolf?!" howled Maria. Mac covered his ears and Kelly cringed.

"Definitely a *howler* monkey," muttered Mac.

"In a way I suppose a were—a weremonkey is an accurate description. Although the change is not lunar controlled."

"You've got to admit that's kind of cool," said Mac to Maria.

"It's horrible!" she replied.

"At least it's not permanent," reasoned Charlie. "We hope."

"Maria, you should change back to normal once your anxiety level goes down. I'm not surprised it has stayed elevated all this time. This was quite a shock to you, I'm sure, and the longer you stay in this condition, the more stress it creates. Try some relaxation exercises. Have you ever done yoga-style stretches? Or meditation? Look those up online and you'll see what to do."

"Parents are getting restless," Ms. Sabbith warned.

They heard a man's loud but muffled voice coming from the den, and Kelly shifted uneasily in her chair. Then she got up and went over to Maria and Dr. Sharma. "I take yoga classes and meditation," she said. "I'll help you."

"Oh, good." Dr. Sharma looked relieved, but then glanced anxiously at the hallway. "I should go. I'll be back in a bit, but I'll stall to give you time to work on this. Play along with the story when your parents come out, all right? We'll get you out of this mess. I promise, Maria. You can count on me."

Leaving Maria looking calmer and more optimistic, Dr. Sharma disappeared to the den.

Kelly guided Maria through the basic techniques that would allow her to grow calm. After several minutes, the beard and fur melted away.

"You did it!" exclaimed Charlie.

Maria opened her eyes and sat up. She touched her chin and head and patted her backside. "It's gone!" she cried. "Oh, Kelly! Thank you! I'm so relieved." She blew out a breath, then checked the lock screen of her bracelet. It had deactivated, and she swiftly released the latch. She slid the bracelet off and thrust it at Charlie. "Here—it's all yours."

Kelly went back to her chair and stared sulkily out the window. Soon the den door opened again and the adult voices became more distinct, especially the man's. "That's my dad," she said, though everyone had figured that out by now. She stood abruptly, a nervous look on her face. Mr. Parker appeared and stopped just outside the room to shoot off a retort to Dr. Sharma. He had strawberry-blond hair with a receding hairline, and his face was red with anger or sunburn—it was hard to tell which. He wore a pink polo shirt, khaki pants, and golf shoes, and looked extremely annoyed.

Charlie watched Kelly curiously. Kelly was fidgeting with her hair, anxiously pulling it in and out of a hair tie. She'd never seen Kelly act like that before. Knowing that Kelly's parents were getting divorced, Charlie felt a wave of compassion for her sort-of friend. She went over to her and touched her elbow. "Are you okay?" she whispered, keeping her eye on Mr. Parker.

"Yeah."

Mr. Parker waved his hand dismissively toward the other parents, then bellowed out, "Kelly! Do you have some sort of machine to give back to them?"

"No," said Kelly. "It—mine didn't work."

"Well, come on, then, and quit wasting my time."

Kelly let out a breath and closed her eyes briefly. "I've got to go."

"Bye," said Charlie, feeling helpless. Still, there was a part of Charlie that wanted to tell Kelly she wouldn't be in this mess if she'd just gone home yesterday when Charlie had told her to.

Mac's mom came out of the hallway next and pushed past Mr. Parker into the living room, shooting a disdainful glance at the man as she did so, like she'd spent more than enough time with him today. Mrs. Barnes was tall and slender, dressed in a sleek black pantsuit with a pinstriped, button-down blouse. Her skin was dark brown like Mac's, and she wore her short hair in a natural afro. "Hello," she said. "I'm Claudia Barnes. You must be Charlie."

"Yes," said Charlie. She glanced at Mac and then back to his mother. "I'm sorry about . . . everything."

"Well, it's over now," said Mrs. Barnes. She peered at Maria. "I don't see any fur."

"I got the bracelet off. The simulator thing, I mean," said Maria. "So it's all gone now."

Charlie nodded. "Yep. Just an illusion."

"All right," Ms. Sabbith said. "Mac, if you turn over the equipment, you're free to go with your mom."

"Ooo-kay," he said, and reluctantly stood up. He unclipped his device from his arm and handed it to Ms. Sabbith. "Bye, I guess," he said.

"Bye," echoed Charlie and Maria.

Mac and his mother walked out together.

Maria's mother finished talking with Dr. Sharma and came into the living room.

Maytée looked at Maria, who now wore the scarf loosely around her neck, and let out a breath of relief. "It's gone. *Dios mío*, child. You had me worried."

Maria smiled weakly. "Sorry, Mamá."

Maytée shook her head and almost smiled. "It's okay. Come on. *¡Vamos!*"

Maria stood up quickly.

"Here," Charlie said to Dr. Sharma, holding out Maria's device. "This one is hers."

"Thank you." Dr. Sharma smiled politely at Maria's mother as the two prepared to go. "And thank you, ma'am," she said.

Maria turned to Charlie. "See you tomorrow, Chuck," she said brightly. "Big make-up game after school. Can't wait."

Charlie had forgotten about their soccer game. "Me too," she said, trying to sound enthusiastic.

Maytée looked over her daughter thoroughly, inspecting her neck and head. "I still don't quite understand how a simulator could make that seem so real," she said, sounding a bit suspicious still.

"Science and technology are amazing," said Ms. Sabbith firmly. "It's wonderful when kids get so interested in them, isn't it?"

"I suppose that's true," said Maria's mom, softening a bit. "I'll let you know if I have any other concerns. And thank you."

Finally only Dr. Wilde and her children remained with Dr. Sharma and Ms. Sabbith. They reconvened around the dining table and let out a collective breath of relief.

"I think we did it," said Ms. Sabbith.

Dr. Sharma nodded. "Nice work, Diana," she said. "Mr. Parker seemed to settle down after you took responsibility for being careless with the college's simulators. He was angry at Kelly, but he believed our story. He seemed more upset about being pulled away from his golf game."

"I hope this will die down by tomorrow," said Mrs. Wilde.

"I think it will," said Dr. Sharma. She laid the devices out in front of her. "Wait—where's Kelly's?

"That's another problem," explained Ms. Sabbith.

"What? Why?"

"She said it was a dud. She threw it away."

"She did what?" said Dr. Sharma, alarmed. "Which one did she have?"

"The Mark Four, I believe."

Dr. Sharma's face turned hard. "The Mark Four—that was my creation. And I can assure you it is *not* a dud."

CHAPTER 11

To the Warehouse

Charlie wasn't sure what to think about Kelly and the Mark Four. It was just like her to carelessly throw something away if it didn't suit her needs. But Dr. Sharma seemed sure that the device couldn't possibly be a dud—even though she admitted she'd never had a chance to test it. After some debate Dr. Sharma reluctantly concluded that there was a possibility Kelly was right. And it wouldn't matter much either way since it was on its way to the dump by now.

"So what's next?" Charlie's mom asked Dr. Sharma. "I'm anxious about Charles."

"He's next." Dr. Sharma caught Ms. Sabbith's eye. "Erica and I will head out to the warehouse to see what if anything is happening there. Hopefully we'll at least get a clue to Charles's whereabouts." She paused and turned to Mrs. Wilde. "I know you'll want to stay home with Andy, but we'd like to have Charlie with us so she can talk us through the layout of the property while Erica scouts around the property and inside."

Charlie's mom blinked. "I'm not sure about that," she said.

"It'll really help us figure out what's happening."

Dr. Wilde turned to Charlie, and Charlie could see the

indecision on her mother's face. "It's fine, Mom," she said. "I'll be fine. I was there when it was teeming with soldiers and I came away from that no problem."

"That's true," Mrs. Wilde admitted.

Andy came creeping down the stairs from his room. "I'm hungry," he said. "What's for lunch?"

Mrs. Wilde stood up automatically to help him, still frowning. "I'm just thinking it through, Charlie," she said. "I mean, it's one thing having you in the loop from the safety of home, but totally something else having you be a part of some stealth mission. It feels risky."

Charlie was about to point out to her mother that their home wasn't exactly a place of safety either, since the soldiers had broken in, but Ms. Sabbith jumped in.

"It's just a recon effort at this point, Dr. Wilde," she said. "Charlie won't be going inside. We're just trying to gather intelligence. Maybe stick a camera on a tree somewhere to observe the exterior."

"I'll have my bracelet in case anything bad happens," Charlie pointed out.

Dr. Wilde studied the other women, then sighed. "All right, that sounds safe enough."

"And if you don't mind, we'd like to test Charlie's abilities. Since the soldiers are animal hybrids, seeing Charlie's abilities in action may give us a better idea of what to expect with them."

"You can't really force-test my abilities," Charlie pointed out. "I mean, we can, but the powers aren't always there—I can't just turn them on when I want. They kick in at certain times. Like the 'fight or flight' intuition that animals have. So you can't, you know, ask me to lift up a Dumpster or something."

"Ew," said Andy, sitting down with his lunch. "Why would you want to do that anyway?"

Charlie frowned at him. "Besides, I've already tried them all, and they seem as powerful as the actual animals'."

"Ah, I didn't know that." Dr. Sharma grew thoughtful. She looked at Mac's and Maria's devices, then handed them to Ms. Sabbith, who packed them in her duffel bag.

"But if any of the abilities do activate, I'll show you," Charlie said. "You should have seen Maria—she was really getting good at swinging through the trees last night. And Mac helped me fight in the warehouse—I didn't mention it before because I didn't want to get him in trouble, but it doesn't matter now. His bracelet gives him a protective suit. He was just starting to figure out what else he could do. He was pretty bummed that he had to give the device back, if you couldn't tell." Charlie looked at Dr. Sharma. "What are you going to do with them both now? Use them yourself to rescue my dad?"

Ms. Sabbith and Dr. Sharma exchanged a look of mild alarm. "Um," said Dr. Sharma, "I'm going to keep them out of Dr. Gray's hands. That's the most important thing. But . . . I haven't thought through everything yet. We're still working on a plan of action. We'll know more once we see what we're dealing with."

"Oh," said Charlie. But she could tell Dr. Sharma and Ms. Sabbith didn't seem excited about using the devices on themselves.

Ms. Sabbith finished packing up her bag and looked at Charlie. "Ready?"

"Ready," said Charlie. A knot in her stomach closed tighter, like a fist was grabbing her from the inside. So that her mom would let her go, she'd pretended like it was no big deal to have to fight soldiers, but she knew how hard it was and didn't want to go looking for trouble. Soon she and the two women were off, heading for the old abandoned warehouse that Gray's soldiers had taken over.

On the way Charlie explained how she and Maria and Kelly had followed the white van with Mac inside it all the way down a residential street, then over a dirt road. She told them about the empty horse barn and the big outbuilding they'd snuck around.

"Did you happen to get the license plate number of the van?" asked Dr. Sharma.

"No," said Charlie. "I didn't really think about that." She could still picture the silhouette of Mac's head through the tinted back window of the vehicle and him shouting for help. It was painful to remember how terrified he'd sounded, even though he was safe now. She wished her father were just as safe.

Dr. Sharma turned down the street and drove to the end where the dirt two-track began. They couldn't see the old buildings because of the brush. Ms. Sabbith rummaged through her bag, pulling out microphones and earpieces and some other strange electronics.

"We'll keep the car here," said Dr. Sharma, "near the houses, so it looks like we're visiting someone in the neighborhood. Erica, I'll stay here with Charlie. Let us know what you see."

Ms. Sabbith handed a set of basic wireless earpieces and a tiny microphone to Dr. Sharma. She explained how to use them. Then, loaded with high-power binoculars and other curious-looking gear, Ms. Sabbith slipped on a more advanced-looking earpiece that had a mike attached. She set off through the desert brush toward the buildings. Dr. Sharma gave one earpiece to Charlie and clipped the microphone to the sunroof between them. "Just put this in your ear. We'll share the microphone."

Charlie watched how Dr. Sharma put her earpiece in, then did the same with hers, and listened in.

"Can you hear me, Erica?" asked Dr. Sharma.

Charlie could hear the doctor next to her, but her voice didn't come through the earpiece.

"Roger that. I'm nearing the horse barn, in sight of the building. Approaching, heading clockwise around it."

"The door is on the back side of the building," Charlie said.

"Got it. Thanks, Charlie."

"And the soldiers we met inside there were pretty beefy, so if they're still there, be careful."

There was silence on the other end. Charlie imagined Ms. Sabbith skirting the building in much the same way she and Maria and Kelly had done.

Suddenly there was an urgent whisper that Charlie couldn't understand. Dr. Sharma sat up sharply. "What's happening?" she barked into the device.

There was silence for another tense moment. Then Ms. Sabbith whispered through her microphone, "White van pulling out of the outbuilding, heading your way. Warehouse doors left open. I'm going inside. You might want to duck."

"Get down, Charlie," said Dr. Sharma. "All the way on the floor." Charlie unbuckled her seat belt and shrank down. Dr. Sharma watched for a second, then flattened herself over the console and seats. They heard the rattling van approach and enter the neighborhood. Charlie stayed down as it roared past.

"The place is abandoned!" said Ms. Sabbith through the mike. "Totally cleaned out. They're not coming back. Follow that van!"

"Get over here, now!" shouted Dr. Sharma, sitting up again and making the car roar to life.

"I'm too far away! Don't lose them—it's our only chance! Go!"

"Not leaving you here. Top speed!"

"On my way!"

Charlie felt her heart race, her pulse pounding in her ears. The Mark Five grew warm. She clicked through and saw the cheetah was animated. She got back up on her seat and turned to look at Dr. Sharma. There was no way she would let Charlie go after the van—not after the doctor had promised Mrs. Wilde that Charlie would stay in the car the whole time. But it seemed like none of the adults really understood yet what Charlie could do. Charlie knew she could run fast enough to keep up with the van. At the very least she could follow it to the corner to see which direction it was heading in. That would be better than nothing.

Impulsively Charlie grabbed the microphone clip from the sunroof and slammed open the door. The van was speeding up the street, growing smaller in the distance. Charlie lunged outside and started running at top speed, microphone in hand. "I'm following them!" she said into it, not realizing at first that Dr. Sharma couldn't hear her since they were sharing a device. "I'll tell you how to find me."

There was an instant of silence. Then, "Charlie?" It was Ms. Sabbith's voice.

"Yes, it's me!" said Charlie. "My speed ability kicked in. I'm following the white van, so hurry up!"

Ms. Sabbith muttered a word Charlie wasn't allowed to say. Then, "Got it! I'm almost to the car."

Charlie smirked. It was kind of fun being in charge again.

"Do *not* let them see you!" added Ms. Sabbith harshly. "If you blow our cover, we are in serious trouble."

Charlie's smile faded fast. She couldn't mess this up. If she got caught, Dr. Gray would know she and the others were trying to save her dad. But if she lost sight of the van, they might never find him. She slowed when she got close and hid for a moment behind a giant saguaro cactus as the vehicle's left blinker began flashing. Then the white van turned and sped away.

CHAPTER 12

Despair

Dr. Gray paced the floor of his new, hastily set-up office. His phone was pressed against his ear. Dr. Wilde wasn't tied up anymore—he'd been taken to the lab across the hall to work. But Dr. Goldstein still was, lying on a sofa at the back of the room and trying to regain his strength. A soldier was guarding him and roughly helping him sip from a cup of broth.

"We're staying here," Dr. Gray said into the phone. He paused for a long moment, listening. Then, "No. I understand the concerns about the compromised warehouse, Prowl, but think it through. They'll assume we've gone far away—why wouldn't we? And while they go in search of us elsewhere or even back to Chicago, we won't waste another minute packing up and moving the operation again. We'll be right under their noses in this half-dead town and they'll never know. It's— What's that?" He listened again.

On the couch Jack Goldstein showed no signs that he could hear Dr. Gray. He finished the broth and turned away from the soldier, then closed his eyes.

"And you're sure no one saw you leave?" Dr. Gray asked. "Has there been any sign of police? Anything?" He waited a beat, then said, "Good. Maybe the other little brats were smart enough not to tell their parents after all. It's too bad they've got the prototypes, but we don't need them anymore now that we've got Charles." He glanced at Dr. Goldstein lying motionless. "And Jack ought to be up and around in a day or so. Then we can finally put this plan in motion. I've waited so long for this."

There was yearning in his voice, which was all the more unsettling to Jack. But he'd heard plenty of it in his time as Gray's prisoner.

There was another length of silence, and then Dr. Gray stopped pacing in front of his desk. "Yes, all right. The abandoned bank building in the business park. All the way at the top. See you soon."

The scientist hung up his phone and went to the window that overlooked the most dismal part of Navarro Junction, with the faint outline of Phoenix in the valley beyond. He hoped his instincts were right. It had been twenty-four hours since the children had escaped. If the police hadn't come to the warehouse by now, they weren't going to. Nobody had reported them—the Wildes were playing by his rules. No one would find them here. He'd bet his life's work on it.

On the sofa Jack remained still as a stone. His face was expressionless, but his heart was heavy. After weeks of torture, being dragged across the country, starved, and beaten for not helping Victor, Dr. Goldstein could hardly hang on to his last shreds of hope. Surely Quinn would figure out soon that he hadn't made it to Peru. She had to.

But when Charles had arrived yesterday as a captive, too, Jack had lost all hope of Gray giving up on his plan—the man was more determined than ever now that he had the kids as leverage. Jack couldn't possibly refuse to help Gray any longer with young Charlie's life at stake. There was no more holding out. Victor Gray's insane revolution was beginning, and Jack, alongside Charles, was forced to help him. It was against everything he stood for.

All he could do was hope that Charles's wife remembered the plan the three biologists had put in place. That she knew enough to call Quinn. But it had been so long since they'd made those arrangements. Would Mrs. Wilde possibly recall it?

After all the trauma Jack had been through lately, he didn't expect anything to go his way. His career, maybe even his life, was over. Instead of pulling DNA from fossils in Peru, he'd be creating DNA-altering devices that would change humanity . . . and not for the better.

He stayed still and silent, and hoped for a miracle.

In the lab across the hall Charles stood at a table looking over the instruments as a group of soldiers unpacked them. He wore an expression of complete devastation as he watched them. One of them noticed—a woman whose fingers ended in long sharp claws. She brought a large microscope over to Charles's station and set down in front of him. "Let me know what other supplies you need," she said quietly. "My name is Zed. I'll be assisting you and Dr. Goldstein."

Charles barely looked at her. He couldn't believe he was here or that this was happening to him. Was his family okay? Was Dr. Gray telling the truth about Charlie? What about these soldiers, covered to hide the permanent alterations Dr. Gray had made to their bodies? Had they volunteered for this? It was beyond comprehension.

"Do you know anything about the state . . . of my family? My children?" Charles asked her, desperate for information. Had Diana picked up on his clue to check the safe? It was hardly likely—they must have been in complete shock by the call.

Zed frowned and didn't answer. She glanced over her shoulder and kept moving as Cyke, the large male soldier who'd guarded them in Gray's office overnight, brought several boxes of equipment to the station. Charles stared at Cyke's facial structure, which had clearly been changed more than some of the others. "Did you volunteer for this experiment?" Charles asked him. "How long have you been like this?"

Cyke did a full body shudder and stared at the biologist like he'd said something terribly offensive. "You can unpack these," he said coldly. He went away, leaving Charles alone.

After a few minutes, with the boxes distributed to the various workstations, most of the soldiers dispersed, leaving Cyke to stand guard at the lab door and Zed unpacking things at the station next to Charles. After a while she carried a box of instruments over to Charles and set it down in front of him, facing away from Cyke. "Your daughter is fine," she said under her breath.

Charles's eyes widened, but he said nothing. Zed turned and went away, leaving Charles wondering why the soldier had taken pity on him. But very grateful that she had.

CHAPTER 13

Relocating

"They turned left on Ellsworth Ave," whispered Charlie into the microphone as she peered from behind the cactus. Once the white van disappeared, she ran to the corner and turned left to follow it. She sped up her pace, not wanting them to be out of sight for long so she wouldn't lose track of them. Within a minute or two she'd caught up again. She strained to see their license plate and managed to get part of it. "License plate starts with CX4," she said.

"I'm in the car," said Ms. Sabbith. "Be careful!"

"I'm being careful," said Charlie, her voice jiggling as she sprinted down a four-lane road, hoping the few drivers in the area didn't notice how oddly fast she was going. "Did you hear me? Left on Ellsworth. Then right on Brown, heading toward the freeway."

"I heard you and we're on the way. You could've told Dr. Sharma what you were doing, you know."

"Sorry. I forgot she wouldn't be able to hear me through the mike. They're going halfway around the traffic circle. Straight, I mean—you know? Not taking the freeway exit."

"You mean they're staying on Brown Road?"

"Yes."

"So they're not leaving town—that's surprising."

Charlie moved stealthily as the van slowed to navigate the curves, then darted after them once more, continuing to try to stay hidden from ordinary traffic as well so other drivers wouldn't be suspicious of her speed. Being a superhero came with a whole host of problems, no doubt about that. "Heading past the high school toward Red Mountain," Charlie said.

"We're not far behind you now," said Ms. Sabbith. "You're doing great."

"Rest of the license plate is R701. CX4R701. Got it?"

"Got it," said Ms. Sabbith. Charlie could hear Dr. Sharma in the background now, sounding pleased with her. Ms. Sabbith went on. "Okay, I see you. We're going to come up alongside you and pull over. You jump in and we'll keep going. You've gotta be quick so we don't lose sight of the van. Okay?"

"I can definitely be quick," said Charlie. "There's a stoplight coming up." She glanced back, searching the traffic for Dr. Sharma's car. She spotted it but then began running again when the light changed and the van sped off.

Finally Dr. Sharma's car caught up and rode alongside her. But Charlie didn't want to waste time waiting for them to stop. Feeling her fingers tingling, she leaped at the moving car, sticking to the side. Ms. Sabbith recoiled, surprised, then realized what had just

happened. She quickly threw open the door and yanked Charlie into the vehicle. Dr. Sharma sped up again.

"Wow!" said Ms. Sabbith. "That was incredible."

"Fantastic!" agreed Dr. Sharma as she glided through traffic to catch up to the van. "Your father would be so pleased—not just with how the bracelet works, but with how well you are using it."

Charlie caught her breath and put her seat belt on, her eyes stinging a little with the kind words. "Thanks. I like the gecko power because I can tell when it activates." She explained the tingling sensation.

"You've done well, Charlie," said Dr. Sharma, glancing quickly over her shoulder. "I have to admit, I didn't expect you to be so responsible with the device. You used good instincts in taking the mike, too. Though I would have preferred to know what you were up to. I almost went after you, but once I saw you running like that, I figured it out."

"Sorry about that," said Charlie, "but we couldn't let them out of our sight. And besides, I wanted to show you what I can do." She lifted her chin. "I really want you to trust me. I know what I'm doing."

Ms. Sabbith laughed. "Hey, don't look at me—I trust you. I think you've done an excellent job so far."

"I hear you, Charlie," said Dr. Sharma. "And you're proving yourself. But it's not that simple. You're a minor using an untested device that isn't even supposed to exist. This is tricky."

"But it's stuck on me, so what else am I supposed to do? Besides, I'm actually getting better at using it, so there's no reason to worry. I'm stronger, faster, and probably better at fighting and defending myself and my friends than any of you. And you're going to need me to rescue my dad. Unless you have a better idea."

"I know you're faster, for sure," Dr. Sharma said carefully, moving through traffic, "and I don't have a problem with you defending yourself or others. But I am not your mother, and I'm not so sure she's keen on the idea of putting you in danger." She hesitated, then said, "We don't even know if we'll need to do any fighting. Maybe we'll be able to go in and get your dad without any altercations."

Charlie raised an eyebrow. "You don't watch many superhero movies, do you?" But at least Dr. Sharma seemed open to Charlie using the device. So there was that.

They trailed behind the white van several more minutes to the outskirts of Navarro Junction. Eventually they found themselves in a quiet, tired-looking business park where a few eight- to ten-story-tall office buildings made up the entirety of the skyline. The van pulled into an alley behind an old abandoned bank building. A rusty gate opened mechanically and the van pulled through. Dr. Sharma glided her car past the alley and went around the block, passing a few smaller buildings and a restaurant. Then she turned down the alley from the opposite direction and came to another mechanical gate but didn't attempt to go through it. Instead, she guided the vehicle into the shadows next to some Dumpsters and a pile of office-type junk, about fifty paces from the soldiers.

This section of Navarro Junction felt like it had been forgotten. There was no one else around at the moment. Dr. Sharma kept the windows rolled up but opened the sunroof, and Ms. Sabbith propped a larger microphone on top of the car, hoping to pick up bits of conversation. She programmed the earpieces to connect with the new mike.

They watched, peering between pieces of junk and the trash receptacles. Three soldiers got out of the van and cautiously looked around, then opened the back of the vehicle and began to unload it. Ms. Sabbith took photos of the soldiers whenever she had an unobstructed shot.

Charlie could hear wisps of their conversation through her ear-piece.

"Equipment goes to the ninth floor," the smallest soldier of the three called out to the others. "The elevator's halfway down the hall. Don't worry about being seen—the whole building is vacant."

One of the others grunted and they continued unloading the van in silence.

"Have you seen these particular soldiers before?" Dr. Sharma asked.

Charlie studied them. "That's Prowl, the leopard man," she

said, pointing to the smallest one. He was slinking around, not carrying much but moving lithely in and out of the building. He had a new face mask on today, or at least the tear in the old one had been fixed.

The other two were slow and bumbling, but they could carry a lot more. "That man and woman were in the warehouse too. At least one of them is some type of cattle—he's superbeefy and was making lowing sounds when I was fighting him. I'm not sure about the other one. They almost took me out, but I was too fast for them. I don't know their names."

The soldiers emptied the van over the next quarter of an hour and brought the items inside. Dr. Sharma scanned the side of the building, looking through windows for signs of activity. "Ninth floor is the top," she noted.

Most of the old bank's window shades were pulled, making the building seem even more unfriendly. Charlie looked at the other structures in the area, trying to be like Dr. Sharma and make closer observations of her surroundings. It seemed like a good thing for a superhero to do. Charlie counted four cars in the parking lot across the street, with dozens of open spaces. There weren't any people walking around, even though it was the middle of a weekday. She could smell food cooking—perhaps from the restaurant nearby—so the business park wasn't completely abandoned. The Dumpster lids were lying flat, so either the businesses didn't have much trash or the receptacles had been emptied recently. It was amazing the things she noticed just by looking around instead of at her phone, like she usually did when she was in a car.

At last the van was empty. Prowl returned alone to lock it up, then went back inside the building.

Dr. Sharma started the vehicle and backed out of the alley. She drove slowly around the block, scanning the building from all sides, and then she looked at the neighboring buildings. Spying something across the street that pleased her, she smiled. "Aha," she said. She stopped the car. "There's an office for lease in the building across from the one Gray is in," she said, pointing to the sign in a window on the sixth floor. Erica, can you take care of securing that as our home base?"

"Got it," Ms. Sabbith said, taking down the phone number and website address on the sign. "I'll see if we can take possession of it immediately."

"Great. We'll need your surveillance equipment set up ASAP." She gave one last look at the bank building, then reentered traffic and began driving back toward Charlie's house. "We're lucky they didn't venture too far from the warehouse," she said.

"I wonder why," said Ms. Sabbith. "They could have gone anywhere."

"It's not easy to travel with an entire lab. And they've already moved the lab once and probably don't want to do it again."

"Makes sense."

When they arrived at Charlie's house, Dr. Sharma went in with her. "Thank you, Charlie. You did great work today. Tomorrow I want you to have an extremely normal Thursday."

Charlie frowned. "But we haven't found my father yet."

"We very nearly have, I suspect. He's in that building."

"Are you sure?" Charlie's heart surged. "How do you know?"

"I'm not positive, but it makes sense. We'll be spying on them in no time, don't worry." She glanced sidelong at Charlie. "I'll let you come if your mom says it's okay."

Charlie wanted that more than anything. "Can't you tell her you need me or something? She'll trust you."

Dr. Sharma's mouth twitched. As she followed Charlie to update Mrs. Wilde on what they'd found, she said, "We'll see."

That evening, only the three Wildes remained in their house. Everyone still felt on edge—it had been more than twenty-four hours and Charlie's father hadn't been found yet. But they were comforted by how sure Dr. Sharma was of his whereabouts. And what she'd said made sense.

Charlie and Andy did the homework they hadn't gotten to the previous night and prepared to go to school as usual the next day. Once in bed Charlie tried reading the comic book that Maria had let her borrow, now that Andy was done with it. But she couldn't concentrate. The drawings blurred and a tear slipped down Charlie's cheek. She missed her dad. What if he wasn't okay? She hoped Dr. Sharma and Ms. Sabbith were busy finding him right now.

After a while she turned out her light. She had to appear normal at school tomorrow. Go to classes, make up the soccer game that had been canceled due to rain the other day. Pretend like her world wasn't all torn up. If she could pull it off, it might be an Oscar-worthy performance. At least she'd have help from her friends.

CHAPTER 14

Just a Normal Day

Charlie's mom insisted on driving the kids to school on Thursday. Once there Charlie went straight to her first-hour class and waited outside the door for her friends to show up. Maria and Mac arrived first. When they saw Charlie, they ran to greet her.

"Did they find your dad?" asked Maria.

"Not yet."

Mac pulled the Talos Global envelope from inside his Windbreaker and shoved it at Charlie. "Here's this for Dr. Sharma."

"Did you find out anything more?" asked Charlie.

"Not really," said Mac. "I didn't want my parents to catch me looking through it after what happened yesterday. And since we don't have the bracelets anymore, it's not much use. I don't want to get in trouble again."

"I still have stuff to figure out with my bracelet," Charlie reminded them. "And there might be clues about how we can stop Dr. Gray. Maybe we can read more at lunchtime."

"Sure," said Mac, and Maria agreed.

Charlie clutched the envelope to her chest as Kelly came up.

"What are you doing?" asked Kelly. She eyed the envelope.

"Mac was just giving that back to Charlie," said Maria. "How are your parents reacting? Did you get in trouble?"

"My dad exploded once we got into the car. He . . . yells. A lot." She dropped her gaze. "My mom's in Cabo. She couldn't care less."

"What's Cabo?" asked Charlie.

"Cabo San Lucas," said Maria. "It's in Mexico. Resort city for the western US."

"Cool." Charlie adjusted her grip on the envelope. "Sorry about your dad, Kelly."

"It's fine. Whatever. I finally convinced him I never took a simulator in the first place and it was all a big misunderstanding. Still, I've never been in trouble like *that* before. And my dad says he doesn't trust your parents because he thinks they're irresponsible, leaving weird science junk sitting around your house for us to get into. So he doesn't want me hanging out with you anymore."

Charlie recoiled. "Oh."

"And now he's sending me to Cabo tomorrow night to be with my mother for spring break." She sounded angry about it.

"Why is that a bad thing?" asked Mac. "I thought it was really swanky there."

"I hate the ocean." Kelly crossed her arms and scowled. "All those jellyfish stinging and seaweed grabbing your ankles. It's smelly and the salt water makes my hair gross. I'll be stuck in the condo the whole week while my mother goes out with her obnoxious friends and ignores me as usual."

Mac raised an eyebrow, and Maria seemed to be rendered speechless.

Charlie was still stinging from Kelly's comment. No one had ever been forbidden to hang out with her before. It felt awful. All she wanted was to change the subject. "I keep forgetting it's spring break already next week," she murmured. "It comes so early here."

"So does the end of the school year," said Maria. "We get out in the middle of May. My cousins in Ohio don't get out until, like, the middle of June or something. Crazy."

"Yeah, but we start in August," lamented Mac.

"That's early," said Charlie. "Back home . . . ." She trailed off. Navarro Junction was home now. And while of course she still loved Amari dearly, her new best friends were here. Her new secret life with the bracelet was here too. She turned abruptly to Kelly. "Did you find your device?"

"What? Me? No. I'm not looking through disgusting garbage for a dud bracelet."

Charlie frowned, remembering how Dr. Sharma had been so sure at first that her device wasn't a dud, and how crestfallen she'd been to admit maybe it was after all. She at least deserved to have it back. "But it wasn't yours to throw away. It belongs to Dr. Sharma."

"She can search through the dump, then, because the trash was picked up yesterday."

"Ooo-kay," said Charlie as the first bell rang. The four of them went inside the classroom. Mac and Charlie headed to the back, where their desks were next to each other. "I hope they find your dad soon," whispered Mac, crouching in the aisle next to Charlie's seat.

Charlie looked around warily as others began to float into the room. "They think they know where he is," she whispered back. "In that big old bank building at the edge of town. But they haven't actually seen him there. The warehouse is totally cleared out and abandoned. We caught the white van leaving and followed it."

"Wow. That's crazy."

"Yeah."

Mac went to his seat and sat down.

Charlie slid the Talos Global envelope into her backpack, then looked at Mac. "Did you get a new phone yet?"

"Not yet. I've got to lie low for a bit until the whole thing from yesterday dies down. I figured I'd better hold off on telling my mom about my stolen iPad and phone."

"Good plan. But what if she texts or calls you?"

Mac shrugged. "I hope she doesn't need an answer."

The rest of the students came pouring into the seats surrounding them. Charlie faced forward and tried to concentrate on math, all the while willing her phone to vibrate in her pocket with news of her father. But it didn't come.

At lunch Charlie, Maria, and Mac ate quickly. Charlie filled them in on what she hadn't had time to tell them before school. Maria and Mac asked a lot of questions Charlie didn't know the answers to, like what exactly Dr. Gray wanted her dad to do for him.

"We don't really know yet," she told them. "But we hope to find out soon. Dr. Sharma and Ms. Sabbith are setting up a home base across from the bank building where they think Dr. Gray is keeping my dad. We're going to spy on them. Do a little recon." Charlie sniffed, feeling pretty savvy using that word.

"I hope you hear good news soon," said Maria. "I don't know how you can even concentrate."

"It helps a lot hanging out with you," Charlie admitted. "For a minute or two I almost forgot he was abducted."

After they finished lunch, they went outside and found a secluded spot in the courtyard to study the contents of the envelope, this time to search for information about the Mark Five. Each of them took a section of pages to flip through. A few minutes into it Charlie came across a page that had "Mark Five: In-Process Notes" written at the top. She scoured it.

It mentioned the animal abilities, which Charlie skimmed— she already knew about those. Then she got to the section on the bracelet's modes. "Listen," she said. "Finally some information we can use."

Maria and Mac stopped reading the documents in their hands and looked up.

"'The Mark Five exhibits three modes.

"'Dormant Mode. In the dormant mode the device is reactionary and only allows abilities to be activated when it senses that the user needs them. The user has no control over the selection of abilities and cannot choose to activate any. If the device senses the user is under attack, it will automatically switch to defense mode.

"'Defense Mode. In defense mode the device is still reactionary, but it also allows the user to choose to use abilities by activating them on the dial. In this mode the device also goes on lockdown and cannot be removed from the user's arm without being keyed in.

"'Battle Mode. In battle mode a soldier initiates the device manually during combat. This mode allows the user free range of all the abilities.'"

Charlie looked up.

"So *that's* what happened when you destroyed the bathroom," exclaimed Mac.

"Shh!" said Maria, looking around guardedly for teachers patrolling the area.

"Part. Of. The bathroom," Charlie said through tight lips.

"He's only saying it like that now to tease you," Maria told Charlie. "You should have seen him when Kelly found out. He totally defended you."

"Kelly knows?" exclaimed Charlie. She glanced around, realizing she'd said that a little too loudly, but Kelly wasn't in sight.

"After you left my house the other day," said Maria, looking guilty, "she guessed it. I said you didn't do it, but I don't think she believed me."

"Anyway," said Mac impatiently, poking his finger at the paper, "what's this Battle Mode? It sounds cool, like you can just choose your abilities instead of hoping the right one activates."

"Me want," said Charlie.

"But more important," said Maria, "does it say what the access code is so we can deactivate Defense Mode? Maybe then you can go into Battle Mode."

"Good point." Charlie quickly scanned the rest of the page as the bell sounded, ending lunch period. "Dang it," she muttered. She picked up her backpack with one hand and the envelope with the other, searching the next page as the three got up to go to class. "Ahh, I think . . . Yes! Here it is," she said, quickly looking over the code as they merged into the crowd of students.

Maria put her hand on Charlie's arm. "Awesome! Let us know if you're able to deactivate it. Here comes Kelly. I'm not sure . . . if . . ." She trailed off, a look of consternation on her face.

"If I should tell her all of this? I think you're right. Lately something with her seems . . . odd."

"What else is new?" Mac griped.

"Well, you don't have to be mean about it," Maria said to him. She turned back to Charlie. "I noticed it too."

Mac shrugged and the three parted ways.

Kelly caught up with Charlie to walk to fifth period. "What've you been doing?" she asked.

Charlie glanced around uneasily and hurried to put the papers back into the envelope. "Nothing much—just reading about . . . You know." She stuffed the envelope into her backpack and swung the strap over her shoulder as she jostled through the crowd.

"Ooh," said Kelly knowingly. Her cell phone rang and she frowned at it. Then she waved Charlie to continue without her and answered it.

Charlie went to class. Halfway through, Kelly came in and dropped a note on the teacher's desk, then went to her seat. Her eyes were red, like she'd been crying.

When fifth period was over, Charlie and Kelly fell in step to go to theater class, and Charlie glanced sidelong at her. "Are you all right?"

Kelly averted her gaze as they crossed the courtyard. "Yeah. Just had a phone fight with my mom. Nobody listens to me." She stomped on a bee that had alighted on some clover. "I'm sorry about your dad. I hope he's okay."

"Thanks." Charlie's eyes teared up a little, but she fought back the emotion. "I'm sorry about your parental problems too. Are you ready for the game?"

"More than ready," said Kelly, and her face clouded. "I can't wait to kick the crap out of that ball and pretend it's my . . . Never mind."

Her *what*? Mother? Her father? Charlie was surprised at first that that was where her mind led her, but then, after thinking it through, she wasn't. Kelly was having a really hard time with her parents and their divorce. And they didn't seem to be very supportive of Kelly right now—in fact, they acted like Kelly was just an annoyance in their lives. And it sounded like things were getting uglier and uglier for her.

"Are you sure you're okay?" Charlie asked.

Kelly was silent for a moment as they walked into the theater building. "I mean, I'm fine, I guess," she said quietly. "They're either yelling at me or totally ignoring me. Usually ignoring. So I suppose that's not the worst thing." But she said it like it really was the worst thing. And for a person like Kelly, who wanted, even needed, a lot of attention, it was probably really hard.

Before Charlie could respond, Kelly pulled away and walked quickly to her fan club, squealing, "Darlings, did you hear what the next show will be? I can't wait for Mr. Anderson to tell you all!"

Charlie shook her head a little in amazement. Kelly was the best actor Charlie had ever seen. She'd turned off her feelings just like that, and she was amazingly convincing. Even Charlie got caught up in her excitement. It was becoming harder and harder to figure out when Kelly was being her true self and when she was faking.

Sara, Charlie's friend who had been the stage manager for the last show, sidled up to her and watched Kelly, too. "Do you think she really knows what the next show is? Or is she just pretending in order to make herself look special?"

Charlie sighed, perplexed by the complex girl. With parents like Kelly had, maybe acting and playing to her fan club was the only way Kelly could feel important. The theater was her place to get the attention her parents weren't giving her. "I honestly have no idea what Kelly is trying to do most of the time."

CHAPTER 15

Disaster on the Field

After school Charlie headed straight outside toward the locker room, checking her phone as she walked. There was just one text message from her mom, reminding Charlie to check in after school to make sure she was okay. Charlie texted that all was normal.

"I'll see you at your game," replied Mrs. Wilde. "Picking up Andy and heading over."

Charlie smiled, though it felt bittersweet. Her mom had been so busy working ever since they'd moved here that Charlie was starting to get used to her missing things. It was sad that it took *this* kind of situation with Dad to change all that. "So your leave of absence is happening? Starting now?" Charlie texted.

"Yep!" Mrs. Wilde replied. "Through spring break for sure and then we'll see. So I'm all yours."

That made Charlie think about her dad and his job, and she grew worried. "What about Dad? What will happen with his job if he's not there?"

"I called in sick for him for the rest of this week. He has spring break next week like you, so we're covered for a while. Don't worry, sweetie! I love you."

"I love you too." Charlie pressed Send and blinked away a second round of tears for the day, reminding herself to act normal. She shoved her backpack and phone into her locker and changed into her sports tank, soccer uniform, shin guards, and cleats. Teammates around her were doing the same.

Maria and Charlie slammed their locker doors shut at the same time and were the first ones outside. They ran together to get a ball and started passing it back and forth as the opposing team's bus pulled into the parking lot. The field, which had been flooded two days ago from a little bit of rain, was dry as a bone today. The desert was a crazy place. Charlie was learning that more and more all the time.

"Did you deactivate your bracelet?" Maria asked in a low voice, chipping the ball to Charlie from close range.

"Not yet. I haven't had time. I don't want anybody to see me messing with it."

"Good move."

"Is there anything else you want to know about the Mark Two before I hand over the envelope to Dr. Sharma?" Charlie asked.

"No thanks—I'm good. It was fun to have the abilities but not the fur and the tail. I'm glad to be rid of it and let you take on the bad guys."

Charlie smiled as the rest of their team joined them on the field. The opposing team soon followed. Maria and Charlie and the rest of Summit's players all went over to circle around Coach

Candy for some final encouraging words.

The stands had filled up with parents and friends. Mac watched the action from his usual spot, looking a little lost and bored without his phone or iPad. Charlie's mom and brother sat in the section next to Mac. The absence of Charlie's dad was particularly glaring, and a wave of sadness washed over Charlie. Maria's mom and stepdad, along with Maria's three stepbrothers, sat a few rows in front of her family.

Charlie didn't see Kelly's dad anywhere. Did she have any siblings or any other family who might come and watch her play? Charlie didn't know—but she did remember that no one from Kelly's family had come to see her in the musical either, which was really sad because she was so talented. Charlie would make a point of asking sometime. Maybe Kelly just needed somebody to truly care about what was going on in her life, like parents were supposed to do. Charlie knew now that in public Kelly liked to pretend everything was perfect. But it was clearly far from that.

The starters took their places and the game began. Charlie lagged a bit—she just wasn't able to focus like usual. But Kelly and Maria were tearing up the field, making some excellent plays together. The opposing team soon caught on to their strategy, though, and started doubling up the defense on them. That only seemed to spur Kelly on. She pushed roughly through a crowd of opponents, who then went after Maria to stop her from teaming up with Kelly.

But it didn't matter. Kelly had the ball and she didn't need any help. As Maria charged through the opposing team trying to catch up, Kelly took the ball to the box. And as Maria broke free, Kelly faced off with the goalie and defenders and slammed the ball into the net before anybody could block it. As the crowd erupted, a defensive player stepped into Maria's path. Too late to stop, Maria jumped wildly and went flying into the air above the other players' heads. Charlie, focused on the goal, barely saw it out of the corner of her eye. She joined the crowd in roaring approval for Kelly.

"Yes!" shouted Charlie. "Great job, Kel!" She turned around and ran toward her position on the field as the opposing team regrouped on their side. That's when she noticed Maria was down.

"Charlie!" howled Maria. "Help!"

Maria's voice sounded frightened and very odd. Charlie's bracelet grew warm and she ran fast, dodging her teammates, some of whom were also heading over to Maria to see what had happened. When Charlie reached Maria's side, she gasped.

"What is going *on*?" exclaimed Charlie. Maria's beard and fur were back! Charlie dropped to her knees and whipped off her shirt, glad she'd worn her sports tank underneath today. "Stand back, everybody!" she shouted. "Make room!" She flung the shirt on Maria's face and desperately looked around. She waved and caught her mother's eye in the crowd and motioned her to come over.

Being a doctor, Mrs. Wilde was usually on alert for injuries at sports events, and she bolted onto the field. Coach Candy was coming toward them as well, and Ken and Maytée and the boys were standing up, looking anxious and straining to see.

Charlie bent to Maria's ear. "How did this happen? You gave the bracelet back!"

"I don't know," moaned Maria. "The tail is there too—I can feel it bunched up in my shorts. This is horrible!"

"Well, breathe! Meditate! Do those yoga things!"

"Stop yelling—that's not helping!"

"Right," said Charlie, trying to calm down, but people were crowding around. "Okay. Phew. Here we go. Breathe, Maria. Very calm. Everything is calm. How the heck . . . What caused it? Was it just adrenaline or what? Did you get hurt?"

"Shh," said Maria. "We'll talk about that later, okay?"

"Right," said Charlie again. She stayed nearby to try to block others from getting too close.

Charlie's mom pushed through the crowd. She quickly greeted Coach Candy and reminded her who she was. "If you could get the team to move way back and give us some space, that would help so much," she said to Coach and a few others.

Mom knelt next to Maria's head as Charlie moved down and grasped Maria's hand. She tried not to cringe when she felt a patch of fur there, too. "What happened?" Mrs. Wilde asked.

"She turned into a weremonkey again," Charlie said in a harsh whisper. "Without the bracelet!"

"Om," said Maria forcefully. "Ommm."

Mrs. Wilde's eyes widened, but her words came out calm. "All right," she said slowly. "Let's think about meadows and sweet little kittens."

"I prefer puppies," said Maria, her voice muffled under Charlie's shirt.

"Puppies . . . napping on your stomach while you read a book," said Mrs. Wilde. She smiled weakly and gave Charlie a look begging for help.

"Puppies walking on cute wobbly feet," said Charlie, and shrugged anxiously at her mother.

"In . . . a meadow," said Mrs. Wilde, cringing.

"All of them breathing very softly and evenly," said Charlie. "And doing . . . yoga . . ." She was so stressed out, she could feel her bracelet grow even warmer.

Coach Candy returned. "How are we doing?" she asked.

"She's just catching her breath now," said Mrs. Wilde. "I'll finish checking her over, but we should be good to go shortly."

"Thanks, Dr. Wilde." Coach Candy frowned, seeing the shirt still covering Maria's face, but she retreated again.

Desperately Charlie looked around to make sure they still had privacy, and her eyes landed on Maria's mother, who was coming over. "Oh no," she whispered. "Keep working it, Maria. I'll go take care of your mom."

"My mom is coming?" Maria screeched. "If she finds out this fur thing happened again, we're toast!"

"No. It's fine. Be calm. I'll be back in a few."

"Tell her not to embarrass me!"

"Okay," said Charlie uncertainly. She sprinted over to Maria's mom. "Hi, Mrs. Torres! Hey, did you see that? Crazy! Anyway, Maria's fine. She's just catching her breath. My mom's with her. I'm not sure if you know she's an ER doctor—she says everything's good. No concussion or anything like that—Maria just fell hard on her back and got the wind knocked out of her. She wants to keep playing."

"Are you sure?" Maytée said, concerned. "She's been down a long time."

"I'm sure," said Charlie. "She told me to tell you she's okay and, um . . . not to embarrass her."

Maytée emitted a relieved laugh. "It figures. Sounds like typical Maria. She'd want to keep playing even if she'd broken her neck. *Gracias*, Charlie."

"No problem. She's a fighter."

Mrs. Torres turned to go back to her seat.

Charlie caught Mac's eye in the stands, and gave him a look of panic. He tensed and shook his head like he didn't understand. Charlie cupped her chin and drew her hand downward in a cone shape to make an air beard. Mac frowned, then his face exploded in shock. He sat there helpless as Charlie turned back and ran to her mother's side.

Kelly was next to Maria now, too, having figured out what had happened. She held her hand and was talking gently. Charlie watched them. Soon the T-shirt began moving the slightest bit, flattening against Maria's face.

"There," said Kelly, peeking under the shirt, then pulling it away. "We did it." She looked up and saw Charlie and handed the shirt to her.

"Is it gone?" asked Maria, feeling under her bum. She sat up.

"Looks that way," said Charlie. She put the shirt back on. "Do you think you should sit out the rest of the game?"

Maria waved to her mom and stepdad to confirm she was okay, and the crowd cheered. "I guess I'd better," she said. "I don't want that to happen again. Why did it, though? I don't understand."

"No idea," said Charlie.

"I'll call Dr. Sharma and see if she knows why it happened without the device," said Mrs. Wilde. "Meanwhile, let's get the game going. I'll let your coach know that I want you to sit out as a precaution."

"Okay. Thanks, Mrs. Dr. Wilde."

"You're welcome. Limp a little so it looks real." Mrs. Wilde helped Maria to her feet and walked her to the sidelines.

"Do you think . . . ," Charlie began, turning to look at Kelly.

The truth of what had happened to Maria, without her wearing the bracelet, began to sink in.

"That the weremonkey thing is permanent?" asked Kelly. "Gosh, I hope not. That would be the worst."

They watched Maria take a seat, then parted and went back to their positions. Coach Candy subbed in another halfback to take Maria's place.

Despite her powers Charlie couldn't find her energy. She could run fast, but she stumbled over the ball or kicked it out of bounds. The wind had been let out of Kelly's sails, too. Their team lost 4–3. The loss felt like an ominous sign of even worse things to come.

CHAPTER 16

Really Not Funny Anymore

After the game Maria, Mac, Kelly, Charlie, and their families gathered in the parking lot. Maria convinced her mom to let her go over to Charlie's house to do homework and have dinner. "That way Mrs. Dr. Wilde can keep an eye on my injuries," she said.

"Just don't mess around with any more science experiments," warned Maytée.

"I won't."

"I think we'll all be more careful," said Mrs. Wilde, resting a gentle hand on Maytée's forearm. "Kelly and Mac, you're both welcome to come over, too," said Charlie's mom.

"Sure," said Mac.

"I have other plans, thank you," said Kelly. Her warmth from when she was helping Maria had faded, and she was back to being icy again. "In fact," she said, looking away, "I need to go now. See you tomorrow, everybody." She picked up her backpack.

"Do you want a ride?" asked Maria's mom.

"No, thanks, I'm good," said Kelly, smiling politely.

The group said their good-byes and Kelly jogged toward her

home alone. Maria's parents and stepbrothers went to their car, and Mrs. Wilde walked over to hers with Andy, Charlie, Maria, and Mac following.

Once inside the car, with the doors closed, Maria let out a huge sigh of relief. "Good grief," she moaned, flopping back against the seat. "That was a disaster!"

"What triggered it?" asked Mac. "I saw you fly through the air."

"Me too," said Andy. "You looked cool."

"I was just playing hard. The other team came at me. I tried to get around them and just sort of leaped into the air and kept going and going until I landed flat on my back. It was insane. I didn't realize what had happened at first."

"But you gave the device back," said Mac. "I don't get how this could happen without it. Unless . . ."

Charlie cringed. "Don't say it. There's no way it changed her permanently." The thought was unfathomable. "We're going to fix this, Maria. Mom, did you call Dr. Sharma?"

"Yes, once the game resumed. She wants to take a look at Maria, so we're heading downtown to the home base they're setting up."

"Do you think they'll be able to find Dad? It's a big building."

"I hope so. I'm sure they'll tell us more once we get there."

"What about food?" asked Andy.

"Dr. Sharma's picking up dinner for everybody."

"Good," said Charlie. "I'm starving." She glanced at Maria, who was quieter than usual. A tear slid out of her eye. Charlie squeezed her hand. "It's going to be okay," she told her. But even Charlie was beginning to doubt it. How awful it must feel for Maria to not know if or when she was going to change again.

Maria stared ahead, unseeing. "I'm a monster," she whispered. "I'm like one of *them*—those awful hybrid soldiers."

Mrs. Wilde parked behind the building in a small lot and checked her text messages from Dr. Sharma for the directions to the correct office. They went inside and up to the sixth floor. Then they counted the doors to the right one and stopped in front of it.

"'Water and Sewage Treatment Complaints Office'?" said Maria, reading the fading stenciled sign on the door.

Mrs. Wilde looked mystified, but she tried the door and it opened.

Immediately in front of them was a receptionist's counter. On it was a small sign next to a bell, inviting customers to ring for service. Next to the bell was a small decorative vase with clear and black stones in it, a few pens, and a clipboard with a waiting list. A few names were written on the list and crossed out. Behind the receptionist work area was a full wall with a door off to the left.

"Are you sure this is it?" Charlie whispered.

"Ms. Sabbith said this office was used for something else until recently," said Mrs. Wilde under her breath. "I'm sure this is the right place."

Mac went up to the counter and dinged the bell. They all waited.

A few moments later Dr. Sharma opened the door. "You found us. Come on in."

Curious, the party followed her back behind the counter and through the door. "Ms. Sabbith rigged the door to lock automatically when it closes," Dr. Sharma explained, "so remember that when you come and go. We should keep it closed for everyone's safety in case we get discovered and need to hide inside. I'll give you a key to it, Diana. If someone rings the bell when you're back here in the surveillance area, use caution in deciding whether to open it and let them in."

"We're going to need to hide?" said Andy uncertainly.

Mrs. Wilde glanced at him and rested her hand on his shoulder. "Probably not, buddy. It's just in case."

Dr. Sharma closed the door firmly and they heard a loud click of the lock.

When they turned around, they found themselves in the surveillance area. Ms. Sabbith, unloading thin TV monitors encased in bubble wrap from a box, waved in greeting. The place was slightly chaotic, with partitions and office furniture and electronics strewn everywhere, but there were a few cleared tables and chairs set up.

Dr. Sharma and Ms. Sabbith took a dinner break with the

others, and everyone ate quickly as Mrs. Wilde caught them up on what had happened at the soccer game.

Maria kept staring off into space, looking sad, and didn't eat much. Charlie lost her appetite halfway through, and even Mac set his fork down when he saw how upset his friend was. Andy finished off Charlie's food in addition to his own.

Later Dr. Sharma beckoned Maria over to a desk. Mrs. Wilde joined them. The two devices the agents had collected rested in front of them. Charlie hovered nearby, listening.

Maria looked imploringly at Dr. Sharma. "Why did this happen when I wasn't wearing the bracelet?"

Dr. Sharma glanced at Mrs. Wilde, then looked solemnly at Maria. She pursed her lips, then picked up the Mark Two and turned it slowly in her hand. "I don't know for sure because I didn't work on this device. But my guess is that the bracelet permanently changed your DNA. It's similar to Dr. Gray's Mark One, except his soldiers' physical bodies don't change back like yours does. The Mark Two must be different in that it responds to your body's signals—you look like your regular self when everything is fine, but when you sense danger, your body automatically changes to give you the abilities and features of your corresponding animal."

Maria didn't say anything.

Dr. Sharma went on. "Like Gray's soldiers, you don't have to keep wearing the device for basic monkey abilities to kick in. Nubia might have embedded other components in it that could enhance the wearer's skills, I don't know. It's got some buttons, so I assume there's a reason for them."

"But . . . wait," said Maria. "Go back to what you said about the DNA thing. What do you mean, 'permanently'? Like *permanently* permanent? Do you mean you can't fix me?"

"I'm not sure yet," admitted Dr. Sharma. "I believe I can. But I'll have to do some research to see if there's a way to reverse the effects or possibly make a new device with your original DNA that will return you to your old self."

Maria and Mrs. Wilde stared. "How long will something like that take?" asked Mrs. Wilde.

"Again, I'm not sure. It'll definitely help if I can locate Nubia. Still no luck there." Dr. Sharma's face clouded. "And I've been trying to reach Jack, but he's not responding to my calls or emails. I'm worried that Victor has gotten him, too, since he managed to get Jack's device."

"You said Jack was going to Peru to do research, right?" asked Mrs. Wilde. "Maybe he's in a remote area and doesn't have a signal."

"Perhaps. But I fear the worst. Anyway, I'm going to work on your case right now, Maria, while Erica sets up the equipment. I hope to have some answers for you soon."

Mac looked over at Maria, horrified. "You're like the Hulk," he whispered.

Maria buried her face in her hands. "Only not nearly that cool."

Dr. Sharma gave her a sympathetic smile. "Perhaps Nubia didn't intend for the actual physical traits to accompany the animal's special ability. Unfortunately, she didn't get far enough in the process to eliminate that problem. Maybe she was on the verge of it, though—don't give up hope. Try not to get into situations where you'll feel trapped or scared or overly excited. If you can stay relatively calm, it might never happen again."

Charlie and Maria stared at each other in horror, no doubt thinking the same thing. What about soccer? What about just being a sixth grader and living a normal life?

"It's a terrible way to live, though," murmured Charlie's mother. She gave Maria's arm a reassuring squeeze. "Once we have Charles back, I'm sure he can help Quinn work on this. Don't worry."

"Yeah," said Andy, who'd crept up to listen in, "my dad can do pretty much anything."

"Please don't tell my parents about this," said Maria. "They'll *freak*."

Dr. Sharma looked solemn. "If we reach the point where we have to tell them, I'll take responsibility. And we'll take care of you and your family. You will have our full support. For now, though, I prefer they didn't know about this either."

Tapping her chin thoughtfully, she turned to Ms. Sabbith. "I've already got a few ideas on how to try to change Maria's DNA back to what it was before. But I'm going to need some lab instruments.

And . . . some very specific materials. High-clearance stuff that an ordinary civilian can't exactly order online, if you know what I mean."

Ms. Sabbith looked sidelong at Dr. Sharma. "Would it be stuff that Talos Global happens to have back in Chicago?"

"You read my mind."

Ms. Sabbith grinned. "You can count on me. I'll go back and try to snag whatever you need."

"Great. I'll do some research and build a list of supplies over the next day or two," Dr. Sharma said. "That'll give you time to set up the cameras and teach me how to control them before you go."

Mac and Charlie exchanged an intrigued glance. Cameras?

"It won't take long," said Ms. Sabbith. She turned to Maria. "Dr. Sharma's a great scientist. She's going to fix you. Believe it."

Maria looked relieved. "Good. Thanks."

Ms. Sabbith went back to her work, and Dr. Sharma opened her briefcase and began to study some files, apparently re-familiarizing herself with the work she and the other biologists had done ten years before. At the sight of the files Charlie was reminded of the envelope, and the access code she'd found after lunch. She could finally deactivate Defense Mode and try out Battle Mode.

"Hey, Dr. Sharma," said Charlie, spying her backpack and going over to it, "I've got that Talos Global envelope for you.

Maybe the Project Chimera papers have a clue that will help you know how to get Maria back to normal." She opened the flap.

"Oh yes!" exclaimed Dr. Sharma, turning to look at her. "I'm glad you brought it. There might be some important information in there."

Charlie rummaged through her backpack. She moved a few books and homework folders around, and then frowned. "Where is it? I put it in here after lunch, didn't I?"

Mac and Maria shrugged. "You were holding it in your hand when we split up after lunch," said Mac.

"I put it away right after that," said Charlie. "I'm sure of it."

"Did you take it out again to get the access code?" asked Mac.

"No," said Charlie. "I didn't have a chance to. And I forgot about it once Maria's problem started." She pulled everything out of the backpack, but came up empty-handed and frustrated. "I could have sworn I put it in here as I was walking to class with Kelly. But maybe I pulled it out to make room for something else and accidentally left it somewhere." She shook her head. "I wouldn't be that careless with something so important."

"Then where did it go?" asked Mac.

Charlie was truly puzzled. "Andy, you didn't touch it, did you?"

"Nope. What is it?"

"A manila envelope that says 'Talos Global' on the outside. It had some really important papers and a Project Chimera file in it, with information about all the devices. Where the heck . . . ?"

"What's manila?" asked Andy.

"It's like yellowy-tan. . . ." She trailed off, looked totally bewildered, then searched through everything again, even though it was obvious the envelope wasn't there. Finally she gave up. "Maybe it's in my locker," she said, feeling helpless and unsettled. She repacked her things, mentally going through her afternoon, trying to remember the last time she saw it. "I'll go to school early tomorrow and look for it."

"When you find it, let me know right away," said Dr. Sharma, looking concerned. "Potentially for Maria's sake, of course, but also because we don't want anyone reading what's in there."

Near the windows that overlooked the bank building, Ms. Sabbith set a briefcase on the table and opened it. She glanced over her shoulder and saw Maria looking melancholy and Charlie looking frazzled. "Come on over here," she said to the kids. "Let me show you what we're doing."

Charlie, Mac, Maria, and Andy obeyed and watched curiously as Ms. Sabbith pulled some tiny wrapped items from the briefcase. The kids grew even more curious when they realized what she was unpacking. It was a set of insects. Real ones, or so they appeared, and actual size.

"They're synthetic," said Ms. Sabbith. There was a dragonfly, a brown roach, a small spider, and a ladybug.

"What are these for?" asked Maria. She scrunched up her nose at the roach.

"You'll see." Ms. Sabbith picked up her cell phone, opened an app, and pressed a few buttons. The roach skittered over the table toward the children.

"Yuck!" said Andy, jumping backward.

"Disgusting!" said Mac. He cringed, but cautiously moved closer to see how they worked. "Cool technology inside gross bugs," he moaned. "I'm so conflicted."

Ms. Sabbith laughed and instructed the kids to watch a large monitor on a table nearby, then she moved the roach around. She made it run to the edge of the table and lean over, then turned its head from side to side. On the screen was a moving picture of the inside of the room.

"It's a camera?" asked Charlie. "Are these the ones Dr. Sharma mentioned?"

"Yes. They're drones—well, technically, only the ones that fly are called drones. But they're all decoys that'll help us spy on Dr. Gray. The roach and dragonfly are big enough to hold microphones as well as cameras." She pulled something else much bigger out of the case. It was a beautiful red cardinal. Ms. Sabbith messed around with her phone some more, and soon the cardinal's eyes opened. It hopped so convincingly that, for a moment, Charlie thought it had to be real. Then it took off and flew around the room. The computer monitor showed everything the cardinal could see.

"Wow!" said Mac. "It looks like an actual bird!"

"These little guys are going to help us a lot." She looked at some plastic crates on the ground that held more screens. "Do any of you know how to set up a monitor?"

"I do." Mac was eager to have his hands on such quality merchandise. He and the others helped set up the equipment, and soon there was an insect's view on each screen. Ms. Sabbith messed around with her phone app and began switching camera views and monitors, trying each one out on the big screen, so they could have a closer look at whichever drone's camera they needed. Then she set up a laptop computer on a table and switched to using that to control the drones and monitors.

"Why are you doing both?" asked Mac.

"I want the phone set up in case we need to go mobile without looking suspicious," said Ms. Sabbith. "Also to use as a backup. But mainly we'll work from the laptop. We'll mount the monitors on the wall later and connect the sound to come through my computer speakers."

"Increíble," said Maria under her breath, forgetting about her personal problems for the moment. "But how are you going to get the cameras over there?"

"I'll show you in a bit," Ms. Sabbith said. She checked her watch and went to the window. It was getting dark outside. Then she pulled a thin, portable window shade from a duffel bag on the floor, unrolled it, and attached it to one of the windows. It was see-through from their side. Ms. Sabbith pointed to the ninth floor, where the soldiers had said they'd be. There were lights on in some of the rooms, though the shades were still drawn. "Now you can stand in front of this window and look outside without anyone being able to see you. That'll do until we can get something more permanent. But finding Dr. Wilde takes priority at the moment."

Ms. Sabbith donned a baseball cap and sunglasses. She picked up her cell phone, the roach, and the spider. "Quinn, I'm heading over to get the non-flyers planted where we need them."

Dr. Sharma glanced up at her, then nodded and went back to her research.

The kids crowded in front of the screened window, and soon they could see Ms. Sabbith crossing the street below. She went into the back entrance of the bank building, where Charlie had seen the soldiers unloading equipment the previous day. From their location on the sixth floor of this building, they couldn't see anything inside the main floor of the bank building. But it didn't take long for Ms. Sabbith to come striding back outside. A few minutes later she returned to home base.

"Let's turn these on," Ms. Sabbith said. She pushed a few buttons on the computer and two of the monitors lit up. She moved the roach cam to the big screen. "The main floor was empty, so it was no problem to plant both insects in the elevator. I sent them up to the ninth floor. I'm going to leave the spider in the elevator for now so we can see who's coming and going. But the roach is heading out into the hallway. Let's have a look around."

Their view on the roach screen was of a long corridor with a few doorways. There were some soldiers standing and talking at the far end. Ms. Sabbith made the roach skitter down one side, staying close to the wall. When it came to a door, she guided it underneath. It was dark and quiet. They couldn't make out much on the screen.

"I think I'll just park you here out of the way for now until I get these others set up," Ms. Sabbith murmured as she worked. She glanced out the window and up at the ninth floor across the street. It was nearly dark out now. A few lights burned in the windows. "Time for the flyers."

Ms. Sabbith proceeded to pick up the ladybug and put it in the cardinal's beak. Then she opened the window a few inches—as far as it would go—and slid the cardinal out. She set it on the ledge and left it there, then went back to the computer to make the drone fly through the evening toward the top floor of the bank building.

Mac watched intently everything she was doing. Ms. Sabbith landed the bird on the middle windowsill of one of the three lit-up windows that had its shade drawn, then carefully maneuvered it to deposit the ladybug onto the sill. Then she made the ladybug walk up the edge of the window frame to a spot where the shade was torn, which gave her a good view into the room. With a few quick keystrokes Ms. Sabbith directed the ladybug cam to be displayed on the big screen, and it showed an empty laboratory with several stations and high-tech equipment. "Aha," she said. "Now we're getting somewhere. Still no biologist, though."

By now Mac had pulled up a chair next to Ms. Sabbith, who was fast becoming his new hero. "Doesn't the ladybug fly?" he asked.

"Yes, but I didn't want to risk it—it's windy and dark and she's so tiny."

Mac nodded thoughtfully.

Leaving the ladybug in its prime spot, Ms. Sabbith took the cardinal controls and flew the bird to a tall palm tree that bordered the parking lot at the back of the bank building. She pointed the bird's camera at the back door that the soldiers had used. Then she set the bird to rotate its head every ten seconds to scan the parking lot before turning back to the door. "Okay. The cardinal is in place. Now for the dragonfly."

Ms. Sabbith sent the dragonfly out the window and flying to the top of the building and out of sight. "Hit Control-Shift-Plus for me, will you, Mac?"

"Sure," said Mac. He did it, and a light from the dragonfly began pinging on the screen.

"That'll help us find a way inside."

Mac nodded and sat up straight, inching his chair closer to Ms. Sabbith's. He watched every keystroke command the woman made, no doubt memorizing it. Charlie could tell he was itching to do more. She and Maria exchanged a smile as they watched him silently geek out.

Ms. Sabbith was quiet for a moment, concentrating hard on landing the dragonfly exactly where she wanted it.

"There's a vent!" Mac said.

"Yep," said Ms. Sabbith. "Good eye, kid. Good eye."

Mac grinned. Ms. Sabbith crawled the dragonfly over the flat roof to the vent and slowly let it flutter down inside it.

Andy, who'd been mesmerized, spoke up. "Why is there a hole in the roof? Doesn't the rain get inside?"

"It lets the heat out. There's a tented cap over the space and our dragonfly is just small enough to crawl under it. So generally no rain can get inside. It's hard to see how that works in the dark, though." She shifted in her chair and squinted at the screen. "This is going to take a while," she told the kids. "And it'll probably be boring."

Mrs. Wilde, who had been helping Dr. Sharma sort through the files she'd brought, looked up. When she saw the monitors were working, she came over. Her face was strained as she waited for evidence of her missing husband. "Since it's going to be a bit before Ms. Sabbith finds anything, maybe you kids should get your homework done. Don't you have a test, Charlie?"

"Yeah," Charlie said. She didn't mention that she actually had two tests the next day. And she didn't feel like studying.

"I'll let you know when I find something exciting," Ms. Sabbith promised.

The four kids reluctantly left the area and went to the table where they'd had dinner to pull out their homework. "At least tomorrow's our last day of school for a while," said Mac.

Charlie could hardly keep track of what day it was. Everything was messed up. She started studying some notes from her English class but her mind wandered back to her school day, and she began wondering again where the Talos Global envelope could be. Had she left it in theater class? She remembered seeing it when she'd put away her script of the new musical they were going to do. She looked up quickly. "Oh, Mom—I forgot to tell you our final musical for the school year is going to be *The Sound of Music*."

"Nice choice," said Mrs. Wilde.

"Is Kelly playing the lead?" asked Maria.

"We haven't had auditions yet—they're not until Monday after spring break. But probably."

They chatted a little more about school as they worked. Their conversation was strained as they tried to act normal, and they all kept looking over at the screens, hoping to catch a glimpse of Mr. Wilde—he just had to be there.

Just when Mrs. Wilde was ready to call it a night and head home, Ms. Sabbith muttered under her breath. "Annnd . . . we're in. Where, I'm not sure. But we're somewhere above the ceiling on the ninth floor." The screen lightened up considerably, and she maneuvered the dragonfly to rest on the air vent grate. Then she tipped the dragonfly forward so it could look down into the room, being careful not to let him fall through. It panned the area.

Ms. Sabbith stopped it abruptly when the monitor showed something moving. She focused and sucked in a breath. "Diana," she said, turning to the woman, "I think we found him."

Everyone came running over to the monitors. Charlie's mom leaned forward and gasped.

The dragonfly cam zoomed in and focused on two men who were tied to chairs and looking beat up.

One of them was Charlie's father.

CHAPTER 17

The Non-Rescue Plan

"Dad!" cried Charlie and Andy together.

"Charles!" cried their mom.

Everyone stared in horror at the two prisoners. "What did they do to them?" asked Maria. "Your dad is all beat up."

"Who's that other guy?" asked Mac. The second man's face was in the shadows, and his body was thin and weak-looking.

Dr. Sharma came over too, and peered more closely. Her expression darkened. "Just as I feared. It's Jack." She put her hand to her forehead and turned around, like she couldn't believe what she was seeing. Then she turned back to the screen. "That's Dr. Jack Goldstein. And clearly he's not in Peru." She shook her head. "He's practically emaciated. They must have had him all this time."

Everyone gathered around to get a closer look. "Can we go in and get them?" asked Mrs. Wilde. "It doesn't look like anybody else is in there."

Ms. Sabbith made the dragonfly pivot, showing a soldier at the door. "I think we need to assess a few things before we rush in." There was a desk in the room, but no one was sitting there at the moment.

"One step at a time," agreed Dr. Sharma. "Let's see our scientists again. Erica, can you zoom in on Charles's face?"

Ms. Sabbith did so. Though the picture was grainy, they could make out a few scabbed-over cuts and bruises.

"Those bruises look a few days old," said Charlie's mom. "No fresh ones that I can see."

"So?" asked Charlie. Andy just stared at their father. His bottom lip trembled.

"So that means they're not currently getting assaulted," said Mrs. Wilde. "Or at least they haven't been probably since Tuesday when they abducted Charles."

"Logically, then," said Ms. Sabbith, "it follows that they're somehow complying with Dr. Gray's wishes."

"But my dad would never help a bad person like Dr. Gray," said Charlie.

"Yeah," said Andy tearfully.

"Unless Gray threatened him," said Dr. Sharma. "Whatever the case, we still have no idea how many soldiers are here and what they're doing. Our plan for now is to watch them for a while. If either of the scientists look like they're in serious danger, we'll drop everything and figure out a way to go in. But if they are not being tortured—beyond this, anyway—we need to sit tight and observe. Figure out when Dr. Gray and the soldiers are most vulnerable. We also need to know exactly what Dr. Gray is up to and what he's capable of."

"I just want this to be over," said Mrs. Wilde.

Dr. Sharma put a hand on her arm. "Respectfully, Diana, I know how much you want your husband safe and home again. We all want that. And that will happen. But we're dealing with unknown factors here. What we know from Charlie and her friends is that there are at least six soldiers, which means we're outnumbered. So we need to gather more information and come up with a plan. And while we obviously want to put an end to this whole project, our first priority is to get Charles and Jack out of there safely. So for now we wait and watch without them detecting us, and go from there." She paused. "Does that make sense?"

Slowly Charlie's mom nodded. "Yes," she said quietly. She put her hands on her children's shoulders.

"But my dad will be safe, right?" asked Andy.

"Yes, I believe he will be." Dr. Sharma gave Andy a reassuring smile, but he still looked troubled. "That's why we've got to do this right the first time." She straightened up, then said to Mrs. Wilde, "And now maybe you and the children ought to head home. Tomorrow we should have all the cameras placed where we want them and the microphones on the dragonfly and roach working."

"I can help," said Mrs. Wilde. "Just let me know what you need me to do."

"Great. Get some sleep and we'll talk in the morning. I'll alert you immediately if anything changes."

Ms. Sabbith looked at Mrs. Wilde. "You can be sure we'll have our cameras on your husband and Dr. Goldstein as much as possible." She went to a different table, calling out, "Quinn, I've got the blueprints of the bank building. Let's get to work."

Dr. Sharma flashed a grin and joined her.

Mrs. Wilde took one last look at her husband and Jack on the screen, then she swallowed hard and herded the children to pick up their things so they could go home.

Andy was quiet for most of the ride. When it was just the three of them left, he said, "Dad looked really bad all tied up and with those bruises. Do you think those soldiers are going to hurt him again? I don't like it." He sniffled and whined. "Why can't we just go in there and rescue him?"

"Oh, honey," said Mrs. Wilde, reaching back between the seats to give his leg a reassuring squeeze. "I wish you hadn't seen that. Your dad is going to be just fine. I promise. We're . . . we're going to get him out of there. We just have to wait a little bit."

"Don't worry, buddy," Charlie said, even though she was worried too. "We found him. That's the first step." But she couldn't get the image of her dad tied to that chair out of her head either. It was disturbing enough for her—it was probably even worse for Andy, who didn't seem to be handling this whole mess very well. And what if things didn't quite go the way Dr. Sharma expected? The soldiers were violent. Charlie knew that well enough.

After Andy went to bed, Charlie and her mom stayed up a little longer; Charlie to study some more for her tests the next day, and her mother to sit quietly with her troubled thoughts and a cup of tea. After a while Mrs. Wilde nodded to herself and picked up her phone, then went into another room to make a call.

As Charlie packed up her homework and headed upstairs, she overheard her mom say, "*Hola*, Alejandra, it's Diana Wilde, Andy's mom. Is Juan still interested in having Andy go camping with you?"

On Friday morning Charlie, Andy, and their mom all ate breakfast together. Mrs. Wilde looked a little less tired than she had the past couple of mornings. Charlie had slept better too, knowing her dad had been found. And though his condition was certainly concerning, Charlie hoped her mom was right about the injuries starting to heal—maybe there wouldn't be any more.

Mrs. Wilde sat down at the table next to Andy. "I talked to Juan's mother last night after you went to bed," she said brightly. "They'd still love to have you go with them on their trip. I think it might be fun."

Andy, mouth full of cereal, looked at her. A drip of milk leaked from the corner of his lips, and he hurried to wipe it away with his sleeve. He chewed quickly, then said, "But I need to stay here with you because of Dad."

Mrs. Wilde glanced at Charlie, then back at Andy. "Well, we know where he is now. And there's no sense in all of us having a boring spring break. Right, Charlie?"

Charlie nodded. "I wish my friends were going somewhere cool so I could go with them. But their parents all have to stay home and work." She tried to look nonchalant. "I'd go if I were you, but that's just me."

Andy tilted his head thoughtfully. He took another bite.

"You wouldn't be far away," said Mrs. Wilde. "Just a few hours' drive. You could let us know if there are any cool places for us to go as a family once we're all back together."

"And," added Charlie, "we can keep you updated about what's going on. If we need you, Mom can drive up and get you."

Andy considered the option for another minute as he finished his breakfast, then a small smile played on his lips. "It would be fun," he said. "They're going to be camping and hiking and stuff." He pushed his chair back. "Are you sure you don't need me, Mom?"

"I think now that Dr. Sharma and Ms. Sabbith found Dad, we can take it from here. I'd really like you to go. You deserve some fun. You're a kid, after all."

"But I'm not packed or anything. They're leaving tonight." Andy grew concerned.

"I'll help you get ready after school," said Charlie. "It'll only take a few minutes."

Andy's face lit up. "Okay," he said. "Yeah, I'll go." He whipped out his cell phone. "Can I tell Juan?"

"Sure," said Mrs. Wilde. She grinned at Charlie as Andy texted excitedly.

Charlie grinned back, but then her smile faded. She knew why her mom didn't want Andy around. She was worried about what he'd see on the monitors. She was worried about trouble. Maybe even danger. Charlie hoped they wouldn't have to deal with any of that. But the thought of it made her put her push her cereal bowl away. She wasn't hungry anymore.

Charlie left for school early so she could look for the Talos Global envelope. She checked the Lost and Found table in the office, but it wasn't there. Mr. Anderson was sitting behind the office counter, just as he had been on Charlie's first day of school, working intently on something.

"Hi, Mr. Anderson," she said. Today he wore a brown Hawaiian shirt with pineapples all over it, and he wasn't wearing his bolo tie.

Her drama teacher looked up over his half-glasses and smiled. "Good morning, Charlie."

"You didn't happen to find a big envelope with a bunch of papers inside it in the auditorium yesterday after sixth period, did you?"

"No, I'm sorry, I haven't seen it."

"Thanks." Charlie turned to go.

"Good luck," said Mr. Anderson.

Next she peeked into her seventh-period classroom but didn't see it anywhere. She traced her steps to the PE building and checked her locker there, but it was empty. The envelope was nowhere to be found. Frustrated, Charlie let out a deep sigh. The code that would've allowed her to deactivate Defense Mode and try out Battle Mode had been at her fingertips, and now it was gone. But she was also worried about losing these top secret documents. Granted, anybody just glancing at the papers would likely have no clue what they were actually looking at, but if someone decided to really dive in . . . well, that could be a big problem.

After Charlie left the locker room empty handed, she spotted Maria outside the main entrance walking into the schoolyard. She went to meet her. Maria was wearing jeans and a long-sleeve top with a bright yellow lightweight scarf tied jauntily at her neck. She pointed to it and explained, "Just in case I need to go full-on Sister Maria because of you-know-what."

"Nice one," said Charlie. "Sister Maria. *The Sound of Music*. You should try out—the nun costumes would cover your beard and tail, I'll bet."

Maria flashed her a quizzical look. "What are you talking about?"

Charlie was confused too. "Weren't you talking about Sister Maria from *The Sound of Music*? The musical we're going to do? She, like, becomes a nun and wears a habit thing."

"No, I'm talking about *me* Maria. Looking like a nun except with this scarf instead of a habit. And there's no way I'm trying out for anything—I'm no actor. I'd rather read a comic book any day."

"You're sort of acting out the life of a comic book hero right now, aren't you?"

"Well, I'm not one."

Charlie put a hand on her hip. "That's almost exactly what I said to you last week. And you told me I had responsibilities."

"Aw, shut up, Chuck," Maria said with a small grin. "At least you look normal." Her face grew troubled.

Charlie laughed. "Yeah, sure. Running seventy miles an hour down the sidewalk looks really normal. But I get it."

Maria dropped her gaze and spoke quietly. "You can't possibly get what this is like for me."

Charlie blinked. She of all people could relate to what Maria was going through. "What are you talking about?"

"At least when your bracelet kicks in, it doesn't change your appearance, Charlie. I can't control this, and I don't have a clue when it's going to happen again. It's scary. I'm . . . I'm, like, really stressed out about it. And . . ." Maria clenched her jaw and blinked tears away.

Charlie's heart flooded with concern for her friend. "And what?" she asked.

"And . . . when *it* happens, I look like one of them. The bad guys. I look like a monster. A freak." She waved a hand in front of her face to ward off the tears. "I don't even dare to cry. What if that sets it off?"

Charlie was quiet, thinking things through. She had thought

she'd understood at least some of what Maria was going through. But now she considered it from Maria's perspective. What if Charlie had actually taken on the physical features of the animals from her bracelet? How horrible would it be to grow fur like a cheetah when the speed ability kicked in, or sprout an elephant trunk out of her face when her strength was activated? That would be disastrous.

A new, deeper understanding began to dawn on Charlie. "Wow. You're right," she said softly. "I can't imagine how that feels. I'm . . . really sorry. I don't know what I'm talking about at all."

Maria nodded. "Thanks," she said. "That means a lot. Do you think I can spend extra time with you this week? Then at least if I change again . . . I'll be with people who won't freak out."

"Absolutely," Charlie promised, feeling sure her mother would agree. "We're going to do everything we can to help you." But both of them felt like they weren't any closer to a solution.

They walked to first period together, uncharacteristically quiet, and met up with Mac and Kelly.

Kelly seemed off that morning, too—in fact, she'd seemed a little off ever since Wednesday at Charlie's house. Charlie figured today she was really moody about having to go to Cabo.

"So," Charlie asked brightly, "are you all packed for your trip?"

Kelly shrugged and averted her eyes. "I guess."

Charlie glanced at Mac, who was making a "don't talk about that" face. Charlie raised her eyebrows and fell silent. Maria remained glum and didn't say anything, so Mac and Charlie eventually went to their seats at the back of the room before the bell even rang.

"Tense," muttered Charlie to him.

"Yeah. Maria too—what's up with her?"

"She's really upset about the monkey stuff," said Charlie. "Worried, scared, all of that. She's feeling pretty bad."

"But Dr. Sharma is working on fixing it."

"Yeah, but that doesn't help for now, when she could change at any second. She's scared."

"Maybe we need to help her get her mind off it," said Mac.

"Maybe," said Charlie as the bell rang and their teacher walked in. But she doubted that would help. Their friend was in a really hard spot, and Charlie didn't have time to explain just how bad it was at the moment.

First period dragged, and so did second. In anticipation of spring break, kids were more rowdy than usual, but the four friends weren't feeling it. They split up after second hour as usual, and Charlie walked to third period behind Kelly since it was so awkward walking next to her when she'd hardly speak. She took the opportunity to cram for her social studies test as she passed from one building to the next across the courtyard.

During the test Charlie's mind wandered. She couldn't stop thinking about her father and how awful he'd looked tied up in that chair. But seeing him had given her some sense of relief, too. At least she knew that he was okay. Charlie didn't ace the test, that was certain. She handed it in feeling a bit numb and just hoped she'd passed.

In fourth period, when her teacher showed a film, Charlie's mind traveled to her friend again. How awful it must be for Maria to walk around every second of the day hoping not to grow a tail and a beard of fur. And it must be nerve-racking for Maria to fear that it could happen in front of her parents and cause a huge amount of trouble. Not to mention in front of friends at school or even strangers—who knew how people would react to that? One accidental transformation in public could change Maria's life forever . . . and not for the better. If Dr. Sharma couldn't fix the problem, would Maria be forced to wear one of those suits like Dr. Gray's soldiers in order to hide the truth?

Granted, it wasn't quite as bad as being one of those permanently altered soldiers. If Maria could stay calm, changing into a howler monkey wasn't likely to happen. But Maria was not the kind of person who liked to be told to remain calm. That was impossible for a passionate person like her. It was only a matter of time before the power kicked in again. The only question was when.

At lunch Mac tried to distract Maria by talking a lot about how cool the insect cameras were and how he hoped Dr. Sharma and Ms. Sabbith would let him have a chance at the controls. Maria remained subdued. She hadn't changed into a weremonkey all morning, and it seemed she was determined to continue that streak by locking in all her feelings and emotions. She wasn't herself at all.

Charlie engaged with Mac halfheartedly, shooting sympathetic looks at Maria every now and then. She was beginning to feel helpless about making Maria feel better. Mac eventually quieted too, sensing the mood, and seemed a bit stumped about what to do.

In theater class Mr. Anderson went over the passages that the actors needed to memorize for the auditions. The rest of the day crawled, including Charlie's second test in language arts. Thankfully there were no soccer practices or games until school was back in session.

Once the final bell rang, the kids were done. Charlie, Mac, and Maria met up outside the main entrance before heading home. Excited students ran past them. Then they spied Kelly walking out of the building with her head lowered.

"Have a safe trip, Kel," said Maria, going up to her. "Try to have some fun. Maybe the ocean won't be so bad."

Kelly stopped walking. "Maybe," she said with a sigh. "At least I'm getting away from my dad's yelling for a while. I suppose that's something."

Charlie's heart twinged. Kelly didn't seem to like either of her parents at all. And her parents obviously didn't like each other either or they wouldn't be getting divorced. It would be really hard to live like that. "I'm sorry," she said impulsively.

Kelly shrugged like it didn't matter, but she still wouldn't look Charlie in the eye. "See you," she said stiffly. "My plane leaves in a few hours, so . . . bye." She started walking home, leaving the three friends standing there watching her go.

Charlie turned to the others. "Don't forget you can spend as much time as you want this week with me and my mom," she reminded Maria. "You too, Mac, if you want to."

"Why wouldn't I?" said Mac. "The insect cams are practically calling out to me. Learning how they work is my new purpose in life now that I don't have a device anymore."

"And we want to help rescue your dad, of course," said Maria.

"Cool," said Charlie with a smile. "We'll pick you up from Maria's after we drop off Andy."

They both nodded. Charlie left them, heading home, and Mac and Maria went toward Maria's house. The best friends knew exactly how they'd be spending their spring break. Hanging out with Charlie and Dr. Sharma, working to free two captured biologists from a mad scientist. And trying to keep Maria from turning into a weremonkey in front of her parents. You know, normal stuff.

CHAPTER 18

Trying to Be Patient

With everything Andy had witnessed over the past few days, Mrs. Wilde seemed relieved to have him spend time with Juan's family for a while. When Charlie got home from school, she and her mom helped him pack. Then they grabbed his sleeping bag and pillow and threw everything into the car. Charlie and her mom waited while Andy gave extended hugs to Fat Princess and Jessie and a short hug to Big Kitty, who didn't care for the extended kind. Finally he declared he was ready to go to Juan's house. He climbed into their Subaru.

Charlie got in, too, since she and her mom were going to pick up Maria and Mac and head straight to home base after they dropped Andy off.

"Just remember not to talk about any of this," Mrs. Wilde told him as they neared Juan's house.

"I know," said Andy. "I haven't told anybody. Text me if anything happens with Dad."

"I will," Mrs. Wilde promised. "And if you get worried and need to talk about it, you can tell Juan you want some private time and you can FaceTime me or Charlie. But just try to have fun."

Andy smiled. "Okay, Mom."

Mrs. Wilde pulled up to the curb in front of Juan's house. She leaned over to kiss Andy good-bye in the privacy of the car, then she and Charlie got out and helped bring his gear over to the camper in the driveway. Juan's mom, Alejandra, was loading groceries from her car into the camper, and Juan was climbing inside carrying a stack of board games. As they greeted Alejandra, Juan set his pile down and came bouncing out to help Andy carry his stuff inside.

"Thank you so much for inviting Andy," said Mrs. Wilde.

"Juan is so excited Andy could come after all," said Alejandra, pushing a lock of hair behind her ear and grinning as the boys disappeared into the camper, talking a mile a minute. "I'll text you our campsite location once we get to Sedona. We're not quite sure when we're coming back. If the weather is good and the boys are having fun, we won't return until next weekend sometime."

"Plan on that!" called Juan from the camper. The moms laughed.

"Anything works for us," said Mrs. Wilde. "Just text me when you roll back into town. I'll come pick him up."

"Sounds great. I'll keep you posted." Alejandra turned as the boys came tripping out again.

Andy wore an impish grin that Charlie hadn't seen in a while. It made her feel even better about him getting away from the seriousness. "Text us some cool photos," she said. She gave her brother a side hug, and then he hugged their mom too.

"Bye!" he called as he and Juan went back inside the camper. Charlie and Mrs. Wilde waved and headed back to the car.

"Whew," said Mrs. Wilde when they were on their way again. "I'm glad for him."

"Me too," said Charlie. "One less person to worry about."

"That's exactly how it feels."

They picked up Mac and Maria and finally the four of them were heading to the business park.

As they pulled into the lot behind home base, they spotted two black-suited soldiers in the shadows of the deserted alleyway next to the bank building, sneaking cautiously out of the white van and carrying in a few boxes. Everyone stayed in the car until the coast was clear. Then they hurried inside. They took the elevator up to the sixth floor and went down the hall to the home base office. "We did a lot of work in here today while you were in school," Mrs. Wilde told Charlie.

The reception area looked the same as before, but the surveillance area had been transformed. One part of it had been partitioned off as a sleeping room with two cots. In the remainder of the space all the tables, chairs, equipment, and supplies were set up and organized. The monitors hung on the wall between the windows, with the large one in the center, each screen displaying a different drone's view. Instead of the temporary shade that Ms. Sabbith had put up the previous day, all the windows now had some sort of shaded film on them. There was a table for the bank building's blueprints, and Dr. Sharma's desk was covered in research papers and files. The woman sat there organizing things, the drawer standing open. And there was the surveillance control table, where Ms. Sabbith had set up the laptop computer that was tied to the drones.

"Welcome back," said Dr. Sharma, standing up. As she closed the desk drawer, Charlie caught sight of the two devices inside. Dr. Sharma locked the drawer and put the key into her pocket. She went over to the surveillance area. "Erica's been teaching me how to control the drones. She'll be flying back to Chicago this afternoon to start gathering up the supplies we need."

That seemed to cheer Maria a bit. The three kids and Mrs. Wilde went over to the control table to watch. Mac was instantly glued to the lesson and Maria looked on eagerly as well. After a while Charlie grew bored and discovered the pile of blueprints on the table nearby. She went to check them out.

Mrs. Wilde studied the monitors for a moment. "Anything new happening over there?"

"A lot since you left," said Dr. Sharma. "We were right about our hunch. Charles and Jack are working on something along with Victor. Look." She hesitated, looking at the keyboard, then typed a few commands as Ms. Sabbith pointed them out to her. The large center screen switched to give them the ladybug's view through the lab window. It was extra grainy because of the dust powdered on the window—an Arizona desert staple—but the scene was easy enough to make out. Dr. Goldstein sat in a chair at a low workstation, hunched over it and looking terribly weak. Charlie's dad was standing at a lab table next to him, working on something very small with a tweezers-like instrument. Dr. Gray stood across the table from him, examining something. A female soldier was working with them as well. Occasionally they appeared to be chatting. Scattered around the room were a few more soldiers.

"Kids, do you recognize this brute guarding the door?" asked Dr. Sharma, pointing to the lab's entrance on the wall opposite the windows.

"That's Cyke," said Charlie and Maria in unison. Cyke was unmistakable. He stood several inches taller than most people, and his shoulders were huge and broad and muscular. His mouth and nose protruded slightly more than an average person's. Watching him up close on the monitor, they could see he had an occasional nervous tic in the form of a full body shudder that sent his muscles rippling under the fabric. Every now and then he moved side to side a bit restlessly.

"Tell me about him."

Ms. Sabbith showed Dr. Sharma how to zoom in on the soldier and take electronic measurements and screenshots of the man.

"He's huge," said Charlie.

"Yeah, and really strong," said Maria.

Charlie nodded. "He can run pretty fast but not like, you know, a cheetah."

"But the dude cannot climb trees," said Maria, shaking her head.

"Right," said Charlie. "Not at all! Thank goodness." She recalled Tuesday after school when she'd had Maria on her back, climbing the palm trees by the church near Maria's house, with Cyke chasing them. They'd thought for sure they were goners, but Charlie had scrambled up and out of reach, and Cyke had failed to shimmy up the tree even a short distance. He'd stayed on the ground and resorted to shaking the trunk instead.

"Interesting," mused Dr. Sharma, straining her eyes at the screen. Then, with Ms. Sabbith's guidance, she tapped a few keys on the computer to try to get a clearer closeup shot. "It looks like his face is unusually shaped. Any idea what hybrid he is? I'd like to start figuring out all the soldiers so we know what abilities they might have."

"I don't know," said Charlie, "but he snorts."

Mac looked at her. "He snorts?"

"Yeah."

"Hmm." Dr. Sharma reviewed her notes and then, looking at the screenshots she'd taken, pausing on one where they could see Cyke's profile. She zoomed in on his face, and they could see the outline of huge nostrils and teeth. "What has nostrils like this?"

Dr. Sharma asked to herself more than to the children.

But Mac was totally on it. "Seems like a horse to me," he said. "Look at him when he does that shuddering thing. It's like when a fly lands on a horse and he can't swipe it away with his tail."

"I think you might be right, Mac," said Maria, thinking it through. "He's very horselike. Running at a gallop, the strength . . ."

"And not being able to climb a tree," said Charlie.

"Good call," said Dr. Sharma. She began putting the screenshots and measurements into a desktop folder and labeled it "Cyke: Horse-Human Hybrid." "I wonder why he picked a horse? Seems like an odd choice."

"Easy access to DNA?" guessed Ms. Sabbith. No one else had an answer.

"Which insect cams have microphones again?" asked Mac.

"The roach," said Ms. Sabbith, "which is currently stationed in the hallway, and the dragonfly, which we have positioned in Dr. Gray's office. That's where Charles and Jack sleep at night. I'm hoping we'll catch some of their conversations now that Jack seems to be conscious and moving around. Gray isn't gagging them anymore, but he still ties them up at night." She paused. "I think we've got eyes on everything, though I'm not sure where the soldiers sleep or eat. Maybe on the other floors. But I don't care about those rooms. We're focusing on the places where the doctors spend time. At the moment I'm waiting for an opportunity to get the roach into the lab so we can hear what's going on in there. But because it's big, and because it's a roach and everybody hates them, I have to be very careful to keep it hidden. We don't want anybody freaking out and stomping on it, trying to kill it."

"Can't you sneak it under the door like you did in that other room off the hallway?" asked Charlie.

"I tried last night after you left. But the lab door is sealed too tightly and the roach doesn't fit underneath. So I've got to go in when the door is open."

Mac frowned. "Can you take the roach in through the air ducts like you did with the dragonfly?"

"Not really. It's a little heavy because of the microphone, and I don't trust it to climb walls or walk on ceilings or balance on vents. It does better on the floor."

"I know you're still working out a few problems," said Mac, "but this is seriously so cool I can't stand it." His eyes gleamed as he watched everything Ms. Sabbith was showing Dr. Sharma.

"Did you happen to see the soldiers bringing in boxes?" Mrs. Wilde asked Dr. Sharma. "We saw them when we got here."

The scientist pointed to the spider's camera view, which was from the rear upper corner of the elevator. "Yes, I was watching them pile things up at the door on the cardinal cam. They'll be calling the elevator down soon. Let's see if Spidey here can get a look at what's in the boxes." She adjusted the spider cam slightly and waited.

Soon they saw the elevator door open. The two soldiers started piling boxes inside. One was a small female soldier who was bouncing around a little from one foot to the other. She was definitely familiar. Now that Charlie wasn't under attack, she could study her a bit better and noticed that her arms were especially long for a woman her size. Charlie leaned forward. "That's Miko," she said. "She's the chimp who was with Cyke and the catlike soldier."

"Catlike—are you talking about Prowl?" asked Dr. Sharma. "The leopard man you told us about from the warehouse?"

"No, there was another kind of cat in the first fight Maria and I had. Smaller but her claws were really sharp. I think she's that woman by the lab table with my dad and the others. I don't know her name. Do you, Maria?"

"I don't remember anybody saying it," said Maria.

With Miko in the elevator was the beefy, slow-moving man who had been in the warehouse with the beefy, not-quite-as-slow-moving woman and Prowl.

"What animal is that woman supposed to be?" Dr. Sharma asked.

"I'm not sure, but that guy is a cow," said Charlie, wrinkling her nose.

"Charlie," reprimanded her mother.

"No—literally, I mean," said Charlie. "When I fought him before, he started lowing like a sick cow. Or a bull, I guess he must be. Right, Mac?"

Mac sighed. "That would be my guess. I wish I could look it up. I just . . . I really miss my tablet and phone so much."

Mrs. Wilde grew concerned. "You don't have a cell phone, Mac? What happened to it?"

Mac glanced at Charlie, and Charlie quickly looked down. She hadn't mentioned this part to her mom originally, and she'd sort of forgotten about it. "The soldiers—they stole his iPad and iPhone," Charlie told her mother. "We all chipped in to help him get new ones, but he hasn't dared to tell his mother yet because she was mad about the simulators."

"I'm not sure how to tell her they got stolen without her freaking out," said Mac. "And I don't think I can buy a cell phone without a grown-up there because of the monthly charges and junk—I don't know how to do all that billing stuff."

Ms. Sabbith turned to Dr. Sharma. "I can hook him up with some new equipment before I head to Chicago, Quinn."

"Please do—that would be great."

"What's your phone number, Mac?"

Mac blinked. "What? What's happening?"

"We can't have you without a cell phone in case something happens," said Dr. Sharma. "And what if your mother tries to reach you and finds out what happened? You need to act normally, remember? Respond to text messages and phone calls. Be seen working on your iPad if that's your thing."

"Whoa," said Mac, his eyes growing wide. Maria actually

broke out of her somber mood and exchanged a smile with Charlie.

Mac told Ms. Sabbith his cell phone number. "I can bring money tomorrow," he said, "but you'll be gone by then. Do you want me to send it in the mail?"

Ms. Sabbith smiled and headed for the door. "Don't worry about it. I figure Talos Global owes you one after all you went through. Or two, in this case." With a wink she headed to the exit. "Back in a bit. Then I'm off to the airport."

Somehow the promise of a new phone and iPad for Mac lightened everyone's mood, even Maria's. She almost seemed to forget she could turn into a monkey at any moment.

Dr. Sharma stayed at the cameras to practice what she'd learned. She zoomed the spider cam in the elevator toward the side of one of the boxes, trying to focus, but the picture quality suffered. "One of the downsides to having a camera lens the size of a pinpoint, I suppose," she muttered.

Mac nodded sympathetically.

Dr. Sharma leaned forward and squinted, trying to make out the word on the side of the box. "What does that say?"

Maria glanced at the screen. "'Titanium,'" she said.

"Yep," Mac agreed.

"Ah, yes. I think you're right, kids," said the scientist. "No wonder it's taking them so long to move those boxes. They should have used Cyke to drag them around."

"What are they going to do with so much titanium?" asked Charlie's mom.

Dr. Sharma glanced at her. "Make more devices, I imagine." She switched her attention to the hallway roach cam, putting its view in the large center screen, and watched as the soldiers carried boxes down the corridor. She quickly checked the computer's volume to make sure they could hear if the roach picked up any conversation, then maneuvered the vermin down the side of the hallway in the shadows, following them. They stopped at a door and knocked.

"That's the lab door," Dr. Sharma whispered. She strained to listen.

A moment later Cyke opened the door, eyed the soldiers, then let them inside the laboratory.

"All that material headed into the lab—that's not a good sign," muttered Dr. Sharma. She tensed, looking for her chance to slip the roach inside, but there were too many feet shuffling around.

"It's not?" asked Charlie.

"Nope." The scientist moved the roach back to the doorway across the hall from the lab. "The only reason they'd need that much is if they have plans to make a lot of devices."

Ms. Sabbith returned from the store with a new iPhone and iPad and presented them to Mac. "All set up," she said a bit mysteriously, but Mac wasn't about to question his good luck. Then, unceremoniously, she packed up her duffel bag and said good-bye. "Good luck," she said earnestly, turning to Dr. Sharma, Mrs. Wilde, and the children. "If all goes well, I'll be back sometime next week with everything we need to make you better, Maria. Quinn, call me if you think of anything else you need. Are you good with the camera controls?"

"I'm good," said Dr. Sharma. "And Mac probably picked up more from the lesson than I did, so he can help."

Mac nodded confidently.

"Thank you for all you've done to help us," said Mrs. Wilde. The kids thanked her too.

With a wave Erica Sabbith was gone, leaving a scientist, an ER doctor, and three twelve-year-olds to navigate the next steps of their rescue mission.

A short while later Mac was happily jailbreaking his new phone. Dr. Sharma worked at the camera controls, going over all the commands Ms. Sabbith had taught her. Every now and then she'd mutter, "Now how do I . . . ?" and Mac would look up and remind her what to do.

Dusk settled and they grew hungry. "Sooo, dinner, then?" said Mac.

"I'll go pick something up," said Mrs. Wilde, tearing her eyes off the ladybug camera screen. "I could stand to do something useful."

"Thank you, Diana." Dr. Sharma told her where to find the restaurant nearby, whose cooking Charlie had smelled a few days before.

"I'll go with you," said Charlie, who was growing bored with looking at blueprints and watching the screens—not much was happening, and they couldn't hear anything in the lab. And though it was nice to see her father moving around, it was also sort of hard watching him, knowing he didn't have a clue they were right across the street.

"I'll stay here and help Dr. Sharma," said Mac. He set his phone down and picked up his new iPad and looked at it lovingly, then turned it on for the first time. He was in heaven.

Maria looked sidelong at Mac, then at Charlie. "I guess I'll go with you, Charlie."

Charlie looked up the menu online and took sandwich orders from Mac and Dr. Sharma, then her mom placed the takeout order through the website. They got ready to go.

"Stay aware of your surroundings," Dr. Sharma said. "This part of town is quiet, and the soldiers don't seem to venture out much on foot from what we've witnessed the past two days, but just in case they do, you don't want them to catch sight of you."

"We'll be careful," Charlie promised.

"I'll make sure of it," said Mrs. Wilde.

Mrs. Wilde and the girls went out through the reception area and set off down the hallway to the stairwell, passing a business woman plodding up the stairs along the way, looking annoyed. "Elevator's out again," she complained.

Mrs. Wilde nodded sympathetically. Soon they reached the main floor and exited the back door so they wouldn't be seen by any of Dr. Gray's people in the bank building. Under the cover of darkness Mrs. Wilde led them to a small restaurant, which had its door propped open to let in the natural air and perhaps attract a customer or two. The place was empty except for a single worker standing behind a cash wrap and some noise coming from the kitchen. Mrs. Wilde asked about their order, and they waited.

Suddenly Maria cocked her head to one side as if she could hear something, then turned sharply and stared out the shop window. "Did you hear that?" She ran to the open doorway and peered out to the right, then to the left.

Charlie could faintly hear a sad, out-of-tune jingle. She joined Maria. Her mom came over too. "What is it?" she asked.

Maria's face fell as the sound disappeared. "It was an ice cream truck. And now it's gone."

Charlie laughed and shook her head, then realized she hadn't seen a single food truck since she'd left Chicago, so maybe they were a bigger deal out here. And Maria took ice cream very seriously. It made sense, living out here in the desert. She went to the door. "Are you sure it's gone? Maybe it just stopped." If an ice cream truck would cheer Maria up, Charlie was determined to find it. Impulsively she went out the door, checking her pocket to make sure she had money, and ignored her mother's calls for her to return—if she didn't see the truck, she'd come right back. Then she rounded the corner and nearly ran into somebody under the streetlamp.

Two somebodies, actually.

Two very big, beefy somebodies.

CHAPTER 19

Monkey Business

Charlie yelped as she realized who she nearly ran into. She quickly looked away, trying to hide her face from the light. Maybe they wouldn't realize it was her—the girl who'd slammed their heads together in the warehouse earlier that week. Charlie could only be so lucky.

"Excuse me," she muttered, and tried to go back to the restaurant.

"It's the girl!" said the bull soldier with a snort. "Grab her!"

The large woman grabbed Charlie's arm in a strong, vise-like grip and yanked her back.

"Ouch! Watch it!" Charlie felt her device grow warm. She punched at the woman's face, hoping for the strength ability and getting it—and felt her fist slam hard against the woman's nose, which curved up and ended in a sharp point. The soldier's head ricocheted back, but she didn't let go of Charlie's other wrist. In pain, Charlie shook out her stinging hand and tried to wrench herself away, but she was stuck.

"Get her, Braun!" The woman shoved Charlie at her companion.

Braun grabbed Charlie around the waist and lifted her high above his head. Her body was a toothpick in his hands, and he was pinching her tightly. She looked down and noticed he had strange, thick fingers on each hand, like cloven hooves that split open wide.

"Let me go!" Charlie said. She swiped at his head, but her arms were too short to reach him. She kicked blindly, trying to hit him in the face, and looked frantically toward the restaurant. There was no one in sight. Maria must have listened to Charlie's mom.

"Maria!" Charlie shouted. Braun began to lumber slowly back toward the bank building with her in the air overhead.

A second later Maria appeared at the door. Her eyes opened wide. And then a furry beard sprouted from her chin. "Mrs. Dr. Wilde! Hurry!" she shouted, and dashed out the door.

Braun swung Charlie around and she lost sight of Maria for a moment until she came full circle. Maria grimaced and yanked her tail out of her jeans.

"Help me!" shouted Charlie. She reached for one of Braun's cloven hands and tried prying the hoof-fingers apart using her strength ability. Braun started lowing in pain and he yanked that hand away. Charlie pounded his other forearm and twisted in his grip, managing to loosen herself. She fell hard to the ground as the soldiers turned around to face their new surprise monkey attacker.

"You leave her alooone!" howled Maria. She ran hard at the soldiers and sprang into the air . . . jumping right overtop of them and landing on the sidewalk. "Whoops," she said, hopping back up. She turned around and charged again, slamming into the brutes like Charlie might have done. But they went nowhere. Maria bounced off the woman's chest and landed on her back, the wind knocked out of her.

"Try doing monkey things!" Charlie said as she jumped on Braun's back and covered his goggles so he couldn't see. "Swing and use your feet! Remember?"

"Right on, right on," muttered Maria, trying to get her breath back and focus on what she knew she could do.

Charlie's mom came running outside. "Charlie! Look out!"

"I'm trying!" said Charlie as Braun pitched around wildly. "Stay back!"

"Are you sure?" Charlie's mom looked on, horrified. She couldn't help herself and ran up to Braun, kicking him in the leg as hard as she could and slamming her fist into his side.

"I mean it, Mom!" screamed Charlie. "If you don't get back, Andy and I will have zero parents. Do you want that?"

"Okay, good point." Mrs. Wilde retreated, flinching at every move.

"Mega!" cried Braun to his fellow soldier. "Where are you?"

Charlie ripped the soldier's goggles off and threw them down. Then she pounded his ears, jumped to the ground, and scooted out of reach. She took a running start and slammed into the man, sending him flying into a lamppost alongside the street. He hit the ground hard. Charlie bounced backward from the impact and lost her balance.

Maria sprang up. Eyeing Braun warily, she took a few awkward hops, then cringed and leaped over him, reaching as high up the lamppost as she could. She grabbed it and stuck there, then began climbing up it hand over hand, slowly at first and then with a bit more ease. As Braun groaned and sat up below her, Maria swung around the pole, flung her feet out, and slammed them into his face. He wavered and fell to the sidewalk again.

"That's it!" Charlie said encouragingly to Maria. "Now let's get rhino face over here."

Both girls turned to look at Mega, who began plodding toward them, head down as if to charge. She gained speed. Charlie held fast, pushing Maria behind her a little to protect her.

Mrs. Wilde was having a hard time watching. "Leave the children alone!" she shouted.

Mega ignored her.

Desperate to help, Mrs. Wilde reached into her takeout bag. She pulled out a roast beef sandwich and sent it sailing like a torpedo at the woman. It struck her in the back of the head.

Mega turned around, confused at first. Then she saw what it was and gasped. "You're sick!" she said.

"Now, Maria!" cried Charlie. She charged at the soldier while Maria leapfrogged off Charlie's back and kangaroo-kicked the

woman in the face. Charlie slammed into her and tipped her flat on her side. Mega struggled, her arms and legs flailing, but she couldn't get up.

"Let's go!" said Maria. "Back to, uh, Phoenix!"

Charlie and her mom gave Maria puzzled looks, but all three of them ran for the corner. They turned it sharply and kept going a good distance out of their way, taking a few extra unnecessary turns in case anyone was tracking them.

"Are you both okay?" asked Mrs. Wilde, sounding worried.

"I'm fine," said Charlie. "Even if I weren't, I'd heal pretty quickly."

"I'm okay too," said Maria. "No worse off than a tough soccer match, to be honest. Well . . . except for looking like a freak again."

"You know what, Maria?" said Charlie, looking earnestly at her friend.

"What?"

"You look like a superhero to me."

Maria kept hold of Charlie's gaze, studying her. "You mean it?" she said quietly.

"I sure do."

"Thanks." Maria looked back at her tail, springing about as they went, and ran a hand over her beard. She made a face, but she didn't argue with Charlie. And she didn't start crying.

A moment later Charlie asked her, "Why did you say we should go back to Phoenix? That's an hour away."

"I don't know. I was trying to throw them off, I guess. I mean, they're going to report back to Dr. Gray that they saw us near their lab, so now we've got a big mess on our hands. I figured if I gave them some false information, they might be dumb enough to believe that we were just in the neighborhood by accident."

"That was quick thinking," said Mrs. Wilde.

Charlie agreed, but she was still unsettled by the soldiers having seen them. They'd been to her house and Maria's already, so it wasn't like they couldn't come after them if they wanted to. Still, she didn't want Gray to feel threatened or to suspect just how closely they were watching them.

Her mom drew up to a corner of a building near home base and peered around it to see if the coast was clear. Coming quickly toward them was Dr. Sharma. Mrs. Wilde stepped out and waved her down.

"Are you all right?" asked Dr. Sharma. "The cardinal camera showed two big soldiers leave the bank building. Once I realized they were heading in the same direction you went, I started to worry. When you didn't return, I decided I'd better check on you."

"We're fine," said Charlie. "Just a little banged up. No big deal." The others nodded. "Where's Mac?"

"I left him to monitor the cameras," said Dr. Sharma. "So they fought you? They recognized you?"

"Unfortunately, yes," said Charlie. "I made a mistake going out of the restaurant alone. I'm really sorry."

Maria comforted Charlie. "It's my fault, actually," she said.

Dr. Sharma's brow furrowed. "No need to blame anyone. It happened. It just puts a bit of a wrench into things." She grew thoughtful as they hurried down the alley toward their building, everyone feeling a little tense in the darkness.

Charlie was thoughtful too, suddenly struck by one of those surreal moments where you look at yourself and think, *How did I get here? Is this my life?* "So many weird things are happening," she mused. "It's like we suddenly entered a totally different world that I never believed could exist, but here we are, in the middle of it. It's like finding out aliens live among us. Or—"

"Or human-animal hybrids are just the beginning of your problems?" said someone with a strange purring voice from behind a Dumpster. The voice was familiar—a little too familiar.

Everyone froze. Soon a pair of glowing green eyes shone like reflectors in the moonlight. Prowl, his goggles atop his head, moved into the alley, staying near the shadows of the building. Charlie's bracelet pulsed with heat.

"What do you want?" Charlie demanded.

"Hello again, Charlie Wilde," purred the leopard man. "It's so nice to see you. And you've brought me just the person I've been hoping for. How convenient."

Who? What did he mean? "Get behind me!" Charlie whispered to the others. She glanced at Maria, who was still in monkey mode, then Charlie sidestepped in front of her to shield her. But

Maria wasn't having it. She moved forward and joined Charlie in staring down the soldier. Prowl slunk toward them into the light of a streetlamp and rolled his clawed fingers in the air. They glinted. Before Charlie could react, he leaped over her head and pounced . . . on Dr. Quinn Sharma.

CHAPTER 20

Abducted

Dr. Sharma hit the ground hard, knocking the sandwiches out of Mrs. Wilde's hands and sending her reeling backward, too. The biologist's glasses flew off her face and skittered into the adjacent empty parking lot.

It took Charlie a second to realize what had happened. She and Maria whirled around, seeing Prowl crouched on top of Dr. Sharma. "Just happened to be in the neighborhood?" Prowl asked.

"Get off her!" Maria sprang at Prowl, landing on his back. Charlie was right behind and slammed into them, accidentally knocking Maria off. Prowl tightened his grip.

"Let go of me!" shouted Dr. Sharma, swinging her fists at him. Mrs. Wilde ran up to him to try to shove him off, but the cat lashed back and barreled into her, ramming her into the side of the building. She stayed there, stunned and breathless as Prowl bounded back to Dr. Sharma.

.Maria bounced up. She swished her prehensile tail and jumped on top of the Dumpster, then grabbed on to a telephone pole and swung around it. Releasing her grip, she flew downward at Prowl, knocking him to one side, but Prowl sank his claws into

Dr. Sharma's shoulders and didn't let go. The scientist screamed in pain as they rolled.

Charlie felt her fingers tingle. She leaped up and gripped the corner of the nearest building and climbed higher, then pushed herself awkwardly away, trying to twist and land on the soldier. But Prowl rolled the other way at the last second, and Charlie hit the ground hard at an awkward angle. Fire ripped through her shoulder, and she lay stunned.

Maria, using the building as a springboard, ran up the wall to gain height and momentum and leaped at Prowl again, but the leopard man was too agile. He batted her out of the way, sending her crashing to the pavement too. Dr. Sharma lunged, trying to roll the soldier away so she could get up. Charlie staggered to her feet to help but immediately dropped to her knees as pain sliced through her. It was so intense she couldn't breathe. Quickly Prowl grabbed Dr. Sharma, pinned her arms, and began running with her toward the bank building, covering the woman's mouth to stop her screams.

"Get up, Chuck!" shouted Maria, running over to Charlie. "Prowl's kidnapping Dr. Sharma!" She continued after the soldier.

"No!" said Mrs. Wilde, getting to her feet. "Stop! Maria, come back!"

Maria slowed to a stop and looked back with uncertainty. She realized that Charlie hadn't gotten up and came running back to her friend's side and dropped to her knees. "Are you okay?"

Charlie's mom knelt next to her and checked her over.

"It's my shoulder." Charlie writhed and groaned. "It's on fire. Check my bracelet, Maria," she said. "Is the starfish animated?"

Maria quickly clicked to the right screen. "No," she said.

"Ugh. I was afraid of that."

"Oh no!" said Maria. She peered down the alleyway, but Prowl and Dr. Sharma were gone from sight. "What are we going to do now?"

"At least . . . we know . . . where he's taking her," said Charlie, taking quick, sharp breaths as she fought through the pain.

"Your shoulder is dislocated," Mrs. Wilde said. "I need to pop it back in. Then we'll worry about Dr. Sharma."

"Oh, please no," said Charlie. "Is that as horrifying as it sounds?" She'd never dislocated her shoulder before, but she'd seen a soccer friend do it back in Chicago. It wasn't pretty.

"Yes," admitted Mrs. Wilde. "It'll go quickly, though. Come on." She gently helped Charlie to her feet. "Maria, grab the sandwiches if you can find them while I take care of Charlie's shoulder."

"Gladly," said Maria. She covered her ears and turned around so she couldn't see what was happening.

It didn't take long. And as soon as Charlie's shoulder was back in place, she felt tremendous relief and the pain was more manageable. "Whew," said Charlie. "That's better." Gingerly she checked the bracelet and saw the starfish pulsing. "It's working now."

"Maybe it couldn't start healing you until your shoulder was back in place," said Maria, returning with the sandwiches.

"Maybe," agreed Charlie.

"Can you make it to the building?" Mrs. Wilde asked. "Poor Mac has probably seen Prowl with Dr. Sharma on the cameras by now. He'll freak out if we don't show up soon."

Maria carried the sandwiches and the three of them limped together back to home base, trying not to despair over the most recent turn of events.

Mac's head was poking out of the door to the surveillance area, his face awash in fear. "Sheesh!" he exclaimed when he saw them coming. "I'm really glad to see you. What happened?"

"Did you notice where Prowl went?" asked Charlie. "Is Dr. Sharma okay?"

"He took her into the bank building. Come on. I'll show you." Mac ran over to the computer that controlled the drones.

"Are you sure you know what you're doing with that?" asked Maria.

"Yeah. I watched everything Ms. Sabbith did. It's not hard." Nobody tried to stop him from touching the equipment—he was their official tech genius now. He moved the ladybug cam to the big screen. Cyke stood at the door of the laboratory, and they caught sight of Dr. Sharma pulling out of Prowl's grasp and running over to Jack Goldstein in his workstation chair. She touched his face and hugged him gently. Prowl went after her, looking like he was going to pull her away, but another soldier stopped him by putting her hand up.

"That's the claw woman!" Charlie said.

"Her name is Zed," said Mac. "I heard Cyke say it through the roach cam in the hallway when he let her into the room a little while ago."

Maria nodded. "Look—she's letting them hug." Indeed Zed continued to hold Prowl back while looking on quietly as the two biologists reunited. Then Dr. Sharma turned to Charlie's dad and hugged him too. She looked disheveled but not seriously hurt, though she had some bloody spots on her clothing near her shoulders where Prowl's claws had sunk in.

"Whew," said Mrs. Wilde, relieved. "At least she's okay."

"Yes," said Charlie, "but now what are we supposed to do?"

"I'm . . . not sure." Mrs. Wilde watched the screen, then quickly went to the window and began pacing, rubbing her temples as she did so, clearly deep in thought. "Actually, maybe it's not the worst thing in the world that she got captured. Now she can fill in the other two. But how are we supposed to get them out of there?"

While the kids opened their squashed sandwiches and ate, Mrs. Wilde called Ms. Sabbith and got her voice mail. "She's probably on the plane," she muttered, then left a message. She came back and looked over the kids' shoulders at the screens.

"What's happening there?" asked Maria, pointing to the

ladybug view. Prowl and Zed appeared to be having an argument in the lab. "Looks like the cats aren't getting along at the moment."

"It's interesting," said Mac. "Zed showed up with Dr. Gray after you left to get the sandwiches. I think she's helping the scientists or something, but with her claws she can't seem to do much intricate stuff." Mac coughed a few times and pulled out his inhaler. "Dr. Gray seems to be trying to get them to work faster. Tapping his watch, wild gestures, stuff like that." He used his inhaler and put it away again.

"I wonder if Prowl told Dr. Gray about us yet. We need to get the roach in there so we can hear what's going on." Maria got down on the floor and started to do her yoga and meditation exercises to try to turn back into her normal self.

Charlie kept a close eye on the screens.

Mac nudged Charlie with his elbow. "What happened?"

Charlie recounted the altercation near the restaurant and how they'd then run into Prowl, who seemed to be delighted to grab Dr. Sharma rather than Charlie or Maria. "He didn't try to do anything to get my bracelet this time."

"I can't believe we're on our own now," said Maria, looking up from her relaxation exercises. "Everything just changed."

"In a big way," said Mac.

Charlie nodded. What were they supposed to do without Dr. Sharma or Ms. Sabbith?

Mrs. Wilde snapped out of her thoughts. Her eyes landed on

Charlie's Mark Five. Then she turned to Mac and Maria. "You're right—everything is different now. And I think you should put your bracelets back on for your own safety. If Mac had been with us instead of Maria, he would have been in big trouble. He wouldn't have been able to help Charlie against those monsters. Now I really understand why you took the bracelets from the warehouse in the first place." She glanced at the screens. "I don't think the soldiers know where we're camped out, but there's no doubt they'll be watching for us again."

"Sweet," said Mac, jumping to his feet. "Does anybody know where the devices are?"

"I saw them in Dr. Sharma's drawer," said Charlie.

Mac went over to the desk and pulled on the drawer handle. It didn't open. He tugged again. "It's locked," he said, crestfallen.

"Pfft," said Charlie. She got up and joined him. "Stand back." She grabbed on to the handle and yanked on it. The drawer front splintered and came off in her hand.

Charlie stepped aside and Mac peered into it and grabbed the devices. He held the Mark Two out. "Here, Maria."

"I don't want it." Maria didn't open her eyes. She kept breathing deeply.

Mac and Charlie exchanged a look. "She did fine without it today," Charlie said quietly. "Does she even need to wear it at all?"

Mac shrugged. "Dr. Sharma said there might be enhancements. It seems like the scientists wouldn't waste time making a whole fancy clip-on bracelet with a screen and buttons if there's no need to keep wearing it. If it was just a one-time DNA change, wouldn't they have just made an injection or something like that instead?"

Charlie tapped her lips thoughtfully. "Hmm," she said. "Good point."

"I'll bet the device does something extra," Mac said, turning to Maria. "Like make you stronger or more powerful or something."

Maria looked up, her eyes clouded. Then she glanced at the scientists on the monitors, and then at Charlie's mom. "But . . ." She sighed. "I don't know. I don't want enhancements. I want it to disappear."

Mrs. Wilde was watching the children quietly, looking very somber. "You don't have to wear it if you don't want to, Maria," she said. "But with Dr. Sharma captured and Ms. Sabbith two thousand miles away, we need to rethink things and take every precaution to keep ourselves safe. And . . ." She hesitated. "Wearing the bracelet isn't all I want you to do."

Mac slapped his device on his wrist and grinned, then looked up. "What else?"

"You kids need to train."

Mac blinked like he couldn't believe what he'd just heard.

Charlie's eyes widened. "What do you mean?"

"I saw you and Maria in action—you're both more powerful than I expected you to be. And since we're on our own now, I want you three to know how to use the devices and your abilities in every possible way to protect yourselves from attacks. And also . . . to be ready. In case."

"In case of . . . what?" asked Maria.

"In case we need your help to rescue the scientists once Ms. Sabbith gets back."

Charlie could hardly believe what her mother was saying. It seemed logical to Charlie—they *should* practice their skills, but she'd never thought she'd hear her mom saying that. "Do you think Ms. Sabbith will come right back when she finds out what happened?"

"I'm going to ask her about that. But it's also crucial that she gets all the items Dr. Sharma needs in order to fix Maria's problem. That's important too."

Maria stared for a long moment. Then, without a word, she slipped the Mark Two on her wrist.

CHAPTER 21

Trying to Communicate

That night Quinn Sharma sat tied up in a chair next to her former colleagues in Dr. Gray's office. She stared at the floor. Victor faced them, leaning against his desk, arms folded over his chest. Cyke stood guard at the door. Charles was rigid in his chair, his face haggard but expressionless. Jack's eyes were closed, his head propped up by the wall behind him. He looked better than he had in the past few days but still not well.

"It's actually quite nice to have you all here," Victor said. He appeared wistful rather than combative tonight.

Charles was never sure what to expect from the man, but he looked up, and instinct told him to play along. Maybe he could get some information. "It is, isn't it?" he said cautiously, hoping Quinn and Jack would play along too.

Quinn's dark expression flickered. After a beat she lifted her head. "Yes. Great to see everyone after so much time." She struggled to make the words sound like they weren't dead. She shifted in her chair—her shoulders ached where Prowl's claws had sunk in. And she had to force herself not to look at the ceiling vent to see if the dragonfly was still there. She didn't see any reason why

Mac or Diana would move it, but she wasn't in control anymore.

An ER doctor and three kids were. Maybe when Victor left for the night, she could communicate with them. But Cyke was within range too. She wasn't sure how she was going to do it—or even what to tell them if she had the chance. They must be freaking out and wondering what to do. But she saw a glint of possibility now that she'd had a chance in the lab to whisper a few words to the other two about their setup across the street. She was aching to tell them more and start coming up with a plan to get out of here.

She glanced at Jack, whose head had lolled to the side. He was in no condition to escape. He needed to get his strength back first. A few more days at least. She hoped she'd have a chance to tell Diana and the kids not to do anything rash.

"And you, Jack?" asked Victor. "Are you having more fun now?"

Jack lifted his head and glared at Victor. He very nearly lashed out in anger, but then Charles caught his eye.

"Jack's tired," Charles said, speaking carefully for his friend. "But he's starting to feel better. Aren't you, Jack?"

Dr. Goldstein closed his eyes again and turned his head away. "Yeah."

Victor seemed pleased with that. "You've done good work today," he said.

"Maybe you could untie *him*, at least," ventured Dr. Sharma, "so he can sleep more comfortably?"

Victor chuckled under his breath. "No, I don't think so."

Quinn laughed too, as if she'd meant it like a joke. She didn't press it. It was clear to all that while Dr. Gray seemed to enjoy their company, he didn't trust them. They had to find a way to make that happen.

Charles leaned forward, seeing a chance to clue in Quinn, who hadn't been given as much information as he and Jack yet. "I've been meaning to ask you, Victor. What's your endgame? Obviously," he said, throwing a swift glance at Quinn, "you have us working on a new device to improve on your old one, so each soldier can have powers from multiple animals. But why not have us replicate the Mark Five so there are no physical changes? Then your group of soldiers would blend into the world like other people, rather than hiding behind masks."

Quinn's eyes widened the slightest bit and she kept silent, listening.

"Ah," said Victor. "That's a great question. But you don't seem to understand my vision at all, and I'm disappointed by that."

Charles sat back in his chair, confused. "Oh. I—I'm sorry. Can you explain what you mean? So we can all do a better job of taking our work in that direction?"

Victor frowned, almost as if he detected something fishy about the question, but he went on anyway. "I've no interest in hiding anything in the long run," he stressed. "I don't want anyone to *blend in.*"

Quinn looked confused. "I don't follow."

Dr. Gray grew more impassioned. "Eventually I want everyone to see the enhancements. The goal is a chimera race—superior beings!"

Charles and Quinn froze, and Jack opened his eyes and lifted his head again. No one spoke for a moment. And then Jack said incredulously, "*Literal* chimeras?"

"Yes!" cried Dr. Gray. "True chimeras, boasting actual animal features, with no one feeling ashamed or needing to cover up with a suit. My soldiers will have the very best abilities from the animal kingdom!"

Quinn's mouth went dry. She didn't know what to say. She glanced at Charles and Jack. They were speechless as well. Then she turned to Victor. "Fascinating," she said, her voice faint. "I admit I need some time to process that. It's very . . . very . . ." She trailed off.

"Ambitious?" said Dr. Gray, a glint in his eye. "Yes, I know. But now that I have your help, I have renewed hope, renewed excitement that I can see this plan come to fruition. It's my life's dream. I'm fully devoted to seeing it through." His expression softened as he looked at Quinn. "My single-animal soldiers were just the beginning. Now that I have you three to produce devices that offer multiple features, I'll begin testing on my subjects to determine the best combination. And once I've figured that out . . ." His faint smile as he trailed off was sickening. He didn't say what he was planning to do next. Dr. Gray turned sharply to look at Quinn. "Do you understand now?"

Quinn's lungs froze. It was a shocking statement, building an army of soldiers with major physical alterations—and Gray wanted to do so intentionally. She thought about Charles's device, and imagined what Charlie might look like if her five abilities all came with permanent physical changes. It was horrifying.

"Well?" prompted Victor.

Quinn shook free from her thoughts. "Yes, I think I understand now," she said, unable to veil the hint of contempt in her voice.

But Victor didn't seem to notice it. He was lost in his own imaginings.

Dr. Gray worked at his desk into the night. The scientists sat quietly, exchanging looks of horror and despair when he wasn't watching. Eventually Jack nodded off, and so did Charles. Quinn sat alone with her thoughts, and when she couldn't stand the sight of Victor anymore, feigned sleep. Soon Dr. Gray packed up his things for the night. He went to where Cyke stood at the door, then glanced at the scientists and beckoned Cyke to join him in the hallway for a word.

The door clicked shut behind them. Quinn's eyes flew open. Realizing they were alone and not knowing for how long, she quickly turned to the air vent, praying that Diana and the kids were still across the street watching at this late hour. "Diana!" she whispered.

Hearing his wife's name woke Charles from a sound sleep.

"Charlie! Mac! Maria!" Quinn continued. "Listen to me. Just keep an eye on us for a few days until Jack is better. I'll let you know when he's well enough, and then we'll make our move to escape. We'll need your help then. Don't do anything rash in the meantime, and above all, don't get caught!"

She strained forward as far as the chair would let her, trying to see the dragonfly. She could barely detect it when the wings caught the light.

There was a noise at the door, and Quinn quickly sat back, her heart pounding.

"What are you doing?" Charles whispered when no one came in.

"I didn't have a chance to tell you before, but I managed to get a camera in here," she told him. "It's in that vent. Your wife and kids are watching us."

Charles's face twisted. He tried to hold back his emotion, but tears started falling. "They are?" He looked up at the vent. "There?"

"Yes," said Quinn. She choked up too, watching him. He must have been so worried. "They're fine. They can hear us, too." The door handle turned. Charles and Quinn pretended to be asleep.

Cyke stepped inside alone and dimmed the light, but Charles

wasn't tired anymore. His heart soared. His family could see him. They were watching him. It made a huge difference knowing that.

Despite the horror of what Dr. Gray had revealed, Charles felt a ray of hope. Eventually the tears dried on his face and he dozed.

Across the street the dragonfly camera showed everything. But no one was there to see it.

CHAPTER 22

Testing Mac's Device

The next morning Charlie slept in late. When she got up, her mom was sitting at the kitchen table with the newspaper spread open in front of her. Mrs. Wilde looked up when Charlie came down the stairs.

"Look at this," she said, pointing to the top story on page three. "'Unexplained Happenings in Navarro Junction.'" It showed two photos: the grainy one of Charlie climbing the side of the burning house that had been all over the news and a new amateur photo of two large soldiers wearing full black bodysuits lying on the sidewalk on a deserted street.

"Oh no," said Charlie, alarmed. "It's Braun and Mega after Maria and I kicked their butts."

"It sure is," Mrs. Wilde said.

"This news article can't be good. What does it say?"

"Basically that they still haven't identified the 'mysterious youth,' and they're questioning who these people in bodysuits are and what they're doing in Navarro Junction. Whoever took the photo didn't stick around until they woke up, and by the time he sent it to the newspaper and they assigned a reporter to check out the scene, the brutes were gone."

"Do you think we'll have to watch out for news reporters now too?" asked Charlie.

"Not if we're careful. This is tricky enough. I still don't know how we're going to do it with just the four of us."

"We'll figure it out," said Charlie. "Did you hear from Ms. Sabbith?"

"We talked late last night. She was shocked, of course, but she believes there's no imminent danger for Quinn and feels good about the fact that we can keep an eye on them to see if anything escalates. She agrees that it's crucial for her to get the items that'll help with Maria, so she's going to continue with that task while we monitor things. She wants me to call her if anything changes." Mrs. Wilde gave a tired smile. "This is going to drag on for a while, I think."

"That'll give us time to practice our skills. When are we going to go back over there?"

"As soon as you're ready. Are Mac and Maria coming with us today?"

"I'll check."

Charlie texted Mac and Maria on her way upstairs to get ready.

"I have to babysit my stepbrothers all day," said Maria with a sad-face emoji. "My mother is making me. It's like payback for the bracelet thing. Ugh!"

"I can go!" said Mac. "Meet you at your house."

"Great!" replied Charlie. "Bring your device."

"Duh," said Mac.

Maria sent more sad faces. "Aw, you two! Don't let anything cool happen without me."

"We won't," Charlie promised. "Stay calm and hang in there, Maria!"

"Was that a bad monkey joke?" replied Maria.

Charlie cringed. She hadn't meant it to be. "Sorry! I didn't mean it like that. I just meant that I hope today goes all right and you don't have any . . . incidents. I wish you could come with us."

Maria didn't answer at first. After a while she replied, "Me too."

On the weekend the area around their building was even quieter than usual. Mrs. Wilde, Charlie, and Mac snuck inside, taking extra precautions in case soldiers were lurking. But once they reached the office, they could see from the drones that the soldiers were busy in the lab.

They sat down to watch. The scientists were at their stations too, working on various tasks. Dr. Goldstein was still seated, but he looked slightly less sickly today. Charlie's father seemed intent on his work and only paused now and then to glance over his shoulder at the soldiers working behind him or up at Zed, who was stationed at the table in front of him. She faced the scientists, keeping a watchful eye over them.

Dr. Sharma had chosen a spot near the ladybug drone. Not

long after Mac, Charlie, and Mrs. Wilde had started watching, Dr. Sharma lifted her head and acted like she needed to stretch. She looked long and hard into the camera, but she couldn't do much more than that without being noticed.

"Did you see that?" Mac said. "She gave us a look."

"Yeah, but what was it supposed to mean?"

"No idea." Mac slumped again. They watched for a while, but with so many soldiers in the room, there was no chance for any of the scientists to communicate with them.

"I wonder if Dr. Sharma had a chance to tell my dad we're here," said Charlie. "It doesn't seem like they get any time alone to talk."

"I'm sure it's the first thing she'd tell him, given the chance," said Mrs. Wilde. "She knows how much it would mean to us."

"How are we going to figure out what to do if they can't tell us?" asked Charlie.

"I think we need to be patient and observe like Ms. Sabbith said."

Mac and Charlie grew bored when nothing new happened. Mac turned to the roach camera in the hallway, moving it back and forth when the coast was clear, and making it turn and run, trying to get the feel for how the insect moved and reacted to commands.

Charlie watched until the constant movement made her feel queasy. Then she flopped down on the floor and flipped through her device's screens, wishing like crazy that she knew where the

Project Chimera envelope had gone so she could deactivate her bracelet. She wanted to forget that the papers were still out there somewhere. And that somebody could be reading all about the devices . . . and maybe going to the newspaper with the information, like that person who took the photo of the soldiers did. She couldn't stand to think about it. Where *was* it?

After a while Mrs. Wilde got tired of the constantly moving roach camera too, and she shooed Charlie and Mac away from the table. "I'll watch for a while. You two go do . . . something else. Memorize the blueprints so you know your way around the bank building. Or . . . I know. Why don't you figure out what else Mac's device does?"

"Now we're talking," said Mac, warming up to the idea immediately. "I didn't dare to try any training at home in case my parents saw me." He hit the activate button and the liquid silver flowed from it, snaking up his arm and over his body. Within a second or two it hardened into a shell of armor.

Mrs. Wilde looked curiously at his suit, then went back to the screens.

Mac started walking and tripped. "I forgot how weird it feels to move in this," he said. It made a clanking noise. He moved around some more, then ran and slammed into the wall on purpose, startling everyone. "Didn't even hurt," he boasted. He looked at his device, clicked a button, and lifted his helmet off.

"Are you sure your device is based on an animal?" asked

Charlie. "It's so . . . different."

"It would have to be, wouldn't it? If all the devices are injected with animal DNA that means it's some sort. Plus, remember there was the outline of scales the other night?"

"That's right, I almost forgot. And there was that drawing of an armadillo or whatever."

"I haven't figured out the animal yet," Mac insisted, a bit defensively. He started clicking the buttons on his device. "Hey, look. New screens. I don't remember seeing these before." He squinted and read, "'Defense Mode: Protective Shell Activated.'" He looked at Charlie. "You were probably right the other day when you said I just needed to reset it."

Charlie beamed and came over to look. She was reminded by the various tabs that the graphics on this device weren't nearly as far along as the ones on the Mark Five.

Mac came to a new screen. "'Scales,'" he read. "I bet this is the tab I was on last time." He touched the word and instantly his smooth armor became etched with large leaflike scales, with the points of the leaves pointing downward.

"That's it!" said Charlie. "That's what you had before. Do you know how you got here?"

"I'd better redo it to make sure," said Mac.

Charlie peered at the suit, then traced her finger along the thin indented line of the scales. "But what good is this? It's just . . . a design."

Mac didn't answer. He was busy retracing his steps. The scales vanished. A moment later they returned. "Okay, got it," said Mac.

Charlie shrugged. She still didn't understand what good it was. Unless . . . "What does that screen lead to?" she asked.

"A tab that says 'Under Construction,'" said Mac. "Like a website with a broken link. Weird, but I guess it makes sense." He pressed it even though there was nothing there. Surprisingly that brought him to another screen, which read, SCALES: DEFENSIVE. He clicked on it, and the pointy tips of the scales all separated slightly from the suit, fanning out. "Whoa," he said.

"Cool!" said Charlie. She reached out to touch one and quickly pulled her hand away. "Ouch! They're sharp!" She looked at her finger, then looked closer at the scales.

"Yes," said Mac triumphantly under his breath, and looking himself over. "But they don't stick out very far. You have to really try to pick me up or come at me from below to get cut."

"Thank goodness," said Charlie. Knowing that she'd heal quickly if she got hurt, Charlie tentatively bumped her shoulder into Mac. The scales stayed pointed downward and didn't slice into her. "Okay," she said, double-checking to make sure she hadn't been cut. "This is definitely cool because now you can't accidentally hurt us."

"Yeah, it's okay, but it's not very fierce," said Mac. He sounded a little disappointed. "I wonder if there's anything else?"

"I'm going to take a picture and send it to Maria," said Charlie.

As she lined up her camera, Mac clicked through some more screens.

Before Charlie could send the photo, she and Mac got simultaneous text messages.

"I can't get to my phone," said Mac. "It's in my pocket inside the suit."

"It's Maria in our group text," said Charlie, skimming the message. Her face fell. "Uh-oh. She got mad at her stepbrothers and she changed into a monkey again."

"Oh no," said Mac, his face growing concerned. "Ask her if she's okay."

"She says she's locked in her bathroom and the boys are pounding on the door."

"Oh no!" said Mac again.

The text messages kept coming, and Charlie read them to Mac. "Now she says they're making so much noise that she can't concentrate enough to meditate."

Charlie sent some encouraging words so Maria would know they were there, and they waited again. Then another message came in. Charlie read it and looked up. "She wants to know if we can come and help her."

Mac picked up his helmet and looked at Charlie solemnly. "I don't know. Can we?"

Charlie looked at her mother, who was peering intently at the screens. "Mom?"

"Yes?"

"Maria's stuck in monkey mode and needs our help."

"Is she in danger?"

"Not exactly."

Mrs. Wilde shook her head, eyes still glued to the screens. "One sec. Mac, how do you switch the cameras so the cardinal is on the big screen?"

Mac clunked over to her and talked her through the keystroke. "What's going on?" he asked.

"There are a couple of soldiers outside the building. I want to see if the cardinal can pick up their conversation."

Mac checked the volume, but they were too far away from the drone to be heard.

"Mom?" said Charlie again.

"Yes, honey?"

"What about Maria?"

Mrs. Wilde hesitated. "By the time we get to her, she might already be changed back. And if we go, we might miss something important here."

"What if I go by myself?" asked Charlie. "I could run the distance pretty fast."

Charlie's mom turned to look at her. "I know you can, but look where the soldiers are. They'd see you leaving, and we can't risk that. After what happened yesterday, we *really* need to stay hidden. I won't have them grabbing you, too." She offered an apologetic smile. Tell Maria I'm sorry. Keep checking on her, though."

"I will," said Charlie. She turned back to her phone and told Maria what her mother had said. "I'm really sorry," she added at the end. "Maybe if you're superquiet the boys will go away for a few minutes so you can meditate."

Charlie waited, watching her screen. But Maria didn't reply. She waited some more, then called Maria on FaceTime.

Maria answered. Her face was streaked with tears, and she still had a beard and patches of fur on her head and arms. Charlie could hear the boys pounding on the door in the background. "Hi," Maria said, sounding miserable.

"Oh, Maria," said Charlie. "Do you want me to try to help you concentrate and relax?"

"No, that's okay. You and Mac just do whatever important stuff you have to do. I texted Kelly. She's going to call me from Mexico in a minute."

"Oh," said Charlie, feeling even worse. "Okay. Are you sure?"

Maria nodded. "Thanks, though," she added.

"Let me know—"

"Oh! Here she is. Bye!" Maria hung up.

"Bye," said Charlie to the blank screen. She looked up at Mac and her mom, then put her phone away. Later, when she checked in, Maria was too busy playing games with her stepbrothers to talk long. But apparently Kelly had helped her turn back into Maria again.

Because it was Saturday night, the building they were in was deserted of its other business tenants. Charlie's mom kept an eye on the soldiers and said the kids could go outside into the hallway. Mac practiced running in his armored suit up and down the long stretch until he got a bit more accustomed to how that felt. Soon he was less clunky and gaining speed.

After a while Mac became winded and started coughing uncontrollably. Charlie helped him liquefy the suit so he could get to his inhaler. By the time Mac had his asthma under control, everybody was ready to go home.

Weary, they left home base and stopped at the Sugar Plum for a quick dessert to revive them. Charlie had mint chocolate-chip ice cream in a sugar cone and Mac had a piece of warm apple pie because he said that ice cream would just make him start coughing again.

Mrs. Barnes met them in the driveway when they pulled up to Mac's house. He quickly slipped his bracelet into his pocket.

Charlie's mom rolled down the window. "Hi, Claudia. Thanks for letting us borrow Mac."

"Hello, Diana," said Mrs. Barnes. "Is everybody staying out of trouble?"

Mrs. Wilde smiled. "Definitely. No more incidents. The kids will think twice before doing something like that again."

"Good. I just wanted to make sure. Thanks for driving Mac home."

"Anytime. He's great company and such a nice young man."

Mac rolled his eyes at Charlie as he grabbed his things and got out of the car, but he grinned despite his embarrassment.

Charlie grinned back. "Nice young man," she mouthed at him, and put her thumbs up.

Charlie's mom didn't notice their antics and continued. "You know, I'm off work all next week, so he's welcome to come over anytime."

"That's very kind of you," said Mrs. Barnes, warming up a bit more. "Mac's father is headed to a convention in Fresno next week, and I'm closing out a riparian rights case with a huge brief to write, so I'll be swamped. It might be nice for Mac to have a place to hang out so he's not stuck here alone all day."

"Makes you wonder why they call it a brief, I'll bet," joked Mrs. Wilde.

Mrs. Barnes laughed. "You said it."

"We'd love to have him anytime."

"Cool," said Mac. "Thanks for everything, Mrs. Dr. Wilde. Especially the pie." He waved his iPad at Charlie. "See you later." He and his mother turned to go back inside. Mrs. Barnes rested her hand on her son's shoulder as they walked into the house together.

CHAPTER 23

A Minor Breakthrough

First thing Sunday morning, Charlie called Maria, worried that her friend was miffed at her for not being able to come to her rescue. "Are you doing okay?" she asked carefully.

"Yeah," said Maria, sounding sheepish. "I'm sorry I got weird yesterday. I was really worried that the boys would see me. It was fine later once I changed back. And then I felt bad for hanging up on you to talk to Kelly. I was desperate for help."

Charlie relaxed. "Aw, I don't blame you. I wanted to come."

"I was a little mad that Mac didn't respond."

"He had his device activated and was wearing his suit, so he couldn't reach his phone."

"Oh." Maria hesitated, then admitted, "I guess I was a little jealous that you two got to hang out all day and I was stuck home with my stepbrothers. Mac and I didn't even get to go to our Saturday morning movie. So everything felt off and weird and then the monkey thing happened again." She sighed.

"How was Kelly?" asked Charlie.

"She was fine, I guess. In the condo alone. She helped me change back, so that was good. I told her we found your dad, and she seemed happy about that. Then I suggested she at least take a walk on the beach or the boardwalk. She said she'd think about it."

"Maybe that'll help her feel better about everything."

"I hope so," said Maria.

"So . . . do you have to babysit again today?"

"No, thankfully, but I have to be here for Sunday lunch. Can you come?"

Charlie wanted to go. But she wanted to see her father more, and try to figure out how they were going to rescue him. "I'd better not," she said with a sigh. "My mom needs my help."

"I get it," said Maria. "I wish I could help you."

"Did you invite Mac?" Charlie asked.

"Yeah, he's coming."

Now Charlie felt left out. But it was by her choice. And she didn't want her mom to go to home base alone—the way things had been going lately, she might not come back. Her mom needed Charlie for protection, not just for somebody to talk to. Charlie fought the heart-sinking feeling and put on a smile. "Good. Maybe you two can come again tomorrow."

"Definitely," Maria said. "Already asked my mom and it's cool. It sure is easier being with you if I start to change again. And . . . maybe we can even do some training. Like your mom suggested."

"That sounds good. Well, I'll see you two tomorrow, then," said Charlie. She tried not to let her loneliness get her down.

Charlie and her mom spent a quiet day observing the soldiers. Before she left, Ms. Sabbith had started to keep a log of things that seemed habitual—like most of the soldiers taking lunch at the same time every day, or Dr. Gray spending mornings in the lab and going to his office in the afternoons to work privately. A few patterns were beginning to emerge, and Mrs. Wilde added them to the notebook.

Ms. Sabbith texted to check in with them. "Has Dr. Sharma communicated with you yet?"

"Just a few glances at the ladybug cam," replied Mrs. Wilde.

"Hmm. Nothing from the dragonfly? Seemed like there was a moment or two late every evening where Gray left the guys alone in the room. Isn't that happening now?"

Mrs. Wilde pursed her lips. "I didn't know about that. We've left by nine every night because Mac and Maria needed to be home. Maybe we can stay late tonight—it's just Charlie and me today."

There was a short pause before Ms. Sabbith responded. "Or you could just rewind the video and watch it back."

Mrs. Wilde and Charlie looked at each other in surprise. "That's a thing?" asked Charlie.

"Apparently so," said her mom. She laughed ruefully and responded, "How do we do that?"

Ms. Sabbith gave the instructions and apologized for neglecting to mention that feature.

Before they could get started, Mrs. Wilde's phone rang. It was Andy, FaceTiming from camping. "Hey, Mom! Hi, Charlie!" he said. His nose was red from sunburn.

"Is everything okay?" Mrs. Wilde asked, immediately worried.

"Yeah, it's great! I'm having a blast."

"That's a relief. I love that you're having so much fun."

Andy glanced over both shoulders, then said quietly, "Anything new with Dad?"

"Just the updates I've texted you," said Mrs. Wilde. "I'll keep you informed, and don't worry about us. We're doing fine." She showed him the lab screen so he could see Mr. Wilde working, then asked, "What's your favorite thing about Sedona so far? The red rocks?"

"Those are really awesome, but I like the Red Planet Diner. It's like this alien restaurant. . . ." He prattled on about the places they were planning to go in the coming days, like shopping in the Tlaquepaque Village and exploring Slide Rock in Oak Creek Canyon. But the thing he was most looking forward to was taking a day-trip to Bearizona, near Flagstaff. "The animals aren't even in cages," he said, "And you get to drive through to see bears and wolves wandering around, like, right next to you. It sounds crazy. I can't wait."

"Just keep your body parts inside the vehicle, you hear me?"

"Yes, Mom. I'm not stupid."

Mrs. Wilde laughed. "I know. You're pretty smart, actually." She paused, smiling at him and his sunburned nose. "Wear sunblock, too."

"I do! I just forgot to put some on my nose yesterday, that's why it's burned. I did my shoulders, though."

"Good job. I love you, kiddo."

"Love you too, Mom. And you too, Charlie. And Dad—tell him if you see him."

"I will."

They hung up.

"I almost miss him," said Charlie.

"I'm so relieved he's having fun. I think the stress of this would be a bit much for him."

"It's not for me, though," said Charlie.

Mom looked at Charlie for a long moment. "You really are quite mature for twelve."

"Twelve and a half," Charlie said.

Mom laughed. "Because that's a real sign of maturity to keep counting your age in half years."

"Well, at my age, that half year is like five percent of my life, you know. It still matters." She pulled up the calculator on her cell phone and did the math. "Four percent. Okay, not quite five, but still." She grinned cheekily.

Mom ruffled her daughter's hair. "Fair enough. And you're pretty smart with math. Do you ever think about what you want to be? Maybe a scientist or a doctor like Dad and me?"

Charlie closed the calculator app and turned back to the surveillance computer. "Well, that's kind of a silly question, isn't it? I'm going to be a superhero, Mom. Obviously."

"Obviously," Mrs. Wilde repeated. "Okay, Ms. Superhero, see if you can figure out how to rewind the dragonfly footage."

Charlie followed Ms. Sabbith's instructions, and soon she was moving the cursor back to the events of Friday evening. She found the moment the scientists were ushered into the room, and they listened and watched with disgust as Cyke and Dr. Gray tied up her father and the other two for the night. Then Dr. Gray leaned against the front of his desk and started talking.

Charlie and her mother stared. What Dr. Gray said was horrifying. Charlie couldn't understand it at first, but then Dr. Sharma's questions began to clarify his intentions to turn the soldiers into actual chimeras.

"That's crazy," said Charlie.

"Dr. Gray is insane," muttered Mrs. Wilde. "I mean, we knew that already, but this plan—it's frightening!" She shook her head. "What possible reason would he have to do this if he wasn't plotting some sort of attack? He's delusional! We have to stop him."

Charlie nodded, scared. While her mom called Ms. Sabbith back to tell her what they'd witnessed, Charlie texted Mac and Maria the horrible details. After Mrs. Wilde hung up, they looked at each other soberly. Then Charlie's mom nodded at the screen.

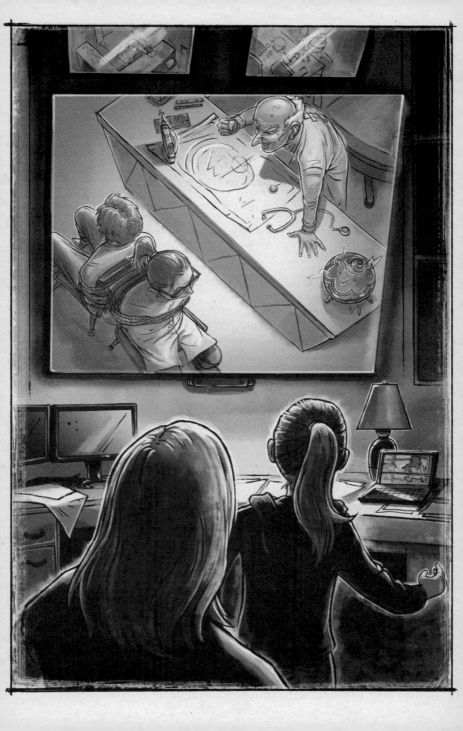

"Keep going," she said. Charlie pressed Play.

When the video came to the part where the scientists slept, Charlie almost turned the footage off. But she moved the tape forward, just in case, and saw Dr. Gray get up to talk to Cyke. She played it, and when the two stepped out, she and her mom heard Dr. Sharma's whispers to them to keep watching, and to wait for Jack Goldstein to get his strength back. That they would work together to coordinate the escape. And then they saw Charles find out about them.

They both broke down when they saw him cry.

CHAPTER 24

Maria Embraces Her Inner Primate

On Monday morning Mac and Maria showed up at the Wilde house eager to be together again, and the four of them set off with lunches packed.

Mac and Maria had researched some spy strategies at Maria's house on Sunday to help them avoid being followed in case some of Dr. Gray's soldiers were scouting the area in search of them. At their suggestion, Mrs. Wilde drove slowly once she reached the downtown area so that all traffic behind her would naturally wish to pass her. Anyone who didn't pass could be trying to follow them. She also agreed to park the Subaru in different areas, like on the street one day, in the parking lot behind the building the next, trying to keep it always in distant sight of the cardinal camera so they could watch for anything suspicious to happen when they weren't near it. And while there weren't many crowds to stick with, which would be the safest way to travel on foot, Maria said they should never walk alone. If they felt they were being followed, they should go inside a shop or walk around the block and see if they could shake whoever was on their tail, because most people heading anywhere have no need to go in a complete square.

Today the coast looked clear. And being Monday, there were a few pedestrians around. Mrs. Wilde parked on the street a block behind home base, in sight of the cardinal cam through the narrow alley.

The four of them headed into the building and up the stairs. Mrs. Wilde unlocked the door and let everyone into the surveillance room.

Charlie, who'd brought along the local paper, laid it out on a table and showed Mac and Maria the recent article. They bent over it and read. Then they talked more about Dr. Gray's crazy plan.

"It's terrible," said Maria. "And even worse, it sounds like the soldiers will be harder to fight if they have more abilities. Um . . . no way." She stood up and shoved her hair behind one ear. "We have to stop him."

Charlie nodded. "That's right. We do." She noticed Maria was wearing her bracelet. She hadn't been sure Maria was going to want to keep it even after she'd put it on the other day, but Maria seemed like she'd made a definite choice now. "Maybe later, once people clear out of the building for the day, we can test your skills."

Maria's look of determination didn't waver. "Okay. Let's see if this device actually makes me stronger."

"Deal," said Charlie.

"I'll show you what I can do too," said Mac. "In the meantime there's something I've been wanting to do." He went over to the camera controls next to Mrs. Wilde.

She looked up at him. "Do you want to take over for a bit?"

"Yes, please," said Mac. He expertly switched to the roach cam.

Mrs. Wilde moved to the desk Dr. Sharma had used for her research and began rummaging around in the broken drawer.

"What are you looking for, Mom?" Charlie asked.

"An extra key to this office. I want you kids to have one just in case you ever get locked out." She pulled open another drawer and found a ring of keys sitting there. "Here we go." She grabbed it and went to try the doors to see which ones would work.

Charlie went to the monitors and watched over Mac's shoulder. "What are you doing?" she asked.

"Practicing the roach controls some more," said Mac. "So that when we see an opportunity, I can move it out of the hallway into the lab like Dr. Sharma was trying to do. If we can get her to notice it, maybe she'll have a chance to tell us more. But first I need to get better at controlling it."

Mrs. Wilde came back to the surveillance area and handed Charlie a set of keys. "Maybe we could stay later tonight to see if they say anything on the dragonfly cam in Gray's office. When do you kids need to be home?"

"Ten o'clock," said Mac. "But that's if I'm walking. Maybe I can get my parents to let me stay later if they know you're driving me home."

"And I can just stay overnight at your house," suggested Maria. "Then I won't have to go home at all."

Mrs. Wilde nodded. "That sounds good, Maria. Mac, check with your parents and we'll give it a try."

Mac practiced his roach maneuvering skills on and off while making notes in the log book. By the time he felt good enough at the controls and ready to sneak the thing into the lab, the soldiers seemed to be more active than usual, and he didn't dare to take any chances. He held back.

Nearby Charlie and Maria studied the plans of the ninth floor of the bank building, identifying the various rooms and trying to figure out which one was the lab and which room was Dr. Gray's office.

"I wonder what's on all the other floors?" said Maria, looking at those plans, too.

"More empty offices, I suppose."

"Or maybe the vault."

"Maybe." Charlie looked through all the blueprints carefully, thinking that if they ever ended up going across the street to rescue the scientists, they'd better know their way around the other floors a little, too.

By seven o'clock their building was quiet. After Mrs. Wilde checked for any straggling workers, she gave the kids the all clear to mess around in the hallway to their hearts' content—as long as they tried not to break anything. Maria, Mac, and Charlie left Mrs. Wilde at the camera controls and headed into the hallway.

"Okay, let's see what this bracelet of yours can do," said Charlie.

"Finally," said Maria.

Mac raised an eyebrow. "This from the girl who never wanted to wear it again two days ago."

Maria sniffed. "I changed my mind. Charlie's mom—she convinced me. She needs me to do this." She started pressing buttons with Charlie looking over her right shoulder and Mac looking over her left. She came to a screen called "Manual Transformation" and cringed. "That's the one I pushed the first time," she said. She clicked it. Her body changed instantly, sporting the same howler monkey features as before.

"So, the bracelet lets you turn on your enhancements in case it doesn't happen naturally," said Charlie. "Wish I could do that with mine." She tried not to sound annoyed.

They soon came across a screen on Maria's device that she'd never seen before. It was an animated picture of a howler monkey bouncing on its feet. With each bounce its arms, legs, and tail grew a little longer. Then the word TURBO flashed once and everything went back to its original size and started over.

"Turbo, *what*?" said Mac. "Cool!"

"What do you suppose this does?" asked Maria, though it sounded as if she had a good idea.

Charlie couldn't take her eyes off the monkey. "I think I can guess," she said in a low voice.

Mac looked at the girls and nodded enthusiastically. "Do you want to click on it?"

Maria closed her eyes. "I hope I don't regret this," she said, and tapped the screen. A second later her arms, legs, and tail all started growing, making her proportions more monkey-like.

"Yikes!" said Charlie.

"Ho-leeeeey," said Mac.

"Whoa." Maria peered down at herself, aghast.

"Does it hurt?" asked Charlie.

"No," said Maria carefully, her voice shaking. "It feels . . . strange."

"I think it's stopping now," said Mac.

He and Charlie took a step back and looked at Maria. She was now a few inches taller than them, her limbs all stretched out. Her shirtsleeves now only reached just past her elbows, and her jeans were like capris. Her furry arms and legs were exposed. Her tail curled and hung nearly to the ground.

Charlie had no idea how Maria would react to this. "It's going to be okay," she said automatically, and searched Maria's face for signs of tears. But Maria was examining herself all over. She tested the spring in her step and swished her tail left and right and left again. And then she examined her fingers, which had grown longer too. "Well," she said, "Turbo monkey mode seems to be a thing. Let's hope it can help stop that maniac, Dr. Gray."

With that, she took a few tentative steps, trying to get used to walking on longer legs, then tried running up and down the hallway. She did a handspring, a front flip, and ran up the wall and vaulted backward off it, landing a bit unsteady but triumphant. She practiced a few more, growing better with each one.

Charlie and Mac exchanged a relieved glance—Maria seemed to be embracing the changes. All Charlie could hope for now was that Maria could just as easily switch out of Turbo Mode. Because if *this* look was the new normal, there'd be no way to cover it up with a scarf.

CHAPTER 25

Making Progress

Monday evening flew by. Mac joined the action by showing Maria the new stuff he'd discovered about his device.

"What animal are you?" Maria said. It was the question of the week.

"I still don't know. It's mostly just a defensive kind, I guess," said Mac sheepishly. "Even the scales can't really hurt anybody unless they're really trying to rough me up." He tried not to reveal how disappointed he was that he didn't seem to have any kind of offensive attack feature, but Charlie knew he was feeling it.

"Show her how sharp the scales are," suggested Charlie.

Mac went to tap the "Under Construction" screen like he'd done before. But this time he hit a different spot on the screen. Instead of the scales pushing out slightly like they'd done before, something totally new and shocking happened: his metallic fingers morphed into thick long claws with sharp points, and more claws extended from his feet.

"Oh my gosh!" shrieked Charlie.

"What?" Mac shouted, sounding delighted and freaked out at the same time.

Maria jumped back. "Your hands!" she cried.

Mac looked at the spikes that had taken the place of his fingers, and the girls examined him too. His new fingerclaws were rock hard and they curved slightly.

"Wow!" said Maria. "Those'll hurt in a fight."

Mac smiled. "You think?" He turned his wrists to view the claws from all angles. "They look sharp."

"I bet you can dig and climb with those things," said Charlie. "And fight, too, of course."

"Yes!" said Mac. He ran to the wall to tap it. It left a scratch. "Oops," he said. They looked around the hallway to see if there was anything he could try to climb, but there was nothing that he could attempt without destroying it.

"We'll have to find a place to test that out so you can train," said Maria.

Just then Charlie's mom poked her head into the hallway and did a double take at the sight of Mac and Maria. "My goodness!" she exclaimed. "Look at you two!" She came out and started toward them. "I was just about to give you the ten-minute warning—it's almost time to get Mac home. But let me see you! Come on—twirl!"

Maria and Mac laughed and Charlie shook her head, embarrassed. But the two slowly turned around, then showed Mrs. Wilde the new features they'd discovered.

"This is really impressive," Mrs. Wilde said. "Both of you.

I could hear some banging around out here. How has training gone?"

"Great!" said Maria. "Dr. Sharma was right about the enhanced features. I'll be even tougher now."

Mrs. Wilde smiled. "Good. I'm going to pack up. Do you have enough time to change back to yourself now, Maria? Or do you want to wait until we get to our house?"

"I'll try now," Maria said.

"You should practice more so you get faster at it," suggested Mac.

"That's not a bad idea," said Maria.

Mrs. Wilde gave her a thumbs-up and retreated to the office. Maria looked exhausted and sweaty, but she was smiling. When she clicked off the Turbo Mode, her arms, legs, and tail shrank back to their normal sizes immediately, which was a relief to Charlie and the others.

While Maria sat quietly to try to make the fur and tail go away, Mac swiftly changed back and grabbed his iPad. "I'll bet I can figure out this animal now that I've seen those claws," he said excitedly. "I already have an idea of what it might be from a video I saw one time—I just can't remember what it's called. . . ." He typed in the search bar.

Charlie left them alone and went inside to where her mother was, near the surveillance laptop, jotting down a few notes in the log book. "Any word from Dr. Sharma or Dad?"

"Not today." Mrs. Wilde's eyes looked red-rimmed from staring at the screens for hours. "Dr. Gray hasn't left them alone for the night yet—they're still in the lab. He's working them really hard." She sounded worried. "I was really hoping they'd be back in there for the night by now so we could see if they had a chance to tell us anything."

"It's all right, though," said Charlie, "isn't it? Because we can watch the video tomorrow."

"True. I just . . ." She looked wistfully at the screen with the ladybug cam stationed outside the lab window. It showed the scientists at their stations with a few soldiers around. "I just miss your dad. And I was hoping maybe he'd have a chance to at least give me a sign . . . or something."

Charlie felt a wave of emotion come over her. Even though her dad was there on the screen, right across the street, she missed him, too. She hugged her mom, then reached out and began massaging her shoulders.

"Oh, honey, that's sweet of you," said Mrs. Wilde. "Thank you." After a minute they gathered up their things and met Mac and Maria in the hallway.

"Pangolin!" shouted Mac. He jumped to his feet. "Yesss! Oh man, this is so much better than an armadillo. What a relief!"

Charlie, Maria, and Mrs. Wilde crowded around Mac's iPad to see what a pangolin looked like, and Mac played a short video for them as they waited for the elevator. It showed the animal curled in a ball and a lion trying unsuccessfully to eat it.

"That is so cool!" said Maria, and the others agreed.

The group headed to the car, with Maria and Mac in the back-seat chattering excitedly about their new powers and the things they needed to practice, and Charlie and her mom in the front, being quiet together.

On Tuesday morning Mrs. Wilde decided she needed a break. "How about I drop you off at the movies this morning?" she asked the girls at breakfast. "I have to run some errands—it'll be fun to act like a normal person again, won't it? We can head over to home base after that."

"Yes!" said Charlie. She turned to Maria. "Maybe we can see a suspenseful one that triggers your monkey power, like we did a few weeks ago, to try to get my bracelet to activate. That'll give you a chance to practice changing back. With the scientists all being held hostage, who knows how long it'll be before they can work on a solution to your DNA problem. So you might as well try to get better at changing."

"I don't know," said Maria, looking alarmed by the idea at first. "What if someone sees me?"

"We'll be in the dark," Charlie said. "And you can scrunch down in the seat and keep your scarf on."

After thinking it over, Maria nodded. "Actually, that's a great idea."

They picked up Mac and told him the plan. Mrs. Wilde dropped off the three kids at the ten o'clock matinee, and Maria picked the scariest movie for them to go see.

As expected, throughout the movie at the most stressful parts, Maria changed into a weremonkey. The first time, Charlie and Mac tried to help her calm down enough so that she was able to change back, but their whispers were unappreciated by others in the audience. After that, whenever it happened, Maria waved them off. And by the end of the movie, at the last superscary moment when she changed into a weremonkey again, Maria was able to change back before the lights came on, which felt like record time.

When they were walking to the lobby after the show, Maria said she'd missed some important parts of the movie, but it was totally worth it to have had the practice changing. She was feeling better about it. "Maybe next time I can work on not getting scared at all so I don't change."

"But you need to change if you ever have to fight the soldiers," Mac pointed out.

"Oh, trust me," Maria said. "If those soldiers come after us again, I'll be scared enough not to be able to stop it. Besides, I can turn it on if I need it. I just can't turn it off."

Just then they ran into Vanessa from the soccer team coming into the theater with a few other kids from school, which jolted them back to their old familiar world. It felt strange.

"I miss soccer already," Vanessa said to Maria and Charlie.

"I was thinking we could get the team together and kick the ball around this Saturday. Are you feeling better, Maria?"

"Yeah, I'm fine now," said Maria. "That sounds great."

Mac looked bored and pulled out his phone.

"Kelly's on vacation somewhere, right? When does she get home?" asked Vanessa.

"Friday morning," said Maria. "I'm sure she'll want to join us."

"Definitely," said Charlie. She knew if Kelly was stuck with her mother in a place she didn't like for a week, she'd be raring to take her anger out on a soccer ball.

"Cool," said Vanessa. "Let's say eleven o'clock on the school field."

"I can't make it at eleven," said Maria. "Mac and I have plans. How about three o'clock?" Mac, typing on his phone, glanced at Maria and smiled. Charlie remembered they always went to the morning matinee on Saturdays.

The group agreed on another time, and then Vanessa and her friends continued on to their movie. Maria, Mac, and Charlie saw Mrs. Wilde pull up to the curb outside the theater and headed out into the warm sunshine. "How was it?"

"It was dark and scary," said Charlie. "I forgot how warm and sunny it is here in the real world."

"Back in Chicago," Mrs. Wilde said, "we'd be out of our minds to get a beautiful day like this on spring break. And here we have them almost every day."

"Get used to it," said Mac. "Just don't forget how nice it is now when we hit a hundred and eighteen in July."

"Did you ever try frying an egg on the sidewalk when it gets that hot?" asked Charlie. "Or is that just a big joke?"

"Oh, we've all tried it," said Maria. "It makes a mess on the sidewalk. It's better to use a black cast-iron skillet and set it on a flat surface. It works in, like, an hour when it's that hot."

"Yeah," said Mac. "The black skillet draws more heat in. It works."

Mrs. Wilde laughed. "That's fascinating. It makes sense, though. Gotta love science."

"Don't forget to put some salt on it or it tastes really gross when it's done," said Maria.

They grabbed lunch, sitting outside on the restaurant's patio, talking quietly about the devices and their powers. Maria wondered aloud about how Kelly was doing. "Do you think we can show her what we can do with our bracelets when she gets home? Or is that too risky?"

"It might make her feel bad that hers didn't work," Mac pointed out.

"That reminds me—Dr. Sharma never had a chance to look for it," Maria mused. "It's probably buried deep in a landfill by now."

Talking about searching for the bracelet reminded Charlie that she had never found the Talos Global papers. "I never found the envelope either," said Charlie glumly. "I searched everywhere."

"Maybe Kelly has them both," joked Mac, and they all laughed.

Maria fake-punched him. "I'd almost believe you, but she didn't mention a word about it to me when we FaceTimed the other day. If she's as bored as she says she is, and she actually had the device, you'd think she'd at least mess around with it."

Charlie wrinkled up her nose. She wouldn't put it past Kelly to have secretly held on to the bracelet. But she kept that to herself.

"When is Andy coming home?" she asked her mom.

"They're thinking Saturday, according to Andy's latest text message."

"That's nice for him to have a friend like that to spend the week with," said Maria. "My stepbrothers are gone for the rest of the week, too. They went up to the Grand Canyon with their mom."

"I haven't been anywhere fun yet," Charlie lamented.

"We'll take a trip as a family this summer after this mess is over," said Mrs. Wilde. "I think we're all going to need a vacation by then."

Charlie smiled. "Tell me about it."

Feeling refreshed, Charlie's mom paid the bill and the foursome headed for home base to see if anything new was happening.

CHAPTER 26

Exterminated

Mac was on a mission. He went straight to the cameras and zoomed in on the laboratory scene. "I am going to get the roach in there today," he said, determined.

Mega stood guard at the door. Charlie's dad, Dr. Sharma, and Dr. Goldstein, who was apparently able to stand now, were working at their usual stations near one another. Some of the remaining stations were occupied by Zed, Prowl, and a soldier none of them had seen before.

"Who's *that* guy?" asked Maria, pointing.

"I don't know," said Mrs. Wilde. "He showed up for the first time the other day. I can't tell what animal he's been fused with—he's just been working in the lab. It appears Gray has put soldiers on the job of creating the shells and clasps for new devices. Maybe so they'll be ready for when the scientists finish putting together the inner mechanisms." She narrowed her eyes and glanced at the roach cam screen in the hallway, which showed Dr. Gray walking to the lab. "Watch closely now—see what Charles does," she said. "Here comes Gray."

Back on the ladybug monitor Mega moved aside and opened

the door. At her first movement Charlie's dad smoothly slid what he was working on to a compartment below the counter and pulled out a different project that seemed identical—at least through the blurry, superzoomed camera lens.

"What is he doing?" asked Charlie. "It seems like he's working on something on the sly."

Mrs. Wilde clenched her fists together and sat forward. "That's the way, honey," she whispered. "I think so too. He's got to be plotting something!"

"Cool," breathed Mac and Maria together. Their eyes were glued to the screen.

Dr. Gray approached the biologists. He seemed almost happy to be chatting with them, and they all responded in kind, like they had done in Dr. Gray's office. They even laughed together at one particular moment.

It was almost horrifying for Charlie to watch her dad behave that way with the man who had abducted him and was keeping him captive. "Why do they keep acting like that?" Charlie asked. It made her stomach hurt. "I wish we could hear them."

"Me too," said Mac. "This is tricky, though." He bit his lip and made a face as the lab door closed tightly again without giving him a chance to sneak the roach inside.

"I'm sure Dr. Sharma has had a chance to tell Jack and your father at least a little about what we're doing here," said Mrs. Wilde. "So they're playing along until we can help get them out of there. Gray thinks they're on board with him, despite their initial reluctance." She paused, then glanced at the visitors. "That's all just a wild guess, of course," she said. "Trying to fill in the gaps in the story so I don't go crazy wondering."

"That reminds me," said Charlie. "We need to watch last night's footage on the dragonfly."

"Can we do that in a bit?" asked Mac as he checked to make sure the laptop speaker volume was turned up.

"Sure, if you think you've got an opportunity to move the roach," said Mrs. Wilde.

Mac switched the big-screen camera to the hallway roach, who sat in the shadowy corner of a doorway across from the lab. He made it look right and left. Seeing the hallway was clear, he practiced the moves he'd worked on before to warm up his fingers. "It's risky with all those big feet stomping around by the door," said Mac. "But I think I can do it. Especially since Mega is guarding the lab today—she's not as quick as Cyke."

"I agree you should go for it—the roach cam isn't doing us much good in the hallway."

"I'll do my best, Mrs. Dr. Wilde." Mac glanced at the others, who were crowded around him at the controls, and poked his elbows out a little to create space as he prepared to get to work. Maria and Charlie took a half step back and kept their eyes on Dr. Gray, trying to read his movements.

Mac guided the roach across the width of the hallway to wait just outside the lab door. "I'm going to hug the wall and see if we can get the roach to sneak around the doorjamb."

"This is kind of like a video game," said Maria. "You totally got this."

"It's actually the highlight of my technological career," said Mac in all earnestness.

They watched the smaller laboratory screen, waiting for Dr. Gray to leave. When he went to the door, Mac called for silence.

Through the roach they could see and hear the door to the lab open. Mac tensed up, then swiftly guided it around the doorjamb, keeping it as flush to the wall as he could. Mega sidestepped so Dr. Gray could get by, nearly brushing against the roach, but Mac gunned the controls. "Come on," he muttered. The onlookers tensed too. The roach moved more slowly along the baseboard of the lab than anyone was hoping for, but Mac got it safely past Mega's big feet and was trying to get it to a shadowy corner before anyone saw it.

But then it caught Prowl's eye. He watched it, mesmerized, and crept toward it.

"Oh no," Charlie cried out, pointing to the ladybug cam. "Look out for Prowl—he's like Fat Princess going after it!"

Mac slammed the roach to a stop, cringed, and waited. "Here's hoping Prowl is enough of a cat that he'll get bored and forget about it."

"I'm pretty sure he won't," said Charlie. "Oh, this is awful!"

She and the others couldn't peel their eyes off the screen. Soon Prowl appeared in the roach camera, coming straight for it.

Mac muttered under his breath, then gunned the roach forward once more, but the game was on. Prowl batted at it, sending it skittering across the floor.

"Nooo!" cried Maria, Mac, and Charlie in unison. Mrs. Wilde gripped the back of Mac's chair until her knuckles turned white.

They could hear some commotion in the lab through the roach's microphone. Did Dr. Sharma see what was happening? Charlie tore her eyes away from the roach cam to check the ladybug's view of things. There she saw Dr. Sharma standing, watching in horror, unable to do anything to stop it. In desperation the biologist called, "Prowl! Can you help me over here?"

But the soldier ignored her. He ripped off his goggles and mask, crept forward, and pounced. Then he batted the roach around a few times and flipped it into the air. He opened his mouth, revealing larger than normal incisors, and swallowed the bug camera whole.

Everyone stared, dumbstruck.

Dr. Sharma looked stricken and turned silently back to her station.

"My goodness," whispered Mrs. Wilde. "Did you see that?"

Charlie and the others all nodded. Mac's mouth slacked. The roach camera went dark, but the sound was still working. It wasn't long before they could hear the gurgling of Prowl's stomach.

Mac gave a pained look. "Once it hits the liquid in Prowl's stomach, the electronics are done for."

"Isn't it already done for?" whispered Maria.

"Not if I can help it." Mac jabbed his fingers on the controls, trying to get the roach to climb up Prowl's esophagus. The others watched the ladybug cam. "If we can hit his gag reflex, he might puke us up."

"Like a hair ball!" said Charlie.

"You can do it, Mac!" cried Maria.

Prowl picked up his mask and began to put it back on when his face got a funny look on it. He pounded his chest, making it sound like thunder through the mike. "Oh no," Mac said again. "Hang on, roach!"

But the roach couldn't hang on. When the sound cut out abruptly, everyone knew the roach was dead meat. After several attempts to revive it, Mac gave up. He flipped the ladybug cam to the big screen and repositioned it to focus on Prowl, who was on his hands and knees on the floor, his back arched high. A few minutes later Prowl expelled all the contents of his stomach onto the lab floor. Then he coughed once and walked away.

"That was . . . incredibly gross," said Maria. The others nodded. "Do you think the roach came out?"

"It doesn't matter now," said Mac, dejected. "It's too late."

Within minutes another unidentified soldier came along, cleaned up the mess, and dumped it all into the trash bin. Mac dropped his head into his hands for a brief moment, and the others knew enough not to say anything to him.

Just as Charlie's mom suggested they all take a little break, Charlie's phone chimed. She pulled it out of her pocket and studied it.

"Everybody," Charlie said, "I just got a weird text message from Sara. It says 'Kelly??' and there's a link to an article." She moved so that everyone could gather around to see it and clicked on the link.

Her eyes flew open wide, and she read the title aloud. "Brave Twelve-Year-Old Rescues Three in Cabo."

CHAPTER 27

Kelly Resurfaces

"It's got to be Kelly," Charlie said. "Do you think she still has the bracelet after all? I always kind of suspected . . ." She scrolled to the article, revealing the first paragraph, and began reading.

"'Three teenage swimmers can thank a young girl from Arizona for their lives after venturing into a riptide yesterday afternoon—'"

"*¡Eso no es posible!*" Maria exclaimed. "Swimmers? It can't be Kelly."

"Shh!" said Mac, hanging over Charlie's shoulder and reading ahead.

"'—and nearly drowning,'" continued Charlie. "'"When we realized what was happening," said one, "we called out for help, but it was already almost too late. We thought we were shark bait." But according to bystanders on the beach who were heeding the surf warnings, the young girl appeared from the direction of the boardwalk and ran into the water toward them. She pulled all three to safety on the beach. "It was miraculous," said Marvin Toomey from Bakersfield, California, who was in Cabo San Lucas with his family for spring break. "I didn't even hear anyone calling for help, much less see those teens struggling out there.""

Charlie scrolled down, revealing a photo.

There in the photo was Kelly Parker, grinning from ear to ear. She was sandwiched between two boys and a girl who looked to be about fifteen or sixteen, and one of the boys was planting a kiss on Kelly's cheek.

On Kelly's wrist was the missing bracelet.

"Unbelievable," said Mac under his breath.

"There it is," muttered Mrs. Wilde, sounding disgusted. "She totally lied." She started pacing.

Charlie kept scrolling and read further.

""'I didn't do anything much,' the hero said modestly. She gave her name as Kelly Parker from Navarro Junction, Arizona. "I heard them calling for help and I don't know—I didn't think about it. I went to help them. That's just the kind of person I am, I guess.' Parker, twelve, was also in Cabo San Lucas for spring break, staying with her mother, who was not with her at the time of the rescue.'"

Charlie stared at the words. "She told us she hates the ocean."

"She's not even a good swimmer," murmured Maria.

"Yeah, but she's got the device," said Mac. "She's got to have some ocean creature ability in order to pull off a rescue like that. But what the stink is she doing, telling everybody her name?

Posing for photos?" He seemed truly upset. "She knows what kind of trouble that can lead to."

Mrs. Wilde stopped pacing and watched the kids react.

"After all we did to keep Charlie a secret from the reporters," fumed Maria, "and Kelly *knew* we did that and *why* it was important to not say anything."

Charlie was quiet. She felt . . . betrayed. Then she turned to her mom. "What does this mean? For us?" She grew scared, wondering what Dr. Gray would do if he heard about this.

Mrs. Wilde returned to study the article. "We'll find out soon enough, I guess," she said angrily. "Maybe the story will die down." She turned to look at Charlie, Maria, and Mac. "Which one of you has the best shot at convincing Kelly to stay quiet from now on?"

"Maria," said Mac and Charlie together.

"Text her, please," said Mrs. Wilde. "Tell her if she says another word to anybody about this incident, I'm telling her parents everything."

"I'm not sure that'll work," said Charlie. "She's not exactly getting along with her parents right now so she might not really care."

"She seemed upset enough when her dad yelled at her after he had to miss his golf game to pick her up." Mrs. Wilde's eyes narrowed. "Besides, she really makes me mad. Lying about such a powerful, secret device? Not okay." Without another word she went back to the cameras and began messing around with them like Mac had shown her.

Charlie watched her, wide-eyed. Her mom rarely lost her cool. But she didn't blame her. What Kelly had done could expose them all and maybe even put the scientists in danger if Gray found out and felt threatened.

A few minutes later came Kelly's reply. "'Tell Charlie's mom,'" Maria read out loud, "'that if she does anything to me or my bracelet, I'm telling the press everything about *Charlie*. And I mean everything.'"

Mrs. Wilde sighed heavily, then wrinkled up her nose. "Well, I guess I should have seen that coming."

"Yep," said Maria. "She definitely doesn't scare easily."

Charlie's mom fumed for another moment, then shook her head. "I say we leave her alone for now. People will forget about this soon enough. They always do. Besides, we have work to do." She let out another frustrated sigh, then took a deep breath and blew it out slowly. The anger cleared from her face. "Let's review the dragonfly footage from last night."

They did so and found nothing. The scientists had retired late and Dr. Gray didn't stick around. A soldier remained inside the room at the door the whole time. All they caught sight of was a furtive glance at the dragonfly cam from Dr. Sharma and Charles, which, while comforting, gave them nothing new to go on.

"I'm getting tired of this," muttered Mrs. Wilde. She thought for a moment, then looked at Mac. "Can you please see if you can figure out how to get the dragonfly into the lab? Not through the door but some other way? There just seems to be more opportunity to pick up information in there, don't you think? Especially if we can get the camera nice and close to Quinn or Charles."

Mac agreed. He took over the controls and carefully maneuvered the dragonfly cam up through the ductwork of Gray's office. He hit the combination of keys that Ms. Sabbith had shown him, making a small light turn on to illuminate the space in front of it. Then he hit another key, and a map and compass appeared on the screen, pinpointing the dragonfly's exact location and direction it was facing. But there were no duct paths leading to the lab that Mac could find. "They must all be covered over or something," he said to no one in particular after a while. "Or just not connected to the ones in Gray's office." He brought the dragonfly back through the ductwork, then found the roof vent where Ms. Sabbith had made it enter the building. Using its light source, and with the quiet nature sounds of evening piping in through its microphone, Mac flew the dragonfly low over the rooftop above the lab to look for a new way in.

The others were grim and quiet—it had been a rough day. After a couple of hours of making no progress, with the girls hovering nearby offering suggestions, Mac sighed and pushed his chair back and rubbed his eyes. "I need a break," he said. He got up and showed Mrs. Wilde how to move the dragonfly back and forth over the roof of the lab, and she took over. Mac went in search of food.

Eating dinner from the supplies Mrs. Wilde had brought, Charlie, Maria, and Mac sat on the floor and began searching social media on their phones for articles about Kelly. Every now and then they blurted out random discoveries—the news had rippled through their school friends pretty quickly, and through the rest of the world. Despite their hopes that the story would die, the article had been shared over two hundred thousand times already and showed no signs of quieting. It had been picked up by dozens of other news outlets and bloggers. People were sharing it across all platforms. Kelly's story was going viral before their eyes, and there was no way to control it. By eight o'clock Kelly was being interviewed live on one of the most watched news outlets in America, talking about the amazing rescue she'd made. Mac joined the internet feed on his iPad.

Then the reporter said, "You're from Navarro Junction, Arizona, where there just happened to be another amazing rescue recently by a mysterious youth. It was someone who saved two people from the second story of a burning house."

"That's correct," said Kelly.

"Oh no," muttered Charlie. Fear seized her. Would Kelly spill the beans about her? Maria grabbed Charlie's and Mac's arms and gripped them tight. What would Kelly say?

"What do you know about that?" asked the reporter.

Kelly smiled assuredly at the camera, almost as if she'd been hoping this question would come up. Almost as if she'd planned for it to happen.

"I happen to know a lot about that," she said. "A whole lot." Then she dipped her head modestly. "That mystery youth . . . was me."

CHAPTER 28

Kelly Goes Wild

"What the heck?" exclaimed Charlie, jumping to her feet. "She did not just say that!"

"Replay it, Mac," Maria instructed. "But I'm pretty sure we heard the same thing."

"How dare she!" Charlie gripped her hair, tugging at it in frustration. "What a . . . UGH!" She couldn't think of a name despicable enough to call Kelly.

Mom parked the dragonfly drone on the roof for the time being and came over to watch the clip. Mac queued it up and rolled it again, and Kelly repeated the words. "That mystery youth . . . was me."

"Yep," said Mac. "She really went there." He shook his head, seemingly appalled by her nerve but at the same time almost admiring it.

"At least that gets the spotlight away from you, Charlie," said Maria. "Maybe this isn't a bad thing."

"B-but she didn't save those people—I did!" Charlie started pacing. "I mean, I don't need the credit or anything. I don't care about that. Not much, anyway," she admitted. "But she totally just lied. I can't believe this."

Mrs. Wilde went to Charlie, offering her a hug. "It feels wrong, doesn't it? You having to be silent about your good deed while somebody steals it away from you without even looking uncomfortable about it. That was a pretty low thing to do. I wonder what made her say it." She smoothed Charlie's hair. The thoughtful, almost sympathetic look on her face made it seem like she knew the answer.

It made the others think. They remained quiet. Soon Charlie sat back down and leaned over Maria's shoulder again, watching her search for more. Maria glanced at her and squeezed her hand. "I guess maybe grown-ups are finally paying attention to Kelly, which is all she really wants. I'm sorry, Chuck."

"It's all right," said Charlie. After a while she added, "I wonder what else Kelly's device does. She has the Mark Four. Did Dr. Sharma ever mention how it works?"

Mrs. Wilde looked up. "I asked her last week when you were in school. She was pretty private about it. I don't blame her—it was her invention after all. Your father was the same way about protecting his projects. I'd hoped to get more specifics once things settled down, but I didn't have a chance to talk about it with her beyond that before she got abducted."

Maria tapped her lips. "Like Mac said, we know now that Kelly has some sort of water creature's ability, like a fish. I wonder what kind."

"It would have to be a powerful fish for her to be able to pull all three of them out of a riptide at once," said Mac.

"Could be an octopus or squid or something," said Charlie. She frowned, still mad at Kelly for what she'd said.

"What about a manta ray? That would be cool," said Maria, really getting into it.

Mac started a search on his phone while his iPad kept track of Kelly. "There are a lot of possibilities in the ocean."

Charlie plopped down on the floor and folded her arms across her chest, frowning. "Maybe she has a second ability to be able to poop owl pellets," she grumbled.

"Well, technically, pellets are vomit," Mac said, but Maria shut him down with a look.

"Maybe her third," continued Charlie, ignoring Mac, "is to act like an annoying peacock, strutting around, being beautiful and highly obnoxious all at the same time. It certainly suits her."

"Pretty sure she already had that ability without the bracelet," said Mac matter-of-factly. "Besides, the colorful ones are males, so . . ."

"Mac, stop," said Maria pointedly.

"I can't help it," Mac replied. "Accuracy is important."

"What are we going to do?" Charlie asked her mom. "With her, I mean?"

"Well," said Mrs. Wilde, "from the sound of that TV inter-view, she's not in this to squeal. She wants fame. And if she keeps the device, she'll get it. But we have enough to do here. We can't worry about her."

"She sure loves an audience," said Maria.

"So I can tell," said Mrs. Wilde. "And she's a great performer. I believed her when she said she threw the device out, and I'm pretty good at telling when somebody's lying. Anyway, since this story is already viral, we'll let her bask in her fame. Meanwhile, behind the scenes, we'll be here trying to stop the bigger evil. Once we have the scientists free, we can deal with her. Maybe she'll do some more good deeds—let's not forget she saved three teenagers from drowning. I'm certainly not mad about that."

"That's true," said Charlie. But she was still really annoyed with Kelly for taking credit for her rescue. "I guess that's better than her using the device for bad things."

"Yes," said Mac firmly. "Knowing her, this whole thing could have gone really badly." He left the words hanging in the air before getting up and going back to the dragonfly camera. Charlie had to wonder if there was still a chance the situation might go that way.

They stayed as late as Mac's parents would allow, but the scientists worked later again. Dr. Gray seemed determined to move as quickly as he could toward world domination. Eventually Mac and Mrs. Wilde gave up trying to find another way in for the dragonfly and parked him back inside Dr. Gray's office vent again.

As the kids and Mrs. Wilde were getting ready to leave for the night, Maria's phone buzzed. "It's another text from Kelly," she said, opening it. She read it to herself, then raised her eyebrows. "Good grief," she muttered. "She's starting to lose it. Maybe all the fame is going to her head."

"What does it say?" asked Charlie.

"It says, 'By the way, tell Charlie the envelope she stole from the warehouse has been really helpful. And maybe she should be more careful about slamming her gym locker door shut. The lock doesn't always catch.'"

CHAPTER 29

Venturing Out

Charlie was getting really tired of Kelly. She was being outright mean, rather than just secretly mean like she'd been before. She'd lied about the bracelet when she knew it was important for Dr. Sharma to have it back. And she'd stolen the top secret documents from Charlie's locker. And why? So she could secretly learn about her bracelet while keeping Charlie and the others from learning about theirs? What kind of friend did those kinds of things? Charlie wanted to write her off as totally horrible. But there was still something about Kelly that made Charlie hesitate. The girl had been through a lot lately. Maybe all the turmoil from her parents' divorce combined with her newfound fame was messing her up and making her act so awful. Still, Charlie didn't know how much more she could take when Kelly wasn't acting anything like a friend.

Before they went home, Mrs. Wilde dialed Ms. Sabbith on speakerphone to tell her about Kelly and the media and the text messages. The engineer said she'd just seen the TV news clip.

"This is troubling," Ms. Sabbith said gravely. "Kelly seems unstable, and obviously I'm worried for her. But I'm more concerned about Dr. Gray finding out. He's been so secretive for years—I'm afraid if he sees Kelly flaunting her hybrid powers, and worse, if she lets the world know a device like this exists, he'll get even more paranoid. Will he worry that others will be able to track him down through her? And if so, does that put our scientists in danger? After all, he threatened to hurt them if you called the police."

Mrs. Wilde glanced at the kids. They all felt uneasy. "What do you recommend we do?" she asked. "When can you come back?"

Ms. Sabbith blew out a consternated breath. "I have everything I need from Dr. Sharma's list except for one crucial component," she said. "It's being delivered to me at our lab on Saturday—I have to do it over the weekend so no one else here intercepts it. As soon as I've got it, I'll fly right out to you with all the equipment. Has Quinn been able to communicate at all with you since the first time?"

"Not really," Mrs. Wilde said. "We're still trying."

"If you can somehow give them a sign to wait to make a move until Monday that would be great. Maybe you can put something up in the window for them to see. Then we'll cross our fingers that Kelly doesn't do anything else and hope that Gray isn't paying attention to what she's already done. I know that's a lot of wishful thinking, though, so you should be prepared to make a move without me, just in case the scientists have to make a break for it."

"Gosh, I hope we'll be ready," Mrs. Wilde said, her voice grim.

"But the situation seems stable over there, and Jack isn't moving around very quickly yet. Fingers crossed that things go our way."

Wednesday was filled with new developments at home base.

"I have an idea for the window sign," said Maria when they arrived. "Your dad likes phone number puzzles, right?"

"Yes," said Charlie. "What's your idea?"

"Well, we don't want Dr. Gray or the soldiers to suspect anything if they happen to glance out the window and see it, so we can't just write, 'Don't try escaping until next week!' or anything obvious."

"Right."

"So, what if we do a cipher in the form of a For Lease sign using a fake company name? Then the phone number can be the date?"

"I'm not sure I get it," said Charlie.

"I'll show you what I mean." They found a large piece of cardboard. Maria carefully wrote, "Grand Escapes Leasing Co," on the top in block letters, then paused. "Monday is March thirteenth," she said. "March is the third month, so we can make the phone number (313) 555-0313. What do you think?"

Charlie nodded. "That's perfect. It even looks like a professional company phone number, so the soldiers and Dr. Gray wouldn't think anything of it. But if Dr. Sharma sees it in our window, she'll know it's got to be a message."

275

They showed it to Charlie's mom for her approval. Then they removed part of the window film that Ms. Sabbith had put up and slid the sign behind it, propped on the sill.

While the girls worked on that project, Mac finally found a way to get the dragonfly into the lab through the vents. He kept it hidden, balancing on the grates above Mr. Wilde's workstation. Now the group could hear conversations, but so far the only talk was about mundane things like the weather or what was for lunch or vague references to supplies needed to continue the work. None of the soldiers discussed anything secretive, probably because the scientists were in earshot, and none of the scientists would talk about anything risky at all, most likely because the soldiers were hovering around them constantly.

If only they could figure out how to get Dr. Sharma's attention and let her know the camera was in the lab now. There seemed to be more opportunities here for instructions to get whispered in passing or written on notes and held up to the camera but only if the scientists knew the dragonfly was there.

Once, around lunchtime when there were only a few soldiers in the lab with the scientists and all was quiet, Mac tried making the dragonfly's wings buzz against the metal grate. It sounded ridiculously loud to them, but that was because the microphone was right there. But Mr. Wilde didn't look up. Mac thought about having the dragonfly swoop down to get their attention but didn't dare risk being seen by anyone else. They needed this camera and couldn't afford to lose another one. So they waited. Like always. But at least while they waited the kids could train. And it was time to dig in and take their training to the next level—somewhere Mac's claws could dig in deep without destroying the office building.

That afternoon Mrs. Wilde drove the kids to the Superstition Mountains nearby and parked at one of the trails that didn't seem to have many hikers. They set out to find a private area where they could test out their skills. As soon as they saw an area of huge boulders near a sheer rock wall a little ways off the trail, they went toward it. Mrs. Wilde stayed behind to keep a lookout in case anyone started toward them.

"I did some more research on the pangolin," Mac said to the girls. "Their claws are supposed to be able to dig through concrete."

"That's amazing!" said Maria.

"I can't wait to see what you can do to this mountain," said Charlie.

Mac beamed. He used his inhaler, then tapped his device to release the liquid suit. When it hardened, he clicked through his bracelet screen to find the claw feature. Once his fingers transformed into claws, he tapped hard against the mountainside to see what would happen. They made a small divot in the rock. He wound up like a pitcher and slammed his claws into the rock. They sank in deep.

He tugged, but they were stuck fast. "Uh-oh," he said under

his breath. He pulled and wriggled until they came free, and he breathed a sigh of relief. "Maybe not quite so much force," he said. He hit the mountainside again, and this time the claws sank only a little way. He bent his knees and hung by one hand, testing their ability to support him. He held. Then he did the same with his other hand and slowly began climbing. He used the claws on his feet, too, trying to get used to that strange feeling.

Maria climbed the boulders, still looking like her normal self. When she reached the top, she grinned back at the others, then cringed and ran off the edge, changing into a weremonkey in mid-flight. She landed and looked around cautiously, then jumped to a lower boulder. A natural hunk of rock jutted out of the rock face above her. She leaped and swung from it. With her other hand she clicked her bracelet into Turbo Mode. When her legs, arms, and tail were fully extended, she continued swinging, jumping, and climbing all over the area.

It was fun for Charlie to watch her friends figure stuff out for the first time, but she knew that she needed more practice too. So after a few minutes she kicked off her shoes and followed what Maria had done: climbing up the boulder pile and jumping off but toward the rock face instead, letting the bracelet kick in on its own. With fingers and toes tingling she hit low on the side of the mountain and stuck there, then worked on becoming more quick and agile with her climbing.

They spent the afternoon working on their various skills.

Mrs. Wilde came to watch their progress for a while. "You're doing great!" she called out to them. "I'm trying not to have a heart attack watching you. Charlie, aren't you a little high off the ground? No?"

Charlie laughed and crawled down the rock face to the ground. Then she went over to her mom. "That was fun," she said, her face streaked with dirt and sweat. The others followed, turning off the enhancements that they could.

Once Maria had changed back to normal, they went back to home base to check the cameras. With the roach cam destroyed, the dragonfly keeping eyes and ears on the scientists, and the ladybug on the window with a different view of the lab, there was no longer a camera in Dr. Gray's office. Mac occasionally brought the elevator spider cam out into the hallway. They caught Dr. Gray going into his office and not coming out for several hours at a time, and they debated whether to try to put the spider cam on him in there. But ultimately they decided it was more important to keep tabs on who was coming and going, especially now that new soldiers seemed to be showing up. They needed to get a solid count of them in order to know what they'd be facing when they went on their rescue mission.

On Thursday the kids returned to the Superstition Mountains and spent much of the day training, then they went to home base for the evening.

"It's good we're learning to use our devices better," remarked Charlie, "but I still don't know how to throw a punch very well. I always feel awkward."

"Same," said Mac. "I bet we can teach ourselves, though." While they were resting up, he pulled up some videos on self-defense and martial arts, thinking that if they just learned some key moves it would help. After watching several videos, they started practicing techniques.

On the other side of the room Mrs. Wilde skimmed through the day's footage, finding nothing of note, then held the dragonfly poised on the ceiling grate for an opportunity to alert Mr. Wilde to its presence above them.

Meanwhile, Mac activated his device. "Try punching me," he said to the girls. "It won't hurt." The girls practiced throwing punches like they'd just learned. Once they figured out punching, they moved to doing kicks on Mac.

When they grew tired, Charlie offered the same opportunity to Mac, so he could get some basic training in too.

"What? No! I can't punch you," Mac said.

"Don't be silly," said Charlie. "I'll work on blocking your punches. And if you accidentally hurt me, the pain won't last long. I'll heal right away."

"Are you sure?" asked Mac, looking skeptical. "My mom would kill me if she heard I punched my friend."

"We won't tell her. Besides, you need to practice too."

Finally Charlie convinced Mac to fight her. He worked on his punches and kicks, with Charlie trying to block them. Slowly but surely they were learning how to use their devices and their fighting skills like experts.

When Mac unintentionally landed a well-placed punch to Charlie's jaw, knocking her to the floor, Maria gasped. Mrs. Wilde looked up from the drone controls, then jumped to her feet, upsetting the laptop, and ran over to make sure Charlie was okay.

The dragonfly teetered on the edge of the ceiling vent grate, then it fell through and plopped onto Mr. Wilde's workstation, directly in front of him.

CHAPTER 30

A Gift from Above

Charles stared at the insect on the lab table in front of him, startled by its abrupt landing. It didn't move. He looked up at the ceiling and noticed the grate. His eyes widened as he realized what it must be. Swiftly he cupped his hand over it and swept it into his lab coat pocket. His heart raced as he tried to be casual about checking around him to see if anybody had noticed.

He glanced at Quinn, who was bent over her station, doing some precise measuring. Jack was occupied too. When his eyes landed on Zed, he saw she was watching him, but she looked away quickly. Had she seen it? No one came over. No one said anything.

Charles dropped his gaze and refocused on the device he was working on. His heart pounded as he tried to figure out what had just happened. Quinn had told him that the dragonfly camera was in Dr. Gray's office. And she'd managed to share with him and Jack the incident with the roach camera and what that whole ruckus with Prowl was about. They'd all been devastated by that. Victor wasn't giving them any opportunity to talk privately in his office at night.

Charles knew about the ladybug camera as well, but Dr. Gray

seemed to get fidgety when the scientists were away from their stations, and for any of them to go and stand by the ladybug window for a few moments seemed suspicious. Still, Quinn had caught a glimpse of the sign that someone had put in the window across the street, and she'd told him and Jack to take a look when they had a chance. Throughout the previous day they thought they'd figured it out, and managed to whisper about it for a minute at breakfast. Grand Escapes—that was clear enough. And 3/13 was this coming Monday.

Now that Charles had the dragonfly camera, he could tell Diana and Charlie that they got the message. He hoped the drone hadn't been broken by the fall, because it certainly wasn't moving or acting alive.

Once he'd gathered his wits, he signaled to Braun that he needed to use the restroom. The soldier grunted and walked with Charles, then stood outside the door to wait.

It was a small bathroom and not soundproof. There was a crack under the door, and Charles could hear the restless man shuffling his feet on the other side. Still, he had to take a chance. He lifted the dragonfly and looked into the camera. "Diana," he whispered. "I hope you're there. We're doing okay." He paused to listen, but all seemed clear. "We saw your sign. Jack's feeling stronger every day, and we're planning our escape for Monday. Let's try for the evening, once we're settled into Gray's office for the night. We'll have to get loose of our ropes, but we'll only have one guard in the immediate area to overcome. And hopefully by then we can convince Victor that we're solidly on his side and he doesn't need to tie us up anymore." He glanced away, then looked back at the camera. "I'll fill you in on more whenever I can. I hope you're all doing okay."

Charles knew he didn't have much longer before the soldier would get impatient. Just as he was about to tell Diana he loved her, voices erupted in the hallway, and he could hear Dr. Gray sounding angry. Braun pounded on the door. "Hurry up!" he said.

Charles quickly put the dragonfly back into his pocket. He flushed the toilet and ran the water, then emerged, seeing a few other soldiers heading for the lab. "What's going on?"

"Dr. Gray just called a meeting," said the soldier. "Come on."

Fear struck Charles. Had Zed told him about the dragonfly? Braun grabbed Charles by the arm and they hurried into the lab, where everyone was gathered around the head of the operation. Braun pushed Charles to the front of the group and let go of him. Charles stumbled and righted himself just a few feet from Victor. His throat tightened.

Dr. Gray held his hands up for silence and looked around the room. "We have a situation, scientists," he said gravely.

Charles swallowed hard and stared at Victor, trying not to flinch. Then, in the quiet, a slight whirring sound came from his lab coat pocket. The dragonfly began to move.

CHAPTER 31

Communication Breakthrough

It hadn't taken long for Mrs. Wilde and the others to realize that the dragonfly wasn't where they'd left it. When they'd heard Mr. Wilde whispering to them through the computer speakers, they'd run back to the controls, Charlie's injured jaw forgotten. But by the time they'd gotten there, Charles had stopped talking.

Mrs. Wilde looked at the screen and saw that it was mostly dark and fuzzy. "What happened?" she muttered. "What are we looking at?" The four of them could hear a muffled voice, but they couldn't really see anything. Mrs. Wilde quickly touched some keys to try to get the dragonfly to pivot. The voice in the lab ceased, and all was quiet. Mrs. Wilde turned the dragonfly's face upward and soon the screen grew lighter. They could see part of a person.

Charlie gasped when she realized who it was. "Mom, stop!" She pointed to the screen, which was now a partial shot of Mr. Wilde's shoulder and face. "The dragonfly is in Dad's *pocket*. Don't make it move! Somebody might notice!"

Mrs. Wilde froze. "How did it get in there? I was only away from the controls for a couple minutes!"

"We can watch the tape back later to figure that out," said Mac.

"But Charlie's right. It must have fallen from the grate. I hope nobody else saw."

"Shh," said Maria as they heard Dr. Gray's voice break the silence again, clearer now that the microphone wasn't pressed against the fabric of Charles's lab coat.

Mrs. Wilde moved over and motioned for Mac to take the controls. Expertly he adjusted the ladybug on the window to try to get a better view of the gathering, since the dragonfly gave them only a partial, limited view of Mr. Wilde's face and not much else.

"Everybody's there," he whispered.

Maria counted them all, saw a few unfamiliar faces, and made a note in the log book while they listened.

"There's a girl in the news who's doing heroic things," said Dr. Gray angrily, "and she's wearing one of our devices. It isn't your daughter this time, Charles." Dr. Gray held up a tablet and played the clip of Kelly's TV interview in Cabo.

Mr. Wilde glanced into his pocket, his eyes wide, then looked away.

"Dad must recognize Kelly," said Charlie quietly. She bit her thumbnail anxiously. "He saw her in the musical."

When the clip finished, Dr. Gray narrowed his eyes at Charles. "Obviously she's one of your daughter's friends who stole the prototypes from the warehouse. But she's being quite a bit more of a pest than Charlie was. At least your daughter knows not to talk about the bracelets. This one can't shut up."

Charlie stared at the screen.

Mr. Wilde didn't say anything.

Gray went on. "If she finds out where we are, she can lead people straight to us." He glared at Charles. "We can't let that happen."

Charles lifted his chin. "It won't. Nobody knows we're here."

"Don't play games, Charles. Braun and Mega saw Charlie and your wife and one of the other juveniles. Prowl fought them when they were with Dr. Sharma. So they know we're in this area."

"They also know better than to tell anyone about it," said Charles, trying to appease him. "Obviously they've listened and agreed to your request—and they know what the consequences are. So I don't think you need to worry about this twelve-year-old leading anybody to us. Besides, according to the news interview, she's not even anywhere near here. And she didn't mention the bracelet, so I think we can remain calm."

Dr. Gray looked shiftily from Charles to Quinn and back to Charles again, as if he was trying to decide if he could trust that this wasn't a big deal. "But if this girl keeps up her antics, and people learn about the device and want to know where she got it, it wouldn't take much for her to lead them to your family . . . and your family can point them to me, or at least give them my name. If that happens, don't forget it'll be you who suffers."

"I know." Charles's face didn't waver. "And they know. It's not going to be a problem."

Dr. Gray seemed to want to believe him. He studied the scientists a moment longer. "I do *not* want to move this operation again," he muttered. Then he barked, "Work faster!" He turned on his heel and went out of the lab. A couple of soldiers followed him. The rest dispersed around the room.

Charlie and the others could hear Mr. Wilde sigh in relief. They traveled in his pocket back to his station.

When it was clear that all was quiet in the lab again, with everyone appearing to work as quickly as they could, Mac rewound the footage to the part they'd missed. They watched the dragonfly falling and Charles whispering into it, confirming they'd seen their sign and they would plan on an escape on Monday night.

Everyone sat back in relief. At least they had that part of the plan figured out. And Mr. Wilde had done an amazing job to calm down Dr. Gray, so that was good, too.

Mrs. Wilde looked at the kids. "Now we're getting somewhere." She checked the time, then said, "It's late. Tomorrow we'll talk to Ms. Sabbith and start figuring out how we can help them on Monday. But for now . . . I've had enough. Let's call it a night."

On Friday Maria's mother announced that she'd hardly seen Maria all week, and she insisted that Maria stay home. She invited Mac and Charlie to hang out there with them. Maria was wary in case she changed into a weremonkey, but at least she was getting better at changing back to her old self quickly now. Knowing that Mrs.

Wilde and Ms. Sabbith would be busy working out a plan today, and there wouldn't be any action happening until Monday, Charlie and Mac decided to accept. "We can try to figure out what Kelly's animal power is," said Maria.

"And there's always good food," Mac pointed out. After having hurried meals and sandwiches every day for a week, the kids were looking forward to whatever Maria's grandmother had in store for them.

They hung out together in Maria's bedroom and researched various fish and other water creatures, but they couldn't come to an agreement on what they thought Kelly's animal might be. Mac insisted it had to be big and strong to allow her to rescue three teens at once, so he found a website of colossal sea creatures and read about them. Every now and then he'd exclaim the name of one, like Portuguese man-of-war, or lion's mane jellyfish, or giant isopod. Maria was more focused on the rescue part of Kelly's animal and looked up what the smartest sea creatures were. She came up with octopus, sea lion, dolphin, otter, and penguin.

Charlie let them argue while she checked to see if Kelly had done anything new. Last night Dr. Gray had said in no uncertain terms that if Kelly did something that would lead people to discover what he was doing, it would be Charlie's dad who would suffer. She was worried about him. And worried about what Kelly was going to do next. Because Charlie didn't believe for a moment that Kelly was done showing off.

"Nothing new from Kelly," Charlie announced after she'd checked her usual online channels. "That's a relief."

"Probably because she's flying home this morning," said Maria.

"Oh." Charlie had forgotten that. There wasn't much Kelly could do up in the air—or at least Charlie hoped not.

"She'll probably find a way to kick out the pilots and land the plane or something," grumbled Mac, swiping through another website filled with possibilities. "Oh! Blue whale! Whaddaya think?"

The girls shrugged. Having so many options was making it even harder to figure out.

That afternoon the three emerged from Maria's bedroom and discovered her *abuela* Yolanda already working on the evening's feast. With the Torres dogs underfoot, the kids crowded into the kitchen and helped Yolanda peel, slice, pound, and fry the plantains that would be used with garlic and pork rinds to make *mofongo*. They watched as she prepared her famous caramel flan for dessert, and they cut up a mountain of peppers and onions to go with the *churrasco*.

That evening the table was packed with the whole Torres family plus Mac and Charlie. Maria's three stepbrothers were back from their trip to the Grand Canyon and full of stories about all the wildlife they'd seen—especially the huge elk that had wandered across the road right in front of their car.

The conversation turned to Kelly and how her face was plastered all over their mom's social media. "How did she do those rescues?" the youngest stepbrother asked Maria.

"I don't have a clue about how she managed the house fire one," Charlie said, trying not to sound snide or sarcastic. Mac squelched a grin and kicked her under the table.

"She must be a great swimmer to have saved those people in Cabo," Maria said lightly.

"She's so cool," said the middle brother.

The oldest agreed. "Everybody is talking about her and I'm like, 'I know her.'" He laughed and his face flushed.

Mac smiled politely and said with false enthusiasm, "Yes, she sure is great."

They moved on to talk about Puerto Rico and Maria's extended family who lived there, and then discussed how much they'd miss Yolanda when she went back home again.

It felt just about perfect being there, laughing and having fun. Charlie almost forgot about how much she missed her dad.

As they were finishing up the meal, Maria's mother pushed her chair back and reached into her pocket. "Sorry everyone," she said apologetically. "Somebody keeps calling me, so I'd better take it." She pulled out her phone, looked at it, and frowned. "Hmm. It's Kelly's mother." She got up and walked to a quieter part of the house to answer.

Maria and Charlie looked at each other. Had they both gotten that prickly feeling at the backs of their necks? Mac looked over, too, uneasiness apparent in his eyes.

They didn't have to wait long. After a few minutes, Maytée came back into the dining room, a stricken look on her face. "Have any of you seen Kelly since she and her mom got home from Mexico this morning?"

Charlie, Maria, and Mac all shook their heads solemnly as their hearts raced—something bad must have happened. "Why, Mamá?" asked Maria. "Is something wrong?" Her eyes went wide and she reached under the table and grabbed Charlie's hand, both of them feeling the effects of their abilities beginning to kick in. Maria's hand began to sweat in Charlie's, and Charlie could tell she was worried about changing. But they had to find out what was going on.

"Kelly didn't show up for dinner," said Maytée, "and her mom found a note in her bedroom. It looks like she ran away from home."

"What?" exclaimed Mac.

Charlie echoed his shock. "Why?"

Maria didn't say anything. She started breathing deeply to stop herself from changing.

"Do you need help?" Charlie whispered in her ear.

Maria shook her head, but a second later she was tipping her chair over and running for the bathroom. "I'm fine, everyone!"

she called out behind her as her mother started following her. "Just need the bathroom!"

Maytée returned to the table, still in shock from the phone call, and the boys started talking over one another, wondering why Kelly would do something like that.

Mac and Charlie looked at each other, eyes wide. What was Kelly trying to prove by running away from home? Was it really that bad for her there with her parents? Or did this have something to do with her newfound powers?

Maybe it was both.

That evening Charlie alternated between reading and googling Kelly as she waited for her mom to come home.

"Hey, kiddo," Mrs. Wilde said, poking her head into her room. "Did you have a good day?"

Charlie nodded. She'd called her mom on her way home from Maria's to tell her about Kelly going missing. "How about your day? Anything new? Yolanda sent a plate of food home for you. I put it in the fridge."

"Oh, that's so kind of her." Mrs. Wilde's smile was tired. "Your dad managed to talk in private through the dragonfly cam a couple times today and told us some stuff that'll help. He also said he loves and misses you."

"Aw, Dad," said Charlie. Tears sprang to her eyes.

"Then Ms. Sabbith and I FaceTimed for a couple hours. We've

been working on a rescue plan for Monday evening. She and I will talk you kids through everything tomorrow night, once she gets back. Can Mac and Maria spend the day with us?"

Charlie nodded. "I'm sure they'll skip their movie to come with us. We just have that soccer scrimmage at three."

"Got it. Also, Juan's mom texted me, saying that they'll be coming home first thing tomorrow, so we can pick Andy up around ten. We can get Maria and Mac then too."

"Okay, I'll tell them."

Mrs. Wilde kissed Charlie on the forehead and went to bed.

Before Charlie turned off her light for the night, she pulled her laptop onto the bed and googled Kelly's name one last time. There were lots of entries that Charlie had already clicked on. But the top one was new. It was the most recent, posted just minutes before. It read, "Wonderkid Kelly Parker Visits *LIVE*, *TONIGHT* to Reveal Her Secrets to Saving the World!"

"Oh no!" Charlie whispered, scrambling to sit up. "Kelly, what are you doing?" Charlie knew that *LIVE*, *TONIGHT* was a Friday night internet show with a live studio audience and millions of viewers. The host liked to have guests who would do shocking, provocative stunts. Some speculated that the show was rigged, but fans didn't care. Charlie's mom and dad generally didn't allow her to watch it because it was too adult, but she'd seen clips of it before. She clicked on the link. While she waited for the feed to start, she group-texted Mac and Maria.

"Are you watching *LIVE, TONIGHT*? That's where Kelly is."

Mac replied immediately. "Going there now."

Maria didn't respond. It was almost eleven—Charlie thought she might be asleep already. She called Mac. "Are you on?"

"Doing some quick research before it starts," he said. "They film in Los Angeles. Do you think I should I call Kelly's mom?"

"Do you have her number?"

"I can find it."

"Yeah, maybe you'd better. I'll text that info to Maria. I think she's asleep."

"Will do," said Mac. "I'll call you back."

"Okay."

They hung up. Charlie sent Maria a text message letting her know what was up and giving her a link so she could find the show in the morning. Then she settled in to watch.

CHAPTER 32

The Showstopper

A band onstage began playing, and the audience cheered. The host, a young college-age genius named Silas Beck, with an angular fringe haircut, skinny jeans, and diamond-studded high-tops, emerged from behind a curtain. He jumped around on the stage in time with the music, making the audience rise to their feet and scream.

He opened the show with some commentary and showed a few clips of shocking things that viewers had caught on camera and sent in. Some of the videos had clearly been doctored to look even more outrageous, but the crowd didn't care.

Charlie watched. She didn't understand why people were so crazy about this guy, but whatever. Then Silas introduced his guest.

"Tonight we have an amazing young talent for you. You may have heard of Kelly Parker in the past few days after she saved three people from drowning off the coast of Mexico."

The crowd whooped.

"Since then we've learned that wasn't her first feat of bravery. She revealed that she also saved two people from a burning house in Arizona." The grainy photo of Charlie went up on the screen.

"My hair is *brown*," muttered Charlie. "That doesn't look remotely like her." At least not to Charlie it didn't. But Silas's audience seemed to accept it.

"The most exciting thing," he continued, "is that Kelly told our producers that she has special animal powers that no one else has, which enabled her to perform those shocking rescues. And tonight, exclusively," he said, pausing dramatically, "she's here to reveal what they are. Let's bring her out!"

Charlie's heart sank and she dropped her head into her hands. "No, no, no, Kelly," she muttered. "You told them you have animal powers? Shut up. Shut up!"

She lifted her head and watched two stagehands escort Kelly to stand with the host. Silas raised a skeptical eyebrow at Kelly, then shook her hand. "It's nice to meet you," said Silas. "Congratulations on your instant fame."

"Thank you," said Kelly. She was casually dressed in a red tank-style shirt and white shorts, but she looked nervous and her voice sounded a bit more strained than usual. She flipped her hair behind her shoulder and stood straight, slightly angled toward the camera. The Mark Four device rested comfortably on her wrist.

"Don't mention the device," whispered Charlie. She couldn't stop staring at it. It seemed bigger than life. Were normal people noticing it too?

"So, 'animal powers'?" said Silas quizzically, doing air quotes with his fingers.

"That's right. You know, like abilities animals have that humans . . . don't have."

"Tell us more," said Silas. "Where did you get them?" He had a slight smirk on his face, and he glanced directly at the camera after he said it, as if he had a secret with the audience. He seemed slimy.

"Don't answer that!" Charlie said to the screen.

"I—I don't want to talk about that," said Kelly. "I just have them. I can do things that other people can't do."

Charlie let out a breath. But she knew this was far from over.

"Which animals do these abilities come from?" asked Silas. "You can at least tell us that, can't you?"

"Um," said Kelly, squirming a little, "a lizard. The—the climbing one."

Charlie glared at the screen.

"And what about saving the swimmers? That was definitely not a lizard power."

The audience laughed.

"That was from a dolphin," said Kelly.

"Dolphin," Charlie muttered. Maria had been on the right track.

"So, these powers," Silas said sarcastically, "do they just come naturally to you? Were you born like this—able to climb the side of a house? Able to pull three people out of a riptide? Like, did Baby Kelly pull drowning kittens out of a river one day and it all exploded from there?"

The audience laughed harder.

Kelly looked repulsed by Silas and shocked by the audience's reaction. Charlie almost felt sorry for her in that moment, because the host was being kind of a jerk. The audience loved it. They were jerks, too. No wonder Charlie's parents didn't like her to watch this horrible show.

Silas kept badgering her. "C'mon, Kelly. How did you do that? Can you climb that wall for us right now?"

"No, she can't," Charlie informed the screen, feeling a little bit of anger rise again, "because she's a lying liarhead."

"Look," Kelly said through gritted teeth, "I'm here to reveal another power."

"Well! Aren't you sassy, trying to run my show?" Silas panned the audience, prompting them to react in laughter again. "Let's get right to it, then."

Kelly, seeming rattled, nodded once. "Great," she said. She let out a breath, clearly trying to regain her composure.

Charlie's phone rang. She dived for it. It was Mac. She answered and could hear the show running in the background at his house. "This is a train wreck," said Charlie, and moaned. "If she mentions the device, my dad's in big trouble!"

"Maybe Dr. Gray won't see this," said Mac weakly, but they

both knew Gray must be watching Kelly as closely as they were now.

"Maybe," said Charlie. But she knew her dad's fate rested in Kelly's hands.

Silas's assistants wheeled out a large speckle-painted board and set it up center stage. The board had a white background with lots of brown, orange, and yellow globs of paint on it. It looked to Charlie like something Andy could do blindfolded in about three minutes.

Silas led Kelly over to it and stepped to one side. "Okay, let's see your new heroic ability! How is Kelly Parker going to save the world next? Audience, let's give her some encouragement."

The crowd began clapping methodically and chanting, "Kel-ly! Kel-ly! Kel-ly!"

Kelly appeared to relax a little now that she had the audience on her side again, and she placed herself in front of the board. She faced the people and smiled her fake star smile. Then she took a quick glance at her bracelet and clasped her hands behind her back.

"Look," said Mac over the phone. "I'll bet she's programming the bracelet to do something."

"As long as she doesn't mention it," muttered Charlie. "But after this show won't people start demanding to know how she's doing it? How long can Kelly keep the bracelet a secret?"

"Hopefully until after Monday night at least," said Mac. He sounded worried, too.

They watched as the audience chanted faster and clapped louder. Finally Kelly took a deep breath and held it. She closed her eyes. Over the course of less than a minute, her skin began to change colors to match the camouflage pattern on the wall behind her.

"Whoa!" cried Mac. "What kind of animal does that?"

"I don't know," said Charlie. "Chameleon, maybe?"

"Nah, not like that."

"Shh. Listen. They like it."

The crowd's chanting and clapping rolled into applause and cheers. But after the way Silas had set up the new power as something that will save other people, like the first two abilities had, a few hecklers in the front row of the audience seemed to be expecting something more.

"Hey, Kelly! How does that save anybody?" shouted one of them.

"That doesn't seem very heroic," said another.

"It's just an illusion—a light trick!" cried someone else. "Show us the lizard!"

A few others said it too. Then one started chanting, "Climb the wall! Climb the wall!"

Kelly's eyes flew open. She looked scared.

Charlie gasped. "Oh no," she whispered.

The rest of the audience shouted down the hecklers, but that only made them more boisterous.

"What the heck is wrong with them?" asked Mac.

"I don't know," muttered Charlie. They seemed out of control.

The hecklers started bumping into people around them, and the people shoved back. Things began to escalate.

Kelly looked at Silas, who was trying not to appear concerned for the sake of the internet audience, but Charlie could tell he wasn't liking where things were going. A security guard approached the hecklers, but they began pushing through the crowd to get away from him. Silas walked over to Kelly. "Look," he said in her ear, "it might calm them down if you climb the wall. Can you do it or not?" Her mike picked up everything.

Kelly expelled a shocked breath and she blustered, "What I just did was pretty incredible."

"It was incredible, obviously, but they think it's a trick."

Kelly stepped away from the wall and her face turned from spotted to beet red, matching her shirt. "I'm not, um . . . equipped for the climbing ability right now," said Kelly, forgetting to keep her voice down.

"Or ever," muttered Charlie, who kept alternating between sympathy for and anger at the girl.

Kelly blustered some more, trying to turn the blame on Silas. "These things take concentration! Maybe if you could have given me more time to prepare, but no, you just *had* to send your people out to Arizona to get me *today* before the other networks could have me on . . . so it's not my fault."

The hecklers were being caged in by the audience. Others trying to get out of the way pushed onto the stage.

"Well, we'll certainly get the views once word gets out about this audience," he said.

Charlie and Mac stared in shocked silence as one of the hecklers broke loose and stumbled onto the stage. "You're a fraud!" he shouted to Kelly before a guard tackled him. "This whole show is rigged."

"I am not a fraud!" Kelly shrank back as more security guards came in from outside to stop the brawl. A look of horror grew on her face. "Make this stop," she whispered softer to Silas.

People in the audience started shouting at the hecklers, "Leave her alone! She's just a kid!"

"All right, everyone!" Silas finally yelled into his microphone. He raised a hand in the air, trying to gain control and salvage the show. "Thank you, Kelly! Let's give the kid a hand." When that didn't get the audience's attention, Silas took Kelly by the arm. "Come on," he said with a forced smile, searching for his stagehands. "Let's help her find the way out." He started pulling her by the wrist, his hand on her device. The camera zoomed in.

"Don't touch that! Let go of me!" cried Kelly, wrenching away. "I can walk by myself."

Charlie gasped. It seemed so obvious to her that the bracelet was the reason for everything, but she knew that was just because she knew about it. And with her dad's life depending on it staying a secret, she knew she was overly focused on it. But still . . . "This is a disaster," she whispered.

"It's going to be okay," Mac insisted. "Look, she's almost offstage. It's practically over. Nobody is going to make the connection to the bracelet, Charlie—trust me."

"Okay," Charlie said weakly.

Just then two stagehands ran up and grabbed on to Kelly's arms to speed up her exit. The three started pushing her backstage.

"I told you to get away from me!" she yelled, kicking out when they lifted her off her feet. "Keep your hands off my bracelet!" She pulled her arm away and quickly punched the device's screen.

"Nooo!" cried Charlie, falling back into her pillows and clutching her head in despair.

But Kelly wasn't done. With no warning two spikes appeared on her heels. She slammed one into Silas's thigh as hard as she could and pulled it out. He screamed and let go of her, falling to the floor. Kelly stared. The stagehands left her and rushed to help him. Silas stopped moving, but he didn't stop screaming.

"Shut it down! Shut it down!" cried the producer to the camera operators.

Kelly stepped backward, watching Silas in horror, then looked at the bloody spike on her heel. Before anybody could come after her, she turned and ran backstage to the exit, and disappeared out into the world.

CHAPTER 33

On the Run

Charlie was aghast. "She said 'bracelet.' And she pressed on it to activate those spikes—whatever they were. There's no way people won't notice that. And what the heck did she do to Silas? This is horrible!" She couldn't believe it. Was Dr. Gray watching? Maybe Mac was right and he wouldn't see it, at least not right away. But the news would get out. "I'll be right back," she said to Mac. "Don't hang up."

Charlie grabbed the laptop and ran to wake her mother. Quickly she told her what had happened and handed the computer to her so she could replay the show. Then Charlie went back to her room to grab her phone. "I'm back," she said.

Mac was still there, clicking on his iPad on the other end. "Poison, I'll bet," he muttered. "Not from her mouth, though, like snake fangs. Her heels? What animal has poisonous heels?" He typed some more and then said, "Ahh."

"What is it?" asked Charlie.

"Platypus," said Mac, almost in disbelief. "So dolphin, platypus, and whatever that camouflage thing was. Wow."

"Is the camera still rolling?" asked Charlie. "I can't believe this just happened."

"There are now twenty-seven million viewers and counting," reported Mac. He was quiet a moment, then said, "Insane."

"Seriously."

"I mean about the platypus. I had no idea they had poisonous spurs on the backs of their feet. And it's only the males that have them." He snickered.

Charlie sighed. "Mac, focus. Kelly could have killed that guy." The thought made her stomach hurt. Charlie went back to her mom's room. She hovered near the door so her conversation with Mac wouldn't interfere with her mom's ability to hear the show.

"He's still screaming," said Mac. "That's a good sign that he's not dead." He typed some more, then said, "No reported human deaths from platypus venom, but get this—not even morphine can take the excruciating pain away. It lasts for weeks, and can paralyze small animals. *Wow.*"

"Where do you think she went?"

"I don't know, but people aren't going to like her after this. Silas Beck has some pretty crazy obsessed fans."

"I hope she's okay." Charlie bit her lip. She'd done her share of injuring soldiers, but that was very different from what had just happened to an internet star on live broadcast in front of millions of people.

"Yeah," said Mac solemnly, and the clicking stopped. "I do too. Did Maria ever reply?"

"No."

"I'll check in with her in the morning," said Mac.

"Cool. Let me know if Kelly tries contacting her or anything. . . . I don't think me texting her directly will do any good, do you?"

"Not after what she said about you last time."

"Did Kelly's mom pick up when you called?"

"Yeah. She was shocked that Kelly was on the show but grateful for the tip. They're going to try to track her down."

"Good." Charlie glanced at her mom, who was glued to the screen with a look of consternation on her face. "I can't stand this," Charlie said. "It's giving me a stomachache. I'm ready for this to be over."

"Me too. I'll see you tomorrow?"

"Yeah, around ten. My mom's going to fill us in on the plan once Ms. Sabbith gets back." She paused and cringed, overhearing the hecklers coming from her laptop. "She's watching now. I'll let you know if anything changes."

"Okay."

They hung up. Charlie watched her mom from the doorway for a moment, then decided she didn't want to hear again how it all ended and went to her room to wait. She climbed into bed and glanced at her device. She hadn't noticed that it had grown warm during the horrifying events on the show, and now she saw that, ironically, the gecko was animated. Too bad Kelly couldn't have used Charlie's ability remotely. Maybe then the whole device-revealing, platypus-stabbing incident wouldn't have happened.

Despite the excitement it was now after midnight and Charlie's eyelids were heavy. She shrank down and rolled to her side, promising herself she'd just take a nap for a couple of minutes until her mom came in.

The next thing she knew, it was morning.

CHAPTER 34

The Chase Is On

Three soldiers charged into Victor Gray's office early Saturday morning, waking the scientists with a start. They began untying them.

"What's going on?" asked Charles.

"Another meeting," said Braun with a snort. He helped the others finish untying Jack and Quinn.

"Has something happened?" Charles asked.

"Something with the girl," said Cyke. "I'm not sure what."

Worried, Charles grabbed his lab coat, taking a quick peek to make sure the dragonfly was still in place, and put it on. The soldiers escorted the scientists out of Dr. Gray's office and to the lab, where everyone else was already gathered around.

As soon as there was silence, Victor tapped on a keyboard and pointed to a monitor. A show began playing.

Ten minutes later Dr. Gray stopped the video, abruptly interrupting Silas Beck's screams. He went back a minute or two and replayed the moment where Kelly Parker clicked on her device and spikes emerged from her heels. Then he stopped it again.

Charles and Quinn exchanged a look of horror. Victor stared

at them and Jack. No one spoke for a long moment. Then Charles sighed. "Victor," he said softly. "I know you're thinking people will notice that she's using a device to activate her powers. I understand your concern. You think she'll tell people how she obtained the bracelet. After all, she's not trying to hide it. But even if she says something, that doesn't change the fact that Kelly still doesn't know where we are. She can't lead anyone to us." He glanced at the soldiers, then added, "And I know how badly you want us to finish our work and how you don't want to waste any more time by having to move somewhere else."

Victor rolled his fingers on the table and looked at Charles. "You know me well. But there's an easy solution to this problem."

"Is there?" Charles glanced at his fellow scientists, a feeling of dread building inside him. What was Victor plotting now?

"Yes," he said. He turned to his soldiers. "Braun, Cyke, and Mega, I want you three to go find Kelly Parker and bring her to me." He rubbed his hands together almost gleefully. "Then she won't be able to tell anyone anything." His eyes narrowed and his expression softened. "Only take her by force if necessary. First I want you to try to convince her to join us willingly. What she did with those poison spurs was . . . well, remarkable. Wasn't it?" He looked at Charles.

Charles's stomach churned. He didn't know what to say. Not long ago Victor had told Charles that he would never stoop to experiment on children. Now he was talking about abducting one like it was an ordinary thing. The man was growing more irrational by the day. Charles had to play along, as much as he despised doing so—he had to keep Dr. Gray thinking that he was trustworthy so escaping would be easier. "Yes," he said faintly. "Remarkable."

"She'll make a great soldier. An excellent addition to our team." Victor smiled wanly and peered at the others. "Come on," he barked, and clapped his hands sharply. "What are you waiting for? Find her! And don't come back without her. The rest of you hurry down to finish breakfast and get ready for a full day's work!"

The three largest soldiers set off to track down Kelly, while the others scattered after Dr. Gray, down the stairs to the floor below. The scientists suddenly found themselves without their usual escorts, alone in the lab except for Zed, who stayed back to guard the door.

Quinn gripped Charles's arm and motioned for the men to follow her to their workstations. "Change of plans," she said under her breath. "We have to make our move. Today, while the big monsters are gone. It's our best chance. Can you let Diana and the kids know?"

"They can probably hear us now if they're watching," said Charles in a low voice. "Do you think they'd be there yet?"

"It's early. Probably not yet. Should we try for this evening?"

Jack shook his head slightly. "I'm afraid the goons might be back with Kelly by then. We need to go as soon as possible. Like when the first group is eating lunch at noon."

Quinn stopped at her station and glanced at Zed, who was glaring at them. Quinn nodded slightly to the other scientists and didn't say anything else.

Jack went to his station and Charles to his, and they focused on their work. Soon the soldiers began trickling into the lab. Whenever there was a distraction at the door, the scientists confirmed their plans.

Once they'd figured out what they were going to do, Charles saw Miko talking quietly to Dr. Gray and preparing to go somewhere. Dr. Gray shrugged and nodded and waved her off, then headed out toward his office. Before Miko could leave for her mysterious destination, Charles flagged her down, telling her he needed a restroom break. She took him and bounced around impatiently outside the door while Charles secretly confirmed the change of plans through the dragonfly camera.

When he was finished, Miko brought him back to the lab. Once he went inside, she took off running down the hallway and leaping over the banister of the stairwell, quickly climbing down. She went outside, crossed the street, and climbed on top of that building. And then she waited, smiling to herself.

She hadn't noticed the cardinal.

CHAPTER 35

Coming Together

When Charlie came downstairs in her pajamas, Mrs. Wilde looked up from her coffee and the newspaper. "Good morning," she said. Her face was drawn and her eyes weary, but she smiled.

"I fell asleep before you finished," Charlie said, feeling anxious. "Did you watch all of it?"

"Yes. That was pretty horrifying. Are you okay?"

Charlie nodded. "I think so. Did you notice that Kelly mentioned the bracelet and then you could see her use it to activate the spikes in her heels? I'm worried about Dad. Do you think Dr. Gray watched it? What's he going to do to him?"

Mrs. Wilde held her hand up to stop the barrage of questions. "First, do you really think Dr. Gray watches *LIVE, TONIGHT*?" she assured her. "Chances are he won't hear about it until today. And second, like your dad said to Dr. Gray the other day, this still doesn't mean Kelly can lead anyone to him. She doesn't even know his name, does she?"

"Well, no," Charlie admitted. "I don't think so."

"And we're not going to tell Kelly where they are, are we?"

"No," Charlie said again. She felt a little bit better.

"I've already talked with Ms. Sabbith this morning. She agrees we should stick to the plan. She said Dad is good at talking to Dr. Gray. He'll calm him down if anything happens. Remember, Dr. Gray needs your dad—he's not going to hurt him as long as he still needs him."

Charlie sighed, relieved. "Okay." She got some breakfast and sat down at the table. "What about that show host guy, Silas—he didn't, like, die or anything, did he?"

"No, he's stable in the hospital. Sounds like there's nothing they can do for him but have him ride it out."

"What are the *LIVE, TONIGHT* people going to do to Kelly?"

"I don't know. But it's pretty clear to me from the footage that they were handling her roughly before the encounter, which made me really angry. She was acting in self-defense. Besides, she's disappeared. They'll have to find her first." Mrs. Wilde leaned over and smoothed Charlie's hair out of her face. "Do you have any idea what sort of animal the spikes came from?"

"Mac thinks it's a platypus."

"Those cute little things? It's hard to believe such a friendly-looking creature could do that much harm."

"You just never know with animals," Charlie said.

"That's for sure." Mrs. Wilde stood up. "I'm going to get ready.

Alejandra texted that they're on the way home."

"I'll get ready in a minute." She gave her mom an impromptu hug.

Mrs. Wilde smiled and held Charlie tightly. "Thanks, kiddo," she said. "I needed that."

"Me too," said Charlie.

As she got ready, Charlie thought about the interesting week—not only the drama but also her relationship with her mother. Charlie felt closer to her than she'd felt in a long time. The resentment she'd had over how much her mother was working had dissipated. All this craziness had forced them to be together so much . . . and they'd found they actually really liked it. But would it last? Once Andy was home and her dad was safe and her mom went back to her crazy hospital schedule, things would go back to normal. It would almost feel bittersweet if Charlie didn't want her dad back so badly.

Andy, wearing an extreme tan and smelling like a campfire among other things, couldn't stop talking on the way to Maria's. He told them all about his trip, even the parts he'd mentioned before, and about his favorite adventures they'd done. "There's way cooler stuff in Arizona than in Chicago," he declared.

Charlie tried to listen to everything he said, but her mind kept going back to the now familiar worry about Dr. Gray. She really just wanted to hurry and pick up Mac and Maria and get to home base so they could see if anything had happened.

Mrs. Wilde filled in Andy on what was going on with their dad. Then she asked casually, "Did you hear what happened with Kelly?"

"No," said Andy. "What?"

"She sort of became famous overnight."

"For what?"

"She used her device's powers to save some teenagers from drowning, and she got interviewed, and that went viral, and then she went on some late show and now the world knows about her." Mrs. Wilde left out the violent parts.

"Why did she do a dumb thing like that? We're not supposed to talk about the bracelets!"

Charlie smiled and reached behind her to pat her brother on the leg. "Exactly."

"Besides, I thought she threw the bracelet out," said Andy. "Why did she lie?"

"We're not sure," said their mom carefully, and glanced at Charlie. "But maybe she'll come back and explain. She's sort of . . . on the run, I guess you could say."

"Oh." Andy grew silent. "I hope she makes it back okay."

"Yeah," said Charlie.

They stopped to pick up Mac and Maria, then ran into the grocery store to get some food supplies for the day. It was almost eleven by the time they got to home base.

When they got out of the car, they proceeded with an abundance of caution as usual, looking right and left as they made their way into the building, knowing that home base was still the safest place they could hide in case things went crazy. They saw no one.

Unfortunately, they forgot to look up.

CHAPTER 36

No Time to Lose

Inside home base, as Mrs. Wilde and the four kids were entering the surveillance room, Mac went to the screens and muttered under his breath.

"What's wrong?" asked Mrs. Wilde. The rest of them set down their supplies and hurried over to the monitors.

"There's Miko on the cardinal cam, climbing down the side of our building. Did anyone see her?"

"No," said Charlie. "We were extra careful."

"She saw us, though, I'll bet."

"Oh no," murmured Maria. "What are we going to do?" Then she glanced at her backside as her tail pushed out. She sighed. "Here we go again."

"This is not good." Mrs. Wilde's expression flickered with deep concern and doubt. "I wasn't planning on them being able to find us. Now Miko's going to alert everybody over there. This changes everything." She went to the window and looked up at the building across the street, but of course she wasn't able to see anything. "Kids, we might have to relocate. I'll call Erica. If her component arrived as planned, she should already be on her way to the airport. While I do that, why don't you check the footage from last night and this morning?"

"Already on it," said Mac. He rolled through the footage in reverse.

Charlie stood over his shoulder, straining to see if anything unusual had happened in the early hours of the day. "Wait—stop. They're all gathered in the lab." She swallowed hard. "Gray knows about Kelly. He must know!"

Mac stopped rewinding and they watched, while Mrs. Wilde stayed by the windows to talk to Ms. Sabbith.

"Mom!" Charlie called out. "He saw the show."

They continued watching through the rest of the footage, listening to Dr. Gray's new orders, and then caught a rare moment when the three scientists had had time to speak freely.

They were talking about a noon escape today instead of on Monday, from the lab instead of Gray's office, and the kids began to realize that Mrs. Wilde hadn't yet explained what the plan was going to be. And then they remembered that Ms. Sabbith wasn't there yet to help enact it.

And finally they realized that noon, the hour of escape, was exactly twelve minutes away.

"Mom!" Charlie called out in a panic.

Her mom put the phone down. "What is it? What's happening?"

"They going to try to escape today! Like, *now*. We have to go!"

"But—" said Mrs. Wilde. "But Erica says we need to pack up

and get out of here because of Miko—she says we have to protect ourselves first or no one's left to do the rescue!" She ran over to where the kids stood around the monitor just as Miko was walking with Charles into the hallway on the video from earlier.

"Quiet, everybody," said Mac. "He's going to tell us their plan."

Charlie looked at the time and jiggled her foot. "Eight minutes till noon," she said. She could feel her bracelet grow warm. Maria was fully transformed.

Finally Mr. Wilde was alone. He held the dragonfly up to his face and whispered, "The first shift of soldiers goes to lunch at noon with Dr. Gray on the eighth floor. We'll be in the lab with the rest of them—Prowl, Miko, Zed, and a couple of new soldiers that Dr. Gray has been training and experimenting on. We won't make a move until we see you, just in case you aren't able to pull this off. But once you show up, we'll help fight them off, grab as much of the technology as we can to slow Gray down, and get out of here. Take the elevator for the surprise effect—the soldiers use the stairs for lunch." He hesitated and looked around, then gave a strained smile. "We can do this. Today's our best chance."

"Six minutes, Mom," said Charlie. "You heard him. We have to go."

"Charlie, just wait a second." Mrs. Wilde took a breath. "Listen to me. Our home base is compromised. Erica's not here yet. This is all very sudden." She put her face in her hands for a moment, then looked up. "I don't know what to do. I can't leave Andy here alone—not now that Miko found our building. And we can't take him with us because it's not safe." She raked her fingers through her hair, her expression filled with indecision.

"Mom," said Charlie again. "Maria and I know the floor plans. You've seen us train—you know how good we are. We can do this." She jiggled her foot. Mac took a hit on his inhaler, and Maria clicked to the Turbo screen and waited to see what Charlie's mom would say.

Mrs. Wilde's expression was agonized. She cringed and shook her head. "Kids," she said, "I'm calling off the rescue operation. We have a new huge threat to us. Ms. Sabbith said we need to get ourselves and the equipment out of here. This whole thing—it's just too big. Too dangerous. I'm sorry."

"What?" cried Charlie. "But what about Dad?"

"Charlie, please try to understand. Dad said they wouldn't try anything if they don't hear us coming—he knows this is a big change in plans and that we might not be able to pull it off. And I've made my decision. This isn't smart. Let's just . . . gather up the computer and screens and our other stuff before Miko comes back here with her friends. Erika will be here by tonight. Then we'll regroup and try this again—from a safe location." She turned and went over to Dr. Sharma's desk and started piling things up. "Get the blueprints," she called to them. "Save the electronics for last so we can keep an eye out for Miko. Andy, come help me get some

322

empty boxes." She went back to the partitioned area where the boxes were. Andy followed, looking over his shoulder wide-eyed at Charlie, afraid to say anything.

Charlie stared after them, shocked. Her mom had gone full-on coward, just like that—just because of Miko, who might have seen them go into a building. But she didn't know where in the building they were, did she? She'd have to go through six floors to find them, and even if she did manage to suspect there was something different going on in the Water and Sewage Treatment Complaints Office, she'd meet up with a locked door. Charlie watched the video, which Mac had switched to live. On the ladybug screen she could see her dad checking the clock, and Dr. Sharma biting her lip anxiously and glancing at the ladybug camera. Her heart twisted. Charlie looked at Mac and Maria, and they looked back at her, disappointment clear in their eyes. "I'm sorry about my mom."

Maria touched her arm. "It's okay." She hesitated, then added, "I didn't realize just how much I wanted to rescue the scientists until your mom told us we can't. I mean, here we have these abilities. . . . We can save your dad."

"And we have a responsibility," Mac added. "Not just to rescue them but to stop Dr. Gray."

"And we've been training for this," said Charlie passionately. "Ms. Sabbith is pretty smart and tough, but we don't need her." She glanced over toward the partitioned area, then looked at her dad once more, who was now reaching under his workstation counter and slipping the secret thing he'd been working on into his pocket. He was preparing to go. This was their best chance, he'd said. Charlie couldn't let him down.

She eyed the partitioned area. Her mom was still back there with Andy. She leaned in. "We have to do this without her," she said in a low voice. "Now's our only chance. But we've got to scram. Right now. Are you with me?"

Mac and Maria stared at Charlie. Their faces lit up and they nodded.

"Let's go." Charlie led, with Mac and Maria right behind.

By the time Mrs. Wilde came back, they were gone.

CHAPTER 37

Going for It

The decision to go rescue the scientists against her mom's wishes felt reckless but also freeing. Like Maria had told Charlie before, when you have something special to offer the world, you have an obligation to do it. And the scientists were counting on them. The world was counting on them! They might not have another chance like this, with the three biggest brutes gone for a while. Charlie, Maria, and Mac ran outside with a fresh burst of energy. And Charlie began formulating a plan.

As they went down the alley toward the bank building, Mac activated his suit. Maria, in full Turbo Mode, jumped a few times, then tried a couple of parkour moves. She ran up the side of a building and sprang off it, landing on a lone parked car, then rebounded to grab a street sign with one hand and her tail. She flipped around the sign and landed just in front of Charlie and Mac and kept in stride with them.

"Looking good, Maria," said Charlie. She clicked through her device. The cheetah and elephant were pulsing with life. That was a good start.

"I'm feeling good," said Maria, bouncing around. "Confident.

We did great stuff this week to prepare. I may look ridiculous and awful, but it's a cool sort of awful when you really think about it."

"Like I said the other day," said Charlie, "you look like a superhero to me." She looked at Mac. "Aren't you going to activate your scales for protection?"

"I move better and faster without them," he said, "so I'll wait until we get there. What's our plan? Are we just going to rush in there and start fighting? Who do you want me to go after?"

"I've been thinking about it," said Charlie. "Let's stay together if we can. Okay? We'll keep it simple. We know there's a guard at the door inside the lab."

"Zed's there now," said Mac.

"Got it. We also know my dad and the others won't do anything until they hear us, so we've got to make some noise. We'll rush in, hopefully surprise the soldiers, and get to the biologists so we can protect them as we fight our way out. The bad guys won't know what's happening at first—we'll be a wall of terror coming at them."

Mac snorted. "Right. They'll probably kick our butts."

Maria poked him with her elbow. It bounced off Mac's armor and she rubbed it. "Well, if they try kicking your butt, they'll definitely be hurting."

"Hey, that gives me an idea," said Charlie. "Mac, you can go after Prowl and Zed since they have claws—they won't be able to hurt you. Maria, use your tail and your swinging abilities to knock the soldiers out of commission, but stay out of reach if you can so they don't hurt you. I'll do what I can with my abilities—I've only got strength and speed activated so far, but hopefully the others will turn on if I need them."

"Got it," said Maria, and Mac nodded.

While they talked through the plan, they tried to sneak past the cardinal even though they knew Charlie's mom had probably noticed they were gone by now. She'd see them soon enough, one way or another. Then they slipped into the back door of the bank building, found the elevator, and hit the button for the ninth floor. Feeling guilty, Charlie looked up at the spider cam, mouthed, "Sorry," and blew a kiss in case her mom was watching.

Maria tapped the elevator wall nervously on the ride up. When they reached the ninth floor, they peered out. There was no one in the hallway. Charlie tried to get her bearings—things looked a little different in real life than they did on the cameras and blueprints. But soon she figured it out.

"There's the lab door," Charlie whispered, pointing down the hallway. "That's where we want to go."

Mac and Maria nodded.

She looked at her friends. "Are you ready?"

"Ready," said Maria.

"Almost," said Mac. He clicked his device. His scales appeared and fanned slightly away from his body. He tapped through a few screens and his fingers and tips of his feet morphed into pangolin claws. "Okay, I'm ready."

"Cool," said Maria. "I didn't know you could do both at the same time."

"Multitalented, that's me," Mac whispered.

They snuck out of the elevator and stayed together, running as quietly as they could, though Mac still clanked a little in his suit of armor. They managed to make it all the way to the lab door without anyone seeing them.

Charlie made eye contact with her friends, and then she yanked open the lab door and they all yelled. Zed jumped, startled, and turned around to see who was there. Her claws came out and her body blocked the entrance. She screeched in alarm.

"Dad!" Charlie called, and she threw a punch at the woman's face.

Zed's head snapped back, but she dug her claws into the frame and stayed blocking the doorway. She yowled, freeing her hands, and started swiping wildly. Charlie dodged to avoid her, and Mac stepped in. He bent over and plowed into her. Zed stumbled backward, caught herself, and then swung at Mac, her claws scraping loudly against his suit. As Charlie tried to get around her into the lab, Zed put her head down and slammed into Mac. He went flying, knocking into Charlie and Maria, and landed in the hallway, curled to one side. The sharp edges of his scales beveled out farther

328

than they'd done before and gleamed.

The girls didn't have time to comment on that new development. Maria leapfrogged over Charlie through the doorway, giving Zed a sharp kick in the face before she landed inside the room. Charlie scrambled in after her.

Zed slammed the lab door shut so Mac couldn't follow them in.

"Hey!" shouted Charlie as other soldiers in the lab realized what was happening. Maria hopped onto a lab table and jumped on Zed, while Charlie ran to the door and ripped it right off its hinges. She tossed it aside and helped Mac to his feet, then they both charged back in. Maria was cowering, bleeding from claw scratches, and Zed was on the floor. One of the new soldiers ran toward them from the back of the lab, while others were diving to contain the scientists. Charlie whipped her head around, looking for her dad. She spotted him being held down by Prowl. "We're coming!" she cried.

Still on the floor, Zed reached for the communication device attached to her suit. "We're under attack!" she screeched into it. "Get up here!"

"She's calling Dr. Gray and the other soldiers!" shouted Dr. Sharma from another part of the lab, where Miko had her pinned to the wall. Miko twisted the woman's arm harder, and Dr. Sharma cried out in pain.

Mac dove at Zed, trying to keep her away from the girls. Maria dodged the new soldier while Charlie came at him, unsure what kind of hybrid she was facing, but hoping he was so new that he wouldn't be very good at fighting yet. She put her hands out and caught him as he tried to grab her. She lifted him up, and hearing commotion from incoming soldiers in the hallway, she pivoted and flung him out the door. He bowled down Dr. Gray and two other new soldiers, sending them sprawling.

"Let's go!" said Charlie. The three kids regrouped and started for the back of the room to where Prowl held Mr. Wilde. Dr. Gray and the three new soldiers got up and came barreling into the lab. Miko, holding Dr. Sharma, inched her way along the windows toward Prowl.

"Look," said Maria in a low voice to her friends as Miko got closer and started plotting with Prowl. "If we take her out, she can't tell anybody what she knows, know what I mean?"

"It might be too late for that," said Charlie, catching her breath. "But we may as well—she's not as strong as the others, so hopefully she'll be easy to handle."

Maria peeled off from the other two and hopped up onto a workstation, running down the length of it. At the end she sprang at Miko, trying to knock her off balance so Dr. Sharma could get away. Miko tried to dodge her but didn't want to let go of Quinn, and all three of them tumbled to the ground. Charlie ran to pull Dr. Sharma from the others while the two primates tussled on the floor. But Prowl saw her and Mac coming. He threw Dr. Wilde on the floor and hissed at Charlie, coming toward her.

Maria freed herself from Miko, jumped onto a lab table and gazed perplexedly at the ceiling, as if looking for something to grab on to so she could use her swinging momentum. Miko jumped onto the workstation next to her, and Maria sprang up and punched at a ceiling tile. It popped up, leaving the rectangular metal grid empty in that space. "Aha," she muttered. She jumped up and swung on it with one hand, testing its ability to hold her, then swung back and shot forward, managing to clock Miko in the jaw with her foot and knocking the soldier off the table. With Miko temporarily down Maria quickly hopped around the lab knocking out ceiling tiles every few yards.

Meanwhile, Prowl struck out at Charlie. She squirmed and dodged and tried to signal to her dad to run for it. Mac caught up to her and slammed into Prowl, but that sent him reeling backward into a workstation. He grabbed the corner of it, then used his pangolin claws to chip off a hunk of the tabletop. When Prowl pounced on Charlie, Mac swung as hard as he could, slamming it into Prowl's shoulder. He stumbled and tripped over Charlie.

"Good idea!" Charlie said, scrambling to her feet. She kicked her foot into the leopard man's stomach as hard as she could, leaving him doubled over.

"That's gonna hurt for a while," said Mac. He and Charlie high-fived and looked around for Dr. Wilde. He had gone over to Dr. Goldstein, and now he and Dr. Sharma were fighting off the new soldier who'd been guarding Jack. "Come on," Charlie

said to Mac. "He looks hurt!"

While Maria duked it out with Miko overhead, the other two zigzagged through the wreckage to Dr. Goldstein. "Are you okay?" Charlie asked the man.

He nodded and pushed himself under a table, out of the way. "Go help your dad!" he said. He looked at Mac and smiled weakly. "Nice suit," he said.

Mac clicked off his helmet. A look of awe came over his face as if he'd just realized he was actually meeting the Mark Three's creator. "You made it," he said with a grin.

"Mac, pay attention!" shouted Charlie. "Dr. Goldstein, stay hidden."

Dr. Gray and two of the new soldiers were coming toward them. "Fang!" he cried. "Morph! Attack those children!"

Charlie's eyes widened when she noticed the woman Dr. Gray had called Morph. She had a giant crablike claw for one hand, and she wore a different bodysuit from everybody else. Was this one of Dr. Gray's new experiments he'd talked about—one with multiple animal abilities? If so, she didn't look quite finished with only one claw. Charlie didn't wait to see what the woman could do. She let her hand fly like she'd learned in the videos they'd watched, striking Morph in the throat. The soldier's eyes bulged and she dropped to the floor.

"I've got Dr. Gray!" cried Mac, whirling around to face the enemy. With renewed fervor Mac ran forward, claws raised. Dr.

Gray saw him coming and paled. He stepped behind the taller soldier, Fang, as Mac attacked. Fang batted him away with a wolflike howl, then veered off toward Charlie, her dad, and Dr. Sharma.

Charlie turned to face Fang; he was a tall, thin man who was making a curious hissing sound now instead of a howl, which was totally confusing. Was he a wolf? Or a snake? Or . . . both? Her father struggled to his feet and limped over to help. "These two are new chimeras!" he called to Charlie. "Multiple animals and abilities!"

"That explains a lot!" said Charlie. "And be careful, Dad! Stay back!" Charlie laid into Fang. He crouched, then snapped forward into Charlie, appearing to open his mouth beneath his mask. Fangs ripped through the fabric, tearing a gaping hole there. The fangs gleamed and connected. Immediately Charlie felt a sharp sting in her shoulder that almost became debilitating within seconds. She yelped in pain and dropped to the floor, rolling around and clutching her shoulder. "Ugh, poisonous snake!" Charlie cried, trying to warn the others as the man started after Dr. Sharma. "Run, Dad! Run, Dr. Sharma!" The scientists obeyed, sliding under the table with Dr. Goldstein.

Across the room Maria had just knocked Miko out cold and was on her way to help when she heard Charlie. She jumped up, nimbly grabbing on to the ceiling tile grids, and began swinging swiftly across the room toward them, out of the reach of the soldiers but slapping them with her tail and kicking at every opportunity, even swatting Dr. Gray on the back of the head. She let go and sailed into the thin rattlesnake soldier, her feet smashing him in the chest. The soldier went down and lay still, his mask ripped farther across his face and down his neck, revealing a snake head. But a pop of gray wolflike fur poked out at his neck.

As Charlie writhed in pain, Maria landed at her side. She immediately pushed Charlie's short sleeve up to look at her injury and watched in awe as Charlie's body seemed to reject the rattlesnake venom. Clear liquid shot out of the pierced skin onto the floor. Charlie moaned and rolled, still clutching her shoulder in pain.

"Whoa!" Maria said. "You should be feeling better soon, *chica*. Hang in there."

Even with the venom forced out of her body, Charlie was too weak to get up. "I'm okay," she muttered. "What's the body count?"

"Miko, Zed, and the snake guy are down. Prowl's waking up. Dr. Gray is . . ." Maria looked around. "Where did he go?"

Just then Mac cried out for help. Maria shot up, then bounded over to where he was fighting the short, clawed soldier named Morph. Charlie lay still a moment longer, then took a deep breath and sat up. Prowl was coming her way. She staggered to her feet and groaned, then summoned her strength and charged at him, socking him in the face. She expected him to go flying, but the leopard man dug his claws into her shoulders like he'd done before in the warehouse, ripping through her skin right where the snake man had struck her. "Yow!" she screamed, dizzy with pain. She tried to shake him off but he stuck fast. Charlie yelled in his face and threw her head forward, trying to strike his forehead. She hated Prowl more than any of them. They tumbled to the floor.

Morph chased after Mac, and when she reached him, her pincer-claw hand shot out like a bullet, striking Mac in the helmet. It sent him flying through the air. He crashed to the ground and slid into the wall.

Maria sprang at the woman, knocking her to the floor. Mac found his footing and staggered back, striking Morph with his pangolin hand. She stopped moving.

Mac ran to help Charlie, and Maria took to the ceiling to aid her as well. Maria flipped and sailed at Prowl, but he released one hand from Charlie's shoulder and batted at her, sending her crashing to the floor, hurt. Maria lay still.

"Oh, no you don't!" cried Mac, running to them. He swung his claws at the leopard man, clocking him a good one and knocking him out.

Grimacing, Charlie pried Prowl's claws out of her shoulders, spun him around, and grabbed him by the suit at the back of his neck. He dangled in the air. She spotted Morph getting back up.

With all her strength Charlie flung Prowl across the room at her.

"Bull's-eye," said Mac.

The lab was suddenly and eerily silent. All the soldiers were out cold or writhing on the floor. Dr. Gray had disappeared. Charlie, Mac, and Maria looked around, a bit dazed, then dashed over to the scientists.

"Come on," Charlie urged them, "Let's get you out of here." Charlie helped her father to his feet. "Can you run?"

"I think so."

"I can carry you, but I might have to drop you if somebody comes at me."

"Let's try it this way first." He glanced at the workstations. Materials were flung everywhere. Charles started picking up a few pieces.

"Dad, we don't have time!" said Charlie. She wanted to grab stuff too, but they'd barely gotten through this. "We need to get you to safety before they wake up!"

Meanwhile Maria had helped Dr. Sharma to her feet. Mac clicked his device, made the scales disappear, and took Dr. Goldstein's arm. "Stick close by me," said Mac, "but not too close, in case the scales come out. They're sharp."

Dr. Goldstein half-smiled as they limped along. "Got it," he said.

Charlie and her dad followed them out with a few small

components. "At least some of it was destroyed," he said, lunging for another piece that caught his eye as they hurried out. "Are you okay?"

"I'm fine, Dad," said Charlie. "The healing power works really well."

When they heard some soldiers stirring, they turned sharply. Morph and Fang had regained consciousness and were coming after them. Charlie sighed. "Overeager newbies," she muttered. Behind them came Zed. Charlie let go of her father. "Stand back," she said, preparing to fight. "Mac, take the snake-wolf dude! Maria, go after Morph! I'll get the cat woman."

Mac ran at the snake-wolf man. The soldier struck out with his fangs, but Mac slammed one of his claw hands into Fang's mouth, breaking one of the fangs off. The man hissed and howled, curling into a heap onto the floor.

Maria ran up the wall in an arc and pushed off at Morph, soaring straight into her and sending them both flying into the opposite wall. They dropped to the floor. Maria lay still for a moment, groaning in pain, then she crawled away and staggered to her feet.

Charlie stepped toward Zed.

"No, Charlie," called her father. "Wait."

"Dad, I know what I'm doing. You have to trust me."

"I do." He lowered his voice. "But leave Zed alone. I'll explain later."

Zed stopped her approach and regarded Charlie. She lifted her chin slightly, then cased the hallway to see if anyone was watching. The two new soldiers were out cold. "Go," Zed whispered. "All of you. Get out while you can. Gray's coming back."

Charlie's eyes widened. She glanced at her father, who nodded. Charlie regarded Zed for another second, then said to the others, "Let's go."

The six of them shuffled and clunked into the hallway, stumbling into the elevator. "Quickly!" Charlie commanded. Maria punched the button, and they descended. Once on the ground floor, Mac led the way outside, everyone helping each other.

The strange-looking crew hobbled to the back entrance of their building, Charlie helping her father, and Mac and Maria helping the other two battered biologists.

Since the elevator was still out of service, they climbed the stairs slowly, waiting for Jack to keep up. When they reached the sixth floor, they hurried toward their office. A tearful Andy was waiting for them inside, with the door to the surveillance area open. "You have to go back!" he cried. "Mom's still in there!"

"What?" said Charlie, rushing to him. "What are you talking about?"

"Didn't you see her? Dr. Gray came into the lab with a huge box and gathered up all the rest of the supplies. She went to find you and stop him from escaping with everything!"

Maria gasped. "Have you been watching the cardinal cam? Did he get away?"

"I don't think so—he went into the elevator but only went down one floor. I texted Mom and you, Charlie—she replied that she was going to meet you on the eighth floor."

"Oh no!" Charlie pulled her phone out of her pocket and saw the notifications on the screen. In the craziness of the rescue she hadn't noticed them coming in. "Why didn't you call?"

"I didn't know if you'd be able to talk—what if you were hiding or sneaking up on somebody? I figured texting was quieter and faster to get you the information."

Charlie squeezed Andy's shoulder. "Smart boy. You did the right thing." She looked at her friends. "We've got to go back to get her before the soldiers all regain consciousness or my mom's in big trouble."

"Let's go," said Mac.

"Text me if you see Mom!" said Charlie. "And take care of Dad and the scientists!" The three friends set off once more.

This time nobody tried to stop them.

CHAPTER 38

Casualties

Charlie, Maria, and Mac peered down the dimly lit hallway on the eighth floor, where Andy had last seen Dr. Gray exit the elevator. They could make out the silhouettes of Prowl and Miko moving swiftly toward the stairwell, leaving the area clear. But they could hear voices coming from halfway down the hall, where a large round, out-swinging door stood open.

"That must be the bank vault!" whispered Mac, pointing at it.

"Those voices sound like Zed and Dr. Gray," Charlie whispered. She checked her phone, but there were no texts from Andy. That meant Mom was still around here somewhere. Charlie texted her, "We're on the eighth floor looking for you."

Her mother didn't respond. The conversation in the vault grew louder. Heated.

The three waited a moment longer, then crept toward the voices.

When they neared the open vault, Charlie could make out a few phrases.

". . . let them come to us," said Dr. Gray.

"They're *children*," said Zed.

"Dangerous children," said Dr. Gray. "We need them out of the way."

Charlie, Mac, and Maria looked at one another, wide-eyed. He was talking about them!

Just then they heard a scuffling noise. Charlie and the others peeked inside the vault, and they saw Charlie's mother at Zed's feet. She was gagged and tied up, struggling to get loose. Charlie had to stop herself from crying out.

At Dr. Gray's feet was a box of components—all the stuff he'd grabbed from the lab that Charlie and her father had failed to pick up. He held her mom's cell phone and sneered as he typed something. Charlie and the others scooted back from the door, and Charlie put her hand over her phone in her jeans pocket, anticipating a response and wanting to muffle the vibration. She looked at her friends. "What should we do?"

Mac frowned. "I don't know. It feels like a trick. Is he texting you back from your mom's phone? Is he trying to get us to go in there so he can trap us?"

Maria nodded. "I don't think it's a good idea."

"But he has my mother!" Charlie whispered. She felt her phone vibrate and pulled it out to read the text. "I'm here! In the vault! Help!"

"Ugh. He's such a creep," Maria said.

Mac and Charlie nodded. They snuck back to the vault entrance, trying to figure out what to do. "It's just the two of them," Charlie reasoned. "The three of us can totally take them down and be out of here with my mom in a few minutes, tops."

"I don't know," Mac said again. He looked nervously over his shoulder. "This doesn't feel right."

"Well, I can't just stand here," said Charlie. "I have to do something! Are you guys with me or not?"

Maria and Mac exchanged worried glances. "Of course we are," said Maria in a low voice. Mac agreed.

Charlie's eyes shone. "Thanks. I really mean it." She took a breath, then said, "Mac, on my signal go after Zed. Maria and I will take down Gray and then come assist you." Just as Charlie was about to cue the others to attack, a strange figure seemed to step out from the shadows of the safe door in front of them. Charlie wasn't sure what she was seeing at first, but then the person changed color, grabbed her by the shirt, and yanked her up in the air. It was Morph, the pincer-hand woman.

"What the—" Charlie said, flailing, trying to make sense of what was happening. She twisted and saw that Maria had also been picked up by Morph, and Mac was being held by the snake-wolf soldier.

"Hey!" shouted Mac, striking out with his claws, trying to connect with the guy. Charlie's fist shot out, but Morph dodged it. Maria slapped her tail at the pincer woman and pummeled her. It didn't faze her. They marched into the vault.

"Look who we found," said Morph.

Zed narrowed her eyes and said nothing. Dr. Gray smiled. "That didn't take long. Set them down and guard the door, please."

When Charlie's feet hit the floor she ran toward her mother.

"Stand BACK!" roared Dr. Gray.

Charlie skidded to a stop and stared at the man. But she wasn't about to start obeying his demands. She continued forward. "Let's get them!" she yelled to her friends.

She caught Maria and Mac off-guard, but after a second Mac ran at Zed, who sidestepped and skittered past him. Maria and Charlie dived at Dr. Gray.

"Morph, come and help me!" Dr. Gray called out. "Fang, take the tin can over there!" The woman ran to help him.

Fang hissed and struck at Mac, his remaining good fang breaking as he tried to sink it into Mac's armor. Mac swung his claws around, striking the man in the face and knocking him down. The soldier growled deeply and attacked Mac, futilely biting at his arms and legs and pawing at his suit as if trying to rip him apart. Mac flipped on his back and rolled up. His pangolin scales pivoted outward a bit more in defense and gleamed, razor sharp. The soldier hissed and bit down again but soon backed off, the scales proving to be too sharp. Mac rolled and got to his feet, then sent his claw hands beating against the soldier. Fang turned and ran out of the vault.

Charlie barely got in a sharp uppercut to Dr. Gray's jaw before Morph threw a jab with her pincer hand. She hit so hard that the punch knocked Charlie through the air. She hit the wall and slid to the floor, the breath knocked out of her. She saw stars.

Maria, exhausted and injured from the earlier fight, was no match for Morph—she ended up on the floor next to Charlie. Mac ran at her and Zed, but the two managed to tie Mac up without getting cut by his scales. They tied the girls up, too, using steel cables for Charlie. Clearly Dr. Gray had been anticipating this.

Dr. Gray staggered to his feet and grabbed the box of components. "Okay, team," he said. "That should have given Prowl and Miko enough time." But he looked disappointed and angry at his new soldiers. "Next time protect me better. Remember, you're nothing without me."

Morph and Fang cowered, while Zed just looked away and walked out of the vault. Dr. Gray rubbed his jaw gingerly and waved the other soldiers to get out, too. Charlie struggled against the cables, trying to get a good grip so she could break out of them. "Enough time for what?"

"Enough time for them to pay a little visit to your hideout across the street," Gray said with a satisfied smile.

Charlie felt the blood drain from her face. "Oh no," she whispered. Was her dad okay? What about Andy and the others?

Dr. Gray held up his box, almost as if he was taunting her. "And now, thanks to your father and his friends, and my loyal subjects, of course, I think I've got everything I need to begin the next step of my journey. Good-bye forever." He went out in the hallway and started to swing shut the vault door.

"Wait," said Mac, panic rising in his voice. "Where are you going?"

Charlie paled. He was going to lock them in the vault! And leave them . . . forever? To die in here? "Stop!" she cried.

"What's the next step?" Maria hollered out to him. Charlie looked sidelong at her and realized she was desperately trying to cut her ropes using Mac's scales and stall Gray from closing them in.

"Yes," said Charlie as she saw Dr. Gray hesitate. "What's the plan? Come on, you can't just leave us here wondering forever." Charlie gave up trying to get a handhold on the cables and instead took a deep breath and pressed outward with her shoulders, feeling the steel bite into her skin. Then a thin strand of the cable broke—she detected it springing against her back. She kept pressing, breaking one strand at a time.

Dr. Gray hovered in the doorway and looked down his nose at Maria and Charlie as if they were simple children. "Once I figure out the perfect combination of traits, I'll help all my soldiers become chimeras. And then? I'll go into mass production."

"*What?*" said Charlie.

"Did you really think I would stop with them? No, I want to give this gift to the whole world."

Had they heard right? Mac and Maria looked horrified, and Mrs. Wilde stared silent and wide-eyed.

"It'll be miraculous. Sorry you'll miss it." He laughed and continued pulling the heavy door, peering at them one last time before he closed it. "Enjoy your stay—you're going to be here for a while. Even someone as strong as Charlie won't be able to open *this* door."

Managing to break free, Maria, Charlie, and Mac all scrambled to stop the door from closing on them. But it clanged shut just before they slammed into it. Charlie even left a dent, but the door didn't open. They were stuck inside the vault.

"Ugh!" screamed Charlie. Maria made fists and pounded at the door, and Mac backed up and ran at it again, while Charlie ran back to her mother and pulled out the gag. "Are you okay?" she asked, untying her.

Mrs. Wilde nodded. "I'm fine. Did you get Dad and the others out?"

"Yeah, but they're across the street!"

"Give me your phone," said Charlie's mom. "I'll text Andy to check if they're okay. You see what you can do with that door so we can get out of here."

Charlie handed her phone to her mom, then eyed the massive door. "It's so huge," she murmured. Would an elephant be able to open a locked vault? She sure hoped so.

"Mac," said Maria, "get in here with your claws, will you? See if you can rip out any of this metal."

Mac dug his claws into the doorframe and started bending it, slowly peeling back the sheet of metal that covered the lock.

"That's it, Mac!" said Maria. "Keep going!"

Mac pulled harder, ripping the material away and tossing it aside, revealing the dead bolt. Then he hooked his claws and strained at the dead-bolt lock, trying to bend it so he could wriggle it out of its socket. "Charlie, pull me!" he said, and quickly made his scales flatten so she wouldn't get hurt. "If we can bend this a little more, I bet you'll be able to break open the door."

Charlie grabbed Mac around the waist. On his go she pulled him backward. The metal around the door groaned and bent, and then Mac's claws shredded through it. He and Charlie went flying backward, skidding along the vault floor. Mac rolled off Charlie and helped her up.

"You're doing it!" said Maria, peering at the metal. "I can see the long stick of metal starting to bend in there. Can you get your claws inside, Mac?"

While Mac dug in once more, trying to break metal with his pangolin claws, Maria encouraged him, and Charlie focused on the door and tried to channel her inner elephant, telling herself she could do this. Finally Mac managed to bend the inner workings of the huge lock mechanism, at least a little bit. Enough to weaken it. Or at least they hoped so.

Mac backed away from the door, breathing hard from exertion. "Your turn," he said to Charlie.

Charlie nodded. She backed up as far as she could and stared at the vault door, visualizing it collapsing under her strength. Then she ran toward it at top speed and slammed into it, causing a tremendous noise.

The force knocked Charlie out cold. She crumpled to the floor.

But the safe door bent and groaned, and with an extra push from Maria and Mac, it opened.

CHAPTER 39

A Wrench in the Plan

By the time Charlie regained consciousness, she was halfway to the back entrance of home base, being carried by her mom and her friends.

"Whoa," she said, squinting in the sunlight. Her head and shoulder hurt. "Looks like that worked?"

"You're a brute," said Maria admiringly. "You dented the vault door enough to break it open."

"Your starfish is working," said Mac, "so hopefully you'll be feeling okay soon."

"Here's hoping the starfish does magic on concussions," Mrs. Wilde said grimly, eyeing the sixth-floor windows of their building. "We may have another fight on our hands if Prowl and Miko are still up there."

Charlie felt her bruises gingerly. "I'm okay to walk," she said.

They set her down in the alleyway as they hurried around the corner of their building.

As they reached the door, Mrs. Wilde paused and narrowed her eyes, looking across the parking lot. She pointed at someone running fast toward them. "Who's that?" she said, alarmed.

Maria turned sharply. "What the—" Then she slapped a hand to her forehead. "It's Kelly."

"Kelly?" said Charlie, fearing her injury might have affected her hearing.

"How the heck would she know where to find us?" asked Mac.

Maria looked guiltily at the others. "I—I told her last week. Before she went to Cabo and started doing stupid things."

"Oh," said Charlie. She wasn't happy.

"Maybe she can help us," said Mrs. Wilde. "We could use it."

Maria flagged Kelly down and they all quickly went inside the building.

Kelly's clothes were torn, her hair was in tangles, and she had dirt and blood on her face. Tear tracks divided the dust on her cheeks, and she looked exhausted. Even her backpack appeared like it had been dragged through the mud. "Hi," she said miserably between breaths. She bent forward, putting her hands on her knees to steady herself.

"Are you okay?" asked Maria. "What happened to you? How did you get back from Los Angeles?"

"Bus," she said, still breathing hard. "Somebody on it recognized me and alerted the media, who were all there at the bus station waiting when we arrived. Then I ran into those two beefy goons from the warehouse with one other guy. I barely got away from them. I had to hide in an empty trash container until they left, and then I remembered where you were."

Mac's eyes almost bugged out at that last confession, but he didn't say the obvious comment that had come to everyone's mind: Kelly hid in a trash can? She must have been desperate.

"I'm afraid this isn't a safe place anymore for any of us," said Mrs. Wilde, hurrying everybody up the stairs.

"Thanks to Kelly," Charlie muttered.

Kelly looked at her, shocked at first. Then she narrowed her eyes. "Oh, I get it. You're mad I took credit for your burning house rescue. Well, a lot of good that did me."

Anger boiled up in Charlie. "You put my dad and all of us in a lot of danger!"

Mrs. Wilde gave Charlie a warning glance. "We can talk about that later. Kelly, we'll protect you if we can. But right now we need to hustle upstairs."

Charlie pretended she didn't see it. She wasn't feeling generous at all after all the stress Kelly had put them through, and Kelly's selfish attitude wasn't helping. "You'll help us fight if we need to," she demanded. "And we need that envelope back. Right now."

"Fine," said Kelly. "Sheesh." Her weariness showed on her face, and her chin began to tremble. She shrugged her backpack off her shoulder and pulled out the Talos Global envelope. She ignored Charlie's outstretched hand and gave it to Mrs. Wilde. "I don't need your stupid papers anymore, anyway." Kelly swallowed hard and glared at the stairs.

Apparently Maria couldn't hold in her feelings about Kelly either. "And you need to stop lying. Why did you do that to me? To us? That wasn't cool."

Kelly's face cracked. "So you're turning on me now, too, Maria? After all I've done to help you?" Her face turned red and she tried to say something more, but only an ugly sob came out.

"Nobody's turning on you!" Maria said. "But we're mad. You did some pretty crappy things." Mac didn't say anything, but he nodded in solidarity with Maria and Charlie.

"Kids, please," said Mrs. Wilde, sounding exasperated.

"But they're being awful to me!" said Kelly.

"Oh. My. God," said Charlie bitterly.

"Stop." Mrs. Wilde held up her hand, shutting them down. "We're all hurting about this, but the fight's not over! Right now we need to focus. Let's go." She reached the top of the stairs and started jogging to home base.

"Sorry, Mom," Charlie muttered. She ran to take the lead, checking her bracelet as she went. Everything was still activated. She waited at the door while the others caught up and pressed her ear to it, wondering if she could hear anything.

It was silent inside. Maria and Mac joined her at the door. They waited an extra beat while Mac reactivated his scales, then Charlie placed her hand on the doorknob. Slowly she turned it, and Maria peeked in.

"*Ay, dios mio,*" she said under her breath.

In the reception area stood Miko and Prowl. "Welcome home," Prowl purred. "We've been expecting you." Between them they held Andy, who was gagged and tied up.

CHAPTER 40

Hanging by a Thread

Charlie pushed into the room, ready to fight. She stopped when she saw the soldiers with Andy. Anger boiled over. "Leave him alone!"

The rest of the group followed. Mrs. Wilde saw her son and gasped. Andy struggled and twisted, but he was bound too tightly to move much. Tears dripped down his cheeks and soaked into his gag. He gave Charlie and his mother a pleading look. They charged toward them. "What do you want with him?" Mrs. Wilde cried. "Where's Charles?"

"Charles and the others are a little tied up right now," purred Prowl, and Miko laughed. "When we saw you coming on your fancy cameras, we decided Andy needed to stick with us for a while. We won't hurt him if you let us go quietly. We might even release him eventually."

Charlie couldn't breathe. *Eventually?* They were taking Andy hostage. Mrs. Wilde pushed past her. "Just leave him and get out of here! We won't stop you. We promise."

Miko sneered. "Nice try, but we can see we're outnumbered." Then she noticed Kelly hanging behind the others. "Oooh, look,

Prowl! It's the famous one. Cyke said you gave them the slip at the bus station before he could tell you all the things Dr. Gray has to offer you. How nice of the Wildes to deliver you straight to us." She glanced at Prowl, then took a step forward. "How about we make a trade, hmm? If she comes with us, we'll give you the boy back."

Charlie's mouth opened in shock, but she couldn't speak. Kelly looked up sharply. "Why would I want to do that?"

"Dr. Gray thinks you'd be a great addition to our team," said Prowl. He watched her carefully. "He thinks you could play an important role in his plan to change the world."

"Dr. Gray is insane," said Mac under his breath. "Don't trust them, Kelly."

"We'll be keeping them both, thank you," Mrs. Wilde said coolly, but her face was deathly pale. Her fingers trembled.

"Oh, I don't think so," said Miko. "You could be the hero for your friends right now if you come with us."

Charlie could see Kelly's face change. "No, Kelly."

She snarled at Charlie and looked away.

Prowl saw the exchange. "Having a little fight with your friends? I hope they're treating you like a celebrity." He glanced at Miko, then back at Kelly, and said confidentially, "Dr. Gray saw you on the show and he's a big fan."

"They're both staying with us," said Mrs. Wilde sharply. She took a step toward Andy. "Either get out now or we'll take you out."

"Oooh," said Prowl, a small smile playing at his lips. "Pretty confident for someone who doesn't have any enhancements."

"You're asking for trouble," Mac warned.

"Let Andy go," Charlie said forcefully. She made fists and put them in the air.

Kelly frowned and glanced at Miko. After a moment she took a defensive stance too.

Prowl sighed and examined his claws. "Do we really need to do this again?" Then he nodded at Miko, and without further warning, he shoved Andy to the corner behind them while Miko hopped onto the counter and jumped on Mac. Prowl sprang at Mrs. Wilde, knocking her into the wall, the Talos Global envelope ripping apart and contents scattering. She slumped to the floor, dazed. Charlie ran at Prowl, fists flying. He dodged her and leaped at Kelly, knocking her down.

"Get off me!" screamed Kelly, flailing. "I thought you wanted me on your side!"

Prowl eyed her suspiciously, then let up and went after Mac, slamming him into the wall. Charlie whirled around and Miko lunged for her.

Maria bounded up and over the counter and grabbed Andy. She dragged him to the double doors and pushed on them, but they were locked as usual. "Dang it!" she muttered. "Who has keys?"

Nobody had the wherewithal to respond. Mrs. Wilde was still down. Mac swatted at Prowl with his claws, but the leopard man was nimble and managed to keep Mac and Kelly in one corner. Charlie's fist connected with Miko, sending her into the wall, but the soldier rebounded off it and hit Charlie, knocking her into Mac. "Yowch!" she said, rolling away from him.

"Sorry!" said Mac, diving at Miko. But the deft chimp woman skittered miraculously midair and leapfrogged off of Mac's helmet, barely getting scratched by his blades. Mac swung his arm around and caught her in the leg with his claws as she pushed off. She squealed and dropped to the ground, clutching it.

Charlie noticed Prowl ready to attack Mac and slammed into him from behind. He landed hard on Kelly, knocking her flat. She screamed and flailed, swinging her arms and kicking her feet. Charlie went after Miko, while Maria gave up on finding a key to the door. She jumped up on the counter and grabbed the fluorescent light fixture on the ceiling in order for her to get some momentum. But the plastic cover ripped off, sending it to the floor on top of her. She lay still, the wind knocked out of her.

Mrs. Wilde regained her senses. She rubbed her head and blinked a few times, then crawled over to Andy to protect him and stay out of the way. She fumbled through her pockets, searching for her key.

Prowl rolled off Kelly, who was furious. Mac slammed his claws into Prowl. The soldier hissed in pain, then charged at Mac and smashed him into the wall again, clearly frustrated that he couldn't seem to hurt the silver-suited predator.

Charlie leaped to the wall and stuck there, then chased Miko around the perimeter of the room.

Kelly jumped to her feet, angry, and charged at Prowl. Prowl whirled around and faced her, claws fully extended this time. He crouched, waiting to pounce.

"Prowl, no!" shouted Miko. "Dr. Gray said not to hurt her!" She turned suddenly and leaped at Charlie. The two went crashing to the floor and started rolling around in a tussle, knocking Mac down too.

"But she's coming at me!" Prowl argued. Still he retreated, bounding away, and caught sight of Andy and Mrs. Wilde at the door to the surveillance area. Mrs. Wilde was fumbling at the lock with her key. "Oh, no you don't!" Prowl shouted, running over to knock the key away as Kelly pursued him. The key flew across the room, and Miko snagged it from the air. She slid it into her suit. Charlie slugged her, and the woman went crashing into Mrs. Wilde, knocking her away from Andy. Prowl pounced, picked up Andy, and whirled around to face Kelly, holding the boy hostage once more.

Kelly stalked him, eyes on fire.

Prowl hissed, warning her.

Miko rolled and grabbed Charlie, picked her up, and flung her into Mac. Maria was still down. Mrs. Wilde was down, too. Then

Miko saw what was going on with Prowl, Andy, and Kelly. The chimp hopped onto the counter, moving from side to side fearfully, unsure what to do.

Kelly—clearly exhausted, enraged, hurt inside and out—charged like an injured animal, uttering a primal scream. She clicked her device and kicked out wildly at the soldier, but she missed.

"Kelly, stop! Be careful!" cried Maria, sitting up and rubbing her head.

"Andy, watch out!" screamed Charlie, seeing the poisonous spikes.

Kelly, possessed by her desire to obliterate one of the many people who'd hurt her over the recent days, didn't comprehend either of them. She pursued Prowl like nobody else was there. Charlie sprang up and ran toward them, trying to knock Kelly down, trying to keep her away from Andy, but that only made things worse. Kelly spun around from the impact, righted herself, and slammed her foot blindly backward, connecting.

Everyone cringed. They waited for the leopard man's scream of pain.

It came, loud and piercing. He fell to the ground, letting go of Andy.

But then Andy fell, too. He made a small muffled cry before his eyes rolled back in his head and he passed out.

Charlie stared at him as she realized what had just happened.

"No! You hit Andy too!" She dived to the ground at his side while her mother struggled to get to them.

"Andy!" Charlie sobbed, touching his cheek. "Wake up, Andy!" But her brother was limp and lifeless. She cried his name again, tears pouring down her face. Maria helped Charlie's mother up so she could go to him. Miko pulled Prowl away from them all, toward the door. Mrs. Wilde took Andy and cradled him, checking him over.

Charlie got up and turned angrily. "Kelly!" she screamed. "Look what you did! What's wrong with you? I *hate* you!"

Kelly stood frozen, the predatory look on her face draining away. She glanced at Miko and took a step toward the door.

Miko left Prowl, screaming and paralyzed, and reached out to Kelly. "Are you okay?"

Kelly jumped at the touch and took a step back. "I didn't mean to hurt Andy," she said, her voice wavering. "I just . . . I get so angry. And I keep hurting . . . people. . . ."

Maria turned sharply to Kelly and said quietly, "We know you didn't mean it. It's going to be okay. If you take the device off, all of this will stop. It'll all go back to normal."

"Give it to her!" Charlie said, her voice ragged. "You're dangerous!"

Kelly's eyes widened. She looked at the device. Then she shook her head. "I can't give it back." She blinked, then said, "I can't go

361

back to being normal again."

"What are you talking about?" said Maria.

Miko turned to Kelly. "We get it," she said. "You're special now, like us. You're better than other people."

Kelly's bloodshot eyes narrowed, filled with confusion. She turned to Charlie accusingly. "Why should you get to keep your bracelets and not me?"

"Kelly!" Charlie said, her voice thick and gravelly with tears. "Please."

"You want to be more powerful than me," Kelly said. She began shaking. "You turned on me—even you, Maria. And now you all want me to go back to normal while you stay special?"

Maria and Mac exchanged a horrified glance. "Kelly," began Maria. She stepped toward the girl but didn't get too close. Kelly's spurs were still activated, and no one dared get too near her—they didn't know if she'd go primal again.

Kelly backed away. She reached to cradle the device on her wrist, then looked at Miko again, who was moving toward Prowl and the door.

Miko caught her glance. "We can protect you, too, you know," said Miko softly. "We don't hate you, Kelly." She paused, then added, "We're your fans. All of us watched you on *LIVE, TONIGHT*. You were amazing. That's why Dr. Gray sent the soldiers out to find you. He wants you for our team."

Kelly glanced at her. "Really? But . . . what about Prowl?

He's not going to like me much now."

"Prowl will be fine. He knows you didn't intend to hurt anybody."

"Don't listen to her," Maria warned. "We don't hate you. Charlie didn't mean it."

Charlie flashed a burning look at Maria, but she was wise enough to stay quiet. She looked miserably at her limp, silent brother as her mother worked on him, and the rage at Kelly churned inside her again. "Just . . . do something!" Charlie cried. "Go, if you're going to go. I don't care! We have to get help for Andy."

"But we want you to stay," said Maria firmly. She put her hand on Charlie's shoulder.

Kelly faltered, and a pained expression came over her face. "No you don't," she said quietly. "I know pretty well by now when I'm not wanted."

"Let's go," said Miko softly. She moved toward the door. Without taking her eyes off the others, she carefully picked up one of Prowl's arms and dragged him over the tile. "Help me with Prowl, will you? Then maybe we can see about creating a slick bodysuit that'll work with your camo. One of the other soldiers has one already. It's very cool."

Kelly looked at her.

"Kelly," said Maria, her voice filled with worry. "Come on. They're the bad guys! They could hurt you!"

Kelly looked at Maria, then at Charlie, then Andy. She winced and turned away. "Maybe I'm not good either," she said. "And I'm already hurt—you just can't see it. So. I've got nothing to lose. But at least I don't have to sit here and watch Charlie glare at me like that for who knows how long." She hesitated in the silence, then bent and grabbed Prowl's other arm. Together she and Miko pulled the leopard man out into the hallway.

Maria ran after them to the door, but Mac stopped her. "No, Maria. We're done. Enough for now."

Mrs. Wilde got up quickly, lifting Andy in her arms. "Charlie, do you still have the key I gave you? Get this door open and grab me a blanket! He's in shock and he's not breathing well. I think . . ." She gulped down a sob. "I'm worried we're going to lose him."

CHAPTER 41

From Generation to Regeneration

Charlie found her key and unlocked the door. She ran for blankets as Mrs. Wilde carried Andy inside. Mac and Maria followed and hurried to free the scientists, finding Ms. Sabbith tied up with the others. They filled in the kids on what had happened while they set them free.

While Maria fielded questions, Mac went for his iPad. He started typing madly.

Mr. Wilde limped over to see Andy and assist his wife. "Should I call an ambulance?" he asked.

Mrs. Wilde looked flustered in her professional role for the first time. "There's not enough time. If I can get him stabilized . . ." She turned and shouted, "Mac! Look up antidotes for platypus venom!"

"Already on it!" said Mac, typing frantically. After a moment he looked up. "There's no known antidote!" he shouted back.

"That's what I was afraid of." She shook her head and blew out a breath. "He's just so small for such powerful poison. We sat there wasting time. . . ."

Charlie paced nearby. She looked at her bracelet. If only

she could give Andy her healing power! But even if she could, it wouldn't work on him. . . . She froze, mid-thought. Then she turned to her father. "Dad, what's the ID Number for the Mark Five? To deactivate Defense Mode? It's stuck on my arm."

"I . . . I don't remember off the top of my head—it's been years. I'd need my computer, but Dr. Gray has it."

"Mom, where's that Talos Global envelope?"

"I dropped it in the reception area."

Charlie ran out and gathered up the papers. She returned with the mess, spreading it out on a table. "Everyone! Help!"

"What are we looking for?" asked Maria, running to her side.

"The ID Number to take this thing off so I can put it on Andy. I know it was in here—I saw it before Kelly took everything."

"That's brilliant, Charlie," said Mr. Wilde. "Andy has my DNA too."

Mac joined them and Drs. Goldstein and Sharma and Ms. Sabbith came over to help. They picked up several pages at a time, everybody looking quickly and carefully through them. They were all out of order and many had wrinkles and stains.

They searched frantically for several minutes until finally Maria stopped and lifted a page. She stared intently at it. "I've got it!" she cried.

Charlie dropped her papers and started clicking rapidly on her bracelet's buttons, fingers fumbling and going to the wrong screen. "Mac, my fingers won't work," she said, desperate. She held out her arm in front of him.

Mac leaned over it. After all his time trying to figure out the Mark Five's ID Number, he knew Charlie's device almost better than she did.

"Okay, go," said Mac. He held his fingers poised.

Maria read off the eight-digit code. Mac entered it.

"Hang on, Mom!" shouted Charlie. "I'm coming!"

After Mac entered the last digit he pushed the OK button. They all stared, waiting to see what would happen. DEFENSE MODE DEACTIVATED flashed three times before going to the home screen.

"Yes!" The clasp came apart easily. Charlie ran over to her parents and squeezed in between them. Then she put the device on Andy's wrist, fastened it, and slid it up his arm until it was tight against his skin. "Please work. Please work," she breathed. The device went through a series of screens, as if recognizing a new wearer, then an attempt to match DNA.

"Hurry," Charlie begged.

After a moment the screen read: MATCH SUCCESSFUL. DEVICE RESET. POWERS READY TO ACTIVATE. It went back to the animal screen, and Charlie saw that the starfish was lit up, animated, and turning pink, pulsing with life.

"It's working!" said Charlie.

"It's working," echoed Mr. Wilde, as if he couldn't believe after all these years that he'd see his invention save his own child.

Charlie hugged his shoulders, then lifted her shirtsleeves and showed him where Prowl had dug into her earlier that day. Only a few lines remained—traces of scars. "See how fast it works? Plus, I got bit by that snake soldier today, too. I'm almost totally fine now." She looked at her mother. "How is he? Any better yet?"

"His blood pressure is coming back up," Mrs. Wilde said. "His breathing is good." She broke down, covered her face with her hand, and sobbed for a moment, then tried to pull it together.

Within minutes Andy's eyelids fluttered. He grimaced and groaned. "My leg hurts so bad."

"I know, honey," said Mrs. Wilde. "It'll feel better soon. Charlie gave you her bracelet so you can heal superfast."

"She did?" Andy blinked a couple times, then lifted his arm weakly to look at it. "Cool," he said with a smile. Then he closed his eyes and slept.

CHAPTER 42

Cleaning Up

"Hey," said Charlie, coming over to the surveillance area where Ms. Sabbith and Mac sat looking over the footage. "Prowl didn't steal the laptop? That's surprising."

"They left the equipment alone because they were using our cameras to keep track of all of you," said Ms. Sabbith. "When they noticed you coming back faster than they expected—"

"Because we busted out of a freaking bank vault," Mac said proudly.

"Right," said Ms. Sabbith with a sly grin. "Anyway, they panicked and grabbed Andy as a hostage so they could make it out of here. I think our hearts all stopped beating at that point. Certainly your dad's did. He was a mess."

Charlie imagined it and nodded gravely. "But what about Dr. Gray?"

"He's gone. Took his equipment and got away in the van. He didn't even wait for Miko and Prowl to come back with Kelly. Looks like Cyke returned for them later."

"Maybe he'll leave us alone for a while, then," said Maria, joining them. She looked at Ms. Sabbith. "I don't suppose you have the stuff . . . ," she began, and trailed off with a cringe.

Ms. Sabbith smiled. "I've got everything we need. And now we have the scientists to start working on it."

Maria looked up. "Do you really think they can fix me?"

"Positive. We'll get you back to normal if it's the last thing I do."

Maria cracked a smile. "Thanks. That means a lot." She looked at Mac and Charlie, and then a look of alarm came over her face as if she remembered something important. "Did you tell everyone what Dr. Gray said in the vault?"

"What did he say?" asked Ms. Sabbith. She glanced at Dr. Sharma, who looked up from her desk nearby.

With all the excitement of breaking out of the vault and fighting the soldiers over Kelly and Andy's near-death experience, Charlie had forgotten Dr. Gray's chilling plan. Her stomach twisted. "He told us he has everything he needs to take the next step in his plan," she said. "Once he figures out the perfect chimera combination for his soldiers he's going to turn *everyone* into chimeras."

Dr. Sharma stood up, alarmed. "Everyone?"

"That's what he said. The whole world."

The biologist stared at Charlie, shaking her head slightly as though she couldn't believe it. "This is extremely alarming. Jack, Charles, are you hearing this?"

They came over. Dr. Sharma filled them in.

"He said something about mass production, too," added Maria.

"This is devastating," said Mr. Wilde, sinking into a chair.

"We can't let him succeed," said Dr. Goldstein gravely. "It'll be the end of humanity."

"We have to stop him," said Dr. Sharma. "Civilization depends on it."

Charlie felt the weight of the matter like a brick in the pit of her stomach. The scientists weren't joking around—they were truly scared about what Dr. Gray was capable of. She looked at her friends. Did this mean what she thought it meant? That this nightmare wasn't over?

"Are we going to be okay?" asked Mac, his face awash in fear.

Dr. Sharma looked at him, and her face softened. "Of course we are," she assured him. "He has a lot of work ahead of him before he can succeed with this, and we're going to stop him before anything happens. I don't want you kids to be afraid." As the three scientists talked about their options, Charlie and her friends sat quietly, listening. When there was a lull, Charlie touched her dad's sleeve. "Where do you think Dr. Gray went?"

"I don't know, but we're going to find him."

"I gave Ms. Sabbith the license plate number of the van the other day," said Charlie. "Do you think that will help?"

"I'm already working on that," Ms. Sabbith called out, not looking up.

Dr. Wilde looked surprised. "Great job getting it, Charlie. That was smart." He paused, deep in thought, then went on. "You really shocked Gray and the soldiers with how powerful you are. But now they're going to regroup and grow stronger with the information they have and the new technology we created for them. And I'm sure he expects us to try to stop him."

"He has Kelly now, too," Dr. Goldstein pointed out. "She knows things about all of you. I imagine Victor will try to pull information from her to see if he can figure out your vulnerabilities. He's gone mad, but he's not stupid."

"Kelly knows plenty about us," Charlie said.

"And she has the Mark Four," Mac reminded them all. "So Dr. Gray has access to that bracelet if he needs it for the technology or to test her abilities to help decide on the perfect chimera combination."

He turned to Dr. Sharma. "That device has three abilities, right, Dr. Sharma?"

Dr. Sharma pulled away from her notes. "Correct."

"Which animals?" asked Mac, sitting up straighter.

"Dolphin—swimming, not echolocation like Charlie has with the bat."

"Well, I *had*," said Charlie, looking at her empty wrist, but the others didn't notice.

Mac nodded. "We knew that one. What else?"

"Platypus."

"Yup," said Mac. "We got that one right. What's the third one? It's not a chameleon, I'm sure of it."

Despite the severity of the situation Dr. Sharma's tired eyes smiled at Mac's enthusiasm for animals. "It's another water creature."

"Ooh," said Maria. "You used all water creatures? That's cool."

Mac was typing furiously, trying to figure out which water creatures had camouflage abilities. He landed on a page, studied it, and looked up. "Cuttlefish?" he said.

Dr. Sharma nodded. "That's right. You should see all the things the cuttlefish can do. It's an intensely amazing animal." She shook her head regretfully. "I wish I'd questioned Kelly a little more thoroughly when she said she'd thrown the Mark Four away. I might have it back now—and she might be safe at home. Things could have gone so differently."

Mac looked up. "I'm sorry Kelly did that. Your device sounds really great."

Dr. Sharma smiled. "Thanks." She loaded what remained of her files into a box. "I had tons of notes on this animal in particular in that Project Chimera folder envelope. You can read them sometime if you're interested."

After a while Charlie's mom appeared. "Andy's doing much better. Where do we go from here? Do we need to leave?"

"This building? I doubt they're coming back here. They have everything they need from us."

"I mean . . ." Mrs. Wilde's eyes flitted to the kids, then back to her husband. "Do we need to go after them? Or hide from them? Do we need to leave . . . Arizona?"

Everyone was silent. Charlie's heart plummeted. The thought had never occurred to her. Surely they wouldn't have to move away.

Mr. Wilde looked at the other biologists. "I don't know," he admitted finally. "We might. It depends on what they do."

"Dad," said Charlie, "you can't be serious." She looked at her friends, who stared back at her in shock. Charlie had grown closer to Mac and Maria than any other friends she'd ever had—even Amari. And that was saying a lot. Plus, they needed them—if Charlie had to move, Maria and Mac had to come too.

"I don't know," Mr. Wilde repeated. "I think we're safe here for now. Dr. Gray is preoccupied with other things at the moment. He's going to have to regroup and reestablish himself somewhere too, and finish experimenting to find the perfect combination for his chimera. He won't quit. And he knows we know a lot about him and his plans."

"There's a lot we have to consider," said Dr. Sharma. "Gray is much closer to his goal. Unfortunately we've done a good deal of the hard work for him. And like we talked about earlier, he has Kelly now, and she's as unpredictable as they come. I have no idea what she's capable of."

"Maybe Kelly won't stay with them," said Maria, troubled. "I bet she'll come to her senses and just go home. I hope so, anyway."

There was a quiet moment where everyone hoped the same.

Dr. Goldstein, who'd been mostly silent, spoke. "Either way, Gray's next move is bound to be huge. We have to prepare for that. And there's one thing I do know. We can't beat them without the kids. So Charlie, you're going to have to get that device back from your brother when he's done with it."

"Yes sir," said Charlie with a small smile.

"Actually," said Mr. Wilde, "I don't think I will give it back to you, Charlie."

Charlie's face fell. "B-b-but Dad," she sputtered. "Why? I mean . . . I know it's your device and all, but it's, like . . . my destiny! I want to fight Dr. Gray! I want to stop him! I was just getting started—and what about my friends? They need me. This isn't fair!"

Mr. Wilde's mouth hinted at a smile. He fished into his pocket and pulled out a half-finished, shiny new device, even slimmer and more streamlined than the Mark Five, with a larger screen and more buttons. He held it out for Charlie and the others to see. "I've got some work to do on the guts of it," he said, "but that shouldn't take long. I give you the new and improved Mark Six." He handed it to Charlie. "Otherwise known as . . . yours."

CHAPTER 43

A Stronger Team

"A Mark Six?" cried Charlie. "For me?" She high-fived Mac and then glanced guiltily at Maria, who was struggling to smile. Little loose beard hairs still stuck to her shirt. Her prognosis was good according to Ms. Sabbith, but Charlie would still feel uneasy until she heard a definite solution from the scientists. Charlie looked earnestly at her father. "Dr. Sharma said you all might be able to do something about Maria's physical changes. Can you?"

Mr. Wilde opened his mouth to answer, but then he closed it, narrowed his eyes, and pointed at the cardinal cam. A soldier was slipping across the street toward their building.

"Miko?" asked Mrs. Wilde, her face worried.

"No, it's Zed," said Charlie, detecting her smooth, catlike gait.

"What does she want?" muttered Dr. Goldstein. "Did they leave her behind? I thought they were all gone by now."

"She's been kind to us," said Dr. Sharma. "Maybe she needs help."

"She was nice to us, too," Maria said. "In the end, anyway."

Dr. Sharma furrowed her brow. "Maybe . . . maybe she stayed behind on purpose."

"He'll hunt her down," murmured Mr. Wilde. "She's one of his most valuable soldiers."

"Do you trust her?" Mrs. Wilde asked them.

"All I know," said Mr. Wilde, "is that she caught me working on the secret device and didn't turn me in. And she's protected us more than once. So I think . . . maybe . . . yes. We should at least see what she wants."

"All right," said Mrs. Wilde. "If she's coming in peace, you can bring her up here. Mac and Maria, go with Charles to protect him, just in case. Charlie, don't forget you're not wearing a device at the moment, okay? Stay clear in case we have a problem, because there are a lot of soldiers who would love to take you out when you're powerless, after what you did to them."

"Yes, Mom," said Charlie, feeling lost without her device now.

Mr. Wilde, Maria, and Mac went down to the entrance of the building, leaving Charlie and the others to wait anxiously for information. Several minutes later they returned with Zed. Mac had his protective suit on, but his claws weren't out. They marched her into the room.

"She wants to talk to all of us," said Mr. Wilde. They gathered around.

"Thank you for seeing me," Zed said. And then slowly she pulled off her goggles and used her fingernail claws to lift the facial portion of her bodysuit. She pulled it off and shook like a cat. On her head was thick, black cat hair, shiny like a panther's. Her ears came to a point and her nose was shaped like a cat's. Unlike Prowl, her deep brown facial skin was free of any sort of fur, but she had a set of long whiskers that twitched. She was beautiful.

The woman looked straight at the biologists. "Do you recognize me?" she asked hesitantly. "It's good to see you again."

Dr. Sharma squinted at the soldier. "Nubia?" she cried. "What on earth?"

Jack stared. "Nubia," he said. "I—I don't know what to say. I didn't realize . . . What has Gray done to you?"

From near the partition Charlie stared. It wasn't too weird to see an animal-person hybrid anymore, especially since Maria had become one, but this was a bit of a shock. Apparently Zed was the missing Dr. Nubia Jakande.

Maria's eye's widened.

"Yes, that's me," said Nubia. "This is where I've been for some time."

"Willingly?" asked Dr. Goldstein, his critical gaze nearly boring a hole in the soldier.

"Yes," said Nubia again. "I believed in Dr. Gray's plan in the beginning. I offered to be his first test subject." She lifted her chin. "But I don't support him anymore."

Mr. Wilde pulled up a chair for their visitor, and she perched on the edge of it, seeming a bit uncomfortable now that everyone was staring at her.

"Why are you here?" Dr. Sharma asked.

"I want to join your side if you'll have me. I understand if you won't."

"Why now?"

"I've wanted to escape for a while. This was the only time I could get away without Victor coming after me. With everyone scattered and the lab in chaos, I took my chance and hid while they were rounding up soldiers. All those eyes watching—there was never an opportunity before now."

"Do you know where Dr. Gray is going?"

"No—not yet, anyway. I might have a way to find out. I can't speak about that yet, though."

Dr. Sharma narrowed her eyes. "How can we trust you?"

"You know me, Quinn. What Dr. Gray told the kids in the vault today—I was around the corner, listening. I didn't know any of that! Changing everyone in the world to chimeras? Against their will? You know I wouldn't want that. I didn't realize what Gray had become. I guess . . . I guess I was too close to see it. When he asked me to join him, I had no idea what his grand goals were. I should have seen it, but I was tempted by the offer—since our original project was shut down before human trials began, I was excited to experience the results of all of our work." She paused and said softer, "Once he changed my DNA, I couldn't go back to my old life. I gave it all up for this."

She hung her head. "Now that I've left him, I can't return. I took the chance, anyway. My life," she said, sweeping a hand over her suited body, "is possibly ruined forever. Will you let me help you stop him? May I join your side?"

The other biologists grilled the cat woman for a long time. She answered everything without hesitation, and finally the doctors conferred.

"We'd like to have you join us," Dr. Wilde said finally. "We could certainly use your help."

"Thank you," said Nubia with a breath of relief. She turned and looked around. "And now I should apologize to the kids." She spied Charlie standing back by the partition.

Charlie stepped forward and joined Maria and Mac, keeping her hands clasped behind her back to hide her bare wrist, just in case this scientist was bluffing and was about to attack. Charlie didn't trust anybody anymore.

"I'm sorry for fighting against you," said Dr. Jakande. "I hated doing that. I will never hurt any of you again. I promise you that."

"I'm sorry for kicking your butt," said Charlie. Mac snorted and Maria nodded.

Nubia laughed softly. "Yes, you did do that. Very competently, I might add." She paused, looking at the kids. "All right. Is all forgiven? Can you work with me?"

Charlie and the others nodded. She found herself smiling and thinking she was going to like the new member of their team. "Just one more thing," she said, glancing at Maria, who'd remained wide-eyed and hopeful since Dr. Jakande's identity had been revealed.

"What is it?"

"Since you made the Mark Two, do you know of a way to reverse the effects and fix my friend, Maria, so she stops turning into a weremonkey? It's wrecking her social life pretty badly."

This time Nubia let out a hearty laugh. "As a matter of fact, I've been secretly working on something similar for myself for months to see if I can undo what Dr. Gray's Mark One did to me." She opened a pouch on her suit and pulled out some components. "With a little help from my colleagues, it won't take long to finish."

Maria grinned. "That's fantastic!"

Dr. Jakande placed a hand gently on Maria's shoulder, her clawed fingernails retracted. "And maybe we can alter your device to make it so you can turn it on and off, like with the Mark Three. That way you can still use it to fight Dr. Gray, because you've become really skilled with it. Sound good?"

Maria's face flooded with relief. "That would be amazing."

CHAPTER 44

A Disappearing Act

Reality returned to Charlie and her friends. They packed up everything that night and went home. Nubia and the other scientists started their search for a new location to set up a lab, and the other kids went to their respective homes, feeling relief for the first time in nearly two weeks. The next day, Sunday, the three hung out in Maria's shed in her backyard and speculated about Kelly.

"She hasn't responded to any of my text messages since yesterday," Maria said.

"Mine either," said Mac.

"I told her that Andy was okay and that I didn't hate her," said Charlie. "She didn't answer that one either."

Despite that, Maria seemed certain Kelly would come to her senses and go home. "I'll bet you five bucks we'll see her in school tomorrow," Maria said. "With soccer practice and auditions for *The Sound of Music*, there's no way she'll miss it. Her fans will demand it. Trust me."

"I think she has new fans now," said Charlie, feeling a bit glum. Somehow she knew that they might never see Kelly again.

* * *

On Monday morning Maria, Mac, and Charlie met up in front of school and headed toward the math building for first period. As they went, they overheard various students conversing about Kelly and her new fame. Even Vanessa didn't scold Charlie and Maria for missing the soccer scrimmage on Saturday—she only had Kelly to gush over. The three friends didn't join in. Instead, they scoured the campus, looking for her. Just as they were about to enter the math building, Maria spotted Kelly talking to Mr. Anderson outside the theater building. Maria squinted, then pointed her out to Charlie and Mac. "There she is," said Maria under her breath. "Told you. Five bucks, please."

"Do you see that?" Charlie said, looking closely at her. "Are my eyes going crazy or is she, like, pulsating with weird colors?"

"I see it," said Mac. "Is her camouflage acting up or something? That doesn't seem right."

"I have no idea," said Charlie. They watched for a moment, and then Kelly stopped pulsating and started heading down the footpath away from school. She broke into a jog, her bright blond hair bouncing against her back.

"Why is she running in that direction?" asked Mac.

"Maybe she forgot something," said Maria.

"If she did, she's going to be late," said Mac.

Kelly didn't make it back in time for first period.

She didn't show up for second period either. Or third. Or fourth.

She wasn't at lunch. And not one teacher mentioned her.

By the time theater class rolled around, Charlie approached Mr. Anderson before the bell rang. He was looking over a script as the students filed in.

"Hi there, Mr. A.," she said.

"Good afternoon, Ms. Wilde," he said. "Did you find that thing you were looking for before the break?"

"Uh, yeah, thanks. I was just wondering if you've seen Kelly or if you know why she's not here today."

Mr. Anderson didn't look up from the script. "What's that? Who?"

"Kelly. You know—Kelly Parker. Have you seen her?"

Mr. Anderson glanced up at Charlie, confused. His eyes had a glazed look that Charlie had never seen before. "We don't have a student here by that name, do we?"

The bell rang. Mr. Anderson put down the script and stood up, clapping his hands to get everyone's attention.

Charlie stared at him, dumbfounded. It was like he'd been hypnotized. He'd forgotten who Kelly Parker was—his favorite student—and he'd just talked to her earlier that day. Either he'd lost his memory or all of that pulsating with weird colors meant Kelly had a fourth ability that nobody else knew about—not even Dr. Sharma. An ability to make him forget. And if Kelly could use it on Mr. A, she could use it on anybody. Had she done it to her parents to keep them from searching for her? Her other teachers and friends?

What if she could make people forget *other* things—like the fact that Dr. Gray was going to turn everyone into chimeras?

It was the most frightening thing Charlie could imagine.

She whirled around and clutched her throat, trying not to freak out. Then she ran full speed out of the theater to find her friends and family—she had to make sure Kelly hadn't found them first.

RUNNING OUT OF TIME.

TIME FOR AN UPGRADE.

DON'T MISS THE EPIC CONCLUSION
TO THE SERIES:

CHAPTER 1

The New Recruit

It was the middle of May and school was out in Navarro Junction, but that fact barely registered with Kelly Parker. She'd made a risky decision to leave her old life after the spring-break disaster to join Dr. Victor Gray and his soldiers. She sat in the backseat of their white van as it sped along the California freeway, thinking about how much her life had changed in the past few weeks and trying not to feel anxious about the important task she was about to attempt. She tried *not* to think about everything that had gone wrong yesterday on her first mission . . . at SeaWorld.

Kelly wasn't used to failing. But she hadn't anticipated how many problems she'd have using two of her device's animal abilities at once. Remembering what had happened messed with Kelly's head a little as she prepared for today's challenge, but she couldn't seem to stop. She knew how much concentration it took to manipulate her camouflage power to create its hypnotic effect—she should have foreseen the issue. And she should have objected to that kind of mission until she believed without any doubt that she could succeed. She ought to have told Dr. Gray that for her first task, maybe it would be better to go after DNA that *didn't* involve dangerous water animals, or require her to use her dolphin swimming ability while simultaneously trying to use her cuttlefish hypnosis ability.

Kelly's face flushed in frustration and embarrassment. She had never enjoyed swimming, but she liked it even less now. She glanced up at Miko and Dr. Gray, who were in the front seats having a quiet conversation. Kelly hoped it wasn't about what a failure she'd been.

"Stop it," Kelly chided herself under her breath. An accomplished actor, soccer player, and student, she'd never gotten good at any of those things by being negative. This was a challenge, and her competitive nature kicked in as usual. Today was a new day and, despite a few unsettling doubts after the SeaWorld incident, Kelly was feeling reasonably confident about *this* task. Because today they were visiting Safari Park, part of the San Diego Zoo, and staying far away from water. It was Kelly's time to shine and prove to Dr. Gray that she could handle her abilities. And hopefully help erase yesterday from his mind.

They parked. All three got out of the van and started toward the entrance.

Beneath her clothes, Kelly wore her new camo-friendly bodysuit, which worked with her cuttlefish camouflage and allowed her entire body to fully blend into the environment whenever she needed or wanted to. Luckily, while the Mark Four's animal abilities altered her body slightly whenever she was using them, it never permanently changed her appearance, like the M

One had done to Miko and the rest of Dr. Gray's soldiers. She looked like an average almost-seventh grader visiting the zoo. *Above average*, Kelly thought to herself with a smile.

Kelly's long blond hair was slicked back and secured at her neck. She walked assuredly alongside Dr. Gray, who was dressed like a civilian in jeans and a T-shirt instead of his usual lab coat. Miko was wearing her black bodysuit as usual, but with a shirt thrown over it as a disguise. And for the first time in public, at Kelly's urging, Miko had daringly left her mask off, though she kept it with her in a bag in case she needed it. Instead, she wore a floppy sun hat to cover the fur that had taken the place of her human hair. The hat brim conveniently cast shadows over her slightly altered facial structure. She kept her bodysuit zipped up tight to cover the fur on her chin and neck. As a chimpanzee-human hybrid, Miko didn't have much facial fur to draw attention to her like the others, but she still seemed a little nervous to be without the mask she'd worn in public for years. Although she was clearly happy, too. She bounced around the other two and ducked behind them when zoo visitors approached. And with the oversize hat, no one really seemed to notice her. People at the zoo were looking at the animals in their habitats and cages, not at other people . . . or at a hybrid who could pass as an ordinary person.

Once inside the Safari Park gates, the three squinted at the tall sign with arrows showing the different parts of the zoo. "Con- dor Ridge," said Miko, pointing at an arrow. "That's the place we need. This way." She bounded in that direction and almost hopped up to grab a tree branch along the walking path but stopped herself before too many people noticed her extreme enthusiasm. She slowed down and waited, bouncing on the balls of her feet, for Kelly and Dr. Gray to catch up. Kelly could tell Miko was trying to subdue her excitement, but her antics were drawing a bit of unwanted attention. The chimp-woman looked guiltily at Dr. Gray and pulled her hat down farther over her eyes.

Dr. Gray frowned but didn't reprimand her. He was eager for this visit, too. In the past, when working for Talos Global with the other biologists, he'd had a large variety of animal DNA available to him whenever he'd needed it, without having to step foot outside the lab. Now all he had were the samples he'd already used on his soldiers over the years. To expand the collection, he and his soldiers had to gather the DNA the old-fashioned way, directly from the animals themselves, and they weren't always easy to get. Over the past few weeks all he'd successfully gotten was a porcupine quill, which he had been planning to use for Braun's upgrade. Plus a few other bits of animal DNA that he wanted for his own mysterious purposes.

But there had been some failed attempts at collecting the important samples . . . like yesterday. He was angry for expecting too much of the girl—he should have known better than to have her go for the shark right off the bat. But he'd let his excitement and Kelly's self-assuredness get in the way of his better judgment . . .

and, to be truthful, he was in a hurry. Without Zed to help him anymore, he needed every willing soldier he could find. Even the kid.

Hopefully, today would be far easier for Kelly and she'd be able to procure new samples for Dr. Gray to use in his experiments. With any success, Miko would soon be a living, breathing chimera of sorts, having her DNA mixed with a second animal and bringing Dr. Gray one step closer to his ultimate goal. The three continued the lengthy walk up the path to the condor enclosure, all thinking about different aspects of the job before them.

Miko spied a pair of the birds sitting a distance apart on a large rock inside the exhibit. She drew up against the enclosure and grimaced. "Their faces are so uuug-ly," she muttered. "They're even grosser in person. I really hope that part doesn't transfer to me."

"I guess we'll find out eventually if it does," said Dr. Gray lightly.

Miko's eyes bugged out. She turned to Dr. Gray, hoping he was teasing, but it was hard to tell. The soldiers hadn't seen him in a good mood in a while. Not since before the other scientists—the real bad guys, according to Dr. Gray—had come along and started ruining things. Gray continued to feel uneasy about the other Project Chimera scientists, so things had remained tense.

Kelly wasn't paying attention to Miko and Dr. Gray's discussion. She had other things on her mind, like clearing her thoughts to focus. Not messing up. And most important, trying to find the vay into the habitat. As she took in the details of the enclosure, she spied some sort of horned goatlike animal inside. She also saw a sign for an ocelot. She wasn't quite sure what an ocelot was, though from its picture, it looked like a cat-type creature. She hoped it wouldn't attack her while she was busy with the condor. Kelly's hands began to sweat, and she wiped them on her clothes and then ditched those for her suit. "You didn't mention there were other animals in this section," she muttered to Miko.

"I didn't know," said Miko. "Sorry. But they seem . . . friendly."

"The sign says ocelots are carnivores," Kelly said, "and I am made of meat." She was annoyed, but there was nothing she could do about it. She searched the area for a zoo worker. Finally, she spied one carrying a bucket and walking toward what looked like the entrance to the habitat. "You two stay here," Kelly said in a low voice to Dr. Gray and Miko. "Let me do all the talking."

Dr. Gray put a hand on Kelly's shoulder, like Coach Candy, Kelly's soccer coach, used to do sometimes during a pep talk. "Just remain calm and don't panic," he told her. "You only have to use one ability this time. You shouldn't have any problems."

Kelly grimaced. "I'm fine. Please . . . can you stop talking about . . . that? I'll show you I can do this better than anyone." She was one of the few people who didn't seem to walk on eggshells around the doctor, and so far she'd been able to get away with telling him what she thought, at least when it came to her abilities. Maybe

Or perhaps it was because Kelly could do something unique that would really help Dr. Gray collect DNA faster—because things had been going agonizingly slowly recently. They'd had to move the lab for the umpteenth time. Then Dr. Gray had struggled for weeks trying to repair the machine that he'd forced the other scientists to make, which had been smashed to pieces when Charlie and her friends broke in and rescued them.

Whatever the reason, the man didn't argue with Kelly and stayed back with Miko.

Walking down to where the zoo worker was, Kelly clicked her bracelet to activate the cuttlefish camouflage. With each step her body slowly changed to green and brown, blending into the wooden wall structure and foliage that lined the path to the enclosure. Nimbly she hopped over the chained-off area near the entrance to the habitat and concentrated for a moment until she could feel heat rise to her face and her skin begin to pulse. Then she beckoned to the zoo worker. "Excuse me," Kelly called out. The woman looked up and almost didn't see her at first. Then she frowned and started toward her. "You can't be in here."

Soft waves of blue-and-white light rippled over Kelly's face, moving in a steady, mesmerizing pattern and growing stronger with each wave as the woman approached.

"This area is off-limits to park visitors," the worker said, looking startled at Kelly's strange appearance. "I'm sorry, miss. Are you . . ." The woman's face slackened, and she fell silent for a

"No, I'm not lost." Kelly smiled disarmingly as the woman stared at her. "I need to see the condors. I'm sure you understand."

The woman blinked a few times. The handle she was holding slipped from her fingers and the bucket clattered to the ground, unnoticed. She seemed to try to form words to object to Kelly's request but was having trouble. "No, I . . . ," she said softly. "I can't . . ."

"Yes, you can," said Kelly in a soothing voice. "I need to see the condors now." The light show on her face continued. "Just unlock the door and take me inside."

The woman hesitated, but Kelly stood confidently. A moment later the worker was fumbling for her keys, looking bewildered but doing what Kelly asked. She opened the door.

Kelly kept the waves of light pulsing over her skin as she went in after the woman. She looked around cautiously for the nearest condor, wanting to stay as close as possible to the exit in case anything unexpected happened. She located the ones they'd seen resting on the rocks nearby, and approached one of the huge birds. As she drew near, the zoo worker followed. Kelly gazed in awe at the condor's size. The bird turned its ugly pink head and stared at her but stayed where it was. Kelly, still pulsing, glanced around her. Out of the corner of her eye she noticed one of the horned sheepy-goat things about thirty yards away. She didn't focus on it, knowing she needed to keep her concentration. She turned back o the condor, who seemed to be entranced by her now, too. "Hi, bird," she said. "This will only hurt for a few seconds." Slowly she reached out, cringed, then gripped a couple of feathers. They were bigger and coarser than she'd imagined. Quickly she yanked them from the condor's wing and backed up a few steps.

The condor hissed and rose, spreading its dark wings wide and showing a stripe of white underneath. Each wing was longer than she was tall—the span was *enormous*. Kelly felt her heart pounding. She reminded herself that her research said condors don't attack prey. Then she saw the sheepy-goat coming closer. She had a moment of panic and clicked her device to deploy her platypus spikes on her heels, just in case it charged. Thankfully the condor settled again, and the horned creature got distracted by something in the dirt and stopped to eat it.

Kelly blew out a deep breath. She slipped the feathers into a clear plastic pouch and put it in her camo-friendly waist pack. Slowly she turned away, checking to see how many of the zoo visitors had noticed her. She might have to do some mind control on the way out, too. Miko was still standing by the cage but not looking straight at Kelly for fear of being hypnotized. The chimp-woman's fingers curled around the railing as if it was all she could do not to climb up the cage and start swinging on the enclosure netting.

Kelly kept the pulsing going. She reached the door with the zoo worker walking complacently alongside her. "Thank you," Kelly said as she went out. "You'll forget about me in a minute. Okay?"

The woman looked troubled but nodded. "Okay," she said.

Kelly smiled, then began walking toward the crowds. She broke her concentration and let the hypnotic pulses fade. Her body returned to its nearly invisible camouflage state as she blended into the rocky background. She clicked off her platypus spikes. Then she clicked off the cuttlefish ability. Kelly appeared to emerge from the wall looking quite normal again. A few people close by watched her with puzzled looks, but they didn't do or say anything—they'd been close enough to have fallen under the mesmerizing spell too. Kelly rejoined her companions and handed her bag to Dr. Gray, who swiftly slid it into his pocket.

"Well done," the scientist quietly praised, though he was glancing around carefully and turning to leave. "That went smoothly."

"I told you I could do it."

"Yes, you did. I'm thrilled. A definite success."

"That was great, Kelly," said Miko. "You were such a pro."

"Thanks," said Kelly, puffing up from the praise as they moved swiftly away from the attraction. "I've gotten really good at hypnotizing," she said, impassioned. Now that she'd succeeded, she felt a sudden need to explain what had gone wrong yesterday. "You see, I just hadn't ever had a chance to practice swimming and hypnotizing at once. I guess . . . I thought I could do it."

"This mission was a much better one to start with," said Dr. Gray.

"Yeah," said Kelly. "At least it wasn't in a shark-infested pool this time, right?" She fell in step with Dr. Gray, feeling a fresh surge of confidence now that she'd managed this task without a hitch.

"The setting today was much improved," agreed Dr. Gray, and Miko nodded behind them.

Relieved, Kelly glanced at Dr. Gray a bit sheepishly. "Look," she said, "I'm sorry we got kicked out of SeaWorld before we could go in search of that jellyfish you're looking for. Hopefully, Cyke and Prowl are having better luck finding it today." Cyke, a horse hybrid, and Prowl, a leopard hybrid, were two of Dr. Gray's other prized soldiers. "This job was a cinch compared to the shark incident."

"It's not your fault," said Dr. Gray, beginning to sound a bit impatient. "I made a mistake in judgment yesterday. I should have had you start with this, clearly the easier job. But I was overeager for the shark DNA. I've wanted to experiment with it for so long but hadn't been able to obtain a sample until you came along—the Mark Four's abilities are perfect for that kind of predator." He frowned. "I let my eagerness overrule my hesitations."

"Besides," Miko added, "nobody thought that you'd actually need to go *into* the pool, you know."

Dr. Gray grimaced and shook his head, like the whole thing had been a cluster of mishaps and mistakes. "Just forget about it. We'll try again at another aquarium when you're ready, Kelly. For now, with what you've accomplished, Miko will soon be able to get her condor wings. And . . . ," he said, pressing his lips into a small smirk, "her pink bald head."

"Ugh, no!" said Miko, hopping along, but it was clear she enjoyed seeing Dr. Gray lighten up a bit for once. "Now you're just being mean, teasing me like that." She stayed close to Kelly, still careful to keep her face hidden, then said abruptly, "What time is it? Do you want me to tell Cyke we're finished here, and we'll be on our way shortly to pick them up? Are they just going to meet us in the SeaWorld parking lot since Kelly is banned for life?"

Kelly rolled her eyes and elbowed the chimp-woman, half-annoyed and half-embarrassed that Miko brought up *that* part again. But then she chuckled reluctantly. "Kelly Parker. Banned from SeaWorld. It's kind of funny, isn't it?"

"Kind of inconvenient is more like it," said Dr. Gray matter-of-factly. "But it won't be too hard to find shark DNA elsewhere, and with you being a child . . . well, you're much less suspicious-looking."

Miko patted Kelly's shoulder reassuringly. "It would have gone flawlessly if you hadn't hit the trainer ladder. That's what made you lose your concentration, wasn't it?"

"I suppose," muttered Kelly.

Dr. Gray gave a rude snort of laughter as they walked, as if he were remembering the scene. Reluctantly Kelly had to admit that the part where the aquarium workers hauled her out of the shark pool must have been quite a sight to witness.

The doctor soon became preoccupied and thoughtful again. "I imagine Dr. Sharma chose to use the cuttlefish for the Mark Four because of its amazing camouflage ability. You were clever to realize how to take full advantage of that power by replicating the animal's hypnotic pulsating feature. That kind of ingenuity is valuable to me. How did you know you could do it? Did Dr. Sharma tell you?"

Kelly beamed from the rare compliment. "I don't know what Dr. Sharma meant to do with the cuttlefish ability. She never said anything to me. When I originally read about it in the Project Chimera papers and tried it out the first time, I thought all I could do was camouflage. Even when I went to LA to be on *LIVE, TONIGHT*, I didn't know the ability could expand to hypnosis or I would have used it then to get that creepy host to let go of me." She frowned a moment, remembering, then shook her head slightly. "It wasn't until I was on the bus ride back to Arizona that I started studying more about cuttlefish. That's when I found out they can use that camouflage technique not only to hide but also to mesmerize their prey. I figured I should at least give it a shot, so I practiced when the lady next to me fell asleep—I used my phone camera to see if I could get the pulsating stripe thing going. Once the lady woke up, I tried it on her and it sort of worked. She was really confused at least. Enough for me to know there was something to it."

"I'll bet she was freaked out," said Miko with a chimpy laugh.

The walkway they were on rejoined the main road that would take them to the exit.

"Anyway," Kelly continued, "after I joined your team, I knew I had to do something to keep my parents from worrying about me, and everyone at school from looking for me. So I kept practicing while you guys were looking for a place to go next. I managed to hypnotize Mega in the backseat of the van." Kelly snorted. "But don't say anything; I never told her. I was really nervous to use it on my teachers, but when it worked on Mr. Anderson, who knows me better than practically anyone, I knew it could actually work on my parents, too. And it did. They . . ." Her expression flickered. "They pretty much forgot all about me."

Don't miss the *New York Times* bestselling series from

LISA McMANN

THE UNWANTEDS QUESTS

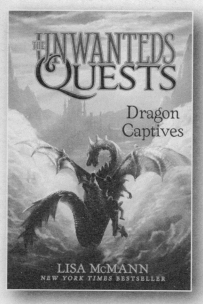

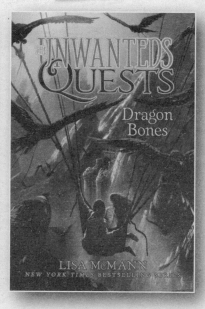